C J West

Dinner at Deadman's

Nicole,
Congratulations!
I hope you enjoy this.
CJ West

22 West Books, Sheldonville, MA
www.22wb.com

© Copyright 2012, CJ West

All rights reserved.
No part of this book may be reproduced, stored in a retrieval system, or transmitted by any means, electronic, mechanical, photocopying, recording, or otherwise, without written permission from the publisher.

Requests for permission to make copies of any part of the work should be mailed to the following address: Permissions, 22 West Books, P.O. Box 155, Sheldonville, MA 02070-0155.

The following is a work of fiction. Lorado Martin is loosely based on a real person. All other characters and events are of the author's creation and used fictitiously. This book in no way represents real people living or dead.

Cover design by Sandpiper Artisans
Cover photo by CJ West

ISBN 10: 0-9767788-6-6
ISBN 13: 978-0-9767788-6-8

Acknowledgments

Special thanks to my brother, Ed Martin, who is pictured on the cover and loosely portrayed in this book by his nickname, Lorado. During the creation of this book, Lorado invited me to work alongside his crew and get to know the ins and outs of his work in construction and estate sales. Many of the items described in this book came from estate sales we worked together and some of them are pictured on the book cover.

Thanks to the many families and recovered narcotics users who told me their stories so I could create realistic characters and situations for this novel. The stories were difficult to hear and many sections of this book were difficult to write knowing that similar stories are being played out across our world every day.

Thanks to Jim Stevens from GiftsToGive for allowing me to mention his charity within these pages, even more so for the great work they do every single day.

Thank you to my beta readers Cindy-Lee Samuel, Gwyneth Martin, Nancy Violette, and Tina Sa.

Other Books by CJ West

The End of Marking Time (standalone)

<u>Randy Black Series</u>
Sin & Vengeance
A Demon Awaits
Gretchen Greene

Addicted to Love (standalone)
Taking Stock (standalone)

To my brother, a gentle soul in a large and rugged package.

Drugs, not Money, are the root of all evil,
Lee Lofland

Chapter One

February 17th. Nineteen degrees on a Friday night and I was tucked in a dead lady's bed trying to convince myself the pressure in my gut wasn't worth risking the cold oak and then the bathroom tiles. Sound miserable? Not for me. I wasn't thinking about the punk heir or how silly I looked in a pink comforter covered with big red roses. I was a pig, belly deep in mud. No part of me wanted to move because I'd been treasure hunting all day. Everything was sore, especially my right elbow, but I wouldn't change a thing.

You're probably laughing. Picturing a fat guy in a pink blanket who fancied himself a pirate. I was no swashbuckler. Unwanted treasure was my specialty. New England might not have had gold or oil, but it was packed with loot.

My ancestors were either cowards or laggards. They landed on the Mayflower and walked inland far enough to get away from the Atlantic storm surge, but not so far they couldn't run back to the boat if the Indians attacked. I couldn't run back. I could walk if I lost a few pounds. Okay, probably not.

Every winter New Englanders dreamed of moving to Florida or South Carolina. Adventurous souls picked some island the rest of us had never heard of like Turks and Caicos. Not me. The South Coast was exactly where I belonged. New Bedford was the whaling capital of the world. Every old geezer who croaked had some scrimshaw or an oil lamp or something that had been around a few hundred years.

In the old days, people had a bottle dump at the back corner of the foundation. Old timers scoured the woods and picked through old homesteads that had rotted into the ground. My grandparents took me along sometimes. They built tiers of wooden shelves in their cellar, a spooky mildew-coated place that had one of the last stone foundations built in the area. They collected thousands of bottles from two-toned brown jugs to tiny blue medicine bottles. One day I found a Fairbanks & Beard soda bottle and my grandfather gave me ten bucks for it. Ten bucks for something I dug out of the ground! I was hooked.

I didn't wait for houses to fall down and their foundations to fill with leaves like my grandparents did. Yuppie kids called me even before their last parent was buried. They saw a house worth two hundred thousand, some cash, and investments. They browsed the jewelry and they were done. The rest of the stuff was just in the way. A bunch of junk that kept them from the big score. They wanted everything gone so buyers could start looking at the house.

That was my domain. All the stuff they didn't want. Some of it was worth a whole lot more than that old F & B bottle with the green glass and jagged top. I'd dedicated my last thirty years to learning the difference.

At forty miles per hour, I could spot a barrel of Lincoln Logs in somebody's trash and slam the brakes in time to swing around and pick them out before the garbage truck got there. Put me in an old lady's house and I was in heaven.

Everyone had some useless crap that never should have been made in the first place. Once that was gone, every single thing left was useful to somebody. The trick was matching them up. Every fork, can opener, end table, and cheesy 1970's lamp was dying to make someone happy.

In about a week, I could have a house open for sale. Posted on Craigslist. In the *Standard Times* classifieds. A cardboard sign on every main road.

The people would fill the place shoulder to shoulder. Browsing. Smiling and sharing reminders of their childhood. Kids would pick up useless junk and laugh. An hour later, an old lady would buy the very same piece. Young and old alike were struck with a combination of nostalgia and bargain fever, but every person who walked through the door had one problem. They were all trying to forget someone died in that house not long ago.

Death never bothered me much.

There's nothing wrong with dead stuff. Road kill could make a great hat if the bumper didn't poke a hole in the pelt. It was awful hard to mess up a raccoon's tail with a car and those rings looked pisser dangling down the back of your neck. When you were seventeen anyway. Or maybe twenty. The raccoon didn't care. He was gone.

People were different. They knew death was coming and didn't want to entertain the thought any longer than necessary. Sometimes they got angry when they died. Sometimes I could feel it. That night, working in Mrs. Newbury's house, I swore the old lady was watching me. And she wasn't happy about me rummaging through her stuff.

It wasn't like she didn't know I was coming. My parents had known her a long time. They went to school together back when Rochester kids went to New Bedford High. Decades ago.

A year ago she'd hired me to replace her kitchen cabinets. And she walked me through the house when I was done. Showed me her treasures. Pieces of scrimshaw squirreled away in the attic. Plates I had to Google to find out what they were worth. Mrs. Newbury had some great stuff. She knew her grandson, Newb, wouldn't appreciate any of it. Her telling me was a sign she wanted me to make sure the valuable pieces weren't thrown away.

Sometime between showing me her house and dying, she'd gotten angry and decided to take it out on my stomach. Maybe I was sleeping on Mr. Newbury's side of the bed, but that shouldn't have mattered. They were together in Heaven. Or at least they should have been.

Maybe she'd changed her mind about me selling her stuff to strangers. The closet cramped with fifty years of floral dresses and skirts. Two bureaus overflowing with scarves and socks and underwear. Boxes, purses, and shoetrees pressed into every available space. The clutter slumped against the walls parted just enough to reveal the oak flooring along the weaving path

Mrs. Newbury followed to the bathroom. The night light's glow gleamed off those precious few boards and my gaze fell there as I struggled to sleep in spite of being haunted.

Old people got out of bed to pee a lot. Well, they couldn't pee a lot. That's why they got up so often. Anyway, the thing they feared most was a fall at night when no one could hear them and come to help. If you'd seen my big blue coffee cup, you'd know I needed to get up a time or two myself. And at three hundred twenty pounds, when I fell there was damage. So I left the night light on even though I wasn't keen on anyone seeing me wrapped in the old lady's pink comforter. I'd have been under the pink sheets and rose-patterned blankets, too, if I wasn't so worried about bedbugs. The look wouldn't have changed. Only the temperature.

It'd be just like Roxie to swing by for a little action and snap a picture from the doorway. She was a whiz with the Internet. She'd email it to all our friends before I could get dressed and chase her home.

Giving her a key to job sites was a risk, but who knows what'd happen in those old neighborhoods. Junkies read the obits. They'd hack out every length of copper from the cellar if they thought no one was home. If they caught me sleeping and roughed me up, maybe she'd call the cops and save my ass. More likely she'd come by to give me a piece of hers. Sadly, three days after Valentine's my stomach hurt so much I hoped she wouldn't come.

My gut rumbled and I pulled the comforter tighter. Damned unromantic.

Wind whistled against the toothless exterior and found its way in through gaps around the windows. I'd pitched the kid a siding and window replacement job, but the only thing the vulture wanted was his grandmother's place gone in a rush. Forsythia slapped the shingles and tickled the glass. The bushes could have been cut back enough in a day so you could see the street from the windows. The briars and scrub out back mowed with a brush cutter in three hours. Two hundred bucks to triple the yard and jack up the sale price at least three times that. No deal. No cash was going into grandma's house. He wanted me to wring out every penny. Every cent he could get without lifting a finger or spending a dime.

Thankless cheapskate I worked for. Even worse when he worked for me.

A knot in my gut twisted so tight I forgot my annoyance with the kid.

The cramps forced me to wrestle out of the comforter and lumber down the path, hunched over in the dark, cradling my gut in my arms. On my second step, something jabbed the meat of my right foot. It pressed in so deeply, I hopped and crashed my right shoulder into the doorframe.

I swiped at the sole of my foot, feeling for blood, expecting a staple or a tack. A bit of broken plastic was all I found. It bounced into a corner for me to step on again later. The jostling hurt so much I thought my stomach was going to erupt horizontally. I wished I'd just kept walking and let the plastic burrow its way in. It would have been a lot less painful.

Four hobbled steps carried me through the hall into a bathroom that had been designed for tiny old people. Her toilet was wedged in a corner between the closet and the window. I leaned against the wall. Ignored the ceramic toilet paper dispenser digging into my knee. The cold air rushing through the window. I balanced there in the dark as the pain radiated lower.

Giving birth had to feel like this. It hurt too much to push. It hurt too much not to push.

The contents of my bowels willed themselves free with a liquid rush that went on far longer than should have been humanly possible. Stuff I'd eaten days ago freed itself from my body in a torrent that released so much pressure it felt as good as any orgasm.

Then my entire body seized in a cramp that folded me in half.

Women complain about cramps like it's the end of the world. If this was what having a period was like, I'd take back every menstrual joke I ever told.

Forty minutes later, I was still sitting there with the seat jammed so firmly into my backside the impression wouldn't fade for a week. I'll spare you the details, but stuff kept squirting out of me until I swore my intestines were inside out, hanging down there in the bowl getting a rinse.

I hate doctors almost as much as I hate health plans and the government sponsored socialist crap that forced me to pay for something I didn't want so some lowlife could get free healthcare. My right elbow had hurt for two years before that night, and I hadn't seen a doctor yet. I'd rather wake up wincing in pain than pay some rich boy two hundred bucks to talk with me for seven minutes.

That night it hurt so badly I might have called an ambulance if I could have gotten my pants back on. Might have driven myself in if I could have taken a step away from the porcelain throne, but I was tethered by unrelenting cramps and the fear of my insides splashing all over everything if I stood up.

I clutched my gut and leaned forward, praying that somehow the pain would pass and I'd make it back to bed. Sleep would set me right. Little did I know sleep was coming in a rush. A nasty cramp hunched me right over forward and my foot slipped.

The bolt of pain in my groin erased any memory of the cramps. Blinding, mind-erasing pain that only men experience. My arms shot down to catch myself on the seat and free my crushed testicle.

The toilet seat broke free under my weight and I leapfrogged forward. The sharp edge of the vanity creased my forehead. That was the last pain I felt that night. My vision faded like an old tube TV, closing in from the outside to a point of light. As I lost consciousness, I had the distinct feeling the old woman was cackling with delight.

Chapter Two

Voices.

Last I knew I was facedown between the toilet and the vanity with my pants around my ankles. I reached behind me, but up wasn't up anymore. A firm mattress stopped my hand from reaching my backside, and I felt like I was about to fall face first. The tiny tiles of Mrs. Newbury's bathroom floor were gone. My mind did a mental flip and reoriented me to my new surroundings, but I still had the strongest urge to pull up my pants and the strange female voices in the room set my heart thumping. The last moments I remembered were not pretty. Some people looked better naked. I was not one of them, not in two thousand twelve at least.

The panicked search for my clothes set off a paralyzing ache in my frontal lobe. The pain wasn't from my ding on the counter. It was ten beers and two Papa Smurfs hangover pain.

My pants had been replaced by a thin blanket and an even thinner johnny. To my left, a blurry nurse fiddled with some equipment. Thirty bucks an hour and probably billed to my insurance at fifty. She adjusted the flow of saline solution into a tube. That plastic bag of salt water was another hundred bucks. I could have shaken some table salt into tap water and drank it for around five cents.

The needle she had poked into my arm, the tape, the tubes, and the hanger, another twenty bucks.

"Just relax, Mr. Martin."

A strip of gauze was taped to my forehead. I fumbled to peel it back.

"Pull that off I'll have to bandage you up again."

A familiar hand rested on my bicep. "You got some stitches. Who knew your head was that soft?"

Roxie. I tried to turn my head, but it only throbbed. "Funny," I said. I didn't remember her coming in, but she must have found me on the bathroom floor. She'd never let me live that down, and if I knew her, she had pictures on her camera. My condition must have been serious because she hadn't jabbed me about finding my pants around my ankles yet.

"I have you to thank for getting me incarcerated?"

"It wasn't easy, let me tell you."

I could hear her broad smile.

"That bathroom was way too small for six guys to get a hand on you. After they cleaned your backside and buckled your pants." A giggle escaped her lips. "Boy, they were lining up for that job. I had to hold them back."

I waited for a crack about pictures, but it didn't come.

"That place is crammed with junk. It took forever to wheel you out."

A male voice came into the room. My head hurt a bit less, but I was too embarrassed to open my eyes. I pictured myself facedown. Paramedics cleaning me up and dressing me then I remembered how much I hurt myself on the toilet seat. My hand shot to my crotch before I remembered I wasn't alone.

"Nothing slows you down, does it?"

The boys were back to normal. "I'll explain later," I mumbled.

"No need. We iced you down this morning." She wouldn't have let that go so easily if we were alone.

My eyes stretched open. A slim doctor faced me from the foot of the bed with my chart in his left hand, a smirk on his face, and one eye on Roxie's ample cleavage. Big, fake, perky boobs. Impervious to the force of gravity and the ravages of time. They were expensive, but she thanked me by wearing a sweater open wide enough to lay them out on display on that February morning.

My aunts complained about the fake blond hair. They didn't realize that dudes didn't care how a woman's hair got the color they like. Mostly we didn't even know. I had three hundred relatives with brown hair. Enough already. The blonde livened things up.

I didn't begrudge the doc a peek. Most guys couldn't resist. What I was jealous of was the hundred breast exams he did every year. Lucky bastard.

He started talking and my mental cash register started ringing at thirty bucks a minute. He asked how I was feeling. Told me I had an acute intestinal problem. Rocket scientist. It got interesting when he asked how many cups of coffee I had.

"Two."

"So about twelve ounces?"

"No." I held out my hands, approximating the size of my big blue mug.

"You drink out of a soccer ball?" he asked.

"Don't put it past him," Roxie said.

Her comment gave the doc an excuse to get another eye full.

"It's a travel mug. I filled it twice." My head throbbed so I stopped talking and held up my hands again. "A pint?" I offered.

"That looks more like a half gallon."

That night I checked. That cup held a liter and a half. But what did it matter? I drank that much coffee every day. Why would it upset my stomach all of a sudden?

The doc wrote something on my chart and started asking me what I'd eaten the day before. He assumed I had food poisoning, and if he could determine the source, he'd know if it was bacterial, viral, or even botulism. It sounded scary, but aside from my pounding head, I felt fine. Sunlight came in from outside and I hadn't been to the bathroom since early morning. I was ready to pull the tube out of my arm and go.

He wasn't eager to let me turn the meter off.

"Roxie made me an omelet. She never lets me cook unless we're on vacation." I told him I'd hit Dunkies twice, Mickey D's for lunch, and ordered a pizza for dinner at Mrs. Newbury's house. I didn't mention that I had eaten cereal from the old Lady's pantry. I knew she liked it. The flakes were still fresh, not like the two-year-old cereal we used to find at my grandmother's house.

The doc kept nodding for me to go on. He expected me to say I'd eaten raw seafood or some meat that had been out on the counter overnight. My trail of fast food, coffee, and Coke didn't give him much to go on. I didn't admit to eating at Deadman's—that's what Roxie and I call an estate sale—because he already looked at me like a buffoon. Roxie wouldn't knowingly eat at Deadman's, but I never threw away unopened canned goods, not unless the cans were rusted. It was a slippery slope to cereal, crackers, and other munchies that were already open.

"Mr. Martin, this isn't a joke. You were severely dehydrated. Without treatment you could have suffered serious complications."

He got me thinking someone had messed with my food. I had a cast iron stomach that never failed. I could eat a seafood platter for two at the Pondo without slowing down. The only thing new in my routine was Mrs. Newbury's house. She couldn't touch me from the funeral home. So who did? I wondered who I'd pissed off on my crew. Which antique dealer didn't like the way I haggled.

"I want you to follow up with your primary care doctor in two days."

Not a chance.

"I don't think he has one," Roxie said.

Traitor.

He asked when my last office visit was and she told him I hadn't seen a doctor since we'd been dating. She did some mental math and answered, "Seventeen years."

The doc looked like I'd just insulted his mother.

Probably because I knew the truth. They charged my insurance company two thousand bucks to tell me I was dehydrated and pump my veins full of salty water. I could have achieved the same result with three glasses of water and a few bananas. I had to give him credit for stitching my forehead. I could stitch my own arm, but I could never get the angle to stitch my own forehead.

"I'm ordering a cholesterol test, Mr. Martin."

He raised his hands before I could object. "You've already got a co-pay for your visit. It's not going to cost you another cent."

Did Roxie tell him how cheap I was while I was out?

"Anything else bothering you?" he asked.

Nice guy for a doctor. Sure he was jacking up his fee to my insurance company, but he seemed like he wanted to help.

"His elbow has been hurting for years."

The doctor gave me a scalding look then came around and handled my arm. He bent it, asked where it hurt, and seemed to instantly recognize the problem.

"Probably tendonitis," he said and recommended a RICE program. Not food. Rest, Ice, Compression, and Elevation. My brother Chris had told me seventeen times I needed ice and ibuprofen.

The doc told me to take it easy and fill my big mug with water a few times. He shook Roxie's hand, probably to check her jiggle, and left.

I was still reeling. Trying to collect the energy to get out of that bed and go home. When the nurse came over with a tray of rubber bands and tubes, I started getting queasy. I didn't mind blood as long as it isn't mine, but when she came close enough for me to see the needles, my skin flushed and my head pounded.

She swabbed me, but before she could tap a vein, my phone rang. Roxie lifted my jeans off the chair in the corner, fished the pockets, and handed over my phone in time for me to answer.

"Hey. Boss."

"What's happening, Speedy?"

The hesitation was painful. Speedy lost his mind shooting heroin. He was a great worker, but the part of his brain that put words together had been thrown into ultra slow motion by the drugs. "They got in."

"Is it bad?"

"Glass."

The nurse waited with her tools while I waited for Speedy to make his point. "Glass everywhere. You're not going to like it."

"I'll be there in thirty," I said and hung up.

"You're not going anywhere," the nurse ordered.

"Take your blood, Vampira, and I'm gone."

Chapter Three

Deadman's had many things, but half-ton pickups were hard to find. The women were always the last to go, and eighty-year-old grandmas didn't drive pickups. The old women kept tools, sporting goods, and books lying around long after their husbands died, but sold their trucks well before I got involved.

After a shower and a change of clothes, Roxie dropped me off at my blue station wagon from, you guessed it, Deadman's. It had twenty thousand miles when I got it for replacing a sliding door and a few windows to help some young kids sell a place they couldn't afford to put money into. The car was pristine when they handed it over, but by the morning I climbed in with a raging headache, the floor mats hadn't seen daylight in years.

Why? Roxie called it an obsession. My father, a sickness.

Once I got into a few places, I started seeing value in everything. People had good stuff. A house full. By the time they died, most people had stuff packed so tightly you could barely navigate the basement. Not everything had value. But eighty-percent of it was worth something to someone. At the end of every sale came a time when I needed to make a decision about every single item that remained. Trash or treasure?

That's why every crevice in my car brimmed with miscellaneous junk. On any given day, I could stop at an antique dealer and sell something for gas money. I couldn't take on a passenger in my four door, but I could pull out a tree stand, hand you a quahog rake, or sell you a lamp. If you asked for a specific tool, I probably didn't have it, but I could hand you some wasp killer, or something heavy to pound a nail. It just might have been a pipe wrench instead of a hammer.

My gas mileage may have suffered a little, but I didn't care.

A few quick turns from Mrs. Newbury's brought me to Route 18 then Route 140, and in twenty minutes, I wheeled the station wagon in front of a brick facade that had once been a thriving hospital.

Plywood sealed off all the lower windows. Shattered beer bottles and cleaved bricks littered the ground along the foundation. Evidence of how hard the little bastards had worked to smash the double quarter-inch panes, mostly unmolested by the local cops. They had smashed and tagged away at the building for years and it was going to take a lot more than fresh no-trespassing signs to stop them.

Saplings had sprouted all over the landscape, and we had to chainsaw our way to many of the doors to change the padlocks. Dilapidated fascia and broken windows let leaves blow inside. Every time I walked on the property, my stomach jittered. Doubly true that day.

"Speedy," I yelled.

He didn't answer.

His red Toyota faced the exit. The bed held a spare tire and an empty gas can, but no tools. He was learning. In the old days, he'd leave my tools in the back of his truck and park in front of one of the holes we were renovating. We worked for the state building halfway houses, drug treatment centers, and homeless shelters. Try putting one of these in suburbia and the NIMBYs will be ten miles up your backside. So the services ended up where the clients came from. Rough places full of drugs and prostitution. Foreclosed houses on every block. The kind of place where the rules became flexible based on how needy the residents were.

Speedy was comfortable in these neighborhoods because he didn't own anything worth stealing. But every time he turned his back, my tools walked off. After four times, it seemed he'd finally learned.

In the leaves outside the service entrance, I found plastic wrappers with a familiar green and blue pattern. Cheap cigars. Kids bought them, removed the tobacco, and stuffed them with marijuana. New wrappers meant new visitors, but they couldn't have gotten past the padlock. The heavy plywood door was intact. I scratched my head and dialed Speedy.

When he didn't answer, I assumed it was the masonry blocking his cell service. I stepped inside and clicked on my light. A pile of shredded tobacco greeted me on the landing. The kids couldn't wait three steps to light up.

I thought I heard shuffling on the second floor and headed up.

"Speedy!"

"Down here. Electrical room."

I turned around in search of my hardest working helper.

The light caught the bare cinderblocks on my way downstairs. The old hospital had been gutted twelve years ago for a complete remodel until someone complained about asbestos and the project came to a halt. The building sat idle until my little brother helped me win a grant to turn this place into a psych treatment unit. At six million it was my biggest project ever. If we got the place up and running, it would push me onto the state's A-list. If we didn't, the junkies would have fifty more windows to break and a half mile of copper pipe to scrap courtesy of the commonwealth and my failed company.

My flashlight beam played on the entrance to the morgue and the autopsy room. Dark. Barren. The new design wouldn't include either.

Speedy's light flickered ahead and I turned into the electrical room.

"Bad news. Boss."

Speedy shuffled from behind a breaker rack and waggled his beam across the concrete floor. "What's up, Speedy?"

He steadied his beam on a four-inch conduit above the rack.

Every single wire had been pulled. Not snipped off, pulled back through the conduit and hauled out of the building. With the high price of copper, the heavy gauge wire they stole overnight would fetch hundreds for the junkies and cost me thousands in materials and labor to replace.

"Cock knocker!"

Speedy had been around drugs enough to know the punks were scrapping my copper even if he couldn't do the math to know how much their habits cost me.

"I'll kill the little bastards."

Speedy checked the shadows for eavesdroppers.

"Not really, Speedy," I said. At that moment I wasn't sure if I'd kill them or not, but it was lucky for them they weren't within reach.

Seven racks held all the breakers for the building. Three or four breakers out of about three hundred had an inch of copper hanging out. The rest had been disconnected to preserve that extra inch of wire. The conduit ran up and along the ceiling to the core in the concrete floor. That was where they pried the conduit open and snipped the wires. Fixing the mess would require fifty times the effort.

The transformers remained untouched. Either the punks didn't know how much copper they contained, or didn't think the effort tearing them apart was worth it.

If only the heating system in the mechanical room had been that lucky.

I sent Speedy up there to check for new damage so I didn't have to see how they hacked away at a fifty thousand dollar machine to strip off thirty bucks worth of copper.

While he climbed the stairs, I headed to the broken glass Speedy had found on the second floor.

Glass fragments crunched under my boots fifty feet from the window. The pebbles on the roof outside didn't show footprints, but they might as well have. The punks had climbed the roof and gotten in. Whatever they used to break the glass wasn't on the concrete floor. They must have carried up a hammer or a pry bar.

The plywood and new locks had made it harder for them, but it was going to be a chore to keep them out for good. The only sure way was to staff the hospital day and night. Running three construction shifts would have done it sooner, but that was beyond my tiny company.

Until the hospital was up and running, I played catch up. They busted their way in. I cleaned up and sealed them out. They found a new way in. The game wouldn't end until I finished the renovation or ran out of money.

Hard plastic hit concrete, rattled, then banged again.

A sixty-dollar drill bounced its way to ruin.

I turned for the stairs and hollered, "What's going on, Speedy?"

Feet scuffled down the steps faster than Speedy could move. I hustled to the stairwell and reached it ten steps behind two punks. A skinny kid with a red knit hat lugged a blue plastic toolbox. Speedy's toolbox. The second kid had my orange cordless drill in one hand and a beat up wooden-handled hammer in the other.

If I'd brought the broom I could have lanced the second one when he rounded the corner to the next floor, but he scooted by and plunged into darkness. My flashlight forgotten by the broken window, I stumbled my way down, quickly losing ground to the kids who hustled down the stairs like they lived there.

I could barely breathe when I reached ground level. My lungs screamed so hard I didn't notice the pain in my head or the watery feeling that had returned to my bowels. I'd quit smoking six months prior. My lungs still hadn't gotten the memo.

Sunlight.

I wheezed up the stairs and onto the grass in time to see the kids jump the chain at the end of the parking lot and head west down Main Street. "Stop them." A feeble command given how little air I had in my lungs.

Broad daylight on a Saturday. People everywhere.

The guy walking his fluffy little dog looked my way. I pointed. He shrugged and followed his dog in search of a place to defile my grass.

I trudged inside. Over to my light. Then up three floors to the mechanical room. Speedy lay at the foot of the heating unit in the dark with blood pooling in his scraggly hair. I didn't dare touch it. Working with recovered addicts meant blood could be as dangerous as any power tool. I'd no sooner put my bare hand to his head than a running circular saw blade.

His pulse was strong.

I left him in the dark and dialed 911 at the nearest window.

Chapter Four

Torn.

The paramedics all knew where the old St. John's Hospital was, but could they find the one unlocked door? And would they know the mechanical room was on the top floor? I couldn't take that risk.

I hated leaving Speedy, but I couldn't do much for him except watch and make sure he kept breathing. I took off my coat and laid it over him then leaned the flashlight against the heater and left it glowing against the concrete wall. If he woke up, he'd be able to see. I wasn't sure how much good the coat did. It was fifty degrees inside. Warm enough so he wouldn't freeze, but the coat might have kept him from going into shock. It was the coat's last act for me. After it was covered in Speedy's blood, I didn't want it back.

I didn't mind blood. During hunting season I was the guy who field dressed the deer. I fancied myself a surgeon, but Chris always reminded me that my patients never survived. By the time I finished, I looked like the villain in a chainsaw murder flick.

Speedy's blood scared me to death. He stuck needles in his arm for three years. I did everything I could to help him, but I wasn't going to let him kill me. The coat was a gift. One of many I gave Speedy.

The cop pulled up first and hopped out of his cruiser. A young guy I'd never seen. I briefed him on what happened. Pointed to the chain where the two guys ran. Like the guy with the dog, he turned away from the chase and headed inside, leaving me alone by the building entrance.

"You're gonna need a light," I yelled after him.

He pulled one from his belt and disappeared behind the plywood.

The ambulance arrived three minutes later and I led two EMTs up to the mechanical room to find the cop kneeling beside Speedy with his light angled at the floor.

Once the EMTs arrived, the cop became interested in my story.

Above Speedy and the EMTs, the light showed the dents the junkies pounded into the copper tubing on the exposed end of the heat exchanger. Most of the copper remained sealed inside. The junkies ruined the heat exchanger in a futile attempt to break off the bends in the copper coil. The cop didn't get the injustice.

"They whacked my buddy for his tool box. They could have killed him."

The cop splashed his light around the floor.

I assumed he was looking for the weapon. "The second kid running out had a hammer. It wasn't one of mine. That's assault with intent to murder if you ask me."

He didn't take my charge seriously. Instead he asked if the kid had taken anything else. "My cordless drill. The first guy had Speedy's toolbox."

I described the toolbox and he told me I could come to the station and file a report. The serial numbers would be necessary to recover the stolen tools. When I told him I branded my power tools with an L and a circle, he seemed surprised. The cowboy hat and down home language confused some people into thinking I was slow. Believe it or not, some country boys were actually pretty sharp.

The EMTs revived Speedy, but they couldn't get him on his feet. One of them went down and brought up the stretcher with the help of a fireman.

While they were gone, I showed the cop the cigar wrappers, the little piles of tobacco shavings, and a pile of crap at the base of the cement wall.

"They're spending an awful lot of time in here."

"Are they hurting anything?"

I could have slapped the guy. The punks were probably kids he grew up with. I led him over to a conduit that had been pried loose from the ceiling and showed him where the missing wires should have terminated.

He didn't do the math any better than Speedy.

"They cost me ten thousand bucks last night. You think that's not hurting anything?"

Speedy moaned. His head probably hurt as much as mine after I crashed into the vanity that morning.

They lifted him onto the gurney and strapped him in.

"Are you allergic to any medications?"

I broke away from the cop and pulled the nearest EMT aside.

"Nothing stronger than aspirin."

"Let us do our job, Sir."

"Listen a minute before you really fuck him up."

The EMT glared at me through the haze.

"He was in a construction accident several years back. Shattered his leg. After surgery they prescribed percs. He went from there to heroin. Lost three years of his life."

The paramedic nodded his understanding.

"Dope him up and he'll be no good to anyone until I can get him clean again."

The EMT patted my shoulder regretfully and turned back to the stretcher. The cop led the way out, lighting the stairs on the way down. I followed up the rear and watched the ambulance pull away.

It took less time to file the police report than to board up the two smashed windows. When I was done at the police station I was sure that like the windows, if I was going to stop the druggies from destroying my building, I was going to have to do it myself.

Chapter Five

Jim Stevens was an inspiration even if you didn't like junk, but if you did, he was a sage to be revered. He had a successful career in business then decided to help the less fortunate by turning unwanted household goods into a charitable empire. As I navigated to Cove Street, I admired a consummate connector. A guy who understood that his friends had more high quality stuff than they could ever use. More importantly, it made them feel good to give it to someone who needed it.

Quality junk beat a path to his loading dock seven days a week. The mission of GiftsToGive was all about kids in need. They took in clothes, toys, and books, cleaned and packaged them, and delivered them through social workers to families in need.

The little old ladies I dealt with, or their families, didn't have a lot of toys kicking around. They had lamps and couches and bureaus. Anything you'd need to run a household. A lot of my stuff ended up on Jim's loading dock, but not for the kids. Some of it went to churches and other local charities and some of it ended up in the Saturday yard sale.

The yard sale was meant for local families. It was called a yard sale because everything was priced so cheaply. It was all good stuff Jim got for free. The revenue helped buy the things kids got new from GiftsToGive. Socks, underwear, toothbrushes, school supplies, and birthday presents. Those things every kid wanted new, no matter how little they had. Jim understood those kids, and he did more for them than anyone I've ever known.

The aisles were a tight squeeze, but I didn't care. I went right for the clothing racks, feeling good about buying a kid a few pairs of socks. I also felt good about the insulated jacket I bought for three bucks. Some days I'd pick up a few extra things for Roxie to sell on eBay, but that day my plate was full. I wanted to pay and get back to sorting Mrs. Newbury's stuff.

The two women in front of me in line spoke rapid-fire Spanish. One held up a coat and kept pointing to it. The other disagreed with her about something. I wished I could have understood what they were saying. It sounded like they couldn't afford the items in their cart. I would have offered the three bucks if I understood, but all I could do was watch.

On my right, a woman with cotton-candy hair and an expensive-looking tweed blazer inspected a men's leather jacket. I visited my share of yard sales and I knew a cherry picker when I saw one. People donated leather jackets and hundred-dollar pocketbooks day in and day out. The charity sold them for peanuts. GiftsToGive was trying to help the locals, but they couldn't exclude the few middle class profiteers who showed up.

I couldn't see the labels on the three purses in her cart, but I was pretty sure they'd be for sale online for ten times what she'd paid. I couldn't help thinking Jim should have charged more, but then he'd be pricing out the people he wanted to help. He had a never-ending supply of free merchandise. Quality stuff I could only dream of.

"Hey, Lorado," a voice called from the processing area.

Angel waved from behind a shelf of used sporting goods then scooted sideways through the swinging door that separated the factory from the narrow aisles of the yard sale. Beyond the partitions, the main factory floor spread out to the size of a football field. Angel maneuvered much more easily among the heaping piles of donations. On the narrow yard sale side of the building, the bulky volunteer slowed to a crawl.

He excused himself three times and changed his route twice to make his way from the toys and sporting equipment to my spot at the end of the checkout line.

The pale Hawaiian shirt and green and white plaid shorts clashed not only with each other, but with New England February weather. Meaty and robust, Angel contrasted starkly with the young men he tried to help.

"What's going on, Big Guy?" he asked.

The rotund Italian calling me big didn't set well. I'd gained thirty pounds since I'd quit smoking. Roxie had started complaining and I didn't want to hear it from Angel, too. I had six inches height on him and I told myself that's what he meant.

I rehashed my problems with the hospital renovation, the tools, and Speedy getting whacked over the head. Angel's eyes twitched when I finished. He knew how much the vandalism cost me and he worried what I might do if I caught one of the punks.

He wasn't worried about me getting in trouble with the law. Angel worried that I'd hurt the kids. It's hard to imagine, but Angel heard about a kid breaking houses and stealing for drug money and felt for the kid before the homeowner. He treated every troubled kid he came across like they were his own. I had two recovering addicts working for me and that was enough. They pulled infuriatingly stupid stunts on a regular basis. I didn't know how Angel helped so many strays and kept himself sane.

"Newb been at work?" he asked.

"Not in a week."

Angel rubbed his face and dropped his eyes to the floorboards. He'd seen too many kids spiral out of control and he took every failure personally. Newb was on the edge and it was eating him up.

Angel had lost his son to heroin years earlier and his whole life went haywire. He gained a bunch of weight, his wife left him. He poured his life into helping the kids who still had a chance. He quit his job to coach football and lead two Narcotics Anonymous groups. One in New Bedford, the other in Brockton.

"His grandmother died. Wednesday? Maybe Thursday."

"Shit. I didn't know. He missed group. Not a good thing for Newb."

He looked at me for reassurance, but I couldn't offer any. A family tragedy was a huge risk for a fragile kid like Newb.

"I saw him Friday. At the funeral home."

Angel's eyes prodded me.

"He was ok." What good would it do to tell Angel the kid was whacked?

"Get him back in group, will ya? And tell him I'm sorry about his grandmother."

The woman in front of me paid and the volunteer behind the counter waved me ahead. Angel looped around a clothing rack and waited in the long aisle toward the exit.

The older woman priced my coat at three dollars and took my singles with a curious eye. I assumed she was annoyed I came in so much, or maybe it was just my guilty conscience. GiftsToGive aimed to serve the locals, but wasn't my money helping? Sure, a three-dollar coat was a huge bargain, but did this lady know how many truckloads of stuff I donated? Probably not. If she knew my last coat went to help a recovering addict, she might have given me a smile, but I had my coat and the feeling I'd bought a couple pair of socks. She couldn't take that away from me.

"Got any work?" Angel asked when I stepped into the narrow aisle of household goods.

"Maybe. I've got a big rehab, but I don't have any slack in my budget. What have you got?"

"A genius drywall installer."

"How long has he been clean?"

"Five weeks."

"You're killing me, Angel."

"He's a good guy. You'll like him."

I was a long way from drywall. The graffiti needed to be painted over. The sidewalks cleared. The trees cut down all around the building. The guy Angel was pushing on me would have done any of those things, but I had my hands full with Newb and Speedy on my crew. A guy who'd been clean five weeks was more likely to steal my tools than put in a solid day's work.

"I'll think about it."

Angel gave me a firm and somber shake. He knew I was a sucker for strays and that I treated Newb like a kid brother. That's why he hit me up every time he had a new guy who needed help. We both knew how unstable these guys were right out of detox and Angel had the decency not to push.

Halfway down the aisle I spotted a set of candy dishes I'd pulled from an estate in Fairhaven. Only the best stuff made it to the yard sale and I was proud whenever I plucked something headed for the trash and it wound up on one of Jim's tables. The dishes had been on display three weeks. I wondered how long before they lost their place of honor.

On the wooden stairs to the parking lot, I had the same feeling about Newb. How long could he hold it together before he ended up on the scrap heap?

Chapter Six

Mrs. Newbury's stuff filled every available storage space in her small cape. Before people could buy anything at the sale the following Saturday, they had to be able to see it. The magic of an estate sale was pricing and visibility. The good stuff had to be visible, but for that to happen every drawer and cabinet had to vomit forth its contents to be arranged in some semblance of order. Interesting stuff had to be placed around every corner to make shoppers keep searching and keep buying. With thousands of items vying for placement, I had to constantly decide what to highlight and what to stick in a drawer or a garbage bag.

Everything that walked out the door put cash in my pocket. And it was one less thing I had to carry when the sale was over. The more time I put into sorting and staging, the more money I'd make on the sale and the less time I'd spend cleaning the place out afterward. Roxie understood that I'd lost my entire day running around, but she wasn't pleased when I took my dinner to go and headed to Deadman's.

I hadn't been in the kitchen fifteen minutes when someone knocked on the front door. It had been dark a few hours. I hadn't turned on a single outside light to welcome visitors. I wasn't family. It wasn't my place to tell them Mrs. Newbury had passed on.

I waded to the front door, bracing myself to give the bad news to one of Mrs. Newbury's neighbors. But when I opened it, Cynthia Newbury stood on the porch with her son Nicholas on her hip.

"Do you need something?" I asked. She wasn't strictly entitled to anything, but who was I to deny her? Cynthia was Newb's ex-wife. Nicholas his son. Newb couldn't have been offering much support on what I paid him, especially given the number of times he decided not to show up for work. And I knew better than anyone that most of the stuff in the house was going to be thrown out anyway. So many heirs got into squabbles over stuff, assuming it was worth retail. When they found out how hard it was to sell a couch for a hundred bucks, most of them lightened up.

Cynthia pushed past me and set Nicholas down. She unzipped her coat like she was staying, but I was the only one in the place and we weren't exactly cozy. The twiggy, boyish figure did nothing for me. She'd just lost her job and the first thing that came to mind was that she was looking for someone to take care of her. No way was I up for that gig.

I wanted to grab the kid and keep them both there by the door, but he stripped off his coat and toddled off through the clutter toward the kitchen.

"I saw the ambulance this morning," she said looking back from Nicholas's trail. "I was worried you hurt yourself working in the cellar."

"I'm fine. They think I had food poisoning."

"It must have been really bad if you called an ambulance." She followed Nicholas who stood underneath the kitchen table, peeking through the chairs at his mother's legs. It would have been cute if I had more time.

I didn't bother to tell her Roxie had called 911.

She turned back to me. "And you're already back at work?"

"The sale starts Saturday. I've got a lot to do."

She didn't budge at my suggestion.

Nicholas came out the other side of the table and said, "Gamma. Dink." He reached for the sink, but his little arms couldn't reach the countertop. Good thing. I had silverware sorted up there. A fork in the eye could have blinded the little guy.

Cynthia didn't stress about the hazards all around. My parents and especially my grandmother stressed about every little thing. They'd have gone crazy if I played in a place like this when I was that young. The kid would probably be better off. If he didn't lose an eye first.

"Sorry," she said. "He loves to bring Grandma a drink." She knelt down to Nicholas, "Grandma's gone, Honey."

I would have added, "to Heaven," but that's just me.

Nicholas wouldn't stop reaching for the counter.

"I've got a lot of work to do," I said, but she didn't take my cue.

"You sure you're okay to be working?"

"I'm fine. I've got tons of things to sort." The mess on the kitchen table and counters seemed to make it obvious where I intended to work. Serving platters, a silver tea service, pots and pans, not a single square inch of counter space remained uncovered. Most of it was double and triple stacked.

She stood blocking me and let Nicholas explore the lower cabinets while I waited in the doorway, hands on my hips. When she finally noticed me watching she said, "Do you mind if we stay a while? He really misses his grandma."

I threw up my hands and headed for the living room. No wonder Newb divorced her. The woman couldn't take a hint.

Nicholas clattered around with baking pans he found in the cabinet by the fridge while I paced the living room and looked for space to add shelving for the sale.

The tattered couch cushions guaranteed it wouldn't sell. Someone could cover it, but no one would pay more than twenty bucks for the light green relic. I tipped it on end, leaned it in the corner by the stairs, and lobbed the cushions in that direction.

Mrs. Newbury had some chunky-framed mirrors hung above the couch. I'm not sure when they were in style, but I was pretty sure no one was going to buy those mirrors no matter how cheap I made them. They went in the corner, but not the trash.

Between the mirrors was a paint-by-numbers picture of a deer by a stream. Most people thought paint-by-numbers were cheesy. They might have been right. But my Grandpa West loved painting sailing ships and Grandma West had his paint-by-number creations all over the house. The day Mary Newbury showed me her treasures, we talked about this painting.

I can't remember where it was back then, but I think I convinced her it was worth showing off because she had moved it to the living room.

I took down the deer and stuck it in the corner with the mirrors to make room for my kitchen display. After a quick vacuum job, I went to the back entry and lugged my portable shelves in and started screwing the supports together.

The wide space left by moving the couch allowed me to set up two aisles with double shelves down the center of the room. The kitchenware would go nicely on the shelves or I could feature her collection of Department 57 Christmas decorations. The Department 57 houses were more valuable than her dime-store cookware, but February wasn't a great time to sell Christmas stuff. My golden rule for estate sales was that it's easier to get a million people to give you a dollar than to get one person to give you a million dollars. Cheap stuff sold. Always did.

Nicholas sat on the floor stacking measuring cups worth a quarter max.

Cynthia watched as I went down the basement steps in search of something to spice up my kitchen goods display. My mood improved with every step. An old lady's cellar did to me what smack did to those kids Angel tried to help. Every piece had a history and a value. The pink ceramic bunny with purple ears had to be a school project. It meant a lot to someone, but that piece would be trash or free. The four paper bags stuffed with vinyl albums held a lot more value.

My brain was so busy categorizing stuff that I didn't hear the shuffling upstairs.

"See you later, Lorado," Cynthia called down.

"Lock up on your way out, will ya?"

She said she would and I didn't hear her or Nicholas again. I was glad she got the hint so I could focus on my work in the cellar.

Against the wall, a workbench held a row of plastic storage containers with two hundred little drawers filled with nails, screws, bolts, clamps, anything a handy guy could want around the house. If I had room in the station wagon, I would have loaded the whole collection. Good thing I didn't. Roxie wouldn't let me bring anything else in the house until I had a big sale and made some room. I sighed and thought about pricing the lot. All those pieces were worth well over two hundred bucks retail, but we'd never get anywhere near that.

Further down the bench on a long stainless hook, I found a hand mixer in great condition. Beneath that I found four Pyrex casserole dishes in white. And in the corner between the end of the bench and the concrete wall, I hit the jackpot. A Griswold cast fry pan with a heat ring. The pan was made to cook on a wood stove in the late 1800s and the ring allowed a small gap underneath the cook surface to even out the heat from a wood fire. I had my anchor piece to draw collectors. A bargain at three hundred dollars. Next to it I found another Griswold, this one square. I couldn't believe my luck.

I left the Pyrex and the mixer and hauled my cast iron treasures up for a cleaning.

Chapter Seven

Two hours later there wasn't a spare inch in my kitchen display. The Griswolds hung prominently on the outer ends where every shopper who walked in would see the price tags waving. They were the only items in the lot sporting tags. Not because they'd sell. I didn't even expect to sell them to the collectors during the preview on Friday. I tagged them because they dressed up the place. Next to the Griswolds for two hundred bucks apiece, a Pyrex casserole for three dollars looked like a bargain. It was. Those things retailed for twenty. Truth be told, I'd be glad to take both Griswolds home no matter how much Roxie complained about space.

I settled into the armchair and the place got dark and quiet as I surveyed my work. My elbow throbbed. Most of the stuff wasn't heavy. It wasn't the weight that got me, but the constant repetition of picking things up and moving them around. I thought about the emergency room doc that morning and wondered if there was any ibuprofen in the kitchen.

I expected Mrs. Newbury to come out and make the hair on the back of my neck stand up. Too tired to go home and too creeped out by the silence to sit alone in the dark, I called my little brother to talk about a grant he wanted to write. The phone rang seven times and went to voicemail.

Ten eighteen. Probably writing a novel. What a life. The kid stayed home and wrote books all day, played on the Internet and once in a while worked four or five hours for me. Somehow he made a living at it. If that wasn't bad enough, our mother couldn't stop talking about her son the writer.

Dinner at Deadman's

Whatever.

The cereal escaped Nicholas's play date in the kitchen cabinets. Ever since I was a kid, I had eaten my cereal in a mixing bowl. The old lady's milk was still good, barely, but the sugar wasn't where I'd left it. Mrs. Newbury used the bowl from her silver tea service. Strange for everyday, but when you're about to die why save things for later?

The bowl wasn't on display with the rest of the tea service in the living room. And it wasn't on top of the fridge where I often left mine. It wasn't in any of the cabinets Nicholas could reach either.

The flakes got steadily soggier until I gave up the search and went for the source. She had a bag of clumpy granulated sugar next to the microwave. I chopped it up with a spoon and covered the surface of my bowl like a good heavy snowfall then headed back to the recliner.

Halfway to the bottom of the bowl, when the sugar had sweetened the milk just right, I realized where the sugar bowl had gone. Cynthia had hung around the kitchen table right in front of the tea service until I went downstairs. As soon as I did, she must have grabbed the bowl and taken off. Stupid bimbo. She didn't need to steal a two-dollar bowl. If she'd asked, I would have given her the whole service.

I wondered what else she'd taken and couldn't help getting up and walking around the kitchen, cereal in hand. A used coffee maker, or toaster oven isn't worth much unless you can't afford one. Ditto used cutlery and silverware. She left those sitting in plain sight.

She lived next door and had a key. I considered taking the price tags off the Griswolds in case she came back during the week, but didn't.

I delayed going to sleep, not because I wasn't tired, but because I felt Mrs. Newbury in the house and didn't want to anger her by climbing into her bed. Those Department 57 pieces turned out to be the anchor of my Christmas display in the dining room. The white tablecloth made a perfect snowy landscape, even though I did want to sell the table at some point. In an hour, the room was jazzed for Saint Nick and I slumped off to the pink comforter whether the old lady was going to try to kill me again, or not.

I didn't sleep the first hour. My stomach was fine, but after looking through the house for a few hours, I kept seeing flashes of things I wanted to tag and organize. The plastic hardware bins. A wooden carpenter's box. A cranberry scoop. She had some great pieces, and exhausted as I was, I still had to fight the urge to get out of bed and paw through the cellar.

I dozed off and on, dreaming of pieces I'd sell for big bucks.

A chill rippled up my back. I grabbed the cover, tugged, and the tension drove a spike of pain deep into my elbow. The lights were out, but I was wide awake in an instant. That elbow woke me up more times than I could remember.

The place was silent, dark except for the glowing nightlight.

Clink. Metal on metal.

Ghosts carried heavy chains or banged frying pans. This clink I'd heard many times before, but didn't register what it was until I heard the second one. A tiny metal piece fell and struck sheet metal. It wasn't Mrs. Newbury trying to run me off.

The wood floor chilled my feet when I got out of bed, but luckily, I avoided the plastic bit that jabbed me the night before.

One step into the living room, I picked up the square Griswold. Five pounds, cast iron. I could whack whoever it was fifty times and it wouldn't lose its shape.

Hands fumbled. A heavy tool hit the stovetop with a bang. "Shit."

As I grabbed the narrow shoulder, the cropped head of hair reminded me of someone. I raised the frying pan ready to splatter his head on the countertop until he spun around.

The kid looked at me in slow motion. A second passed, then two, finally recognition lit his eyes. Bad enough he walked the earth with the life sucked out of him. He was completely wasted.

"What the fuck, Newb?" I asked, lowering the fry pan.

Entranced by my voice, he stood and gazed blankly in my direction. This was what zombie apocalypse movies are about. They were all a metaphor for guys like Newb. Sad that kids watched them and didn't get what the writers were saying. Heroin stole Newb's life and no matter how hard we all tried to help him, the dope kept luring him back.

"You're messed up, Newb."

He tried to focus on my eyes.

Four screws lay on the stovetop. The upper cabinet had been emptied, the microwave's power cord detached. The vent pipe was twisted and bent.

"You're stealing from yourself."

He mumbled something I couldn't make out.

"Sit." I pointed to a chair blocked in by the table. He climbed around and sat, wedged into the corner. The screws went in much more quickly than they'd come out for Newb. I pushed the plug back in and tried to pop the vent back into shape, at least enough so a buyer wouldn't complain.

The table legs hopped as Newb pushed past. With my hand clamped around the vent, it took a moment to register what was happening behind me. By the time I let go, I was way behind. Newb faceplanted in the hall, and struggled up and through the door. As I lumbered after him, every dish on my shelves jumped and shook.

Even drugged up, Newb slapped his way out the door faster than I could get across the living room. I went outside more to yell after him to clean up his act than to catch him, but when I opened the door he was sprawled at the foot of the stairs holding his shin. He crawled and squirmed, trying to get away, but made no progress across the lawn.

I jumped all four steps and when I hit the landing, the ground rumbled, or maybe that was me. Either way, my momentum carried me forward and I landed just short of crushing Newb. I latched onto his legs and that was the end. My bicep dug into his calf. I felt his knees grinding together, but Newb was too out of it to feel the pain. He tried to kick away, but his legs barely moved.

"Let me go," he whined.

I caught him, but what the hell was I going to do with him?

Chapter Eight

Newb needed saving from himself.

"Run again and I'll hurt you." I yanked him toward the stairs with my left arm, not letting on that I could barely move my right elbow.

He parked in the recliner and this time I blocked his exit with my big, barefoot carcass.

"Where have you been all week?"

"The city." The kid never looked anyone in the eye. He kept his head down, his eyes lazily scanning the bottom half of the room. He could bolt or attack. Certainly he couldn't be trusted.

"Didn't think about calling me to say you were going to miss work?"

He grunted.

Technically he wasn't stealing. He was stupid and totally classless, pirating his grandmother's house before the ink was dry on his inheritance. The microwave would net him twenty bucks. A buyer would deduct two hundred for the aggravation of replacing it, probably more when you factor in how important a nice kitchen is when selling a house. Especially in this market. Idiot. In the next room was a fry pan he could sell for ten times what he'd get for the microwave. It was lighter and it wasn't mounted to anything.

That's the problem with his situation though. The kid made shitty decisions that kept compounding into deeper trouble.

My decision wasn't any easier. The cops wouldn't help. He was using, but they didn't have the resources to haul him in for that. Angel would want to help, but he'd probably have the kid committed somewhere until he cleaned up. Angel was tough. If Newb refused to go voluntarily, Angel would force the issue. Newb didn't need any more ink on his record.

"Who were you with?"

He didn't budge.

I kicked his sneakers. "Answer me."

"A girl."

"Doper?"

"No. Booze."

"Bullshit, booze. What the hell, Newb? You had it beat."

His head drooped further.

"You trade your life for a good lay?"

"She's hot, man."

Newb had no impulse control whatsoever. Beating up on him was pointless. He'd lost all pride in himself, interest in doing anything, and the dope kept him from feeling pain, physical or otherwise.

I was about to reach for my phone when knuckles rapped on the storm door's huge glass pane. I pointed at Newb to stay in his seat and stepped back to see Cynthia's long dark hair on the landing.

She ignored me and looked around the corner for Newb.

"Are you okay?" she asked.

When he didn't answer, she walked right past me and knelt down at his feet. She rubbed his hand and told him everything would be all right. His ex-wife. Probably hadn't received child support in a year. Still she coddled the guy like a stray kitten.

I knew another guy whose girlfriend turned tricks to keep them in drugs. What was it about these guys? Did they have some animal charisma, or childlike innocence the rest of us were missing? Why did Newb's ex-wife come running next door in the middle of the night to make sure he was okay? My ex-wife wouldn't cross the room if I fell down dying.

The kid had been pounding dope and some junkie bimbo for days. Did Cynthia have any idea? She'd seen him high plenty of times. She'd probably caught him whoring around while they were married, too.

"We've got to get him cleaned up for the funeral."

"We?" I asked.

"It's Tuesday. We've got two days."

Newb rocked forward in his seat. "I gotta go."

I stepped up into his path. "You need help, kid."

"S's waiting. Gotta go," he moaned.

"You don't need her," Cynthia soothed.

She might not have known how many days of work Newb missed, but she'd seen this before. He found a girl, hooked up, doped up, and dropped out of circulation. I wondered how many times she'd gotten him clean and how much she must have loved him to put up with his crap.

Even though Newb could barely move, it was clear he was getting irritated. He had a woman back in the city and he wanted her badly. At that moment, I realized he'd driven to the North End totally whacked.

Cynthia whispered to me that she'd take care of him and stood him up.

"Need to go," Newb mumbled.

"You need a good lay, don't you? I'll take care of you, baby."

My mouth hung open as she guided him out.

How much was manipulation and how much promise? Whacked out like he was, he probably couldn't get it up. She patted his hair as they walked out and he followed her like a puppy hungry for a treat. One arm around her back, the other reaching for her breast.

I couldn't sleep when I crawled back under the pink comforter, but it had nothing to do with the mishmash of junk downstairs.

Chapter Nine

Speedy didn't call until he was about to be discharged, and by the time I walked into the lobby at Tobey, he was waiting in a wheelchair facing the door.

"How you doing, old man?" I asked.

"All right."

He barely moved his head to speak and I knew the EMTs had passed my instructions to the hospital staff. Speedy must have been cursing me. The pain must have been miserable, but when he recovered from his head injury, he wouldn't need a trip to rehab.

"Want a ride?"

He waved me off and made some unintelligible sound. To understand Speedy you had to intensely focus on him when he spoke because he didn't talk much and what he said was often gibberish. Most people didn't put in the effort, myself included.

We hooked elbows and I hoisted him to his feet.

He held his shoulders perfectly still and took measured steps, always leading with his right and stepping even with the left. His left hand guarded the side of his head, seemingly in case it fell off and he needed to catch it. He gingerly lowered himself into my car, mumbled something about the mess, and feebly kicked at a can of wasp spray, a pipe wrench, and a dozen other miscellaneous goodies I might have needed someday.

I started the car and distinctly heard Speedy mumble, "Rat trap."

"Glad to see they took such good care of you."

He didn't say anything the rest of the ride except to complain once about my jerky acceleration. He didn't thank me when I dropped him off and didn't comment on his good fortune to find his truck the way he left it out front of the old hospital. Being clean for Speedy was plodding along an endless dreary path. Nothing excited him the way the drugs could.

I told him to take a few days off, and when he drove away, my regular crew was down to one middle-aged fat guy with a sore elbow. Angel's guy would have been eager to pitch in, but I called someone a bit more dependable and by the time I drove home and showered, my little brother was sitting on my couch, warding off Beta, my one hundred pound English Mastiff. The big-headed, drooly monster wanted to jump up on the couch and lay on him, but the kid is allergic to everything with fur, so he kept a hand on Beta's beefy shoulder and held him at bay.

"Leave Uncle Chris alone." Beta came over to my chair and lay down.

Chris sat back and crossed his legs, but he didn't really want to touch anything covered in fur and that included pretty much everything in our house. He'd be sneezing in twenty minutes, so I wasn't surprised when he prodded me into my pitch. "So some guys attacked you in broad daylight?"

"They didn't go after me, they're not that stupid."

"And you want me to fill in for your crew? Should I be packing?"

The place wasn't that rough. The old hospital had become a magnet for druggies looking for cash or a place to hide out and shoot up. Once it was cleaned up they'd move on. The problem was they could destroy the place faster than we could fix it. They made money selling my copper and they'd do it as long as they got away with it. I didn't have the money to play that game very long. I needed them out in a rush.

"So you have a plan and you need me to do what exactly?"

Chris was thinking I wanted him to take a pry bar to some kid's knees. It was all over his face. He was capable, just not willing. Not like he had anything against violence. Give the kid a shotgun and chase a deer by him and it'll be there on the ground when you catch up. Pissed me off he never seemed to miss. But he didn't want to hurt people without reason. He was nice to everyone, assholes included. I saw it as a major character flaw.

"I need you to help me do some driving and move in some gear."

"You think that's a good idea since stuff is disappearing even while you're there?"

I didn't get a chance to answer.

Tires squealed outside. The two of us made the porch in seconds.

My son Jake stood beside the wagon, swearing, and looking down the one-way street in the wrong direction. Beta pushed by me and leaped the stairs to Jake's side. He growled, ready to rip into anyone who looked menacing. When Beta couldn't find anyone to maul, he chased from the front of the station wagon to the back in wide circles. Finally, the angry dog settled at the foot of the stairs, frustrated and confused, still eager to put his teeth to use.

When Beta stopped prowling and Jake stopped swearing, I finally saw the hole in my windshield.

"Aw. What the hell?"

"I just pulled in," Jake said.

One wheel was wedged into the curb, the other was about eight inches away. Not a terrible parallel parking job for a beginner.

"What happened?"

He told me a square-looking car came tearing up the street the wrong way and a guy leaned out and heaved a brick at him. I asked what kind of car, but he had no idea. Jake could tell you anything about lacrosse or football, but he's not big on cars. He'd just got his license and was in that phase where his mother thought it was cool to send him to the store, and he was happy to get a chance behind the wheel with free gas.

Chris looked in the passenger's side and laughed.

"Something funny?"

"If you threw a brick through my windshield, it would stick out wherever it landed. In your car it blends right in with the mess."

"Wiseass."

"You'll be finding glass fragments two years from now."

I pointed at him across the car. "Beta, kill."

Stupid dog just looked at me.

Jake laughed his way up the stairs.

"You need to move back to the country where it's safe," Chris said.

Roxie picked that exact moment to leave her computer and wander outside on the porch. "I think someone's trying to help me."

"You've got to increase the dose," Chris said.

A running joke in our house. Roxie claimed to be poisoning my food for ten years. Some days I think she's tempted, but moving my junk would cost more than the life insurance policy would pay.

"Did he tell you about his trip to the hospital Saturday?"

When Roxie started telling the story, the world did a one-eighty around me. The brick was no accident and neither was the food poisoning. Someone was trying to kill me, and little old ghost ladies didn't drive cars and throw bricks.

Chapter Ten

"Any idea who it is?" Chris asked from the couch.

That was all I had been thinking about while I called the cops and the glass replacement guys. That and wondering how much I'd have to pay Jake to clean my car. If it was clean, he could take girls out, but he was too smart for that ploy. It was going to run me fifty bucks and that's only because the kid had no experience estimating how long it was going to take to do a job that big.

Roxie sat in my chair, away from the front window.

"Honey," I said. "Those kids at the hospital are just punks. They don't know where we live and they probably couldn't afford the gas to get here."

She glanced at me then down to the carpet. She hated my clientele. The project at the hospital was a reach for respectability. The grants Chris and I wrote together secured funding for much less desirable endeavors. Every remodel had its risks because the foreclosed and abandoned buildings we bought from the city were always in the roughest, dirtiest parts of New Bedford. That's why they were so cheap.

Construction meant constantly guarding tools and building materials. Some places I had to sleep overnight so my tools would still be there in the morning. But that wasn't the worst part.

We turned these places into sober houses, homeless shelters, detox units, places you think would really be doing some good. That's why I started, and that's why I hung on to guys like Speedy and Newb who had a glimmer of making it. But working in these places brought me into contact with the lowest filth our society had to offer.

Standing there outside my dining room, one of the dirtiest scumbags came to mind. A guy with a grudge who wouldn't flinch at throwing a brick, or a grenade for that matter.

Findley was one of those guys you could hear about on the news and shake your head, but not really believe people like him really existed. Being in a room with him made you feel dirty. It wasn't hygiene, or upbringing, or intelligence. Findley was a good-looking guy, a guy who could have attended college and made good money, but somewhere along the line, he went off track.

His eyes shifted all around when you talked to him. Looking for an angle, or an escape, or a way to stab you and take your wallet. You could never be sure, but you could be sure Findley only wanted what he could get from you.

He lived in one of my houses in a sober house program managed by my partner firm. I refurbished the houses, they provided meals, counseling, security, and ran the government funded programs. I got a bit of rent, and they made a tidy income helping addicts and impoverished families recover.

Noble business. Most of the time.

Findley had three young kids living with three different ex-girlfriends. He also had two new girlfriends living in the program house the government subsidized. One older in her thirties, the other not yet in her twenties. The girls each brought a friend or two to live in the house. Findley pumped them full of heroin and pimped them out. All of them.

He blamed me for getting him sent up.

I didn't drop a dime on him, but it was no use explaining that to a guy like Findley. He came out of prison with a grudge and got sent to one of my houses. Just my luck.

I started building homeless shelters after meeting a few families who had run into hard times and for one reason or another needed a place to live. If I were in charge, these people would get a whole lot more than they do. But then there were cases like Findley who came out of the womb expecting the world to hand them a living. Nothing could convince Findley to do a thing to help himself.

Hours after getting out of jail, Findley showed up at the storage unit high. The state had hired me to get his things out of storage. I'd been paying to store his furniture and personal stuff for two years because he came from one of my programs. I couldn't trash it, much as I wanted to.

Findley paid nothing. For the move from the house to storage. For rent on the storage unit. For the move back. Nada. If I moved furniture for most anyone else, they'd pitch in to help. Not this guy. He sat in his car until he didn't like the way we handled something. That was about half the time. Then he came out spewing cusses with his arms flying.

When we finished loading the truck, he went berserk. No matter what we said, he couldn't get control of himself. His big screen television was gone. I knew it was gone a month after he went up. It was hard to miss a plasma screen that big. Quite a contrast to the trash and dope bags on the floor of his place when we moved him out.

My guys sure didn't miss it. Two nights after we moved him to storage I got a call about a lock missing on one of my units. The television was gone along with some other electronics no man should be able to afford while the state was paying his living expenses.

His place was on the second floor. Speedy, Newb, and I hauled everything up without him lifting a finger. When we hauled the mattress up, he went nuts again. Said we'd ruined it. That he was going to sue.

The lowlife did sue. He couldn't afford a lawyer, but that didn't matter. I ended up paying for his new mattress and his lawyer. Losers like Findley would sue for anything and they always seemed to find a sympathetic ear on the bench.

I knew exactly where to find him as soon as I took care of my disappearing tools and copper.

Chapter Eleven

Tools and junk defined me and they littered my car. Riding to the hospital with my kid brother, his tools were hard to find. One cup holder was stuffed with pens with his name on them. The console had about a hundred bookmarks. Other than that, there was nothing in the car except us. Any mud on the bottom of my boots would have shown the second it flaked off.

He said the love of his life was a minimalist. I say it was the divorce that did it to him. Different women. One left him broke. The other tore his heart out from fifteen hundred miles away. Poor kid. He worked way too hard to make everyone happy. Most of the time he succeeded, but he was the one left wanting. He didn't even know he was miserable. He should have been working on a book, but he was driving me to the hospital, spending the afternoon hauling supplies into the old shell to help me out.

He'd rationalize it as exercise. Boy did we get plenty.

The delivery truck had a long boom for lifting building materials to an upper window, saving hours of legwork carrying bulky lumber and drywall up internal staircases. I could have removed one of the upper windows. They were mostly broken anyway, but the punks would have carried the lumber out of the building as fast as we brought it in.

We lugged one hundred sheets of drywall downstairs to the windowless electrical room. The same room that had been savaged for copper. Surrounded on all sides by a thick concrete pour, it was the only place in the compound that could be secured. The punks would break in upstairs no

Dinner at Deadman's

matter how many sheets of plywood and padlocks guarded the exterior, but with a little work, I could keep them away from my materials.

The next delivery packed metal studs, screws, joint compound, and a very solid steel door.

On his fifth trip loaded down with a shoulder full of studs, Chris started to doubt the wisdom of keeping supplies on site. "You really think you can stop them?"

We took a break from lugging studs and set the heavy door into the opening.

"They can still go over," he said.

"True. They could bust through that drywall up there and squeeze through the studs, but if they're going to take anything out of here, they've got to get through this lock."

"And this is different from all those other locks how?"

I let the door swing open, left my tools inside, and led the way upstairs. "You'll see."

I squeezed through the propped-open plywood door and the February sun poked me in the eyes. Forty-five degrees. Sunny. Not the mid February weather you'd expect in New England. The whole year was like that. We had two cold weeks, but the rest of the winter, we worked outside and didn't mind. Al Gore could kiss my ass, but I bet he was smirking in that mansion of his.

A father and daughter stopped on the curb. The father pointed to the plywood covered building. The girl looked old enough to have been born here before the place closed down. I couldn't hear what he was saying, but I was glad our delivery piqued some interest in the neighborhood.

"The neighborhood's getting better already," Chris said, lifting an armful of studs.

"Why you say that?" I asked.

"They didn't steal a single one while we were inside."

"This is just the opening act."

Chris gestured for more, but I didn't give it to him. We hauled studs down to the basement until the pile disappeared then we leaned against the trunk of the Volvo and watched the neighbors pass while we waited for the next truck. I was covered in sweat, panting. The kid wasn't even breathing hard. I wondered how long he could keep pace with Speedy.

A few of the neighbors waved on the way by. Most of them looked at the building, but when they saw us leaning against the car, they moved on. We didn't look like the druggies that had been ravaging the place, but they probably didn't expect the two guys who inked the deal to rehabilitate the old hospital and remove this eyesore from their neighborhood to be the ones hauling plywood and drywall.

"Are you out of your mind?" Chris asked when the first truck pulled in.

"Don't worry."

He shook his head the whole time he carried pipes downstairs. The same copper the junkies labored hours to break free from the structure lay stacked in a pile in the electrical room. Free to pick up and walk off with. No tools required.

Chris didn't say anything when the last truck pulled up, not until the spools of heavy gage wire had been rolled downstairs and stowed away behind the heavy padlock, but he had that look in his eye like I was nuts. My father got that look every time I told him I scored some great collectibles and needed a place to store them.

"You have insurance?" he asked.

"Oh yeah. I have insurance."

Chapter Twelve

The Volvo snaked backwards into a spot along Main Street, and I followed on foot half a block behind. Chris hopped out and skirted the back of the car in his sweatshirt and boots. A yuppie through and through. Compared to me anyway. The sweatshirt wasn't designer label and his work boots were missing a big chunk of the sole in front. If you didn't look too closely, he looked like a yuppie who had been doing a project around the house, needed something, and stopped into the pawnshop for a bargain.

Chris didn't work out in a gym. He lugged firewood, ran the brush cutter, and helped our dad lug iron for whatever project he had going on. He was a hick like me. He hadn't shaved in a few days, but the short haircut and the college-boy talk would have the owner thinking he'd found a score.

The door opened and a bell chimed. It swung closed and swallowed the discussion inside.

It was hard to wait there on the curb. But Chris knew what I wanted, and it wouldn't take him long to find out if it was there.

I learned a long time ago playing poker that people have a hard time connecting events separated by time. I waited three minutes before walking through the door and scooting across the main aisle. I lurked in the front aisle, catching glimpses of the discussion at the back of the store.

Chris stood in front of the counter that partitioned the back rooms from the sales floor. He told the owner he was installing a birdhouse in his backyard and it was too far from the house for his extension cords. He wanted a cordless drill and any other tools he could get cheap.

The gleaming finish of a red Gibson electric guitar caught my eye. Two clarinets in velvet-lined boxes, a few higher end acoustic guitars, and some cheap drums rounded out the music section along the wide aisle where I hid from the shop owner. The clean shelves organized anchor pieces. Cool stuff that would be in the shop for a very long time. It gave the place panache.

It was a showplace more than a shop. The cool stuff bought credibility for the haggler who worked the back counter, helping him pay less for what people brought in and get more for the merchandise he sold out of the back. I inched my way along the outside of the store, my blood pressure rising with each step.

The shop served the same clientele as GiftsToGive, albeit in a very different way. Toasters, coffee pots, and microwave ovens lined the side wall. Some of those came from the homes of the very people who were the big donors to the less fortunate. These kind people (or their neighbors) didn't donate anything that wound up here. Those things walked off just like my drill and Speedy's other tools.

The meaty guy with wavy brown hair falling from his Phillies cap had to know when he bought something from a junkie that it was a local score. He wasn't dumb enough to display my tools on a shelf out front. That's why I set him up to haggle with my little brother before he had time to list my stuff online.

"I don't need anything top of the line," Chris said. "If it's solid and it works, and it's cheap, I'm a happy guy."

"Let me check out back," the man in the cap said, disappearing into a narrow doorway behind the counter. He made a show of scratching his head and thinking about what he might have back there, but those tools had come in within the last twenty-four hours.

Halfway across the store a wide display of synthetic marijuana lined a glass case. Beside that a row of cheap cigars in purple and green plastic wrappers. Seeing them together it was obvious what I had been finding on the floor in the old hospital. The punks bought cigars and Spice here, carried it down the block, and smoked it hidden inside the boarded up shell of the old hospital.

"You're in luck, Buddy," the owner called as he squeezed through the doorway and plunked a drill on the counter. The orange plastic matched the drill I'd lost.

Chris dipped his head and rolled his eyes in my direction. I nodded and he pulled out one of those black plastic pens with his name on it. He clicked it twice, and I wanted to kick him for attracting attention to himself. He was a little OCD. Didn't even realize he was doing it, but it didn't matter, the guy in the Phillies cap was talking to a woman with three gold rings she wanted to sell.

The drill tipped up and his eyes locked on the spot where my brand was burned onto the bottom of the handle. My drill rested on the counter with the shop owner's prints on it.

If not for the wide glass counter I would have reached over and grabbed the jerk by the throat. He didn't even look nervous as he filed the edge of the woman's ring.

He squeezed a single drop of solution on the filings and pronounced the ring 24 karat gold then quoted her a price in pennyweight.

"You should get the price in grams," I said.

The guy snarled at me.

The woman didn't understand what I meant, but she looked interested.

"If you were buying that ring he'd price it in grams."

The guy did his best to look bored. "Grams or pennyweight, the price is still the price."

"They sell in grams because there are thirty-one grams per Troy ounce. They buy in pennyweights because there are twenty pennyweights in a Troy ounce. The little bit of imprecision means they take a little more and give a little less."

The woman inched back from the counter. I'd just cost the guy a sale and his annoyance bubbled under that red hat.

"You a gold expert or something?" he asked sarcastically.

"I deal in collectibles mostly." I handed the woman a card and wrote the name of another shop in New Bedford I dealt with regularly. It was a fifteen-minute drive, but my friend would treat her right.

She looked us both over and decided it was me she could trust. The owner couldn't hide his anger when she stuck out her hand and motioned for her three rings back.

"You don't want to drive all the way to New Bedford for a few extra bucks. It'll cost you that much in gas."

"I think I do," she said and waited with her hand out until he gave her rings back.

The second the door closed, he told me to get out.

"I'm not going anywhere."

For a split second, he sized me up. I knew the look because I'd worked as a bouncer in a strip club for two years. Plenty of guys gave me that look before they hit the floor. This guy had better judgment, probably because he was stone cold sober.

I didn't get frisky because a guy handling this much cash was certainly packing and I wasn't going to shoot him over a stolen drill. I put my hands together in front of my chin so he could get a good look at my forearms.

"Get out or I'm calling the cops."

"Great idea. Want me to dial?" I pulled my phone and asked if he knew the number for the locals.

He looked like a cheating boyfriend who wasn't sure how much his girlfriend knew. He couldn't call the cops to his place with a room full of stolen merchandise. He might if he thought I was clueless, but he couldn't be sure, so he grimaced while he considered his options.

"Chris, that looks a lot like my drill, doesn't it?"

The guy blanched when Chris turned my way.

"Sure looks like the Lorado brand here on the bottom."

The owner knew he'd been played. One of my junkie employees would have bolted, but this guy couldn't, not with fifty thousand dollars of merchandise lining his shelves.

"This guy tried to sell you my stolen drill? We should call the cops, shouldn't we?"

"I didn't know that was stolen."

"Bullshit you didn't. Where's the rest of my stuff?"

He squirmed. "That's all that came in."

I walked to the end of the counter, lifted the bridge, and ducked underneath.

"You can't come back here." He rushed my way.

"Watch me."

Halfway to me he pulled a club from underneath the counter and jabbed for my chest. If he'd pulled a .45 he had a chance, but I wrenched that club, grabbed his wrist, and whipped his arm around his back so hard his forehead slammed down on the counter and cracked the glass. Blood droplets sprayed.

Little brother stepped back and shot me an approving smile.

"Come on back and keep an eye on my friend while I go see if I can find the rest of my tools."

I shoved the owner to the floor and handed Chris the club.

"Don't do anything stupid," I said. "He's the mean one."

The doorway led to a stockroom with shelves lined with tools, appliances and other goodies that were probably just as hot as my stuff. The jerk out front had to be moving it online or to another store well outside the neighborhood.

On the way to my tools, I spotted a stack of Cash for Gold envelopes. No doubt the stuff he shipped to them was smoking hot. Once they melted it down, it would be untraceable.

My toolbox was pretty much intact. There were a few things missing, but nothing I couldn't replace. I brought it out and smacked it down on the counter. Chris let the owner get to his feet and we walked around to the customer side.

"I'm taking my tools."

"Hell you are."

"My brand is right here." I showed him the circled L burned into the handle. "These tools were stolen half a block from here. This weekend. The cops have the report. Why don't you call them and we can talk about the synthetic pot you're selling in exchange for stolen property."

"Spice is legal."

"Receiving stolen goods isn't."

"I didn't know those tools were hot."

I threw him a finger and hung it in his face, daring him to take a swipe at it. He didn't.

"If I find another one of my tools in here I'm going to burn this place down. Hear me?"

He waved me off. What else could he do?

The kid and I walked out with almost everything I'd lost that weekend.

"Why didn't you just call the cops?" Chris asked on the sidewalk.

"I don't want to make any more enemies in the neighborhood than I have to."

"Great job."

Chapter Thirteen

An hour after sunset, the headlights panned across the overgrown shrubs, raked through a mini forest of bare saplings that had sprouted up in the lawn during the years the grass hadn't been mowed, and washed over the plywood-covered windows. No one scattered from the yard, and I didn't catch anyone hanging from the side of the building tagging the new plywood.

I climbed out with my halogen light and checked every window on the ground floor, careful not to bump into anyone lurking in a shadowy corner.

In some places, the saplings were so thick they detoured me twenty feet from the building. The light sliced between the tiny trunks illuminating bricks and trash, but no junkie hoodlums. Around back, the asphalt made progress easier. The clean lines of brick meeting asphalt made it obvious no one was in back. The windows showed no recent signs of damage, so it was an easy walk around front.

Down the uneven concrete stairs at the entrance to the main stairwell, the padlock had been twisted open, the door ajar two inches. I locked the padlock on the ring so I couldn't be locked inside then climbed the stairwell and visited the usual haunts the druggies frequented to defile my building.

The mechanical room on the top floor was silent except for my own labored breaths. No new cigar wrappers littered the open space, but the pile of crap on the concrete floor still waited for someone to clean it up. It didn't smell from across the room, and I didn't venture closer. Someone could have been hiding behind the compressors, but I hadn't heard anything on my way up and hadn't seen any light coming from the room. I bet that I would have heard shuffling if someone was trying to hide from me.

With the interior walls removed, there were no hiding places on the main floors and they cleared easily. I flashed the light over each sheet of plywood and checked the screws to make sure they hadn't been tampered with, but other than that, it was simply a matter of walking the length of each floor and back again.

The autopsy room and the morgue in the basement were the best places for the little criminals to hide. I led with the light, darting it from corner to corner, finding nothing.

Back to the electrical room, I found the padlock had been removed from the new steel door. I walked in to find Chris waiting in a jacket that looked identical to mine. He flashed a light on a cot and a cooler set up in an alcove behind the door.

"Try not to fall off the bucket."

Going in a bucket might seem primitive, but it was a lot easier to clean than what the junkies did upstairs.

"You sure you want to do this?"

I waved him out with my light and he wished me good luck.

The padlock clicked closed on the outside, and I was locked in until morning. My phone worked in one corner of the room. Otherwise, I was on my own.

The cot would have been comfortable had it been about six inches wider, but the blankets were warm and I fell asleep within twenty minutes.

Chapter Fourteen

I stifled fourteen expletives that rushed forth in a string that would have made my grandfather proud. He was a world champion cuss stringer if there was such a thing. Grampy could take a pronoun or two and string together thirty or forty cusswords into a grammatically correct and interesting sentence without need to dilute his fury with proper words. No one in the cold electrical room would take offense to an indelicate word, but a noise at the wrong time might have spoiled my surprise.

My elbow throbbed. I'd banged it on the cot's wooden frame while I slept and the blinding pain had forced me awake. I sat up and reached for the big blue mug to distract myself, but the ache intensified as I became more alert.

This room was designed to hum with voltage, feeding the rest of the building the power it needed. It had been silent for a decade now. The thick concrete walls shielded the street noise leaving me in darkness and silence. Not a cricket, or a mouse, or a drop of water sounded in the thick darkness. I pinched a Devil Dog wrapper in my teeth and pulled with my left hand. The crinkling shrink-wrap sounded like an armed assault after the hours alone. The packaging tore open and dumped the little chocolate cake on my lap. The plastic ruckus echoed off the far wall. When it died, I tuned into the noise that must have startled me into moving moments earlier.

Steel clanked against steel outside the door.

Muffled voices.

The clanking returned, harder this time.

I grabbed my equalizer and pressed myself against the concrete wall behind the door. Something fumbled outside and a heavy hunk of metal clanked to the hall floor. The lock had been beaten and the punks' muffled celebration flowed into the electrical room when the door swung open.

A beam of light swung wide, just missing the cot. It panned around to the stockpile of materials heaped in the center of the room and I heard a gasp.

A second beam lit the silhouette of the lead guy. Scrawny and narrow shouldered. Drugs had sapped his strength. These guys didn't move as slowly as Newb when he was doped, so taking the three of them was going to be no easy feat for a guy with one good arm.

The third guy wedged the crowbar under the door to make it easier to shuttle my copper out. He walked in without a light, his outline lit by the reflections of the other two beams. He was bigger than the others. Luckily, he chose to stand back as his buddies went off about their good fortune.

"Can you believe this, man?" The two beams played along lengths of gleaming copper pipe.

"We're gonna have to beat this stuff up. We can't sell it like this."

Their voices echoed off the thick concrete walls, covering my footsteps as I crept up behind the biggest of the three men.

"How about that contractor Dale knows?"

The instant the contacts reached his neck, I buried the trigger and held it down. The sparks snapped and crackled, lighting him up for a moment with a sharp blue glow. He dropped immediately and I ducked behind a pile of lumber I'd stacked by the door to funnel the punks into the middle of the room where I wanted them.

A light flashed in my direction.

"What's wrong with you, Idiot?"

The kid's nervous system was short-circuited. He couldn't move. Couldn't talk. Couldn't warn his buddy to look out when he came over and kicked him to get him up. The guy bent over and shined his light right in the kid's eyes assuming he'd passed out. They couldn't fathom an ambush inside a locked room and their confusion bought me enough time to get up and zap the second guy.

The leader leaped away when the stun gun crackled. "Who the hell are you?" He backed up toward the copper, deeper into a room with only one exit, which I blocked.

"You're done stealing my copper, Asshole." I crackled the stun gun and waved it menacingly so he could see the blue spark fly. He stumbled on loose lengths of copper tubing and fell on the pile. He recovered quickly though, focusing his light in my eyes to keep me from rushing him.

I had to do something. The other two would be moving again before long. I pushed forward crackling the stun gun to scare him.

He raised a pipe for a moment, but it was a fifteen footer, useless as a weapon. The punk had enough experience ripping out my piping to know he wasn't going to snap that pipe and hit me with the small end. He fumbled around the pile, searching the floor for a weapon with his light.

The first guy, the biggest one, started to rouse himself. I couldn't fight the three of them at once. I rushed to the cot, grabbed my duct tape, and moved behind the big guy where I could block the door and wind the tape around his wrists several times. Two wraps around his ankles was enough to keep him from leaving the cellar.

I tried to move on to the second guy, but the leader chose that moment to make his break. I zapped the second kid again and let him drop. Too much current couldn't have been good for him, but if I let him recover he would have whacked me over the head with a concrete block.

I tossed the stun gun to my left hand and took two running steps to the aisle leading to the open door. He waved his light at me, but with us both at a full run, he couldn't blind me like he had before. And the light made a good target. I lowered my shoulder, crunched through the light, his arm, his ribs. I rode him down, felt the wind blow out of him, but I took his full body weight on my right arm and howled in pain as we went down. This time I let the obscenities fly.

The stun gun bounced at our feet. The kid lurched for it in the dark, but couldn't move with me on top of him. His salvation stayed six inches beyond his fingers. I lay still to catch my breath a second.

The flashlight came out of nowhere. The metal handle bounced off my temple and I could feel the reverberation all the way down my chest. The kid thought he could knock me silly long enough to get up and scramble outside, but all he did was piss me off.

I grabbed his throat so fast and so hard I could see his eyes bulge from pressure and surprise. That was the end for him. I rolled over onto my knees and smashed his face against the concrete floor.

He stopped squirming after the third time.

Chapter Fifteen

"Isn't there a two-dirt-bag, bag limit?" Chris asked when he saw the three of them with their hands taped behind their backs.

"No. It's however many your truck holds."

"And you don't have a truck so you called me to bring dad's?"

"I fix plenty of stuff for him."

"And that compensates us for being involved in kidnapping?"

"Relax, Writer Boy. This is good research."

"I've never spent a night in jail. That'd be good research too, but I'll pass."

I stood the big one up and joined him to his buddy by duct taping their forearms together. Chris picked up one of their lights and inventoried the materials we'd hauled down that day. "The new security system works."

I laughed and told him to help get the pukes up in the truck. He led the way, with the tandem right behind. I followed them up with my bag slung over my right shoulder and the leader walking up the stairs with his hands taped behind his back and my hand clutching the back of his collar.

We couldn't lift them over the tailgate while they were bound together, so Chris cut them apart and I stood back to cut them off if they tried to run. If they'd all run at once the commotion would have alerted every neighbor for three blocks, but the crackling stun gun kept them in line.

"Don't you know you're supposed to rent a white panel van under an assumed name when you do this?"

"I'm too cheap."

Chris saw me favoring my elbow and climbed up into the bed. We folded the big guy and rolled him in.

"What the hell do you think you're doing?" he protested. I'm not sure if he was too dumb to realize what was happening or if he was too scared of the stun gun to resist, but if he'd fought harder, we would have had to beat the crap out of him to get him in the truck. As it was, Chris sliced off a strip of tape, sealed his mouth, and rolled him toward the front.

We hauled the leader up and when he was lying on his back with Chris in between him and the big guy, he kicked Chris in the knee. If it had been his left knee, the one he busted up showing off on the trampoline, it would have buckled and dropped him like a girl. The right leg was damn strong from carrying him everywhere, so the dirty sneaker bounced off.

The maniacal expression that flashed across Little Brother's face transported me back to our cellar when we were kids. Back then, Chris was a hundred pounds. I was two hundred and change and he hit me harder than any grown man has since. He's two hundred plus now. Luckily, he's not nearly as mean as he was.

In that dark truck bed, he moved too fast for me to stop him. He folded his good leg, turning his knee into a battering ram and he fell, simply let himself drop two feet onto the punk's chest. Two hundred pounds drilled down on a spot a bit bigger than my fist.

Ribs cracked. The kid howled out the most horrifically pained noise I've ever heard. The big guy inch-wormed away. Despite the intense pain, the kid barely moved, but Chris wasn't done. He cocked his right and pinned the kid's head down with his left.

"Somebody's gonna get hurt," I said.

We locked eyes and I watched the anger ebb. He knew I was right. The truck bed wouldn't give. The kid would have been lucky to escape with a concussion. Chris would have hit him hard enough to break his wrist.

I was glad when he rolled him over, taped his arms and legs to the big guy, and sealed his mouth shut.

The third guy practically loaded himself. Chris taped his legs to the other two in a star formation and hopped down.

Dinner at Deadman's

They couldn't squawk when we rolled the tarp over them, but panic showed in their faces. The tarp bungeed tight above them made them invisible for the duration of our drive. Almost as good as a panel van and a lot cheaper.

Chris drove us out of the hospital parking lot at 3:30 A.M. At that time of night, no one was downtown to hear us, but even if they were, the punks in back couldn't do much to attract attention. We heard some thumping back there, but their feet were all bound together and their hands were bound behind their backs. Their only free, noise-making appendage was their heads. They could thunk the truck bed a few times, but they'd be unconscious before they attracted anyone's attention at forty miles per hour.

"You should have heard them going off when they walked in and saw the pipe stacked down there," I said.

"I can't believe they came the first night."

"Everyone saw those trucks unload. There's probably more of them around. These three wanted to be sure they got my copper."

Little brother wanted to say I'd done a good job luring them in, but he focused on the curving onramp instead. He looked back at the tarp a few times as we raced down Route 140. At forty degrees and sixty-five miles per hour, those guys had to be freezing back there. Served them right.

We swung east on Route 195 then south on Route 18 and right off again. If you're looking for compassion, Weld Square, New Bedford isn't the place to find it. You can buy passion or at least a passable act, but if you need help from a stranger, you are in the wrong place.

The moment we stopped the truck, two working girls took notice and meandered in our direction. Chris went around back and unclipped the tarp like he was working the pit in his first big car race. He wanted to be out of there before we ran into a cruiser, so I grabbed my bag and got ready.

He was up in the tailgate when Leona called, "Hey, Lorado."

"That's why you wanted to bring them here," Chris called from the bed.

Not many guys cut a figure like mine. Fewer wear a black Stetson here in New England. You could call me memorable. Not a memorable customer. Roxie took good care of me. Leona lived in a sober house I renovated.

When the air conditioner refused to chill the place so cold you needed a sweater, Leona called me. Strange that someone living off the state, getting everything free had so few qualms about calling for every little thing. Put a middle class family in that house, they'd pay rent and never complain that the A/C couldn't chill the place below sixty-eight. Hell, they'd never pay the electric bill to drop it that low.

Leona strutted over in her skin-tight mini dress when I hauled the first punk to the sidewalk. She gawked when I ripped off his shirt and duct taped his wrists around the nearest telephone pole.

Three more girls came over by the time we had the three of them stripped to their underwear, hands and feet bound to a pole or a sign too solid for them to move.

"You expect us to work right here?" a girl in a black dress and four-inch transparent heels asked. "If you do, you got 'em facing the wrong way."

"I'm not hiring you," I said and went into my bag and pulled out three pairs of swim goggles and two cans of spray paint. "When I'm gone, you might convince these guys to cough up some cash to cut them loose. Might be your easiest job tonight."

It was quicker to reattach the tarp with bungee cords than to fold it and stow it in the cab so that's what Chris did. He watched me put swim goggles on each of the guys. The hookers were intrigued. The guys' wallets were presumably in their pants in the gutter. I had no idea how much cash they carried, but it wouldn't be there long once we drove away. That wasn't my concern.

"The kinder, gentler kidnapper?" Chris asked. Then laughed out loud when I sprayed their faces blue, covering the goggles and blinding them.

I gave the red can to the hottest of the three girls. Hot being a relative term. She shook it but not hard enough for the agitator to do its job.

I demonstrated a few swirling blue lines across the men's backs and then handed off my can to a girl in a black mini who looked more eager. A stocky dark-skinned guy stopped beside the girls, unsure what to make of the scene. His friend, a shifty, skinny, white guy moved in close as we boarded the truck and sped away.

Chapter Sixteen

"I'm guessing they won't be back in my hospital anytime soon."

"Those guys are screwed."

The hookers wouldn't hurt them. They weren't violent. They were just desperate for money. It made me queasy thinking about all the fat, smelly guys they serviced. Those guys on the street weren't much different. They were doing what they could to make a buck. Unlikely they'd hurt the punks simply for sport.

"They won't get hurt. Spray painted, yes. Robbed, probably. Seriously injured before the cops cut them loose, probably not."

"You remember that thing about the original Wizard of Oz?" Chris asked as he whipped the truck up Coggeshall.

I didn't.

"Your skin needs to breathe, right. When they covered the Tin Man in paint, his skin couldn't breathe."

I shrugged when he looked my way.

"He died."

That was an "oh, shit" moment. Tattooing the little criminals seemed like the best idea, but I wrote it off because it was permanent. Seeing them go through life with "THIEF" tattooed across their foreheads would have been justice, but most kids outgrew this hoodlum stuff. The ones that lived long enough.

Neither of us said anything for about a mile.

"I don't get you sometimes."

"I'm a guy. What's not to get?" I asked.

"You bust your ass to help these people. We acquire buildings. We put up sober houses and clean houses. You're responsible for twenty-five houses full of recovering addicts and criminals all over the city. You help guys like Newb who are the most useless workers you could ever have on your payroll."

"What's your point?" I asked.

"Then you go and light these guys up. What's that about?"

"It's good for me and them."

"Really?"

"The system coddles these kids. They live better than you or me without spending a nickel because the state is trying to save them. They game the system over and over again and these idiot judges never get tired of hearing the same old crap. Someone needs to slap them upside the head. When they start stealing from me, you bet they're gonna get what's coming."

"What makes Newb and Speedy so different?"

The kid had a point. I'd grown attached to them. Sometimes they fell off the wagon. Shot up and disappeared. They'd sold my tools for drugs more than once. My warehouse had been broken into a dozen times, and I was pretty sure the thieves were guys from my crew. Stuff like Findley's TV disappeared. I assumed inside knowledge, but it was nothing I could prove.

I kept bringing them back. Clean kids would have worked harder. Faster. Better. Smarter. But these guys needed my help. They were sunk without me. Why I chose to help them I couldn't say.

Chris parked the truck and I climbed down.

"That was fun," he said. "Maybe next week we can go for arson and grand theft. Maybe hit a bank and get on the FBI's most wanted list."

"Thanks, man," I said and shut the door. "Work on your driving in the meantime. And get a faster car."

"Watch your butt this week," he said as he pulled away.

Just before dawn I walked past my new windshield and went inside to find Roxie already up and really glad to see me home. I didn't get any sleep until she left for work. Poor Jake made his own breakfast.

Chapter Seventeen

Panic swept over me with the morning sunshine. Beta nudged me. More of a shove considering his head weighed twenty pounds. Roxie and Jake were long gone. My uneasiness had nothing to do with oversleeping or making enemies with the pawnbroker and the kids the night before. I'd left thousands of dollars of material unsecured in that electrical room after the vandals pried the lock off. Anyone could have walked in and hauled off more materials than I could afford to replace.

I jumped out of bed and sent Beta into our tiny backyard. My dad always said with a lawn so small we should have gotten a Chihuahua. He joked that Beta took dumps the size of landmines. I heard dad telling me in that know-it-all voice of his that the yard needed to be cleared. His advice always came back at the most inopportune times.

The coffee brewed in the time it took me to shower, and I dumped the entire pot into my big blue mug. Yes, it all fit.

A note slipped out from under my mug and drifted toward the floor. I snatched it from the air and read Roxie's handwriting. The doctor had found Furosimide and a heavy dose of an over the counter laxative in my system. He thought I had been desperately trying to lose weight, and my strategy backfired. Roxie joked that he didn't know me very well.

All the way to the hospital, I wondered if I was wrong about Findley trying to drug me. He couldn't have expected to kill me with a laxative, could he? The whole thing could have been a prank. Speedy or one of the other guys messing with me. I vowed to keep a close eye on my big blue mug until I figured it out. If it left my sight for too long, I'd dump it and buy a refill.

The cops weren't waiting for me outside the hospital, but I figured we'd have a discussion about my security tactics eventually. I removed the cot and the cooler and any other evidence of my ambush. Then I installed the beefiest lock I owned and turned my electrical room into a vault for valuable building supplies. I probably should have installed a camera down there, but the lighting was impossible and I was pretty sure that once word got around about the hookers spray painting those three guys, I wouldn't have any more problems with supplies walking off my site.

Speedy still suffered from a nasty headache so I worked alone. He didn't think he'd be at work for a few days. No surprise. My guys weren't gung-ho workers. But what could you expect from day labor?

The saplings around the yard needed cutting and chipping, but my elbow was in no shape to run the chainsaw and chipper by myself. Newb was a couple days into coming down cold and was totally useless. I felt for the kid. Ten milligrams of Methadone would have done wonders for him, but a legit detox meant legal complications he couldn't handle.

A few of my tenants had minor maintenance calls, a loose handrail, some caved drywall, and a cracked window one of the women bounced a shoe off, but I ignored those and headed for Mrs. Newbury's place. Junk was my drug of choice. My brother still wanted to talk about his new grant, but the estate sale was only four days away and frankly, digging through the old lady's junk put me at ease.

If my brother had found me down there he might have said I was hiding from the person who was trying to kill me. That might have made sense, but the truth was I was good at spotting treasure in heaps of junk. That's why Mrs. Newbury had toured me all through her home six months earlier. Healthy as she was, she knew even then she wanted me to be the one to sell her treasures. To make sure her prized possessions found homes with people who would enjoy them and not end up in a dump after she'd protected them for decades.

The half of the cellar around the workbench would become Toolville. It's what men expected down here and why they gravitated downstairs, or to the garage and attic while women headed straight for the kitchen then the bedrooms. Mrs. Newbury had been proud of the tiny plastic drawers arranged along the back of the workbench. Her husband had gathered every piece of hardware necessary to maintain their home and arranged them neatly by function and size. The whole collection might fetch twenty bucks. I didn't have the heart to tell her that it was best left behind for the new owners. Thrown in free. I'd put a price on it, but I knew it wouldn't sell.

Mr. Newbury did have some eye-catching antique tools. A manual drill. Large wooden clamps. A custom-made carpenter's box. Those would get prominent placement. People told friends about items like the carpenter's box. And sometimes they drove all the way back to see it one more time. Anything placed within reach and priced to move would probably sell.

The best pieces took center stage on the workbench above the carpenter's box with its wooden sliding drawers and compartments on three levels. Tagged and ready for sale, the newer tools filled every inch of bench space. Two boxes of 25-cent items bookended the collection. My way of getting a million people to give me a dollar each. Once they opened their wallets, they'd fill boxes of items I'd sell for a quarter or fifty cents. It might not sound like much, but every item they took was one less thing I'd have to haul away when the sale was over.

The miscellaneous junk scattered everywhere was the toughest. To most people it was trash, but if a piece caught someone's eye, they'd give me ten times what it was worth. I whirled around and my eyes landed on a pink ceramic rabbit, two old lamps, and lots of boxes that could hold either treasure or trash. Too tired to sift through them, I turned back to the workbench and spotted a problem next to the breaker box.

A single red wire hung loose, a quarter inch from making contact with the screw that should have held it tightly in place. I flicked open my multi-tool, loosened the screw, and tightened the wire down. Somewhere upstairs a phone jack had just come live. I fixed stuff. It's what I did.

Chapter Eighteen

Halfway up the stairs I remembered I'd left the big blue mug on the workbench and went back for it. I still had no idea how the drugs had gotten in there, but I surely didn't want a repeat of Friday night on the bathroom floor. Trudging down and back up the stairs was a small price to pay to keep my insides on the inside. The insulation on that thing was so good, my coffee was still warm hours after it left the pot. A deep swig helped me catch my breath at the top of the stairs just as the mailman stepped in front of the door.

An older guy in postal blue waited for me to meet him at the door.

"You know about Mrs. Newbury?" I asked.

"Sad, isn't it? We still deliver the mail if that's what you're curious about."

"If it starts to pile up, can you tell Cynthia next door?"

"Sure. I know Cynthia. She spent a lot of time over here the last few weeks."

I wondered if that meant she hadn't spent much time here before then, but let it drop and took a stack of mail without looking at the dead woman's bills and advertisements. I wondered if postmen were alert to check for government checks coming to dead people. Seemed like they should be.

"Is the son going to sell the place?" he asked.

"Yeah. We're having an estate sale Saturday The house will go on the market as soon as it's cleaned out." I turned to show off the display of kitchen gear, but he wasn't interested enough to come inside.

"She was one of my favorite customers. So spunky."

Judging by his knobby knees, he wasn't much younger than Mrs. Newbury. He spoke fondly of her, more fondly than her own grandson, but I lost track of what he was saying when a black sedan pulled up to the curb behind him. The muscle head who got out was so pumped up he could barely bend his arms. He strutted across the lawn to Cynthia's house. It seemed she'd traded one type of drug abuser for another.

"...that hip was the beginning of the end."

"I'm sorry," I said, tuning back in. "What happened to her hip?"

"She fell," he said. He went on to tell me that Mrs. Newbury had hip surgery. She spent a few weeks in a rehabilitation facility and then there was a series of physical therapy visits to help her recover her mobility. At some point along the way, she fell ill and Cynthia stayed at the house to care for her until she recovered.

I was torn between listening to the mailman and following the body builder over to Cynthia's to check on Newb. I felt for the old guy. He knew so much about Mrs. Newbury I wondered if he had a crush on her. He looked twenty years younger. Guys just didn't date women that much older. I convinced myself the old guy kept up with neighborhood happenings to keep busy. Once I decided his interest was nothing more than senior citizen gossip, my curiosity died and I was ready for our conversation to die, too.

I closed the door, walked down the steps onto the lawn, and backed my way toward Cynthia's. He'd already delivered Cynthia's mail, so he had no choice but to continue on his route once I crossed into her yard.

The inner door hung open and the body builder's rage rattled the aluminum frame of the storm door. Inside the living room, he towered eight inches above Cynthia and pointed a bowed arm toward the bedroom. His taut, bulging biceps kept him from straightening his arm and making his point. The picture of vitality, I doubted he could move fast enough to take me in a fight.

Most of the conversation was muffled by the door, but the big guy was upset about Newb staying in her house. The guy had issues with his manhood. Deep issues probably related to steroids and his inability to take care of Cynthia's needs.

A petite little thing. She had two useless drugged up guys. I knocked with the purest of intentions. She was way too bony for me. Roxie was more woman than I could handle anyway.

Cynthia spotted me and came over.

The big guy said, "Get him out of here."

I assumed he meant Newb.

"How's he doing?" I asked when she opened the door.

"He's looking rough, but he's going to make it."

"Mind if I come in and see him."

She moved right out of the way and waved me in. Her boyfriend smirked and introduced himself as Chuck Ramshead. Every muscle from his chest to his wrists pushed up from under the tightly stretched T-shirt, but the one that counted was probably limp as licorice. I didn't comment about his last name being a descriptive verb.

Cynthia shimmied between us and led the way to the bedroom. I tried not to gawk at her hot little wiggle. She was way too flat for my taste, and I didn't need a fight with the monster, but her backside deserved attention.

Newb moaned when he heard us coming. The second Cynthia walked in, he begged for help getting off E. He promised anything as he lay in the fetal position, sweating profusely, not even aware I was in the room.

"Will he make the funeral tomorrow?" I asked.

"He'll be sick, but he'll be there."

Newb groaned. He and Nicholas were the last of the family as far as I knew. He was in no shape to handle the arrangements for his grandmother. A few days earlier, he'd handed me the keys to the house and told me to sell everything. I assumed Cynthia had done the rest.

She sat on the bed and rested her hand on the blanket over his feet. She was surprisingly tender. That had to be what enraged her new man.

I drifted closer and a whiff of stale, acidic puke assailed my nose and slapped me back. No way I could have watched Newb shake and puke and piss himself for five days. He was lucky to have an ex-wife who'd take such good care of him. A lot of wives would have tossed him out.

"You're gonna be okay, Newb," I said.

His legs jerked. The poor kid clutched his hamstrings. The pain had such a grip his eyes never ventured above mattress level.

She rinsed a facecloth in a bowl of water and pressed it to his forehead.

Newb was at his worst. He'd get a bit better overnight, but the following day at the funeral, he'd look like he was in line to be buried next.

The agony was too hard to watch. Newb wouldn't be back to work for at least a week. It was the first time I'd seen him go through this, but it wasn't the first time Newb kicked. I wondered why anyone who got clean once would ever go back. Seemed like a monumental screw up to me. I couldn't stand seeing him suffer, so I left him with Cynthia.

The big guy waited on the couch, legs and arms spread wide. How ridiculous to spend life scuttling around like a crab. He preened and flexed, but I couldn't help thinking he should have been working instead of wasting all that time in the gym. He should have seen the patio I installed in the last sober house I renovated. Or the tile job I did last month. Those things were a lot of work, too, but they were useful to more than a panel of judges and a few crazy chicks who wanted a guy so muscled he could barely move.

I left Cynthia with the two druggies and headed back to the old lady's house. The big blue mug waited for me on the kitchen counter. I raised it halfway to my lips before putting it down.

I laughed at myself as I dumped two lukewarm cups of coffee down the sink. The old lady couldn't spike my coffee. I hadn't seen anyone else in the place, but I rinsed my mug clean and filled it with tap water. Something about being there felt dirty. I scrubbed my hands like they'd been covered in grease. My stomach rumbled, but I didn't even look in the fridge on my way to the station wagon.

Chapter Nineteen

When you're spooked and really frazzled, sometimes you need to do something even if it isn't going to solve your problem. That's why I lied to the program manager at the halfway house before I climbed into the attic. The women's detox next door had a better view of Findley's place across the street, but they were tight about anyone going inside, especially a guy. Those girls were messed up for the first seven days. They'd do anything for a fix. Most would still have been tricking if they weren't ordered to clean up. Drugs-for-sex was a way of life. Any guy walking in threw up a big warning flag and I didn't need that kind of scrutiny because I wasn't there to fix anything that day.

The attic had one tiny window on each gable end. It didn't throw much light, but it offered a decent view of Findley's door and my car parked on the street below. Findley wouldn't recognize the wagon. The only time he'd seen me was in the moving truck, hauling his crap out of storage and up the wooden stairs to his place. Just thinking about it boiled my blood. The guy whined and complained for an hour about the way we moved his stuff. The state paid for the moving. And the girls earned the money to buy his big TV and furniture in the first place.

While I waited for Findley to show, I kept an eye on the punks lurking up and down the street. Plenty of my clients came from this neighborhood, and before they were my clients, the guys were drug dealers or thieves. Sometimes both. The .38 clipped inside my belt would chase the punks off, but only after I got down to the sidewalk. Fortunately, the inside of my car looked like a dump and the guys that passed didn't linger.

I had been hunting deer almost thirty years by then. I could climb a tree and sit still for hours. But sitting on that overturned five-gallon bucket by the window, the plastic ring dug into my thighs and after twenty minutes my patience wore thin. Waiting for people wasn't nearly as exciting as waiting for deer. I was feeling woozy from looking down, and I started pacing before the first person came to Findley's door.

A young guy in leather arrived on foot. I missed my chance when he went inside Findley's apartment, but two minutes later I snapped a photo of him coming down the stairs.

The camera didn't zoom close enough to get a clear look at the guy's face. It was a freebie Roxie won online. Like a lot of things she won by entering contests, it wasn't exactly what I needed, but it was good enough.

The guy looked more like a dealer than a junkie. Findley had to pass random drug tests to qualify to live in that apartment, so he probably wasn't using. If he was distributing to other dealers, he was a much bigger fish than I thought. He hadn't been out long, and he was already back to dealing and running girls. Some things never changed.

No one walked down the street for the next fifteen minutes, and the absurdity of my mission started to set in. Photographs wouldn't get Findley arrested. And photographs wouldn't tell me if he drove out to the hospital and spiked my coffee. He had the motivation. And he was truly a scumbag. But it was going to be impossible for me to prove he tried to kill me.

Findley deserved what he had coming to him. What I needed to figure out was whether to deliver in person or send the boys in blue to put him away again.

Footsteps came up the wooden treads. I took two quick steps, picked up a nut driver, and settled in next to the blower. The site manager walked in. She noticed the overturned bucket by the window, but didn't comment.

Chapter Twenty

In some families you could reach thirty years old before setting foot in a funeral home. Not so for Newb. He'd lost his father and mother, his grandfather and now his grandmother. He'd lost his wife, Cynthia, to divorce. As far as I knew, his son Nicholas was the only family he had left, so I expected the two of them to be seated alone in the front row for Mrs. Newbury's service.

Somber music and a stoic funeral director led me into a deep room lined with folding chairs. Cynthia and Newb sat one seat apart with Nicholas between them. Chuck Ramshead sat one row behind in a suit tailored to cover his bulging form. A funeral was the one place his constant sulk was in style. He didn't like Newb being with his woman, and I didn't blame him given the way she flaunted her body when men were around.

The rest of the front row was filled with people I hadn't seen before. Newb hunched forward, the light reflecting off the sweat on his forehead. Cynthia watched him intently and her boyfriend watched her. Nicholas was the only one focused on his great grandmother.

On my way to pay my respects to Mrs. Newbury, the line stopped in front of a collage of photographs. I'd seen the photos of Mr. and Mrs. Newbury from the 1950s and 60s when Cynthia came to retrieve them from the attic. What I hadn't seen was the odd collection of characters in the newer pictures. A sharp looking young couple posed with a polished blonde woman. They didn't resemble Newb in the least. On the opposite side, an older woman wearing a "boys regular" haircut and a polo shirt stood beside a young redhead in a bold flower print dress. If not for the age difference, they could have been dating.

The line moved ahead, pulling me toward the casket, but something tugged at my subconscious and I turned toward Newb. Forty mourners faced me from the seats when I turned around. I wasn't exactly inconspicuous in my black jeans and size fifty sport jacket. I felt forty sets of eyes telling me I was faced the wrong way, but my eyes refused to leave the odd little group in the front row. Newb's five closest relatives filled the seats next to him. Five people Newb had never mentioned. Five people who couldn't have had less in common with Newb if they tried.

A gentleman in a dark suit tapped my elbow and I moved up to face Mrs. Newbury. A delicate little woman. She lay peacefully with a subtle smile on her lips that reminded me of the last day I saw her. Her kind expressions. Her family stories. This wasn't a woman who held a grudge so fiercely she'd reach back from the grave. I felt guilty for considering something so ludicrous and said a little prayer that she'd find peace.

A dozen floral arrangements lined the viewing area and made a convenient place to land my eyes rather than face the seated mourners directly. Newb clutched his stomach. Still days away from feeling well.

I stopped in front of him, placed a hand on his shoulder, and said, "So sorry for your loss, Newb." We both knew his biggest problem was getting off the junk and that he'd be a wreck for the next few days. It was impossible to tell if his grandmother's death affected him at all. When you sat in front of Newb, he had the enthusiasm of a post. Unless he was in pain, his expression rarely changed. He was eternally flat like his emotions had been surgically removed. More correctly, chemically removed.

Cynthia motioned to the young man next to Newb and introduced him as Trig, Newb's half brother. The line to view Mrs. Newbury stretched out the door, so I stepped along the front row and extended my hand. Next to Trig was his wife Suzanne, a beauty with shiny black curls. Next to her, Trig's mom, a blonde hottie about my age.

Newb's father worked on a fishing boat, and when the boat came in, Bernie Newbury hit the bars. Newb had told me plenty of stories about his father and it was easy to blame Bernie for what became of Bernie Jr. The stunning part was looking at three kids who couldn't have been more different. Next in line was Delilah, a shy redhead a few years younger than Newb. Her mother in the last seat couldn't have looked more masculine without facial hair.

Newb's mother had died years earlier, but I'd seen pictures and Newb had told me bits and pieces about her while we worked. The only thing the three women had in common was sleeping with Bernie Newbury. Alcohol had to have played a major role in two of the conceptions. The blonde was either feeling really charitable one night about thirty years ago, or she'd had some major persuading from a bottle. The manly looking redhead had to have used liquor to her advantage. Even Bernie Newbury had higher standards than that.

I made the corner and found a seat eight rows back and waited for the reverend to begin the service, my attention more focused on the amalgamated family in the front row than the words spoken in celebration of Mrs. Newbury's life.

Chapter Twenty-one

The reverend spoke with great finesse about love, loss, and family, when the family in question had been cobbled together haphazardly then torn down until only mismatched pieces remained. His conviction and joy for Mrs. Newbury's journey to meet her Creator pulled my thoughts away from the strange family and the assortment of friends scattered around the funeral home. He shooed away my ridiculous notions that the sweet old lady in the casket had been trying to do me harm and I was left with brooding thoughts of my own mortality.

The mourners left the funeral home robotically, heads down, not buying the reverend's words about celebration. I considered my good fortune to have one of those caring families right out of the 1950s as I climbed into the station wagon alone and joined the line of cars with headlights on and fluorescent orange tags hanging from rearview mirrors.

The procession drove down Pleasant Street to Mount Pleasant and circled the cemetery drive on a day too bright for mourning.

The dance to the gravesite was always the same. I came from a huge family so was practiced in the rituals of funerals, weddings, and the like. Not being a close relative, I pulled off my Stetson and hung back. All people except the closest family did. We learned in school to avoid the front row so we didn't have to sit face to face with the teacher. But the stakes were higher there. No one wanted to be anywhere near that six-foot hole no matter how much they liked the person designated to spend eternity there.

The funeral director called the mourners to gather closer three times before the reverend began his graveside remarks and when he did, I was standing at the very back watching the gathered, hat in hand.

The service could have gone on longer that February day. The weather accommodated, but the remarks were brief. I sang *Amazing Grace* without looking at the funeral program. My eyes played tricks with words sometimes, so I got really good at memorization.

Circling away from the gravesite to intercept Newb and Cynthia at her car, my mind was consumed with the idea that ten thousand years could be an insignificant time period in Heaven when I saw Angel approaching Newb. Cynthia had helped support him graveside, but she'd picked up Nicholas and stepped away from Newb's side. The overcoat helped hide his hunched posture. His blotchy, clammy skin looked to the uninitiated like he'd been crying for his dead grandmother. But Angel would know the scoop at first sight.

I tried to cut him off, but didn't make it three steps.

The problem being iconic is that you can never blend into a crowd. People point out my little brother as the tall guy or the skinny guy or the brown-haired guy. Those descriptions fit half the people standing around him. Being the three hundred twenty pound guy in the cowboy hat in New England made me pretty much a one-of-a-kind item. People want to find me, and boom, there I am. No blending. No skirting the crowd. No saving Newb.

"Excuse me, are you Lorado?" an older woman asked. She stood almost five feet and looked up at me with a sweet smile in spite of my rugged appearance. Her husband, a full foot taller, looked apologetic but didn't offer a path around his wife.

"Guilty," I said with a tentative step toward her.

"I'm Lynne and this is my husband Grant. We live next door, lived, next door to Mrs. Newbury."

I tipped my head forward and touched the brim of my hat. It was one of those gestures that was really cool in movies, but most people couldn't pull off in daily life.

"Cynthia tells us they hired you for the estate sale."

The little woman didn't obstruct my view of the crowd at all. In the distance behind her, a dozen people had gathered around Newb and Cynthia just outside the small tent over the grave. Angel was stymied outside the group, edging his way closer to Newb, but his bulk made moving against the flow of mourners almost impossible.

I nodded to the woman, not remembering what she'd said.

"Could you do a sale for us, too?"

"You're not dead." The couple was about Mrs. Newbury's age and still vigorous. My joke didn't hit too close to home, but didn't earn a smile.

Lynne turned to her husband and asked for help with her eyes.

"She thinks we've got some antiques in the basement that might be worth something," he said. "I think most of it's junk, and I'd like to throw it out. Could you come take a look when you've got some time? We're right across the corner from the Newburys."

I could have held out for a few bucks, but I loved sifting through old stuff, and I was in a rush to help Newb. I agreed to take a look at the stuff in their basement, shook their hands, and left without asking which house was theirs. If they really wanted my help, they'd spot me when I was getting ready for the sale and come over. No skin off my back either way.

The crowd had thinned, but on my way through, I couldn't help noticing how many mourners were older than Mrs. Newbury. These were her neighbors and friends. I stopped for an old man leaning hard on a cane and felt the unfairness of that fall that took Mrs. Newbury too soon.

I skirted the Davis family plot and reached the cluster of people beside the tent as a large family shook hands with Newb and his half siblings in turn and headed for their cars. I tapped Angel before he reached Newb.

"Hey, Lorado."

"That new guy of yours still looking for work?"

"I've always got someone looking for work."

"Whether he wants to or not," I said. Angel didn't disagree. "Speedy got whacked on the head and he's out for a while. I might need to call your friend. Maybe end of the week."

I'd hoped Cynthia would get the idea and shuttle Newb toward the car, but they were busy talking to what was left of Newb's family.

Angel saw me looking in their direction, turned, and once he saw Newb's face, he whirled around. "Did you know about this?"

"What? He's got the flu. Hasn't been at work for a few—"

"Don't shit me, Lorado. He's coming down cold."

At least he was decent enough to keep his voice down. I tried to object, but he shook me off, agitated, his big body rocking with anxiety.

"You should have called me," he said. "If his color is pulled, he'll lose his apartment, and he'll be out on the street."

"You wouldn't," I said. "He can't afford the time or money to detox right now. He's barely making his bills and this will put him under."

"Is this better? Mooching off her? He's one misstep from the gutter."

"She's cleaning him up. He'll be okay."

"Who's going to take care of him when he falls off next time? You? Or that ex-wife of his? What do you think she's getting out of this?"

I assumed she was doing it for love, but it was too ridiculous to say out loud. I didn't know why chicks get this broken wing thing for used up guys like Newb, but they do. I'd seen too many women selling their bodies to keep a guy in drugs or big screen TVs to try to make sense out of it. Wasn't it obvious that a guy who'll ask you to turn tricks on other men wasn't boyfriend material? Lots of them did it. Lots of them.

"She's after something, trust me," Angel said.

"This isn't my call, Angel. You want to help the kid, go ahead. Just don't turn him in. He needs the work and I need him working."

"He needs a lot more than a few days rest and a kick in the butt to get back to work. You ready to help him? To really help him?"

Angel and I both knew that Newb was barely worth what I paid him. Anyone with a pulse could replace the lifeless kid on the job and anyone could do the work with more flair. Not that unskilled labor required flair, but a little personality would have livened the days up considerably. We both wanted to help him in our own way, but Angel was convinced his way was right and he had the law on his side.

Chapter Twenty-two

Angel put his arm around Newb and walked him off behind the tent toward the stone wall that marked the back edge of the property. If he'd have flashed me a look to see if I had his back, I would have been right there, but he plodded along with Angel, content to submit to whatever the big man asked of him.

The kid had the hopes and dreams of a fruit fly. Anything past the next twenty minutes was completely invisible to him. Angel could lecture all he liked, but I'd worked with Newb day in and day out. Nothing could bring joy to that kid like heroin. It made him a slave. He spent everything he had for less and less of a high until he could barely get off E. Getting clean meant being sick for a week. Vomiting. Shakes. Cramps. The drug destroyed him, but he couldn't stand to have fifty extra bucks in his wallet. He couldn't trust himself. The siren song could call him back whenever it wanted him. Newb would be vulnerable to the junk as long as he lived.

I turned away from the heartbreak that was Newb's life, and my eyes fell on a tall, thin figure with a sharp goatee standing in the shadow of a monument at the edge of the cemetery. From a distance the facial hair formation looked like a snake's mouth, and that image couldn't have been more fitting for the sleazy character who'd travelled four miles to lurk at the edge of the crowd. Unlikely he came to pay his respects to Newb, although they traveled in the same circles. More likely he'd seen me outside his apartment and wanted to return the favor by dropping in on me.

I had an inkling Findley had been hunting me, that he'd been all around me for weeks, and I hadn't tuned in to his presence until I saw him in the graveyard. That he'd almost killed me. My mug was safely locked in the station wagon, but I wouldn't touch that coffee again. It would get dumped and refilled at the next Dunkies I passed.

Findley split his attention between me and Newb. Too far away to flank him. Too close to traffic for me to take him head on without him melting away on the sidewalk.

"Lorado."

I heard the words and simultaneously registered the three pokes in my arm, my nerves delivering the words first and the touch second even though they'd been received in the reverse order.

The band from the front row at the funeral home surrounded me with Cynthia as their ringleader.

"Hi." I nodded to the bastard Newbury children and their mothers.

Trig stepped up and offered a hand. Polished in black from his shoes and belt to his tie, with a crisp white shirt and freshly pressed suit, the kid oozed success. The force of his intense eyes compelled you to shake his hand and listen to what he had to say.

"Cynthia tells us you're organizing grandma's things."

"I am." Weird he called her grandma.

"We didn't get a chance to see her while she was sick."

I cut him off because I knew where he was going. Whenever I did an estate sale people wanted something free. I didn't care what he took, but it wasn't my call. "Did you see her much?" I asked.

"Not lately. I was in San Francisco closing a deal last week and I got the news before I flew home."

Sure. Too busy.

His mother stood over one shoulder with a long black coat hanging open to show off a nice black dress, the dark outfit a stark contrast to her golden hair. Suzanne stood by his side, dark hair to match her funeral attire. Both women showed keen interest in the outcome of our conversation. Odd, because Mrs. Newbury didn't have anything valuable. These people could easily afford anything she left behind.

"I know how he feels," Delilah said. "I was at a craft show in Colorado. I left as soon as I got the news and barely got here this morning."

Delilah's mother stood by her side, but she was such a cartoon I had to look away or break out laughing.

"We're not looking for anything valuable," Trig said. "We just want some things to remember her by."

"I'm glad to help, but it's not my call. Everything in that house belongs to Newb." They gave me odd looks, so I corrected myself, "Bernie Junior."

"She was our grandmother, too," Delilah said.

Funny, I hadn't heard of her until today. I wasn't the patriarch of the Newbury family, only the retailer of unwanted goods. It wasn't my job to vet them, and I shouldn't have pressed them at all. Maybe I didn't trust Newb to protect his own interests. And maybe I wanted that fry pan a little too much.

Newb trudged back over with Angel by his side, not looking to join the conversation, but to reconnect with Cynthia so he could get back in bed.

"Hey, Newb," I began, "Trig and Delilah would like some pictures and things from your grandmother's house, but according to the lawyer everything belongs to you. How do you feel about them taking a few things?"

His washed out expression didn't change. "Give them anything they want."

He couldn't have chosen his words less carefully. I doubted he'd ever owned anything he needed to take care of. He couldn't keep the house and had no place to store his grandmother's belongings, but he'd given them license to walk away with anything no matter how valuable. The kid wasn't thinking. That was Newb.

"Can we head over now?"

All I could see was the Griswolds walking away.

Chapter Twenty-three

The bodybuilder had camped out in front of Cynthia's Nissan rather than walk across the grass to listen to the graveside service. Mrs. Newbury was nothing to him. Barely any relation to Cynthia anymore if she hadn't been caring for her the last few weeks.

"You mind?" Newb asked with an eye on the station wagon. Couldn't blame Newb for not wanting to spend time with the muscle head. Chuck hated the idea of his girlfriend nursing Newb back to health. If he'd seen her walk him home the night Newb tried to steal the microwave, he'd never have left the two of them alone.

"We're going to the same place, Buddy Boy. If you can find a seat, I'll take you."

He kicked aside the wasp spray, a few fast food wrappers, and a water bottle, and sat with a half empty bag of potato chips pinched between his lower back and the seat.

We pulled out of the cemetery north on Mount Pleasant and the kid hunched forward, without even a glance at his grandmother's grave. The significance of major life events zipped past Newb unrecognized. I felt a twinge for the poor woman as we passed and we weren't even related.

"How'd things go with Angel?" I asked.

"He knows I'm coming down."

As would anyone who knew anything about heroin. "He going to turn you in?"

"Nah."

Angel must have had said something to the kid in the ten minutes they were alone. Newb wasn't a big talker, so he must have gotten an earful from Angel. The kid wouldn't tell me what that was, but I didn't worry. The meaty Italian only wanted Newb to be okay. The kid didn't complain and I didn't press it. Angel would probably keep tabs on the kid and make sure he stayed out of trouble until he had his feet under him again. That only improved my chances of getting one of my better employees back.

When we drove into his grandmother's neighborhood, I asked him what he felt comfortable giving his half brother and sister.

"Anything they want."

"Are you sure?" I wished I hadn't priced the fry pan.

"They have as much right to her stuff as I do. I don't know why she gave it all to me. If they want something, give it to them."

I parked in front of the little cape and headed onto the lawn. Newb cut across for Cynthia's place. He was hurting, ambling along, but even so, I expected him to give a wave to the three carloads of family unloading at the curb. He didn't look back.

Trig hustled around the car and met me halfway to the front steps. Funeral garb was all wrong for treasure hunting, but Trig and Delilah were eager to get inside and their mothers followed closely behind.

They couldn't get around my bulk in the doorway, but as soon as I stepped in the aisle down the center of the living room, they came in, eyes wide. Both frowned at my displays. Delilah stepped to where the couch had been and looked around in search of it, not that it was small enough to hide somewhere else in the house. The couch wasn't worth anything and it wasn't until they started digging through photo albums and the box of framed photos that I realized she wasn't interested in having the couch, but bothered that it had been moved.

The two of them dug through a box of framed family photos Newb hadn't even looked through yet, sharing the ones they liked with their moms and telling stories about a woman I didn't think they knew.

When the knock came on the door, I was glad to excuse myself.

Lynne's face peeked through the storm door. "I saw you here and was hoping we could borrow you for a few minutes," she said.

"I don't think anyone will miss me," I said and walked to the kitchen and told the family I'd be back in twenty minutes. It felt right giving them space to look through the house on their own terms. I'd misjudged them and felt guilty for my own greed in the face of their loss. If anyone was grieving Mary Newbury, it was Trig and Delilah.

The layout of the Carters' home matched the Newburys' so precisely I assumed it had been built by the same builder. Lynne led me downstairs, and the musty air hit my sinuses long before we reached the cement.

Slick, dark concrete in February didn't bode well for anything stored down here more than a few weeks. Lynne shuffled along to meet Grant by a pile of boxes stacked on the floor. Three tiers of shelves stood along the wall. The light barely penetrated the murk, but once up close it was obvious that whoever stored this stuff was a collector. This wasn't junk. This was treasure.

Dilapidated treasure.

Fourteen tin signs backed the length of the shelves, leaning against the concrete wall. Crush. Pepsi. "The lettering on these signs is 1920's. Pre Depression," I said. "They were worth good money before they rusted."

Grant looked like I'd just exonerated him for a heinous crime. Clearly, he and Lynne had been discussing this collection for a while.

"What about these?" Lynne asked, holding open a cardboard box stuffed with linens.

"Whoever collected this stuff knew what he was doing," I said. "These linens could be cleaned, but the mildew may not come out and they probably aren't worth much anymore."

"Really?" Grant chimed in, needling his wife.

I shrugged to Lynne and kept digging.

"How about these?" Grant asked.

The curios lining the floor in the corner had been valuable once, but mildew stains and peeling veneer made them worthless. "Sorry," I said and shook my head.

Underneath the linens I found several rotting wooden cases. Blob top soda bottles and seltzer bottles from the 1920s packed the cases, chips of wood sticking to their sides.

A smug Grant smirked at the decaying wood, ready to pack up everything in this little corner and haul it off. A less scrupulous dealer would have charged them to haul it all away, but I couldn't do that. I held up a seltzer bottle for Lynne.

"Is that any good?" she asked feebly.

I pointed to the boxes of soda bottles. "Nothing in these boxes is worth a hundred dollars."

"Oh."

Grant was about to condemn the whole collection.

"Every single one of them is worth more," I said.

Lynne picked up a blob top soda bottle and dusted it off, all smiles. "Can you sell these for us?"

"You don't have enough here for a sale."

"I meant when you have the sale across the street," she said.

"That's not up to me. You'll have to talk to Mrs. Newbury's grandson." I'd lobby Newb for that. The bottles would definitely bring collectors. And collectors bought big once they got going. My thirty-three percent on a few dozen soda bottles would really add up.

"Oh, Trig. Such a nice boy. I'm sure he won't mind."

I told her it was up to Bernie Junior and scratched my head on the way to the door wondering how she knew Trig by name.

Chapter Twenty-four

I drove out of that little neighborhood feeling like a complete ass. Trig and Delilah shared stories about their grandmother for well over an hour after I finished advising the Carters. Together the two half siblings took five dollars worth of knickknacks and two dozen pictures. Newb, the guy who had lived next door to his grandmother his whole life, only came to her house to steal the microwave. He gave permission over the phone for the Carters to include their bottles in the sale. He didn't hesitate. Didn't care. Newb had bigger problems than the death of his grandmother.

The whole family thing was backwards in my mind, and on the long drive across town, I was really glad I didn't do something stupid like hide the fry pan.

The sun hadn't quite set when I rolled into the abandoned hospital. I looped around the exterior, dodging saplings on my circuit. To anyone watching my movements carefully, this visit looked identical to the one that ended with three punks duct taped to signposts, stripped mostly naked, and spray painted.

The plastic packaging and tobacco shavings that remained on the concrete floors had been there for days, and the heavy lock on the electrical room door hadn't been tampered with. When I finished my rounds, I decided that four cans of spray paint and a stun gun had taken the place of a security guard quite nicely.

My mood improved throughout the drive home.

I brimmed with pride for my frugal ingenuity. Kicking ass, too. What guy isn't proud when he kicks some butt? I believed every one of those punks needed a good whooping and that I'd done exactly the right thing, until I opened my front door and Beta growled.

Beta loved me. He slept in bed with us and deferred to me as the alpha male even though he probably could have eaten me. Beta barked sometimes before he realized it was me who had come through the door, but a growl meant trouble. If there had been a threat inside, Beta would have been too busy chewing the offending person to come to the door, so that wasn't a worry.

The dog recognized me and stopped growling, but instead of bounding over and jumping with his paws on my chest, knocking me backward, he ducked his head and U-turned for the kitchen.

Sad faces greeted me there.

"That car was back," Roxie said.

"And?" I couldn't imagine they were so grim about a drive by.

Jake sat with his head turned completely away, giving me a scant view of his right ear and not much else. Roxie prodded him to turn, but he didn't.

"What happened with the car? Another brick?"

"Not this time," she said, her sarcasm warning that this time was even more serious.

"So why are you hunkered down in the kitchen? They say something?"

They looked at each other, daring the other to tell the story while I pictured Findley hurling bricks at my family from a speeding car.

"Did you see who was in the car?"

Jake shook his head, more of a jiggle that kept his eyes focused on the back door.

"Show him," Roxie said.

My son turned his head and showed me a massive shiner over his left eye. He'd been keeping still to lessen the pain and keeping it turned away to delay the inevitable questions.

"What happened?"

"I got jumped on the way home."

"How many were there?" Jake was only five ten, but he played offensive line because, for his size, he hit like a truck. No single kid from his school dared take him on.

"Three."

"Recognize any of them?"

He said he didn't. He thought they were older, but he couldn't tell me if older meant upperclassmen or guys out of school. They hadn't taken anything, so it was personal. I felt sick watching him hold his head perfectly still.

Findley was going to pay for sending his thugs after my kid.

Chapter Twenty-five

The snug black jeans and tall black boots led the way upstairs to what would become the triage area. The hospital grant was the biggest project I had ever done, and it required more detailed plans than rehabbing and reconfiguring a three decker, which I did mostly on the fly. The final plans had to be approved before the next grant installment would be released, and that put me at the mercy of a woman I hadn't met until that day.

Denali, the long-legged architect clad in black, had been recommended for her skill. My friend hadn't mentioned her figure, and he was probably sure I'd choke when I saw her up close. Of course he never imagined I had a woman like Roxie at home, so my choking was grossly overestimated.

Denali tapped on her iPad and shot measurements around the space with a laser ruler. She settled at a point in the middle of the room where the security station would be built. Intake rooms would fan around the desk in a semi-circle so that the security officer could see into all the rooms from a single position. The doors would remain open most times and the walls would run directly away from the focal point, assuring that they separated the patients from each other but didn't obstruct the guard's view into any corner of the rooms. Anyone admitted here would be under constant watch for violent outbursts and suicide attempts. Building and maintaining the space was much easier than managing the crazies once the project was up and running, so I was glad to be on the front end of this one.

I looked over Denali's shoulder at the layout. The turtleneck sealed off anything a guy might be peeking at, so she didn't flinch at my presence.

Two of my measures had been off by a full inch. I suspected that was a mile in her circles, but the crude drawings had gotten me the grant with a little creative writing by my little brother. She corrected my mistakes without commentary. My kind of woman.

We moved north into the area dedicated to longer-term care. Precision wasn't as important here. If one patient had a room a few inches wider than his neighbor, it really didn't matter. Not to me anyway.

Denali took her measures precisely and recorded her results while I checked the boarded up windows for signs of tampering.

A voice called from the stairs. "Police. Anyone in here."

"Second floor," I yelled. "Come on up." I moved to the center of the floor so it was obvious even in the gloom, that I wasn't up to no good.

The blue uniform topped the stairs and headed over.

"You Lorado?" the officer asked.

I considered my usual reply, "guilty," but given the escapades in the electrical room a few nights earlier, I decided not to send him the wrong message. "That's me."

He walked over and shook my hand while he gave Denali a cursory look. She was more interested in her laser ruler than anything he had to say.

"Two parents came to the precinct and complained their kids ran into someone here who attacked and spray-painted them. You wouldn't know anything about that would you?"

"I haven't been here much since my associate was whacked in the head with a hammer, robbed, and taken to the hospital. Did you ask those parents if their kids had anything to do with that?"

"We have no reason to suspect their kids attacked your coworker."

"When did they say this happened?"

"Early Tuesday morning."

"How early?"

He didn't like my question. "Two A.M.," he grumbled, leaving no doubt he got my implication and resented it.

I pressed on anyway. When you're right, you're right. "They were trespassing on my property at two A.M. Shouldn't they be arrested for admitting that?"

"I'd appreciate your cooperation, here. You know we're not going to arrest them for trespassing."

"Why not? Isn't trespassing against the law?"

"Those kids were attacked."

"With spray paint? Someone ruins their clothes and you come out here to bust my balls? Do you have any idea how many thousands of dollars worth of copper has been hacked away and stolen out of this building?"

"We're talking about an assault."

"For spray paint? Someone ruined a hundred dollars worth of clothes and you're harassing me? You need to get your priorities straight. What about my man who was hit with a hammer and sent to the hospital? He missed a week's pay. Exactly what are you doing about that?"

Denali stopped measuring and turned toward my angry voice.

"This was a lot worse than paint on some clothes."

"Are you kidding me? Are you trying to tell me they got hurt badly enough by spray paint to compare to the thousands I've lost?"

"I can't share details of the incident until the investigation is complete."

"Investigation?" These guys seriously needed to get their priorities in order. A decent citizen, if you can call Speedy a decent citizen, was attacked and almost killed and they do nothing, but some punks get zapped and taught a lesson and this young cop came over and got all up in my face.

The cop was convinced I was the bad guy. "Do you own a stun gun?"

"I might, but if I wanted protection, I've got a nice .38. You're still missing the fact that those kids didn't belong here at two A.M. Nothing good happens that time of night. If I was here, I would have held them at gunpoint and called you."

"Are you going to cooperate or not?"

"There's nothing I want more that to stop the lawlessness on this little square of property so I can finish this project safely and on budget. You're the one who's not cooperating. You need to arrest those punks so they can't break my windows and steal my copper."

"Do you use spray paint?"

I threw up my hands. "You're free to check the place for spray cans."

He took two steps toward the stairs down to the electrical room. Apparently, the parents got a pretty detailed story from their kids.

"I want you to fingerprint every can," I yelled after him. "If they match those neighborhood derelicts you sure as hell better lock them up."

He kept walking.

"You'd better at least cite them for littering."

He waved over his head. We both knew he wasn't going to help. If you own property and it gets violated, you can't strike back. Everyone knows who you are and why you're doing what you're doing. I caught those little pricks in one night. If the cops were half that productive, my halfway house work would be nil.

All I could do was shake my head as I turned back to Denali and her measurements.

With the cops on their side, it was only a matter of time before those kids got the balls to come back. The hospital needed guarding, but so did Jake and Roxie. It was an easy call where to spend my night.

Chapter Twenty-six

Whenever I threw open the Deadman's store—that's an estate sale to the rest of you—there were two competing pulls customers contended with. Everyone who came through the door knew someone had died. The recently deceased owned a lot of good stuff that had to be sold at a huge discount, because they couldn't use it where they were going. Sinners and saints alike left their stuff behind here on Earth.

The bargains packed customers in, but at some point in their shopping experience, they got the heebie jeebies about the cause of death contaminating the merchandise. Whether their fear was medically justified or a combination of phobia and superstition didn't matter. Freaked out buyers didn't buy. Fortunately, most people were so consumed with the bargains, they forgot about the previous owner being planted six feet under.

When Lynne and Grant Carter arrived at the back door at eight thirty, cars had already packed in all along the sidewalk thanks to a few listings online and in the local paper. The signs along the major roads wouldn't start working until people were up and around, but the early indication suggested the place was going to be jumping all day.

Grant lugged the soda and seltzer bottles, and Lynne followed along brimming with pride. We arranged a special shelf next to the television that displayed twenty bottles Lynne had washed and shined.

"Where do you want the rest of them," Lynne asked.

"We're going to ask a hundred dollars apiece. We won't sell twenty."

"We might get lucky," she said hopefully.

"If we do it'll be a collector and they'll take them by the case," I said. "We'll have to discount them. You realize that, right?"

She told me she'd cleaned over sixty bottles. By the look on Grant's face, he'd been up late helping and still wasn't sure whether I was full of crap, or if I'd turned them on to a little gold mine in their own home.

At nine o'clock, I opened the door and three women came right in past me headed for the kitchen. Car doors opened along both streets and a stream of people flowed onto the lawn and up toward the door.

On my way back in, I noticed the spot where the Griswolds had been. They had sold the night before to one of my collectors along with a bunch of antique tools and a couple decent lamps. The soda bottles were my anchor now. I watched a woman step past them to look at the television I valued at twenty bucks. I pulled a tag from my money belt and prominently tagged one of Mrs. Carter's bottles with $100.

The next woman who turned the corner around my kitchenware shelves picked up the soda bottle and turned it in her hands, inspecting the flaws in the glass. She put it down, but I knew I'd accomplished my mission. Someone would buy a few of those today and that would make Lynne happy. The rest would go to collectors for about sixty bucks each. Not a great return considering what they were worth, but it would be an easy sale and a windfall for Lynne and Grant.

My first sale of the day was a complete surprise. I'd staked out the living room as the place I wanted to move items. I lingered there in the doorway, but my first call came from a woman about my age in the dining room. Being February I hadn't expected much from the Christmas display, but this woman hovered over the ceramic houses like she was ready to fight for them. The ring on her left hand was well over a karat, maybe two.

"How much do you want for these?"

Mrs. Newbury had twenty houses. My research online showed they sold for anywhere from fifteen to seventy-five bucks each. "It depends which one," I said.

"All of it," she said. The man across the dining room table didn't flinch.

There were twenty ceramic houses, figurines, trees, backdrops, little stone walls. All sorts of pieces that could have been put for sale online individually. They would sell, but the packing and shipping would have been a drag.

Twenty times twenty was four hundred. Adding in all the other pieces for a hundred was a great deal. But would she really have five hundred bucks cash? For Christmas displays in February? Not a chance. "Four hundred," I said, expecting her to balk.

"Three fifty," she countered without missing a beat.

"Sold."

She whipped out three sixty in twenties and I handed her ten in change. For the next twenty minutes, we boxed up the houses and her husband carried them out to the car three at a time.

Even before the dining room was clear, a frenzy hit the living room. One couple carrying out twenty-five boxes of stuff signaled to everyone else that Mrs. Newbury's stuff was priced to move. And move it did.

People kept cutting through the dining room to find treasure elsewhere. Anything I highlighted on the table would have sold. Newb was still on the tail end of sweating it out next door. Otherwise, I'd have called and had him create a new display there. I didn't have time. I was swarmed with women asking me to price dishes and utensils.

Across the room Lynne hovered in front of her bottles. She held them out to four different women who all turned away. Finally a couple in denim stopped to hear her spiel. I heard her say "rare" and "the great depression."

Instantly a woman down the aisle picked up some glassware and brought it to me. It was 1970's. Nowhere near the value of the soda bottles. She didn't ask and I didn't tell.

Lynne's enthusiasm helped me sell out a dozen pieces before a voice called me down the hall. I signaled Lynne to watch the living room while I was gone, and she looked proud to have the responsibility, but before I reached the hall, the woman in denim tapped my shoulder.

"The woman over there said you'd take eighty dollars for these." She held a soda bottle in each hand.

"Each." I said.

She nodded.

I held eight fingers to Lynne and her grin was instant. She had her first sale. Cash headed for her pocket and an "I told you so" for her husband that he'd probably never hear the end of.

I reached the bedroom and stopped short at the threshold.

A head of thin, artificially brown hair peeked over a floral dress. A younger woman vigorously shook her head. I pegged them as mother and daughter. Mother in her early sixties had a style that resembled Mrs. Newbury's. She wanted to save money on second hand clothes. Her daughter thought the idea so ridiculous her eyes were filled with pity.

"Do you really want to wear something a dead woman had on?" She'd wasted over a grand on a Versace bag. A thousand bucks for a label that impressed her friends. I'd sell her a bag that served the same purpose for a quarter. The mother was the smart one, hands down.

"She wasn't wearing that when she died," I said.

The daughter whipped around. The mother smiled in appreciation of the support. Between the two of them and the sixty other people who'd been through the bedroom, the place was torn apart with clothes draped over every available surface.

"How much," the mother asked.

"You can't be serious, Mom."

"A dollar," I said. Most of the clothes would end up at GiftsToGive even though they were nice. People like this woman with the Versace bag couldn't imagine buying clothes at an estate sale. Her loss. A dollar for a forty-dollar dress was a steal.

The woman folded the dress and asked, "How much for the bed?"

"One hundred."

"Really, Mom?"

"My bed collapsed last week. What's wrong with this one?"

"The lady probably died in it."

She was right. I did my best not to smile.

The daughter pulled an armful of clothes aside and inspected the rose patterned spread. I didn't expect the mother to use Mrs. Newbury's bedding, but I didn't add fuel to the fire. The girl ran her hand along the frame and stopped at a pair of scuffmarks.

Her mother considered the marks and offered me fifty bucks. I told her she could turn the bed the other way, but the daughter walked around the other side and there were two identical scuffmarks on that side of the frame. I didn't budge from my price and the woman left with a one-dollar dress. I should have taken fifty because I ended up moving the damn bed.

Chapter Twenty-seven

On Sunday at noon, I issued a curb alert. Then I spread a big blue tarp on the front lawn signaling the shift from Lorado the salesman to Lorado the mover. The first item outside was the ceramic bunny. Perfectly painted and preserved, no one would take it, but it said value and whispered that there was better stuff inside. Then came a box of tools that wouldn't survive the first wave, but would get some excitement going. Three claw hammers. Two pounds of miscellaneous open-end wrenches. Screwdrivers of every shape and size. The Christmas tree, still on its stand.

I scoured the house for anything that took up more storage space than it was worth. That's what junk came down to in the end. Everything was worth something to somebody, but it was the waiting to find that somebody that was killer. In the meantime the storage space had to earn its keep.

A red Mazda pulled to the curb and the guy jumped out and rushed for the blue tarp. The first curb alerter, a modern recycler, keeping junk from the landfill and probably hurting the pocketbooks of many corporations around the globe. It only took him fifteen minutes to arrive after I posted the alert and in two more he had an armful of the best stuff, dumped it in his trunk, and came back for a second pass.

"There's plenty of great stuff left inside," I said, huffing down the lawn with another box of ancient sporting goods from the basement.

"Thanks," he said, but his eyes never left the twenty by twenty square packed with freebies.

Three more cars stopped soon after. My curb alert was a success.

Half an hour later I'd stopped hauling free stuff out to the lawn and the house was again packed with bargain hunters, more like ants hauling eighty-two years of treasure out the front door one bag at a time.

"What's with the bags?" a young woman with a little boy on each hip asked.

"The garbage bags are five dollars. Any clothes, shoes, or handbags you can fit inside are yours for five bucks. The smaller bags and boxes are for anything else that isn't marked." I held up a paper shopping bag for her to see. "These are two bucks."

She grabbed a garbage bag and headed for the bedroom. Her kids looked confused for a second, then rushed to catch up. She wasn't going to find much her style. Mrs. Newbury was eighty-two after all. In two minutes she rushed back out and asked for a smaller bag. She filled that one with glassware in two minutes, paid, and led the kids outside to drop her bag and return to the hunt.

"There's still plenty of great stuff downstairs," I said.

"How much are the books?"

"Books are free. Take as many as you want." Little brother would cringe at that, but Mrs. Newbury didn't have any children's books GiftsToGive would have been interested in. Fiction was useless to me. A hardcover fetched a quarter in my circles. They weren't worth hauling around.

Lynne looked at me then the horde of people swarming around stuffing items into paper bags. She got it. If not for them, I'd have to do this tomorrow with moving boxes and a big truck. Thirty people rushed around to get the best stuff before anyone else got it. No matter how much they picked, there was always more around the next corner. I didn't have the heart to tell Lynne these people weren't going to buy her bottles, but I think she had already figured it out for herself.

She hung in the corner for the next three hours, watching them fill bag after bag with glassware, knickknacks, pictures.

When we were down to our last two customers, I walked over.

"I thought we'd do better," she said.

"We're not done. We can put these online. We'll get full value, but we'll have to pack and ship every one. That can be a pain. Or, I can bring them around to some dealers and sell 'em as a lot."

"What can we get?"

"Seventy."

Mrs. Carter lit up.

"Don't quote me. But I think we might do seventy on all of them."

Ten minutes later the entire collection of bottles was stacked in Mrs. Newbury's living room.

The rest of my night was less glamorous. The remaining contents needed to be categorized. Most of the salable stuff already had tags on it. I walked around and boxed about a hundred more good items that would sell online without taking up too much space in my warehouse. The rest would go either to the dump or GiftsToGive. Separating and moving the stuff would take the entire next day and that was if Newb and Speedy were both able to help.

Monday was garbage day, so I got a jump on cleaning the place out by hauling the barrels I'd already filled to the curb. I wandered the cellar for half an hour, looking for treasure, something I'd sell for a hundred or more online, all the while congratulating myself for taking advantage of the municipal trash pickup. I filled two big bags and hauled them over next to Cynthia's barrel.

Half a step back I froze. The silver outline inside the black bag was unmistakable. I sliced the bag open with my multi-tool and pulled out the silver sugar bowl, now caked with hard white crystals from whatever had been spilled into the sugar. You didn't need to be crazy to pick junk out of someone's trash. Once you learned to turn trash into cash, the appeal was hard to resist.

I felt clever on my way to lock up the house. Clever and curious why Cynthia had stolen the sugar bowl then thrown it away. Maybe the kid took it. Or maybe Newb saw her with it and called her out as a thief. Whatever the case, I was glad to have it back even if it was only worth two bucks.

Chapter Twenty-eight

The next morning when the sun rose through the scattered trees that separated the tiny houses in Mrs. Newbury's neighborhood, I was already packing the first load into the station wagon. Newb stumbled over from Cynthia's at about eight o'clock and Speedy showed up a short while later. Neither man looked eager for work. They never looked eager for anything. After dancing with the drug, everyday life took on a mundane tinge, but at least they both showed up on that crisp morning.

Estate was hardly a fitting word to describe what Mrs. Newbury left behind, so hiring Speedy and Newb to help me clean the place out really ate into my profits. But the arrangement allowed me to do what I loved while I waited for the next phase of the hospital project to get moving. It would have been cheaper to come here nights after work and haul the boxes myself, but that was a strain my body couldn't take. Better to take a down day with the crew and save my elbow the wear and tear.

I put the guys to work packing the truck with the best of the leftovers. Things I'd tagged and things I'd boxed the night before. It was enough work to keep them busy three hours. As I drove away, I didn't worry about them running out of work before I got back. If they worked half pace while I was gone, I'd be lucky. For what I paid them it was still a bargain.

Across town, down Route 18 the water came into view. As I neared the South End, it hit me that the city was built to enhance the drug and prostitution problems. The docks on one side brought fisherman streaming to shore laden with cash. The projects on the other housed hopeless men and women eager to score that cash. The two inevitably met in the rundown bars to trade for sex and drugs.

Jim Stevens had located his charity right in the heart of the mess to help the people who really needed a leg up. My time would have been better spent chucking the whole carload in the dump and saving my gas, but I believed in what Jim was doing. Maybe I was a sucker for people who needed my help. Maybe that was why I kept calling Speedy and Newb when I could have easily found more reliable workers.

Angel met me on the loading dock.

"These don't look like they'd fit you," he said when I handed up a trash bag stuffed with Mrs. Newbury's dresses.

"Outgrew 'em," I said, patting my belly and lugging a lamp out of the trunk. Over time I'd gotten to know what ended up in the yard sale and what got handed off to other charities. I liked donating stuff that helped keep the lights on for Jim, and it was a point of pride for me to come back and see something of mine in the yard sale especially if it was gone the next week.

"You travel back in time for this?" he asked when I handed up the lamp.

"Is this how you treat your major donors? It's a wonder—"

"Major donuts? What?"

Angel proceeded to mock every piece I handed him. When the car was empty, he came down the stairs at the end of the platform and leaned on the hood of the station wagon.

"How's Newb?"

"He's good," I said. "He's packing boxes and loading the truck while I'm gone. Cynthia's got him clean and he's moving under his own power."

"You know he needs ninety meetings in ninety days."

"Yeah?" The last syllable refused to stop coming.

"I promised I'd help him, but there might be a few days I can't drive."

"Don't I do enough for the kid?"

"You're the closest thing he's got to a sponsor."

I hesitated, but Angel refused to let me off the hook.

"A couple days, tops. Only if I can't get there."

I shook my head but Angel knew he had me.

He patted my shoulder and stepped back.

"What happened to him anyway?" I asked.

"A little spicy Latin number."

Prostitutes in the movies are hot. You'd want to have them and you wouldn't mind paying. Not so in real life. The women Newb ran with sold themselves for drugs and the combination of streetwalking and opiate abuse took a heavy toll. Still, it wasn't hard to imagine Newb getting distracted by any woman who paid him a little attention.

Angel said the girl's name like he knew her. I wondered if she was one of the kids he helped, but didn't ask. He had a gleam in his eye when he said she wasn't bad looking. According to him, she had neon stripes in her hair and features much too delicate for her line of work. For a guy like Newb with a ten dollar an hour job, no transportation, and a criminal record that spanned ten pages, she sounded way out of his league.

"A freelancer," Angel said.

"What's she doing with Newb?"

"Came up to him in a bar. He said he had a few extra bucks and she wanted to party."

"What was he doing carrying extra cash?" I asked out loud. Newb didn't trust himself with money. He deposited his check every week and withdrew twenty-five bucks. He bought everything he could on his debit card. I knew this because he was always asking for a ride to an ATM. Since prostitutes and dealers didn't accept debit cards, the strategy had helped him steer clear of trouble.

"I don't get it either," Angel said. "Help me keep an eye on him, will you? The kid's got big problems and he's all alone now."

I shook Angel's hand and headed back inside. The kid did have big problems. All it took was a flirtatious smile and a little action to get the kid back on drugs. It took a week of sweating and cramping and vomiting to kick. Newb had done it three times already. Why did he keep going back?

Chapter Twenty-nine

The station wagon rolled backward along the curb and stopped in front of Mrs. Newbury's empty barrels. The pile of garbage the city had hauled away saved me half a load to the dump. I was proud of my small victory as I stacked the empty barrels and lugged them across the lawn. When Newb rumbled out the back and laid a box on the edge of the asphalt behind the truck, my mood deflated. The collection of boxes didn't even approach two man hours. Unless everything inside had been packed, Newb and Speedy had done next to nothing while I was gone.

I lugged the first case of soda bottles to my car and then detoured around to meet Newb by the truck. Speedy never appeared. The guy took more than his share of smoke breaks, so I asked Newb where I could find him.

"Gone."

"Gone where?"

"Had a bad headache."

That was all he said. He stood there, empty and motionless, while I looked over the assembled collection of salable items. Mrs. Newbury had some great stuff. I could fill a little shop with all my treasures if I could just afford to pay rent and someone to work the counter. Someone who'd show up. Someone I could trust with cash. Newb wasn't that guy.

Visions of Speedy and Newb selling my inventory for drugs shattered my dream. I signaled the kid to climb up in the truck. I hefted the boxes and he packed them front to back like an airport luggage handler. Nothing was particularly valuable and I hadn't paid a penny for the entire truckload, but I still cringed when he tossed boxes around.

In an hour we had the truck and the station wagon loaded.

Newb took the truck to the warehouse, and I took the station wagon loaded down with soda and seltzer bottles in search of a buyer. The first guy I called already had a bunch of bottles he wasn't moving. The second guy wasn't interested in bottles at all, but when I got to DeAnna who ran a huge building salvage and antiques market in the south end, she told me she'd take the whole lot if the price was right.

Their place was two miles past the warehouse through city traffic, which meant Newb would get started unloading well before I got there. I didn't rush, and I didn't expect him to get too much done before I arrived.

The deal at the salvage shop was more valuable than the entire load of junk. If I closed it. If not, the bottles would start taking up space like everything else.

DeAnna came to the curb in tight jeans and work boots with her golden retriever by her side. She'd been around the block a few times, running her business on Cape Cod ten years before moving it to an old mill here in the city. She disappeared for a minute and came back with her husband Jim, a guy in his late seventies who hunched and really struggled to get down the walk. I knew if he came all the way outside, the buy was important to them. DeAnna wanted a good price and she wanted her husband's okay to take the whole lot.

Jim held the first bottle up to the light with traffic passing in the background, scratched his chin, and said, "Seventy-five apiece."

They may have scripted the whole thing for my benefit. Or he may have made the offer without consulting his wife. I didn't care.

The cases seemed a lot lighter going over the wood-planked floor of the old mill than they had going into the wagon. I didn't mind lugging them one bit. I'd just made fifteen hundred for two hours work. The deal was even better for Mrs. Carter. She made three grand on something her husband would have thrown away.

The news was too good to sit on. I called Lynne from the car and she was so excited about the sale she couldn't stop thanking me. I felt a bit guilty letting Newb work alone, but I was paying him by the hour. It would take a while to visit the Carters and get back, but my warehouse was surrounded by recovering addicts, not a place you wanted to carry a big wad of extra cash. Newb was used to rough neighborhoods. I told myself he'd be fine and focused on Lynne's enthusiasm for the deal as I drove across town to deliver her cash.

Three thousand dollars of I-told-you-so made Lynne giddy. She jumped in place then hugged me, her head barely clearing my belly. The dirty work shirt didn't slow her down. She clung to me for a full minute, time I would have enjoyed a lot more if she were forty years younger, but her enthusiasm was contagious.

I didn't get a chance to see Mr. Carter that morning, but if his attitude about my junk business hadn't turned around already, I was positive the cash would do the job.

On my way back from the Carter's I felt guilty. I expected Newb to have the truck mostly unloaded and to miss the ordeal of pushing the cart the length of the warehouse over and over again to pack the stuff away.

Newb got paid to work. It shouldn't have bothered me to leave him there alone, but for some reason my gut nagged me all the way across the city. It only got worse when I finally pulled into the lot I called Lower Methadonia, and a guy on foot waved me down.

"Hey, I know you. You're Lorado, right?"

"I am," I said through my window.

"We went to school together. Memorial. Remember?"

"Oh yeah. I thought you looked familiar. You doing okay?"

"Good," he said. "Five days in. How about you?"

"I'm good. I run a small construction business now. My warehouse is around back." I tried to play it down, but I knew exactly what the poor guy felt. His chest had just caved in. We both came from a town of one thousand people. Everyone knew everyone. My parents knew his parents and probably his grandparents. And now I knew he was coming clean off heroin.

He thought I was, too. That we shared a common bond. In an instant he realized his mistake. He'd just told me his darkest secret and he was terrified everyone in town would know within days.

The next time he saw me coming he'd duck and turn away. It had happened three times before. The guy was ashamed of what he'd done, but he was on the right road. I wanted to tell him he should be proud of his progress. That I wouldn't tell anyone in town what he was going through. But he was too mortified to listen, so I just smiled. I didn't offer to shake his hand. Bad idea to shake hands with too many IV drug users. Bad enough I had two of them riding around with me most days.

Several users came out of the clinic on foot headed back for the street.

I rounded the building with my windows rolled up, the Acushnet River shimmering in the background, a slight chop under the steady breeze. The drive around the far side of the building climbed steeply to my second floor loading area and the station wagon chugged hard to get to the top.

Newb stood on the platform inside the flimsy outer door. He couldn't have finished unloading already, but he stood idle, staring blankly as I climbed the incline toward the stairs. Odd behavior even for Newb.

He didn't even try to hide his loafing.

Something was seriously wrong.

Chapter Thirty

Lower Methadonia was not the safest place to store anything valuable. Zombie movies depicted the people who walked around outside my building. They would steal anything, pimp anyone, do anything to get drugs. Even Newb, the guy I trusted with my keys, would steal from his own grandmother. He'd proven that less than a week earlier. Why didn't I get the idiocy of leaving him alone in my warehouse for two hours? It took me several days to understand why it was a stupid idea, but right then I was consumed with worry, speculating about what could stop Newb from unloading the truck and moving my junk inside.

Newb stepped aside and let me push through the flimsy door first.

The loading area was piled high with trash, the heaps slithering down toward the center of the floor. Nothing valuable stayed out here because the junkies kept bashing through the outer door.

The inner overhead door was reinforced and secured with heavy-duty locks, so even when the junkies broke in, they remained where they belonged, on the narrow loading platform, away from my stuff.

The big door was up onto its tracks. No sign of tampering. The locks sat on the crate where I always left them when I went inside.

Even in the gloom, my brain knew something was out of place. Like a presence lurked in wait. For an instant, I wondered if Newb could have been angry about me turning him over to his ex-wife. If he'd let a few junkies in to jump me to get even. As I walked the first gloomy corner with my hands low and ready, I was glad I'd brought Mrs. Carter her money. My share bulged in my pocket. On alert to defend my windfall, I waited for someone to come flying out of the shadows in a blur. But as my eyes adjusted, I learned the problem wasn't something that moved, but a whole bunch of things that had been.

The light streaming in through the factory windows unveiled the catastrophe that had Newb frazzled silent.

On my right a deep stack of windows had been tipped like dominoes and smashed individually. Glass littered the floor in a narrow arc around the useless frames. Far to the right, two of the warehouse windows had been smashed. At the foot of the wall beneath them lay a mangled pile of glass and cords that had once been a variety of glass lamps and light fixtures. Someone had heaved them against the brick wall and struck the windows in the process.

At least forty fixtures lay in the heap.

Six windowpanes needed replacing.

Beyond the fixtures, three tall rows of shelves had been tipped, spilling doorknobs, screws, hinges, nails, any piece of hardware you'd regularly use to rehab a house. Half the boxes and bins had spilled their contents on the pine floor. The materials were so mixed up I felt like scrapping it all and buying replacements rather than paying Newb to sort it all out.

Whoever had been inside had taken pains to inflict as much financial damage as possible. This wasn't junkies. Junkies broke in because they wanted something to sell. Windows and lamps didn't qualify. They wanted power tools and electronics. Stuff I never left lying around.

Across the main aisle, my furniture storage area had taken the brunt of the attack. Every couch and mattress had been knifed, covers slashed, stuffing hanging out. Every bureau had been hacked with a hammer. The vandals had conserved energy, hitting each wooden piece three or four times with enough force to leave deep divots, and in most cases heavy cracks, on the outward facing surfaces. My entire stock of furniture was ruined.

The rehabilitation programs were ready customers for my used furniture, taking an apartment full almost every week. Every piece had come to me at a steep discount and now it was all useless. None of it came with a receipt. Claiming damages would be next to impossible. I had nothing to sell until I found a few more good estates, and I had to pay to move and dump the entire lot.

I'd lost everything I made on those soda bottles and more.

When I reached the back corner of the warehouse, my anger spiked. My junk kingdom had taken the worst abuse. All forty shelves had been tipped. The contents had been hammered and kicked and smashed against the floor and the brick wall.

Forty identical white boxes lay scattered in the aisle. The ray gun inside the first had suffered a direct blow. Smashed plastic bits spilled out of the box. Those had been selling online for twenty bucks apiece. Now every one of them was trash.

When I couldn't look anymore, I turned away and raised my eyes to the back wall. Blue spray paint had been lingering over my head, waiting for me to look up and interpret the swirls. "Fuck off Lorado" had been sprayed over the bricks.

Not junkies.

Three possibilities came to mind.

Findley. My spray-painted friends from the hospital. And Newb.

Findley had shown up at the funeral. He must have seen me outside his place and knew I was onto him. Maybe that was a good thing. Maybe he lost the nerve to kill me knowing I'd be waiting for him, and this was his last attempt to get even and feel like the big man he wanted to be. Too bad for Findley. I wasn't going to forget about the poison or that brick.

Unlikely the spray-paint kids knew my name. The blue paint closely matched the color they had used, but it didn't make sense for them to travel this far to get even with me. They could do a lot more damage in their own backyards.

I felt so guilty for suspecting Newb, I couldn't look at my helper even though I had the strongest urge to check his fingers for blue paint. He'd been here two hours. He had reason to be angry with me, and he wasn't above theft and vandalism. I considered that he'd made a mess to cover something he'd stolen. I'd never notice a few things gone in this disaster, but my stuff took time to sell. If it was easy cash, it was already gone. He'd already proven he wasn't interested in junk by ignoring the Griswolds.

I was no cop, but the first thing I needed to figure out was how the vandal got in. If there was no sign of forced entry, Newb might be my guy.

The windows by my junk empire were two floors up. No way anyone had climbed in there. Along the bricks and down the row of windows, the locked locks and pristine glass confirmed that no one had gotten in that way.

The west wall was the best way to rule Newb out unless he'd gotten clever in the last five days living with his ex. It was my only interior wall. An interior where junkies came to receive their daily dose of Methadone. These same men and women would scavenge or steal anything for a fix and once they were inside the building, only a six-inch barrier of pine and drywall separated them from my stuff.

I'd known this for a long time, so I leaned heavy stuff against the drywall, multiplying the barrier two dozen times over.

Newb followed at a leisurely pace as I inspected sheets of leftover plywood I'd stacked against the wall ten deep. He didn't seem surprised when I stopped at the stack of doors. A jagged hole had been ripped in the drywall five feet up. Someone had squeezed through and apparently climbed over the stack of doors then jumped down on the inside.

Newb shrugged as if to say it wasn't him.

He had the key and didn't need to break through the wall. That's what I read in his lifeless face before he walked away through the warehouse. Sometimes it was hard to tell if Newb was really that simple or if he was covering something more sinister. Most often he was like a little kid. Straightforward if not always honest, but that day I couldn't be sure.

Chapter Thirty-one

"When was the last time someone checked the place?" the officer asked.

It took a minute. With the work at the hospital and the estate sale, I hadn't been downtown in a while. I remembered picking up a toilet float a week earlier. "Tuesday," I said, remembering the half hour I spent crammed into the tiny corner of the bathroom floor while a line of girls formed in the hall.

"In a neighborhood like this, you should keep a better eye on the place. Check the locks at least every two days."

So the break-in was my fault?

The officer saw how annoyed I was and softened his tone. "Anything missing?"

"Hard to tell," I said. "There's so much stuff packed in here. Not stuff your average junkie would sell. Mostly building materials. No copper, of course. The junkies have gotten in before, but they've never done anything like this."

"Could this be personal? Anyone upset with you lately?"

It was a long list, topped by Findley and Newb. I picked up an antique clock and pretended to think. I didn't need the cops complicating my problems, so I told him I couldn't think of anyone who had it in for me. I wasn't not sure how I expected him to solve the case without my help. Maybe I didn't want him to.

"I assume you'll take an inventory and file a list of missing items."

"Sure."

"Check this," Newb said walking toward us. He tossed a can from one hand to the other. "Look what I found."

"Newb!" I yelled.

The kid froze, but had no idea what he'd done wrong.

The cop looked back and forth. He hadn't seen the spray-painted warning yet and I wasn't sure if he'd even consider fingerprinting the can for a robbery. Findley's prints were on file from his time in jail. My best chance to nail him was connecting him to that can, but that chance had been wiped away by my idiot helper.

I led the cop deeper into the warehouse where he could see the spray-painted warning for himself. He bobbed his head in sympathy, but didn't say whether he would have collected the can for evidence or not. My guess was that fingerprint analysis was reserved for rapes and murders. Thinking that kept me from smacking Newb.

We searched the tipped shelves together. The cop browsed the mishmash of items, clearly confused why I had all the useless junk so neatly organized in my warehouse and why anyone wanted to destroy it.

"He had to grab onto these shelves to knock them over. Could we get a print here?" I asked, pointing to a shelf support along the aisle.

He looked at me like I was insane. After that I didn't need him to tell me how backed up the crime lab was or how expensive fingerprint analysis was, but he told me anyway. On his way out he said he had dozens of these cases stacked up, that he'd do what he could, but not to expect miracles.

I pictured him going back to his desk, completing his paperwork and never looking at the file again. A list of stolen items would only waste away in a file somewhere. Nothing in the warehouse was marked with my name or address. Who had time to mark thousands of items?

The smarter solution was to capture the thieves themselves. On video. The high ceilings made an ideal perch for cameras to cover every possible entrance. And with an Internet feed, I'd always have the footage no matter how badly they smashed the cameras. Chris could help me set that up. I decided to ask him later.

Right then I had a big job to do. I picked up a handful of screws from the mess on the floor.

"Grab a screw gun and follow me," I said to Newb.

In ten minutes, we fastened a one-inch sheet of plywood over the hole. Findley could still get in by breaking through further down, especially now that he knew what the inside of my place looked like. If I was going to stop him, I'd have to deal with him head on, but that had to wait for nightfall.

"You hungry, Newb?"

"Starving."

The kid was always starving when I asked. Part of that had to be the weight he lost while he was hooked. Part of that was he couldn't afford to eat out and knew I'd buy.

He piled into the station wagon without bothering to look and sat on a bag of Tootsie Rolls. I guess he knew he was going to be sitting on top of something when he rode with me and had given up trying to move the junk out of the way. I didn't know if that said more about him or me.

Around the corner he asked if we could stop at the bank.

The kid couldn't afford his own car, so I didn't mind driving him places, but it had been quite a while since he'd gotten a check from me. A withdrawal was dangerous for the kid. Cash was more temptation than he could handle.

"What do you need, Newb?"

"Deposit a check."

A boss shouldn't ask his employees about stuff like this, but I felt like a father figure to Newb even if I had a hard time trusting him. "Where's the check from?"

Sometimes the kid was as open as a four year old. He unfolded the check from his pocket and showed it to me.

Pay to the order of Mary Elizabeth Newbury.

The Social Security check was a week old.

"You can't cash this."

"Why not? She left it to me."

"Yeah. She left you everything. But the government isn't going to keep paying her now that she's dead. That money's not yours."

"How are they going to know?"

We waited for six cars before making a left into the parking lot. The idea of my tax money going to Newb's dead grandmother irked me. I couldn't turn the kid in, but it was going to be another of those things that bubbled under the surface, reminding me how unfair life was. That the world handed kids like Newb all they need if they didn't think too much about where it came from.

"They'll find out eventually. Trust me."

When the car stopped, Newb twisted out and walked inside. He didn't hurry like most people would if their boss was waiting. And he didn't care if what he was doing was right or not, only if he could get away with it. He was textbook for an old joke, "How do you get to the homeless shelter? A series of really bad decisions."

Newb's decisions certainly had him headed for trouble.

Chapter Thirty-two

We shared a large mushroom and linguica pizza. Newb devoured his half. He always chowed down when I bought, but this time he hadn't eaten much in a week and his body was calling for all the calories it could get.

I didn't care. Half was plenty for me.

When he got in the car, he held up the bag of Tootsie Rolls he'd been sitting on during the drive over. "Mind?"

"Knock yourself out."

He ate four by the time we made the corner on Coggeshall.

"You're going to have to call and cancel her Social Security." I figured someone should try to help him stay on the straight and narrow. The family he had left didn't seem eager for the job.

"No way. Let them figure it out."

"They're going to sue you when they find out. Maybe send you to jail."

"I ain't got nothing to lose."

"You do, Newb. You have a lot to lose."

"Nothing worth taking."

"Newb, you just inherited a house with no mortgage. It's worth over a hundred grand."

The kid stared at me stunned. Like I was the first to tell him. How could he not know he'd get that much from the sale? Was home ownership such a foreign concept? The kid missed most of his childhood chasing drugs, but he should have known the inheritance was a big deal.

He tensed and I realized that much cash could kill him. Maybe he'd been avoiding thinking about his inheritance because he'd be tempted to party himself to death.

"Don't worry, Newb. I'll help you put it away." I knew a little about investing from my stint in life insurance. The best thing for Newb was to lock that money up tight where he couldn't get it for ten years. Too bad interest rates were in the toilet.

We pulled up and parked beside the box truck at the loading dock. The real work began when we reached the furthest corner of the warehouse.

"Help me get these shelves back up."

We tipped them upright and piled the fallen inventory against the wall. Newb started a pile for broken items and quickly found a mirror, three vases, and four boxes of heavy Pfaltzgraff dinnerware. All smashed. I tried not to look inside the boxes as we slid them to the wall. I didn't have insurance for the contents. Whatever was broken was lost.

At the end of the shelves we cleared and swept a twenty foot wide section of floor and started unloading the truck. The lamps had all gone to GiftsToGive, the ratty couch went out, and the kitchen and dining room sets sold for next to nothing, so the only big pieces we had were the bed and two bureaus at the very back of the truck.

When we'd finished hauling the boxes that filled the rest of the space, Newb and I balanced the first bureau on the cart and wheeled it back.

"Glad she didn't have a piano," Newb said.

"They're impossible to sell. I've smashed twenty of them with a sledge hammer."

"No way."

"Yup. Same with pool tables. I keep the balls, sticks, and the accessories, but you can't sell the stupid things. They're too hard to move."

"Hmm."

The kid wasn't much for conversation, but he was a decent worker when I was around. I found myself talking at him most of the time. He showed so little emotion it was hard to tell if he liked the chatter or not.

The bed moved easily but took three trips. We stacked it against the wall and Newb headed outside. I took a step to follow him, but couldn't help looking at the scratches on the frame that had cost me a hundred bucks. The bed would have sold if that lady's daughter hadn't noticed them.

With the light in front of the windows, the wear patterns resembled something I'd seen on the side of a truck where tie downs wore the gloss off a paint job.

A metal railing would have made sense to keep the old woman from falling out of bed, but the marks didn't come from a railing. They were made by a fabric or mesh. The finish had been rubbed off, not scratched. Underneath the heavy wooden frame, centered in the wear pattern was a fuzzy hole where a screw had been removed.

I couldn't imagine what they'd done to the bed. Even refinished, I'd get maybe one hundred fifty bucks. The mattress needed to move before it started smelling musty and with all I had going on, I didn't have time to strip and refinish the whole piece. I thought about a quick touch up that would be passable enough for someone to give me fifty bucks for it. I was leery about investing more time in that piece and the more I thought about it, the more irritated I was with the Newburys for ruining the bed and myself for not chucking it in the dump when I had the chance.

Chapter Thirty-three

Findley was at a huge disadvantage. He may have known where I worked and where I lived, but I served twelve houses within a five-block radius of his apartment. Two of them happened to be across the street. Not only that, but I maintained the building he lived in. He could never keep me out because I was the guy who changed the locks.

It may seem odd that I had so much work in such a small area, but detox and rehab facilities get located in troubled neighborhoods. Not only did that put the services close to the clientele, but it also solved one of the big problems in the neighborhoods hit hard by drugs: foreclosures. Every time we turned a boarded up three decker into a rehab, we closed down a potential heroin den.

Sometimes I wasn't sure if we were making it better or worse by treating the druggies here. Everyone may have been better off if we shipped them to North Dakota and put them to work far away from the drugs and street corners. Without temptation, recovery would have been a whole lot easier for most of them. And the neighbors would have been a whole lot happier and safer.

Even the station wagon full of junk was at risk of being swiped. It waited two blocks over in the driveway of a house I had finished rehabbing a few weeks earlier. The residents hadn't moved in yet due to a paperwork snafu, so my car wouldn't raise any eyebrows over there. It was also far enough away so Findley, who was always watching the street for customers and cops, wouldn't see it and know I was around.

After shift change at the women's detox, I slipped into the garage and settled in to wait for Findley to come home. The nurses and staff who worked the detox were there for the night, so no one had any reason to come outside and find me. The windows in the overhead door gave me a great vantage of Findley's staircase; though, they were at head height and I had to stand up to see across the street.

My knees started hurting after an hour standing on the concrete floor, so I hunted around and found three gallons of paint to sit on. A stick wedged into the crack at the edge of the overhead door widened the gap enough so I could see the street. A five-gallon can would have fit me better. It didn't take long for that metal rim to start digging into my backside, but I stuck it out and pretty soon the scrawny creep with the angular goatee strutted down the sidewalk.

I stretched to get my joints moving again and slipped out the side door, hustling out into the dark to catch him soon after he disappeared inside his place. I didn't carry a gun. I wasn't planning to kill the guy, but I had over a hundred pounds on him and a roll of duct tape clipped to my belt. It shouldn't have been too hard to teach him a lesson that would keep him away from my big blue mug, my house, and especially my son.

The wooden staircase shook on my way up. The lag bolts, four-by-four posts, and footings held, but the vibration telegraphed my arrival to anyone inside. I slowed halfway up for stealth and maybe to catch my breath. Fire code required a second exit. I'd installed a metal fire escape on the other side of the building, but I wasn't thinking about Findley running. If he did I'd never catch him. Instead I concentrated on the noise in the outer hall.

Two apartments shared the upper floor. When I stepped into the hall connecting their front doors, a dark haired woman gasped and stepped back. One of Findley's girlfriends, though I didn't know how you called someone your girlfriend when you sent her out into the night to have sex with other men.

I waved her past me to the outer door, but she pushed back against the wall and stared. Maybe I should have been thinking about keeping her there so she couldn't run to the cops. Maybe I should have been worried the way she gawked at me, but I couldn't help seeing the swollen patch underneath her left eye and wondering which horrors were worse: the things she did with the men she met on the street or the things she suffered inside the tiny apartment.

She didn't have anything to fear from me. I'd never hit a woman, or at least I hadn't up until then. I didn't want Findley to hear me talking outside his door, so I smiled and waved her out again. Even moved aside, but she wouldn't go. Findley must have told her about me, but it wasn't me she was afraid of in that instant.

The door flew open and whacked me in the shoulder blade, scraping my skin on its way past. Behind me a stocky guy barreled in low and drove his shoulder into my hip. If my feet had been planted, he would have bounced off, but I'd gone off kilter to save the skin on the back of my shoulder and that gave him enough leverage to plow me forward.

We stumbled across the hall and smashed into the opposite wall. The guy tried to wrap me up, but he chose the wrong side. My right elbow hurt when I lifted my coffee, but I could push a small car with my left, and I wrapped that thick forearm around the guy's head and yanked like I wanted to rip it off and kick it across the floor.

Lucky for him the second guy came charging in. With a club.

I wrenched the first guy around by the head, his neck popping. I didn't know which bones were grinding around in his neck, but I felt the vibration up my arm. His stumbling rear end kept the second guy at bay while I figured out how to take on both of them with one good arm in a narrow hall.

Shoving them onto the landing seemed like the best idea. I forced the second guy back, crowded by the first and the door opened behind me. I turned for a second, exposing the back of my head to the guy on the landing, but that didn't matter. Findley rushed out with a baseball bat and slashed at my knee.

No time to dodge. Too much weight holding the guy by the head to pull my leg up out of the way and honestly I just wasn't that fast anymore.

A locked knee risked a ligament tear or worse, so I dropped down and the bat hit low on my hamstring. My leg crumpled and I sagged, buoyed only by my grip on that guy's neck. My anger shot right down my arm, putting everything I had into ripping that guy's head clean off.

Half a beat later the club whacked low against my spine.

The pain ripped through me so intensely, I let go of the punk. He scrambled across the floor on his hands and knees and fell at the hooker's feet, holding his throat, his face red, his breaths ragged.

I should have flashed back to Findley, but a look in the prostitute's eyes forced me to double take. Her glare at the man on the floor was beyond contempt. Murderous rage maybe. She didn't lash out. Didn't try to help me, but I could only imagine the things these three men had done to her.

Findley wound up with the bat. I spun down onto my back, turtle style, raised my leg, and took the strike on the sole of my boot. His bat cracked. The reverberation stung his hands so much he let go of the bat and it fell in one useless-hinged piece. In his moment of distraction, I crunched my other boot through his knee and dropped him on the floor beside me.

I spun forty-five degrees and pushed myself up.

For an instant I congratulated myself. I'd met three guys head on. Two with bats. At my age that was something of a feat. But when I reached a squat, my hands ready, the guy with the club wasn't where he was supposed to be.

Everything went white. Pain blared in the back of my head and I knew he'd scampered around behind me while I was trying to get up.

When white faded to black, I slumped and fell.

Chapter Thirty-four

Mmmm. An overhead door rattled on its tracks. I assumed there were no automatic garage door openers in Heaven, so I was still alive.

My entire right side had been numbed by cold concrete.

Rain pattered.

Wheels splashed.

I opened my eyes and panicked. A plastic bumper closed in. I threw myself over, bound hands tucked under my body, bound feet circling in place as I rolled frantically for the wall. My head hit the stack of paint cans as I reached safety. They wobbled, the top can tipping and smashing down onto my chest as the tires rolled past. The car braked to a stop behind me.

The can kept rolling, over the threshold, and out into the rain.

I recognized my seat from the night before.

Brandy stepped out of her car dressed for the morning shift and saw me lying beaten and taped with my own tape. She screamed loud enough for Findley to hear across the street. The bastard probably had a good laugh.

He could have killed me and dumped me somewhere while I was unconscious, but I guess he was worried someone had seen me come to his place. Dumping me here sent a message. He knew where I'd been watching from and he wasn't playing. If I was going to catch Findley I had to seriously up my game. Brute force worked on those kids in the hospital, but Findley was a bigger fish. Running drugs and girls taught him to protect himself. He had to be clever to survive, small as he was.

My heart rate slowed. The adrenaline rush subsided, then the damage they'd done the night before hit me like a brick. Brandy stood looking down. I wanted to tell her to pull the tape from my mouth and cut my hands and feet free, but my roll to safety had set off flares of pain in my ribs and arms. I hummed and fell slack, my head on the concrete, waiting. Brandy was a nurse. It didn't take her long to understand what had happened. She got right to work on the tape covering my mouth.

That stuff really holds tight. She tugged steadily at one corner. I expected her to rip it off in one quick motion, but she kept even pressure and let it peel away. Blood dripped from my cracked lips. If half the nerves in my body weren't constantly signaling my brain, the pain would have been excruciating. The cool air hit the back of my throat and I took a deep breath in spite of the ache it caused in my ribcage.

"I'll call an ambulance," she said.

"Don't do that." Cops would have arrived before the ambulance with questions about where I'd been and what I'd been doing. I could have lied and said I went to work on a problem next door, but a little investigation would show that no one had requested my services.

"Are you sure?"

"Yeah. Just get me loose. There's a knife on my belt."

Brandy slid the multi-tool from its case. It took her a moment to get a knife blade open then she carefully sliced the tape and peeled it back. She sawed through the tape at my ankles and I was free. I didn't even try to get up. My shoulders ached from a night of bondage and whatever abuse they'd taken while I was out. I've got beef covering me most places, but even I have little protection at my sides and on my back. Lying still, the pain was unbearable. Sitting up was unthinkable.

If I'd just had the foresight to set up a reason for my visit over there, had someone call a problem into the system for me, the cops would be on their way to haul Findley back to jail where he belonged. I hadn't had time to threaten him or even step inside his apartment. If I had any justification for going, Findley might have been facing two to five. But no such luck.

"What do you need?" Brandy asked.

I wanted a perc. A doc would have prescribed them if he'd seen me, but I couldn't ask a nurse charged with treating drug-addicted women to give me a prescription painkiller. That's how many of those women got hooked in the first place.

"Whatever you've got for the pain."

My phone buzzed. Digging it out was excruciating, and when Newb answered, he heard the agony in my voice.

"I'm okay, Newb. What's up?"

"We working?"

The rain pelted down steadily. That day we were planning to cut and chip the saplings around the hospital. No way I could run a chainsaw with all the bruises on my ribs and arms. The rain gave me an excuse to take the day and I told Newb I had nothing for him. I could have put him to work in the warehouse, but getting over there to watch him was more than I was up to. I should have called Angel to let him know, but I didn't have the strength. I called Speedy and told him we weren't working.

He grunted out the equivalent of "obviously" and hung up. Judging by the light outside, it was around eight o'clock. We started by seven, so it made sense for Speedy to assume we weren't working if he hadn't heard from me. He didn't want to be outside in the rain any more than I did.

I felt a little guilty not finding them something to do. The guys needed to work to live, but I couldn't think about that lying on the concrete floor.

Brandy came back with four round orange pills. Ibuprofen. Really? I tried to hide my disappointment and downed the pills with the cup of water she handed me.

"You sure you don't need a doctor?"

"I'll be fine."

She looked down her nose at me, challenging me to get up and prove I was okay. I made it as far as my elbows, thanked her, and sent her on her way. She clicked the door button on the way out and I was glad it came down and stopped the rain from splashing in because I collapsed as soon as I heard her footsteps splash on the concrete path.

The ibuprofen took a while to work so I stayed still. Least that's what I told myself about the next ten minutes on the hard floor. Finally, I rolled over and dragged myself up.

Severe bruises on my right thigh made every step agony. That and moving my torso ignited pain in a dozen places where I'd been beaten or kicked. Then I opened the door and stepped out into the rain for the two-block walk to the station wagon. At least when I got in my car, I could drive home, get dry, and crawl into bed.

That was what I told myself on every slippery step down the hill, along County Street and back up to the future program house where I'd left my car. The beating rain kept my eyes low, but about one hundred feet from the car I could tell it hunched on the right front quarter.

Closer, I saw the problem and stopped in the pouring rain.

The left two tires were gone.

The wagon propped up on blocks.

I could have gone back to the garage and waited for a ride, but the walk had drained most of my energy. A tow wouldn't help. I needed tires and if I left the car here overnight I might need a lot more.

I pushed up the driveway and gingerly pulled myself into the driver's seat. The car wobbled under my weight but thankfully didn't fall. Angel owed me a favor, but before I dialed, I turned over the ignition and could have clapped when the engine fired up.

Angel answered and promised to head right over. I waited with the heater on full blast and the cold rainwater soaking my aching muscles.

The car was another message from Findley. This was his neighborhood, not mine, and he wanted me out. The tires would cost me three hundred bucks. It didn't matter that he'd sold them for twenty or thirty. It was all about the message.

As much as I wanted to rip his head off, the only thing I was capable of that day was waiting for Angel then crawling into bed.

Chapter Thirty-five

"What happened to you?"

"Findley."

"Holy crap. Are you okay?"

I grunted.

"Where are we going?"

I told him I needed tires or my car would be stripped overnight.

He reached in and wiped the dried blood off my left cheek. I guess he was used to cleaning up druggies so they looked good in school or court. But there wasn't much he could do for me. I was wet, bloody, and dirty. Even if he cleaned me up, there was no hiding my pain when I moved.

I lowered myself into his little red Toyota, my hair dripping wet, a tissue pressed to my face. Bad as I felt, I couldn't help thinking that woman was stuck with Findley and his friends and probably had been for months.

"You must be freezing. It's February." Angel cranked the heat.

It was the warmest February I could remember. He'd never heard the story about me pulling lobster pots in the canal with my dad in January, so I told him. "It was about fifteen degrees. Current moving like a mother. You know how it rips through there?"

The way he casually nodded he couldn't have ever stepped foot in the water. The water ripped so fast through the channel when the tide was moving, if the current grabbed you, you didn't have a shot of getting back to land.

"I was reaching for a pot and got my boot wedged between two rocks. I slipped and splashed down."

He laughed, gave me a glance, and went back to driving.

"I went in up to my ears. The only thing dry was my cowboy hat."

"You had to quit?"

"You obviously don't know my father. He said, 'Go sit in the truck,' and started to pull the rest of the pots himself. I froze so bad in the truck, I went back down to speed things up."

Angel drove another few blocks toward the tire place. "So a little rain isn't going to kill you?"

No, but four bruised ribs and a throbbing head made me mighty uncomfortable. The rest of the ride I thought of ways to murder Findley and bury him in a shallow grave in a state park somewhere. Or dump his body beside the highway. I pictured it rolling down an embankment and smiled.

"You must of really pissed him off."

"He thinks I'm the one who got him sent up."

"Does this make you even?" Angel asked, parking in front of the tire shop's floor-to-ceiling windows.

"It's a long story," I said. "Let's save it for the ride back."

Four cheap tires cost me two hundred and fifty-one bucks, plus another five hundred for rims. The tech rushed because he knew me, but it took forty minutes of waiting, slouched and still dripping on a cloth chair. The lady on the other side of the room kept her kids back from me like I was contagious. It hurt to talk. I couldn't tell Angel I wanted to beat Findley to death with the lady listening, so I watched the news on the fifteen-inch television and waited for the tech to pack the tires in Angel's trunk.

The car pulled out onto Coggeshall and the questions began. "So what is this? War?"

"He tried to kill me."

"What? How?" After all he'd seen with users, Angel didn't buy it and I couldn't understand why.

"He poisoned me. I ended up in the emergency room."

"Poisoned you? With what? Drugs?"

"Laxatives and a really strong diuretic."

"That's not going to kill a big guy like you."

"Sent me to the hospital."

"The guy sells heroin. If he wanted you dead, he'd have pumped you full of dope. You wouldn't have woken up this morning."

I didn't have the energy to explain why Findley didn't want to kill me in his own place. "He threw a brick at my car and almost hit my son."

Angel turned serious. Kids were his hot button.

"I went over there last night to kick his ass and tell him to back off. Tell him I knew what he was doing."

"That didn't end well."

Laughing hurt every one of my ribs.

"How are you going to keep him away from Jake?"

"We both know he's dirty. If he doesn't back off, I'm thinking of helping the cops."

"Maybe I can help."

On the rest of the ride, Angel told me how many of Findley's friends he knew. Angel was tied in deeply to the drug community. Only Findley's girls knew more about Findley than Angel did. And Angel knew them all.

We pulled up and the rain increased its fury. We unloaded the tires before we realized Findley and his friends had taken the lugs on the passenger's side. Angel drove me back to the tire store to fetch lugs then stood in the rain and helped me mount the tires.

I owed him big by the time I crawled into bed. It wouldn't take long for him to start calling in favors, but I didn't care.

Right then all I could think about was sleep. A hot shower and two shots of Jack Daniels put me in the mood. I crawled into bed with Beta nuzzling up next to me.

The next thing I remember I saw myself wrapped in that pink comforter. I felt gayer than I had ever felt. Embarrassed even in my dream. The little boy, Newb's kid, kept coming to me with ibuprofen saying, "Grandma drink." Every part of me ached for those pills, but I fought to stay asleep.

Chapter Thirty-six

Beta head-butted me in the ribs one time too many. I pulled myself out of bed, swallowed a handful of ibuprofen, and slogged to the couch with some cold pizza and a big blue mug half-full of Coke. I probably should have been drinking something caffeine free, maybe even a beer to loosen me up, but it wasn't even two o'clock.

Tween comedies, soap operas, and talk shows held my attention for about five seconds, so I thanked God for on-demand cable. Three episodes watching Mike and Franz comb the back roads of rural America for abandoned treasure kept me entertained until Jake came home from school.

The teenage, self-absorbed, hurry-to-the-fridge strides stopped five feet into the living room. "You okay?"

His chiseled muscles went slack, but the kid still didn't have enough body fat to smooth them out. If I had his build and my size, I'd have pummeled all three guys the night before.

Jake ignored my assurance that I was fine.

A few scrapes roughed up my face. I looked better since I'd washed the blood off in the shower, but my stiffness betrayed how much my ribs hurt. I came home from work sore often. Still, the kid looked genuinely worried, as if he knew what had happened at Findley's.

I shooed him off.

He inched back into the room a few minutes later with a 20-ounce protein shake. He had that look Roxie got right before she nagged me to call the doctor. He gulped the shake, his eyes on me while I started another episode of American Pickers.

I felt him watching me, but didn't look over. He wanted to know what happened. I couldn't tell him. Couldn't even hint. I felt guilty he'd gotten involved at all. And worse that I'd let those losers take me by surprise.

When he finally drained his glass and headed for the gym, I settled deeper into the couch. Beta followed him to the door and waited there like he sensed something I didn't.

Beta looked at me expectantly like I'd get up and take him out, but that wasn't going to happen. He gave up eventually then came over and nudged my leg. He wanted me to reach down and pet him. To reassure him that everything would be okay. Bending was out of the question. Breathing hurt. Even thinking about laughing sent painful tremors through my core.

We stayed like that for two hours. Me watching Franz and Mike. The dog uneasy at my feet. Until the door swung open and Roxie came in.

"Don't you look like crap," her voice dripped sarcasm. She played lover and tormenter with equal enthusiasm and talent.

"Squishy crap."

She leaned over and kissed my head knowing she exposed the girls in the process. I closed my eyes and smiled.

"Wow. You are in bad shape. I guess I'm getting a few days off." She didn't want the days off any more than I did, but my ribs hurt so much I couldn't reach up to touch my favorite toys.

"Maybe just one day," I said.

"You want to tell me what happened?"

"Not really."

"You're going to get yourself killed."

"And you're going to miss me."

"Think how you'll feel looking down from heaven to see me with a young stud." She wiggled her way into the kitchen for emphasis.

I cringed knowing she could get one any time she wanted. Why she stayed with me was a mystery. The junk packed in the basement and attic drove her nuts. I'd gained a hundred pounds since we met, but at least I'd stopped smoking. Sometimes I thought she stayed with me because she loved Jake so much. Other times when she snuggled into me and patted my belly I believed she loved me for the guy I was inside, no matter how odd a pair we appeared to be.

Hamburger sizzled on the stove.

I wanted to ask what she was making, but couldn't raise my voice loud enough to be heard over the frying beef.

She chopped lettuce. Filled a bowl with shredded cheese.

I nodded across the vacant dining room.

She saw me, but pretended not to.

The taco shells were the giveaway.

"Can you make it in here, old man?"

I pulled myself up and shuffled to the kitchen, doing my best to keep my torso perfectly still.

"It must have been a wild night."

She lured me to my chair with grilled beef and salsa, still wanting an answer that I wasn't giving.

She spooned two tacos to overflowing, heavy on beef with enough lettuce and tomato to hold a coating of cheese. But instead of setting the plate down, she waggled it in front of me. "Now are you going to tell me what happened? I can't eat all these myself, but Jake's a growing boy. He'll help. Don't forget Beta. He loves tacos."

Holding myself erect hurt. Smelling dinner and not being served was torture. She knew I couldn't chase her. Even if I was healthy—or what normally qualified as healthy for me—she could have grabbed the tacos and made it out the back door long before I caught her. It wouldn't have been the first time she withheld food as punishment.

"It was nothing," I said.

"Well, go make your own dinner if it's nothing."

We traded prodding looks. Me pleading with my hands, her tucking her chin into her shoulder and raising her eyebrows. Me drooling over the tacos, her eyeing my sore ribs.

It didn't take long for me to figure out she could wait a whole lot longer than I could. "I went to see Findley," I offered.

"In the middle of the night?"

She took one of the tacos off my plate and started to slide the remaining one toward me, but waited for me to continue talking before she pushed it within reach.

"I couldn't let him get away with throwing that brick. And poisoning my coffee."

"You don't know it was him."

I crunched through the crispy shell, juices dripping down my fingers and chin. Roxie was right about most things, but she had no idea how much Findley hated me. I didn't need her to believe me. I had my taco and I was happy. When I finished that one, she tempted me into talking again.

"He was standing on the edge of the cemetery at Mrs. Newbury's funeral. And then last night, he and his friends attacked me before I even knocked on his door."

Roxie didn't understand that if you let a guy like Findley push you around you were in for a lot more trouble than if you met him head on.

"Why don't you just tell him you didn't rat him out. It'd all be over."

"He's not going to listen."

"Not now. Probably not."

She hadn't heard what I'd said about Findley attacking me on sight. She acted like the whole thing was my fault, but when she saw me about to growl, she surrendered my second taco and went to the stove to make another.

"I'm worried about Jake," she said from a safe distance.

The boy could handle any kid his age. He was always lifting and running. Nagging Roxie to make healthier food. I couldn't imagine anyone at school giving him trouble. Findley was a completely different story. A problem only I could fix.

Chapter Thirty-seven

The shocks on the old station wagon smoothed out the smaller potholes I splashed through, but every bump rumbled through my body like a freight train. The drivers behind me didn't appreciate my caution around the larger puddles or the slow motion turn I made into the warehouse lot. Palming the wheel was too painful, so I fed it hand to hand along the bottom and drew a few honks as I slowly rolled into the lot.

I hadn't gone to pick up Newb. The kid could have used the money and the place needed a good cleaning, but I needed some time to heal and regroup. A day with my newly acquired junk was the ideal medicine for my flagging spirits.

Going to a warehouse surrounded by desperate heroin addicts wasn't a good idea for someone who could barely move, but I had a .38 tucked in my belt in case they saw me walking like an old fogey and decided to boost my wallet. It may sound extreme, but overwhelming force usually ensures that no one gets hurt. I walked inside confident I wouldn't have to shoot anyone.

The locks held the overhead doors fast. Once I had them open, it took all my strength to lift the inner door high enough to duck under. Through the dark maze of building supplies, the west wall, the one where the druggies loved to break in, was still intact. The bricks on the opposite end still held the message from Findley. That reminder and all the broken glass were going to be around a while.

Mrs. Newbury's stuff was packed in the only neat corner of the whole place. I grabbed a box of her best stuff and struggled with it over to the desk. The answering machine on top was my signal to myself there was good stuff inside. Sometimes with junk it's hard to tell the good stuff from things I was going to donate, so I put something obviously valuable on top, in this case worth five bucks.

It powered right up when I plugged it in. The messages should have been private, but the same curiosity that drove me to dig through people's stuff, forced me to play Mrs. Newbury's messages. And I needed to know the machine worked if I was going to sell it.

The queue was empty, but a quick rewind brought up a week's worth of deleted messages.

"Hi, Cynthia. This is Laura at Home Health Aid checking in on Mary. We haven't visited in a few days. If you need us to come out, please call." A mechanized voice added, "Wednesday. February. Eighth. At ten A.M."

Laura called back every day. Her tone more concerned with each passing day. Mrs. Carter from next door called twice. Mrs. Newbury's doctor also called to say she'd missed an appointment.

She was sick, but from the tone of the messages, I suspected Cynthia hadn't called any of these people back. She couldn't have been that busy taking care of one old woman and her son.

The messages stopped on the fourteenth, the day Mrs. Newbury passed. I remembered the disconnected phone wire in the basement. One of those jacks upstairs hadn't been working, but unlikely the line to the answering machine had been disconnected that way. More likely they unplugged the machine when she died, or maybe accidentally cut the power moving things around.

Still, I couldn't shake the feeling something wasn't right. If Cynthia was in the house, why didn't she return all those calls? I started to wonder if maybe she hadn't been there. If maybe she'd left Mrs. Newbury alone or had someone else watching her.

I picked up the silver sugar bowl and shined the outside with a rag. I thought about going to the sink and washing the sticky residue out of the inside, but lifting myself out of my chair was more than I was up for. I sat back, absently looking at Mrs. Newbury's scuffed bed frame.

Next to the bed was a box thick with documents. Newb must have lugged that box in from the truck because I didn't recognize it. I slid it across the floor with my foot and started leafing through one manila folder after another. You never know what you might find. An old stock certificate. A bond.

Most of the stuff was Newb's. Useless crap. School records. The poor kid's grades were so bad I understood why he didn't graduate.

Another folder held a notarized settlement agreement between him and Cynthia. For a young couple who hadn't worked much, they had been pretty well off. She got everything. The house he inherited from his father. The car. The kid. Newb got hosed. Several pages later I learned how badly. The monthly child support figure was ridiculous. The poor kid had been hooked on heroin when the documents were signed. He couldn't have known what he was agreeing to. Or maybe he was thinking about how much money he made breaking houses while he was high. Twelve hundred a month. No way he could pay that.

His rent was only twenty-five bucks a week. He struggled to keep that apartment, feed himself, and get around. No way he could come up with twelve hundred a month.

I slipped the folder back into place and stared down into the mishmash of junk in the box in front of me. Newb was willing to steal his grandmother's microwave to get high. If Cynthia had been pressuring him for child support he couldn't pay, would he bump off his grandmother to get the DOR off his back?

My phone buzzed and I was so shocked by what I was thinking I almost couldn't answer.

"What's up, Angel?"

"Can you put Newb on?"

"He's not here."

"What?"

Angel sounded freaked.

"You saw me yesterday. I'm in no shape to be working. I'm taking it easy in the warehouse."

"What are you thinking?"

"It's raining. I can't work outside today."

"Newb can't be alone yet."

"I'm not his mother."

"His mother and his father are dead, Lorado. The kid needs help."

How that became my responsibility, I wasn't sure, but Angel was steaming at me for taking the day off. I could have paid the kid to clean up, but maybe I needed the peace and quiet as much as I needed the rest.

"He's probably at his grandmother's."

"He's not answering his phone. I've been chasing him all day."

"Don't worry, Angel. I'm sure he's fine."

All I could think about was that social security check. If he had cashed the whole thing, he could be passed out in an alley or under a bridge somewhere.

"We need to find him. Now."

"I'm in no shape to chase him around the city. Try his grandma's."

Angel muttered a curse and hung up.

Chapter Thirty-eight

Some days I didn't know whether I loved or hated the recovering addicts who worked for me. I had to feel something for Newb because that night I hiked up Mrs. Newbury's back stairs in the dark even though every one of my muscles ached. It would have been so much easier to go home to the couch and a beer. Roxie might have even given me a massage if she was in a good mood.

Angel had called back two minutes after hanging up to apologize and beg for my help. He searched the dive bars and drug hangouts while I drove to the north end. Searching the old lady's house was easier and safer than the shitholes Angel was going into, but he connected with the people in those places. I think we both came away feeling we had the better end of the bargain.

The vacant house lay dark and quiet. No one was home at the Carters' either, so I poked my head in the side window of Mrs. Newbury's place then went around and used my key at the back door. I could have called Angel from the outside, told him the kid wasn't there, and headed for a hot bath, but I was curious to know if he'd been around since we cleaned the place out.

I flipped the light on to make it clear I wasn't hitting the place.

The microwave was still there. A good sign Newb hadn't been around. The counters and floor had been wiped clean. With no table and chairs, the dining room and kitchen looked large. No trash anywhere. The fridge empty and unplugged.

The wooden floors shined all the way into the back bedrooms. Not a baggie or syringe or even a tissue on the floor. The kid hadn't been here since the sale. No wonder, with no furniture, no phone, no food, what would he do. And how would he get here without a car?

I shut the place down and went out the way I came in.

The Carters' lights were still off. The station wagon waited out front, but a movement next door caught my eye. It was a flash. Unconscious mostly, but it brought me around front for a look in Cynthia's yard.

The big guy lugged something heavy inside. I wanted to know what it was badly enough that I dragged myself over. My first guess was that he was moving in. It didn't seem right so soon after the old lady died. Not that I should be the judge of that. Roxie and I had a high school kid and we hadn't bothered to get married. Still, the timing seemed odd.

The hulk stood ten feet inside the door with the kid playing by his feet. Nicholas was a cute little bugger. How can you not be cute when you're four? Chuck didn't share my interest in kids. Nicholas jumped up and down for attention and the big guy didn't even look down. I know some guys aren't happy to deal with a kid that isn't theirs, but he seemed cold.

Neither of them moved to let me in when I knocked. I pulled the storm door open and knocked louder on the glass. The bodybuilder saw me clearly. And he saw that I saw him. He still hesitated before coming over.

He waded around the bags and opened the door. "What?"

"Is Cynthia home?"

"What do you want her for?"

"I want to talk about Newb."

He eased back and looked toward the bedroom, but didn't call for Cynthia. Thirty seconds later I knew why, but in that instant I thought he was being a prick because that was his nature.

I was sure I was going to end up fighting Chuck, so I started looking for weaknesses. The tight T-shirt strained to cover bulging arms and chest. He stood solidly planted on both feet. Both knees firm. Not a bruise anywhere. Muscles that hid under most people's skin, never to be seen, poked out in meaty little tubes, some in grotesque proportions. Veins popped everywhere.

With a two-inch blade and quick hands, you could turn Chuck into a big red fountain, spurting in every direction. Short of going up for murder one, his only weakness seemed to be that his sheer bulk made him slow.

He turned toward a noise in the hall and backed up, not inviting me in, but not blocking me out either. I took the door handle and pulled it closed behind me, stepping into the small living room uninvited.

Nicholas puffed on a plastic beach ball. The brightly colored strips shined. The ball lay limp in spite of the puffs he blew into the valve. He was too weak to pinch the plastic valve open. Chuck didn't notice his struggle. Or care.

A thick red suitcase waited beside the couch. And if that didn't make it clear enough they were taking a vacation, Cynthia stepped into the room in a neon orange bikini.

The bodybuilder snapped a look at me. Warning me not to look at his girl. But what was I supposed to do when she came in wearing three tiny triangles of cloth?

Face it, Cynthia had been married to Newb. By definition she was no prize. She was stringy, with limp hair and a forgettable face. Had the big guy seen Roxie's boob job and silky blonde hair, he wouldn't have been so unnerved when Cynthia came into the room mostly naked.

She did have attitude. You had to give her credit for that.

My muscles hurt so much I wasn't a physical or romantic threat, but that didn't lower his pulse any.

"Have you seen Newb lately?" I asked, getting quickly to the point.

Cynthia wasn't embarrassed standing there mostly nude. There would be other men on the beach. Chuck was going to have a tough vacation if he got this upset every time she walked near a guy in that bikini. The guys were going to look. Maybe not all of them, but certainly a bunch.

"He hasn't been around."

"Angel's worried about him. We haven't seen him all day."

"He hasn't been here. Not since you cleaned the place out."

The big guy shifted his feet as though he were getting ready to drag me outside. I kept it friendly with Cynthia.

"Where are you going?"

"Cancun. I've been tied up every day for weeks with Newb's grandma. A week off will give me a chance to recharge."

"If you need someone to look in on the place, I'd be glad to if I'm in the neighborhood."

I didn't know why I asked. She didn't have much worth stealing, but knowing Newb, she'd seen her share of breaking and entering. Newb might have even targeted her if he knew she was away.

"That'd be great," she said, but didn't offer a key.

The big guy shifted again. I smiled at Nicholas and headed outside.

My cell rang halfway across the lawn.

"Where have you been?"

"My couch," Newb said. "We working tomorrow?"

I could have killed Angel, or thanked him.

Chapter Thirty-nine

"Hey, Kiddo. What's going on?" I asked from the hood of the wagon.

"Clicking keys."

"Want some exercise? You're trying to get in shape, aren't you?"

"You looking for free labor?"

"Speedy didn't show up today. I've got a three-man job and two men."

"I've got a book to write and only one author."

"Help me out, will you? I've got a chipper for the day. Newb and I won't finish without you."

"So you want me to stop what I'm doing so I can save you a couple hundred bucks on a chipper rental?"

"Something like that."

The great thing about our family was that we always helped each other. Chris could never say no. He grumbled plenty, but he was a sucker for someone who needed help. Our dad was the same way. He got too much satisfaction from helping people to care that he was always doing something for someone else. I think doing favors let them feel superior. They both liked to grumble, too.

Thirty minutes later the Volvo pulled up and Chris strolled across the grass pulling on his leather work gloves. My elbow was already killing me, and I was glad to hand off the chainsaw and toss him a pair of safety glasses.

"Don't cut those too long."

The saw revved, drowning me out. He always cut firewood too long for the splitter. Dad wouldn't take it if it was over twenty-four inches. He didn't appreciate my nagging any more than our father's.

Newb followed behind, lugging armloads of logs over to the truck while I dragged the tops of the saplings to the chipper and fed them in. The power of the knives was awesome, grinding and slicing up the branches to three-inch chips as fast as the machine dragged them through.

Chris diced up the saplings as they stood, cutting sixteen inch logs from the top down, using the tree's strength to make it easy to slice them up to fireplace length. By cutting the wood off the stump, he didn't need to constantly bend over and work his back. Newb hustled behind, keeping pace even though he had a thirty-foot roundtrip to the truck with each armload.

My job was the easiest. The branches were a lot lighter than the saw and the logs Newb lugged, but I was the brains and the money behind the operation. I'd put my time in yanking on tools. I stood back while they worked, slipping in behind to drag branches away when they moved on.

Newb really busted it. For a rail-thin guy who'd been hooked on smack a week earlier, he looked good. Steady. Strong. He kept up with the kid and the saw better than I'd hoped. He had some strange ideas about work and finances, but when I paid him, he usually did his job.

We cut three-quarters of the way around the hospital by the time we broke for pizza at the Flat Iron.

Chris stopped on the sidewalk, dusting sawdust off his pants after Newb went inside. "What happened today?"

I let the door close. "Speedy didn't show up."

He brushed the sawdust out of his hair. "He okay?"

"His head's better if that's what you mean. Sometimes these guys just get a wild hair. You know?"

He grabbed the door handle and looked at me with sadness or maybe disappointment. "He fall off the wagon?"

I had no way to tell. Newb had gone off with a girl and gotten hooked because he had a few extra bucks in his pocket and wanted to party. The power of this shit boggled my mind. After seeing Newb convulse and shake coming clean, I couldn't understand how anyone would ever go back to the drug. But they did. The drug owned them. If they weren't careful they slid back. Most of them had to kick it time and time again.

I checked my phone outside the door. No message from Speedy. That could mean he overslept and didn't feel like coming to work or that he was lying in a shooting den somewhere, nodding against a wall.

We trailed inside and found a table on the aisle where we could spread out. Newb came out of the bathroom as we sat down. His hygiene surprised me. For a guy willing to take a needle from anyone and stick it in his arm, washing his hands before lunch seemed like a waste of time, but he never failed to head to the restroom when we went out. I couldn't say that much for myself. To me a little dirt wasn't worth fussing over.

"What do you guys want for toppings?" I asked.

"Any kind of meat is fine," Chris said.

Newb didn't answer. I could never tell if he didn't feel entitled to tell me what he wanted because I was paying or if he didn't have an opinion. The kid sat deadpan. A thirtyish waitress in stretch pants and a black top took my order for three pizzas. Newb didn't check her out. Didn't react when I ordered a veggie, a pepperoni, and a combo of sausage, pepperoni, and linguica.

Chris flashed me a confused look.

"What are you writing?" I asked

He paused, scratched his chin, then understood I didn't want to embarrass Newb. "A short about a social network and a group of vigilantes."

"My kind of story."

"You'd like it. Lots of bad guys get whacked."

Asking Chris what he was writing in front of Newb worried me. The kid spent much of his childhood robbing houses and selling other people's stuff for drug money. Chris had a way of killing off people like Newb in his writing. And he enjoyed it. The kid was already having a rough enough week even if losing his grandmother didn't seem to faze him.

Newb's cell rang and he walked away from the table to answer.

"What's up with him?" Chris asked when he was out of earshot.

"What do you mean?"

"He's half dead."

I shrugged.

"Does he ever say anything? Or smile for God's sake?"

"The drug emptied him."

Chris didn't understand. How could he? Nothing would ever compare to the drug for Newb. Love. Sex. Success. None of that captivated him like the thought of nodding. Why taking a drug that made you fall asleep was worth all the pain I'd never understand. But once Newb rode that high, he didn't desire anything else. I'd asked him once if he could go back and change things if he'd never have started the drug. He told me no. Unequivocally. Years on drugs taught him who he was. It was the most ridiculous bullshit I'd ever heard, but the kid was completely serious.

Newb walked in the front door and my cell rang immediately. I didn't connect the two until I heard Angel's voice. "Can you do me a favor?"

My muscles were already stiffening after sitting down ten minutes. I saw our waitress carrying our first pizza and all I wanted to do was scarf down and lay back on my couch. Angel had other ideas.

"What's up?"

"Newb needs a ride to NA."

"Tonight?"

The kid walked over and sat down. My disgust had to be apparent, but searching Newb's face for recognition was pointless. I couldn't let the kid down. Ninety meetings in ninety days would keep him from going off the rails. I got how important that was. But every muscle ached and I had a bad feeling about going into a meeting with a bunch of hoods. I pictured myself a walking ATM.

Angel told me he had a game to coach.

"Where's the meeting?"

Chapter Forty

Of course the meeting was on Findley's turf. A day dragging branches stiffened up every bruise Findley and his friends pounded into me, and by the time I tipped myself out of the station wagon, I couldn't have outrun a fourth grader. I cursed Angel and Newb for suckering me into coming.

"Where we going, Newb?"

True to form he pointed the way around back of the brick church and led me down a narrow set of granite stairs to the basement. He didn't utter a word. Didn't look back to make sure I was following. Just plodded along.

I wondered if I could ever wind up like Newb.

I liked my beer. I could have two Papa Smurfs and six beers on a Friday at the Pondo and get so wasted Roxie had to drag me out of the place. Sometimes I passed out in her car and she left me there overnight. It wasn't a problem. I could take the booze or leave it. I thought of booze similarly to the way Newb thought about drugs. I used booze to make me feel good. Not to loosen up with one or two, but to get good and ripping drunk.

Outside that door I thought I was better than the druggies I'd see in that basement. They were stupid. Weak. They should have known it was wrong to stick a needle in their arm and shoot heroin into their bloodstream. The idiots ruined their lives. Working beside Newb and Speedy, I'd seen the boneheaded decisions they made. I braced for the worst and followed Newb down a short hall to an open room with a circle of chairs.

I reminded myself not to touch anyone. Any of those people could have had HIV, especially the women. Newb walked right for a cluster of people talking by the coffee. I hung back in the middle of the floor, stranded between the entrance and the knots of people greeting each other like friends.

Newb hugged a thin woman with scraggly black hair. I shivered, imagining she'd slept with two hundred guys for drug money. It could have been a thousand, but Newb didn't seem to care. It was just a friendly hug, still, I never would have gotten cozy with any of the women in that basement.

They broke their embrace and the woman called us to the circle of folding chairs. I headed for the wall, but Newb came over and pulled me to the circle. Hanging back wasn't allowed. I was in or out.

The woman identified me as new and singled me out with a special welcome. She put me on the spot immediately and asked if I had anything to share. I told her I was there to support Newb and a chorus of welcomes followed. I got the feeling they didn't believe me, but I was okay with that.

The meeting started with those who'd been clean for twenty-four hours. I half-listened to the struggles of four new members, but I was intent on the woman leading the group. She had echoes of the emptiness I saw in Newb. Not quite malnourished, but not healthy either. She'd used for sure. I couldn't help wondering what horrible things she'd been through before she came through the program and wound up leading it.

"Twenty-four hic, twenty-four hic, twenty-four hic. That's hard man."

"Hard on the bod, mind, and soul."

"Good lessons on powerlessness."

"True. Humbling."

The voices pinged around faster than I could track them. Maybe I didn't care to track them. I didn't identify with these people. I was just there to make sure Newb stayed straight.

Then a guy in a Nickelback T-shirt said, "I'm looking forward to sleep."

"Yeah," Newb said. "It took me two months to sleep through the night last time."

No wonder the kid looked half dead all the time. How could you go that long without a full night's sleep?

As I started to tune in I kept hearing HP or Higher Power. God wasn't politically correct in a public group. One guy said he didn't believe in God and was immediately met by a chorus of suggestions to let go and put his faith in a Higher Power. That he was powerless to his addiction and only by understanding that, could he overcome his disease.

I didn't buy drug addiction as a disease. I wasn't sure what I thought it was, but the chorus kept offering suggestions to the guy. To use his family or the group as his Higher Power. He had to let go.

Newb kept jumping in and offering help. He was seven days clean and acting like a star. Only the leader, Nickelback called her Rose, offered more direction and suggestions. She knew about meetings and resources online. Clearly she had control of the group, but I'd never seen the kid talk so much. He started a conversation about candy, and I remembered him taking the Tootsie Rolls out of the bag in my car.

I scoffed to myself, but then three other people started talking about chocolate and ice cream. One girl had a half gallon that day. It sounded like trading one problem for another, but no one in that room had a weight problem. Well, no one except me.

Across the room, a yuppie kid, smartass attitude and all, said he needed a few beers to take the edge off.

"A drug is a drug is a drug," Newb said.

Rose smiled across the circle.

Newb was in his element. A leader. I had a glimmer of hope that he'd run a crew for me some day.

Chapter Forty-one

"I have a one-year-old son. Every day clean is a day I'm there for him."

Heads nodded all around. I remembered when Jake was a baby. Roxie wanted me there every minute, and I'd wanted to be there, too. Every little thing he did was a miracle. As I remembered Jake crawling across the carpet, a rough-looking guy with a deep, wavy scar across his forearm caught my eye. The other members of the circle wore tender looks, remembering their kids, but this guy shifted his glare from one twitchy twenty-four hour to another. He wasn't listening, but biding his time. I assumed he was there by court order rather than a desire to get clean.

"I almost killed my eight-year-old son," Nickelback said. "My old lady took my stash. I was so mad I whipped a frying pan at her. Spun like a helicopter. Skimmed right over his head and buried in the wall. I came here the next night."

Every eye shifted except mine and those belonging to the wavy scar.

"HP saved him," Rose said. "It wasn't his time."

"He saved me, too," Nickelback said.

A chorus agreed, but one guy in a red T-shirt said, "I don't believe in God."

"You've got to find HP, man. He worries for me now. I have no fear. It's unbelievable. I was depressed for twenty-five years and now that's all behind me." Nickelback looked on the verge of breaking down.

"You're brainwashed coming to this place," Red T-shirt said.

"Maybe I'm brainwashed, but I don't give a shit."

"Your Higher Power can be anyone, Justin," Rose said. "Your family. The group. Your straight friends. Anyone who can help you stay the path."

The guy shook his head. Every eye, even mine, was on him. He wasn't nearly convinced, but the pressure was palpable.

"You've got to accept that you are powerless to resist the drug," Rose said. "You need to give control to HP and lean on Him to help you through."

The guy started to say something, but Newb cut him off, "The definition of insanity is doing the same thing over and over and expecting different results. If you keep using, you'll keep screwing up."

Funny of Newb to say that a week after falling off.

The guy pushed back in his chair. He didn't believe what he was hearing, but couldn't overcome the wall of eyes aimed in his direction.

"You'd rather have a nod than God," the guy with the scar said. "I can understand that."

Rose spun in her chair. "I think you need to do more listening than talking."

"That's our problem," Nickelback said. "The cravings are part of the disease."

"The good news is that it gets better." The woman who spoke had been quiet until then. She proudly held a keychain that had been given to her by the group. I couldn't remember if the key chains signified ninety days clean or longer, but clearly she was an elder of the group and she looked more together than anyone except Rose. She spoke quietly and commanded the attention of everyone in the room, me included.

"When you get away from the life for a while, you start to see the damage the drugs did. Damage you may never be able to repair, but at least you can stop the wrecking ball from smashing into your family and friends."

Scar didn't respond and the group discussion detoured into the woman's past. Janet was her name, and she'd been in and out of detox twenty times before she decided she wanted to clean up and stay clean. It was two years ago that she earned her ninety-day key chain, but she kept it as a reminder of her decision to make the change stick.

The meeting broke up slowly. I was one of the first people standing because I couldn't wait to get off the hard chair. My butt had been numb thirty minutes, and I was ready to get Newb in the car and get on with my night. But Newb had other ideas. He didn't even look at me. Just got up and walked over to Janet and pretty soon a little cluster formed around them. All I could see were backs.

I turned toward the wall, looking for a place to swear, and I caught something strange in the corner of my eye. Scar tapped the inside of his elbow and one of the twenty-fours who had been heading for the door stopped and turned back.

The men nodded to each other knowingly. The hair on the back of my neck stood up. Stiff and sore as I was, my heart started pumping. Priming me for action. I took a step toward the coffee, and the two of them headed out into the narrow hall that led to the parking lot.

Newb, Janet, and Rose were all deep in conversation.

Nickelback was the next biggest guy in the room. He didn't register my nod, so I pointed at him and gestured toward the hall. I hadn't said a word during the meeting, and he didn't seem keen on talking to me outside. I turned my back and followed Scar and his friend not knowing if Nickelback would come bail me out or not.

Scar had defensive wounds on his hands. He'd been attacked with knives more than once. I assumed he had a habit of selling drugs and instigating trouble. Not the kind of guy you want to brawl with when you could barely move. On the plus side, I outweighed him by a hundred fifty pounds.

The door flung open and there was the exchange clear as day. Tiny baggies passed from man to man. "What the hell?" I yelled. "You can't bring that crap here!"

The twenty-four bolted immediately.

Scar yelled, "Hey," and the kid tossed the baggies back over his shoulder on his way up the stairs. The dealer seethed, collected his goods, and spun toward me, ready to rip me apart for nixing his deal.

"You got a death wish, man?" He blocked the exit, but twenty people remained in the room behind me. Twenty frail people, five or six of them women, but if I backed through the door, I'd have all the help I needed. I wasn't the kind of guy who backed away from a fight, and I wasn't keen on letting this guy walk away.

We squared off. Scar considering an attack. Me waiting for my shouts or my signal to Nickelback to bring help. I couldn't take a shot in the ribs. I'd fold for sure. By the look in Scar's eyes, he wanted to poke a hole between in me rather than merely add another bruise.

The tight hall left no room to maneuver. If he lunged there was no space to dodge, not that I was much on dodging. If anything, the tight quarters gave me a better chance to latch onto the scum.

The buck knife clicked and the door squeaked open at the same time. It was Rose not Nickelback who intervened as the blade glimmered in front of me. "Augustus you want me to drop a dime?"

He inched back.

Prison was a different threat to Augustus than it was to me. He'd probably been. He knew the realities, and he lived on the verge of going back. I wouldn't kill a guy in front of an audience, but Augustus seemed to be weighing his options.

"You bringing drugs in here?" Rose asked.

Augustus glared at me.

I heard footsteps in the doorway and imagined a dozen people crowded behind me. I had nowhere to go and suddenly the idea of twelve witnesses wasn't nearly as comforting.

"Get out of here," Rose yelled.

He took a step back. Found the stairs without turning around.

"Bring that shit back here, and I'll dime you. Count on it."

When the door closed, I turned and thanked the little woman who'd saved me a knife fight.

Newb stepped free of the knot in the doorway. "You make friends everywhere, don't you?"

Chapter Forty-two

Back in the station wagon we wound around to Newb's apartment. Half a block before I pulled over, he turned and stared at me. I couldn't look away from the road with parked cars hemming me in on both sides, but the stern expression was more emotion than I'd seen out of Newb in a very long time.

"He would have left you for dead in that stairway."

"Or vice versa."

Newb looked me over as I stopped at the curb. Something brewed underneath the surface, but he either couldn't find the words or the enthusiasm to let them loose.

"I couldn't let that shit go on. All those people in that circle struggling to get better and he comes in there tempting them with dope. Someone should kill the bastard. Forget diming him."

Newb looked at me like I was from space.

The kid had been in the thick of the conversation. Encouraging everyone to kick, to embrace a Higher Power. How could he back the loser trying to wreck it all?

He looked at me like I was the one with the messed up worldview. I shrugged. "What?"

Nothing.

I prompted with both hands.

His lip quivered, but he kept quiet.

"You know that guy?"

Newb opened his door. "Forget it." He stepped out and thanked me for the ride then trudged up the wooden staircase to the second floor.

Drug dealers are a scourge. A blight that infects young people and steals their lives away, damaging countless others in the process. Did Newb sympathize with Scar? The guy could have been Newb's dealer. That was the only way I could explain it.

I sat a long time and wondered how the two of us could see the guy so differently. Newb fantasized about the drug. Dealers were part of his life. I'd always assumed he would have been better off without them, but his eyes told me different. Newb cared what happened to that lowlife even though he made a living destroying the lives of others. Doing it at a Narcotics Anonymous meeting was low.

I coasted down to the corner so occupied by Newb's acceptance of the dealer that I almost didn't see the girl's head pop out of the car. She'd been leaning in the window. When she jumped away, I saw the same swollen face and brownish hair from Findley's doorway an instant before she bolted.

The car's lights flipped on. Brights flicked in my eyes.

There was only a car width between the parked cars on each side and the station wagon blocked the car from coming up the hill after the girl. We were almost nose to nose when he blasted his horn.

He pounded his steering wheel. Raging inside his car.

She was ripping and running. Maybe that's how she got the black eye.

I dropped into reverse. The transmission whined as I zipped back almost pulling even before she darted down someone's driveway.

He followed me up. Close and fast. Nose to nose.

I stopped and the guy slammed his brakes. Missed front-ending me by two feet. I saw a glimmer disappear into the shadows. Dark Brown or black hair. A red top and a short black skirt.

His grill faced me when I looked back.

He jumped out of his car and took a few steps around the hood. He hesitated there, looking at darkness beyond the empty driveway. He could have pulled in and chased after her. But what if he caught her? Could he slug her and take back his cash? If the cops caught him chasing after his money, he'd have a bigger problem on his hands. If Findley and his boys caught him threatening his girl, it would have been ugly.

He looked at me and mouthed, "fucking bitch." He kicked his front tire on his way back to the driver's seat then backed into a driveway further down the hill, turned, and sped off, his engine gunned in frustration.

I was a bit more curious. The girl could tell me a lot about Findley. Maybe if I had something on her she'd give me something in return. Not likely, but I wheeled around that block and the next, scanning every fence line and shadow.

I followed one girl with a red top for a few dozen yards, the station wagon prowling along until she whipped out her phone and fixed on my front license plate. Her face didn't match the girl I'd seen at Findley's so I drove on and left her to wonder why I had trailed her.

I was thinking I'd be the next almost kidnapping story when I saw another red top hustle across the sidewalk and get in a small red car. I followed half a block back. Without traffic it was easy enough to watch the taillights at each turn. Three blocks later they swung behind an old mill. I assumed there was no way out and blocked the narrow alley with the station wagon then continued around back on foot.

The cracked pavement led to a dark lot that hadn't seen regular use, from employees of the mill anyway, in dozens of years. The drive wound well back from the building, descending to a lower lot, favored by girls like Findley's because it was much lower than the surrounding landscape and proved impossible to see from the street.

My eyes made the corner, and I held the pointed bricks for balance as I looked down at the car. Through the driver's window I caught black and white flashes. Alternating rhythmically. The black hair took shape, bobbing in and out of view, alternating with a white blur I didn't want to look too closely at.

If I had a camera, I might have gone down and snapped a photo thinking I could turn her in or at least threaten to. But what does a blowjob picture do for me besides label me as a perv?

I slipped down the grassy hill. Not that stealth was a big deal. All she could see was his thighs. He was looking out the windshield, directly away from me. And he had more important things on his mind.

Sex for money makes me shiver. I bounced in a strip club for a few years, and the girls offered me sex all the time. Sex for protection or between friends is a lot different than sex for drug money. I didn't feel badly enjoying their hard little bodies, but what this fat guy—I could see he was fat as I got closer—was doing grossed me out.

I wasn't sure if it was better that she was servicing this guy instead of ripping him off or not.

I slipped over to the bumper and alongside, trying to stay in the blind spot outside the rearview mirror. Her bobbing head came clearly into view, but she was leaned across the front seats with her face angled down. The guy faced forward and down, watching her work.

Ten feet closer. No man's land. The door locks were down. I couldn't barge in and rip the girl out as awkward as that would be with the guy's pants down and her half-finished. I needed to grab her before she ran, but I didn't want to fight this guy any more than I wanted to fight the scarred drug dealer. Every muscle was still sore. And I had no beef with the John.

She bobbed some more and I felt ridiculous waiting.

A peeper. A perv.

Finally I stepped up and rapped the glass with my knuckles.

Her head flashed up in surprise.

It wasn't the first time she'd been caught in the act. She was fully clothed at least, expecting my knock meant a bust. If I was a cop, she would have calmly waited to be processed, but recognizing me, she panicked. She must have thought I'd grab her and beat her up to get back at Findley. Or worse. Her eyes went wild looking for a place to run, but the two of them were tangled together behind the steering wheel, and she couldn't get away.

Her fright was nothing compared to the shock on the man's face.

I didn't remember backing up to the grass and sitting down, but that's where he found me.

Chapter Forty-three

I barely saw a dark shape shuffle off across the asphalt, giving me a wide berth on her way back to the street. I couldn't have caught her in a foot race, and I was too stunned to get up and try. The near door opened, and Angel waddled out, tucking in his shirt before easing down on the grass. I heard him sit, but didn't look in his direction.

Angel spent his life helping kids get off drugs. When he couldn't help, he pushed people like me to step up, like at Newb's meeting that night. But that night he paid for a blowjob from a girl tricking for drug money.

It wasn't the first time either. She hopped across the sidewalk and into his car like they'd done this dozens of times. He was enabling. Using. Taking advantage. I felt sick. Maybe it was because they were so mismatched. Angel pushed four hundred pounds. Jovial but hapless. No woman's dream guy. The skinny girl would have been hot if not for the miles. She might not have been a prize, but if not for the money, she would have been repulsed by the thought of touching Angel. Come to think of it, she probably was. But what kind of guys paid prostitutes?

If making me queasy wasn't enough, Angel had also shocked me into letting my best link to Findley get away. I needed to stop him before something happened to Jake or Roxie. The threat boomed in my mind for an instant, quickly replaced by a sickening dread. I couldn't walk away. I had to understand why. If guys like Angel didn't pay for sex, girls like the one in the red top would live very different lives.

He breathed next to me. Wheezy. Penitent.

"What was that?" I asked.

Car brakes squeaked in the distance. I imagined another customer stopping to barter with the girl. Would she rip and run or climb inside and perform? I shivered and looked at Angel. He stared over his tiny car at the drooping chain link fence and the dark trees beyond. I knew he was feeling guilty. No guy wanted to be caught with a prostitute. No one wanted to be the guy who needed a prostitute.

Sex was a sign of success. Angel paid for his and tonight he didn't get his money's worth. I wondered how long it would be before he came back looking for her. Or if there were other girls he frequented.

So many questions I didn't want answers to.

"Tendonitis?" I asked.

He grimaced, and for the first time, I met his eyes. He didn't understand what I meant until I gave him the hand gesture.

He shook his head in disgust and shame, but there was a hint of laughter in his smile. "This isn't bad enough?"

What did he deserve?

He had helped plenty of kids, but he wasn't helping this girl.

The two of them had powerful needs. She was willing to give herself away for drugs. He was willing to pay cash for sex. They fed their desires, one preying on the needs of the other.

When I didn't answer, he asked, "What do you want from me?"

"I just don't get it. You bust your ass to help Newb then you come down here and pay this girl to suck you."

If he'd said he was helping her, I would have gone off.

I wanted to ask him if he'd thought about how many guys she'd slept with and how likely it was she had AIDS. Plenty of women in treatment got the disease, tested positive, and went right back to work. I know a guy who got fired for saving a kid's life. He saw a hooker working the street. He knew she had AIDS because he'd seen her test results. When he saw an eighteen-year-old kid stop and pick her up, he headed them off and told the kid to kick her out.

He was fired the next day for a HIPPA violation. Amazing she had the guts to make a complaint. She'd risk a kid's life then sue because a male nurse divulged her medical information to save him. Unbelievable. How ludicrous that the system backed her up. I felt for the kid. The nurse. The girl in the red top.

I wasn't sure what I felt about Angel.

"It may look like free enterprise, but she's a slave, Angel."

Angel had been looking down at the grass between his feet for a while. He faced me with that silly goatee. "Joanna's been gone a long time." The desperation in his face, even in the dark, was heart wrenching.

Angel had his own problems. A son dead from an overdose. A wife who left him soon after. And life as an overweight, funny-looking, bald guy. The poor guy was lonely. He wasn't getting any without paying for it. I should have felt sorry for him, but I couldn't shake the sick feeling in my gut.

"She was my link to Findley," I said.

"I can fix that."

I hadn't even thought that Angel could pick her up any time he wanted. She'd probably get right back in his car to finish her work. He could drive her right back to me.

"You going to go and get her now?"

"Not her. She won't help you."

I was over three hundred pounds, but when I protested with my hands he looked at me like I was an idiot.

"Anything you can do to her," he said, "Findley will do worse. Can you imagine what he'd do if he found out she helped you?"

Angel knew someone better. When I met her, I began to understand how he knew so much about the drug community.

Chapter Forty-four

The house Angel drove me to the next afternoon looked like any other in the north end. The lawn was neatly trimmed. The landscaping had more than its share of weeds, but the fence stood tall and the trim on the little cape looked crisp and white from a paint job a few years back.

On the way over, Angel had told me we were meeting one of the girls Findley was running before he got sent up. She moved here while he was in prison to start a new life with her daughter, Findley's child.

We followed a walk of stepping stones deeply swallowed by thick grass. The neighborhood had been here a long time. How many of the neighbors knew a former prostitute lived on their block? Did that really matter? It would be ugly business if she turned neighbors into customers. I couldn't imagine she'd ever go back, get desperate for a little extra cash and turn a trick, but when the door swung open, Angel's eyes filled with hope.

Morgan stood about five-six with wispy, bleach-blonde hair swiped every which way, and a draped top, patterned with big checks, like an oversized tablecloth. The neckline dipped far enough to get your attention, but not far enough to show you what you came for.

Angel melted when she patted his arm.

She wasn't gorgeous. Not stacked liked Roxie. But she commanded your attention. It was the vibe. The tilt of her hips. The certainty in her eyes. She wasn't playful or flirty. It was power. She could rock your world if she wanted to. Faced with two oversized, middle-aged guys on her doorstep, Morgan was in complete control.

She invited us in, closed the door, and we stood in a little group facing one another. "Is this the guy, Angel?"

He nodded and she threw her arms around me and didn't let go. I felt her boobs against my chest and her fingernails on my triceps. Either my bruised ribs had healed or my brain chose to focus on pleasure over pain, because for the first time in nearly a week, I moved without my torso aching.

She gave me one last little squeeze then patted my chest as she backed up. "Thank you," she said.

Angel had told me in the car that she believed it was me that dimed Findley. We decided I'd get more out of Morgan playing along than trying to clear my name. So far we were right.

Before I could ask a question, a little girl toddled out of the kitchen in Capri pants and a pink top printed with stuffed animals. Morgan scooped her up and took her down the hall.

The eclectic 1990s furniture could have been mashed together from a bunch of my estate sales. When she'd moved here two years ago, Morgan had nothing. I moved everything out of Findley's place and when he got out of prison, Findley took everything to his new apartment. Morgan had been broke when she stopped hooking, and I bet most of the stuff in this place had been donated to one charity or another then given to her.

Above a pine bookshelf hung a nursing program certificate. Angel nodded at me as I walked over to the kitchen and saw the trappings of normal life with a young kid. Cheerios. Sippy cups. Plastic plates featuring cartoon characters.

For all the stories of donations wasted, gifts cast aside by ungrateful recipients, here was the one that warmed your heart. Morgan was making it proudly on her own. All she needed was some help getting started.

The television started playing a Disney movie, and Morgan's footsteps approached over sticky linoleum. She offered us a drink. I refused even though I'd left the big blue mug in the car. Angel and I split the couch, each filling our half, and Morgan slipped into a mismatched upholstered chair.

My curiosity about her time with Findley wiped away my thoughts about the tablecloth top and the sexy legs wrapped tightly inside those blue jeans.

"What do you want to know?"

"You seem to be doing pretty well," I said.

"You're wondering how a girl who can get a job at St. Luke's and raise a kid wound up working the streets for Findley."

"Something like that," I said.

"He's slick. I was a kid, bouncing around. House to house. Doing drugs. Having fun. He traded me sex for drugs. Once. Then twice."

Plenty of girls took free drinks in bars. I'd bought tons myself. Morgan was attractive. I couldn't understand how she could sell herself, but maybe I also couldn't understand how persuasive Findley was.

"He's not a bad looking guy."

"So you progressed to other guys?" I asked.

"He shared me with his friends."

I felt my eyes bulge.

"I saw them pay. I knew what was happening, but I ignored it. I was living with him. It was how I earned my keep. And they were decent-looking guys at first. It was a few, maybe ten a week."

Angel fidgeted next to me but I didn't look his way.

"The other girls warned me to get out, but I didn't listen."

"How many were there?"

"Three. Four of us. Findley took whichever of us he felt like having. It was mostly me at first because the other girls were out."

"And then you started going out?"

"Yeah." She looked shattered as the memories came. I couldn't imagine how low she felt about giving her body to strangers every night.

I couldn't tell what was going on with Angel. I didn't need to look to know he'd paid for Morgan back then. But he'd helped her somehow or she wouldn't have invited us inside. I couldn't believe she was still servicing him, but the idea sent a rod up my backbone and my legs went numb. Did a former prostitute even want sex? Did she see Angel as a repulsive, sad man, or as an easy buck if things got desperate?

She went on without me prodding and I was thankful because I couldn't have come up with another question.

"The street guys were different. Fat. Ugly. Smelly." She shuddered involuntarily, and Angel stopped moving altogether. "Hot guys don't pay a street girl for a blowjob in a car. They might mess around with a stripper, but they weren't pulling up to the curb to talk to us."

I thought about who Morgan might date. She's a strong seven. Angel's a three on a good day. But he'd had her. Probably dozens of times. A mixture of guilt and embarrassment steamed off him. She fixed on me, not looking further down. I bet Angel wouldn't be back, but I'd been wrong about him before.

"So you quit?"

"That's funny. You don't quit Findley."

The guy's not very tough, but Morgan looked terrified. "You tried." It wasn't a question.

"When I was pregnant, his friends still wanted sex. They complained and he forced me to take care of them."

Sickened, I stared at her, but couldn't help wondering why she'd have Findley's kid after he put her out on the street. The math was a bit tricky, but I guessed she got pregnant soon after meeting him.

"I was disgusted. I needed him for a while and he took it easy on me until Clara was one, but then he wanted more and more money."

"So you ran?"

She nodded through tears. "He threatened to hurt Clara, so I hid her with friends. But even that didn't help. I was desperate for money and went out to turn a few quick ones. One of the guys I got in with took me back to Findley's. He was so desperate to get me back that he'd told all his friends they could do whatever they wanted to me if they brought me back."

A tear streaked down her face and I sat back.

"He kept me inside for two months."

I was glad she didn't say what they did to her, because I probably would have thrown up. Angel still wasn't moving. I wondered if he thought about his money being partly to blame for her torment. If men didn't pay for sex, men like Findley would lose their power over girls like Morgan.

"He threatened to sell Clara if I didn't work."

The tears came faster. I didn't know where to look. What to say. I spotted tissues on the end table and brought her one.

She smiled at the small kindness.

"When he got sent up, I was free." She sniffled. "Now I have a job and a place for Clara and he can't touch me."

The whole time we'd been sitting there, I hadn't asked what I'd come for. The movie still played down the hall, but Clara could come wandering down any minute. At that moment I didn't want Findley behind bars. I wanted him underground. Morgan would have helped me put him there.

"So where is his weakness?"

"Drug buys."

"I thought drugs were a sideline?"

"He went away for running girls. Two of us testified and he served eighteen months. He can pimp all the girls he wants and the state isn't going to do much about it."

"You think they care more about drugs?"

"Not the nickel and dime stuff. The big buys. Help the cops connect him to a big buy and he's all done."

Findley had been trying to kill me over an eighteen-month hitch. And he was just a little fish. Imagine what a big time dealer would have done over a major bust. Jake. Roxie. We'd all have to go into witness protection. They'd probably kill Newb and Angel just for information.

Morgan was cute, but she was out of her mind. I listened to what she had to say about Findley and his money, but I wasn't going to get tangled up with a big time dealer. Not on my life.

Chapter Forty-five

The next morning Newb and I met Chris at the hospital.

"Not bad, Little Brother."

Chris stripped the forms from the low wall that would anchor the curved security desk at the head of the stairs. He carefully smoothed the concrete with his hands. There was something about stone walls and concrete that got him going. I didn't complain. He worked as fast as Speedy and he always showed up when he said he would.

"You should quit writing and work for me fulltime."

"Probably make more," he said tossing a used form aside.

I never understood why the kid threw away so much time writing books. He wrote great stories, but never made any money. He could do other stuff. Years ago he'd been some big computer guy and left that because he loved to write. Two days before he'd helped me mount cameras at three properties and tie them into the Internet. In a few hours, I had Findley under surveillance from three different angles, all from the comfort of home. Well, Chris's room. The kid had potential. Sad he wasted it.

I was glad to have him on board for the day, anyway. Speedy hadn't called me in a while, and I was beginning to wonder when he was coming back.

At least Newb kept showing up. He wasn't nearly as useful, but he was learning. I'd had a few guys on the job who thought being in recovery entitled them to get paid for showing up and hanging around. Newb wasn't like that. He wasn't much for personality, but if I asked him to do something, he did it. Or at least he tried.

I chuckled to myself as I watched him fumble with a tangled extension cord. Stringing temporary lights was a major project when it took five minutes to untangle an extension cord. I didn't say anything. Just watched.

Chris stripped away another section of form.

Newb backed the female end of the cord through one tangle after another. Fighting to get it free. Losing the battle against time.

I walked over. "You doing okay, Newb?"

He yanked and the coils dropped to the floor. The cord finally free.

I grabbed an end and walked it back to the light I'd hung. He didn't seem pleased with his success, so I asked again. "What's going on?"

"They found a buyer."

"For the house?" I thought I heard him grunt. "That's great, Newb."

"Angel thinks so."

Chris looked over. I could read his thoughts from fifty feet away. Newb didn't sound the least bit happy. The kid was selling a house he inherited. Walking into a hundred grand and not happy about it.

I couldn't help asking, "How much they offering?"

"One forty-five."

It didn't sound like a lot, but it was a small house. And it was all free to Newb. "Sounds good to me, kid."

The kid wasn't convinced. He hauled extension cords around and helped me string up the lights, but wasn't much on talking. We hauled steel studs and tools up the concrete stairs, and when I asked him about the house again, mostly because I needed a rest, he told me the hassle of taxes and the death certificate and all the paperwork was killing him.

He was nervous about the closing, and when I offered to help, he told me Angel was going to sit in with him.

When we had everything ready to start framing and I told him to take a break for lunch, he just looked at me. We always went together and I bought. I assumed that was his problem. I handed him a twenty and he disappeared.

I shook my head all the way upstairs to where Chris had the laptop running.

"What did we get?" I asked.

"That depends on who all these people are."

I came around the security desk so if anyone decided to come inside, the video would be faced away from them. He played a video that showed one person after another going up the stairs to Findley's place.

"These times right?" I asked.

"I set the cameras by my phone. The time comes right from Verizon."

A young guy went up and came out two minutes later. The tape cut to another man going up and coming out a little over three minutes later. I watched as the scene replayed over and over. It was always men until almost dark. Then the girls left the apartment and were gone quite a while.

Findley himself left for an hour then came back.

Chris didn't know who these people were and neither did I, but it wasn't a stretch to figure Findley was dealing drugs out of his state subsidized apartment.

"It's a good start," Chris said. "But it doesn't prove anything."

"If I want to see the deals, I need a camera in his place."

"That'd never be admissible," he said.

"You write about murder and now you're a lawyer?"

"Put a camera in his apartment and you're going to need one."

I turned my back on the video and paced away. The kid was right. The video didn't prove anything, but it was obvious those guys weren't all visiting. Anyone with common sense would know Findley was up to no good. What I needed was a vice cop motivated to prove it and make a bust.

Chris ejected the CD and handed it to me. "Careful with that. You think he was pissed before. He finds out you're recording him, he's going to go ballistic."

Chapter Forty-six

As I showered off the grime and sweat of a hard day's work at the hospital, I remembered Morgan telling me about the vice cops she bribed each week with sex. She knew the right guys in the department and was never arrested in three years working the street. Those guys didn't do her any favors. If she'd been arrested, maybe she'd have broken free of Findley sooner. Maybe someone in the system would have helped her.

I couldn't help picturing the girl I saw with Angel as I pulled on my jeans. Angel wanted to help. He dedicated his life to troubled kids after his son died. Still he couldn't resist the pull of cheap sex. If she could get money out of a guy as big-hearted as Angel, prostitution might never end.

All the way down Coggeshall and into the south end, I thought about legalization and what that might mean for the girls working the streets. Anything would be better than working for an abuser like Findley. I'd heard stories of girls being forced to serve as many as forty guys a night. Just thinking about it made me want to puke. Kidnapping. Torture. Forced drug use. The skin on my face and arms turned hot. Half sick. Half needing to hit someone. I was so agitated I could barely keep the station wagon in its lane.

By the time I parked beside Angel, I'd have said anything to get Findley locked up. The problem didn't end with him, but if everyone took action the way I did, a lot fewer women would have been forced to sell themselves.

I didn't think about the problems that might create. The stress in those guys who couldn't get sex even by paying for it. All I could think about at that moment was putting Findley behind bars. Angel assured me he had found the right guy for the job.

We dropped my car, and Angel drove me to a donut shop downtown. I followed him inside and watched him order three Boston Kreme donuts and a Coke. I ordered a single chocolate cruller and a coffee then paid for the entire order.

Angel avoided my eyes when we sat down. He didn't want to talk about what I'd seen. We both knew he couldn't stop. He ate his donuts while I thought about how lucky I was to have Roxie. She was crazy about me and more woman than I could handle. It must have been miserable in Angel's shoes. Sharing a woman that had five or ten other guys a night. Who didn't care who you were. Even drinking my coffee couldn't warm me up.

Alarm bells went off when the tall skinny guy walked in. His head was too long for his body like the California Raisins from those old commercials. Angel looked up then made a point of sipping his Coke. I thought I saw a bulge at the bottom of his windbreaker, but his piece was hidden well enough that I never saw it.

The vice cop ordered a coffee and came casually to our table.

"Rusty, Lorado," Angel said.

The guy made Newb seem emotional. His eyes betrayed nothing, but his body language was cocky. More than confidence. Maybe it was the gun. Or maybe it was the power he wielded over the junkies and pimps spilling over into his talk with us.

"Angel tells me you have a problem." I didn't like where his power trip was headed. I'd worked with enough losers to know Rusty got off on control. If he had an advantage, he'd use it to get something he wanted.

"I've got something that will help you," I said.

"And what do you want out of this?"

I didn't want to owe this guy anything. "Justice."

He nodded and rubbed his chin.

I tried to bury my hatred for Findley. I couldn't give Rusty the satisfaction of knowing how badly I wanted him put away.

Angel saw the tension. He'd stopped eating and watched without moving except to breathe. For a moment I wondered how well he knew this guy and whether he was reconsidering bringing us together.

I pulled the CD out of the big pocket inside my coat and slid it across the table.

Rusty looked at both sides then folded his hands over it. "What is this going to do for me?"

"There is a stream of drug buyers and prostitutes going in and out of a government subsidized apartment. There are some good face shots on there."

"Any drugs visible?"

"No. But it's plenty for a warrant."

"What do you know about getting a warrant?"

My lazy-ass bureaucrat warning light went solid red. You know when you're dealing with someone who can only see the fine print of every policy no matter what common sense dictates? You stand there and explain yourself over and over, but no matter what you say, they refuse to help.

Any idiot watching that video would know Findley was selling drugs. I wanted to slap the guy and tell him so, but I forced myself to breathe.

"I'm not a cop," I said. "But I know Findley is running girls and drugs out of that apartment. If you look at that video, you'll know it, too."

"What's your interest in this Findley guy?"

He wasn't bullshitting me. Any vice cop in New Bedford knew who Findley was. Rusty wasn't surprised by the name. There in the donut shop I didn't know why Rusty played dumb. I assumed it was part of the cop act.

"He tried to kill me. Twice."

"That's homicide. You want me to turn this over to them?"

The homicide cops would have laughed me out of the building. Findley was trying to kill me, and he knew that I knew. We couldn't go on like that. My family wouldn't be safe until Findley was dead or in jail. A drug bust was the easiest way to get him back where he belonged.

"That video will help you bust him for selling heroin. Use it."

Rusty's face instantly showed how little he liked taking orders.

They focus on clothes and toys for kids. The flow of used goods is enough to run a major clothing outlet.

Volunteers wash, inspect, and package so many clothes that Jim can tell you what colors are popular with girls of various ages and even what brands are in fashion. If you just look at the shelves you can see the colors morph from pink to purple as children grow and have more voice over what they wear.

They didn't call me to look at clothes. They ushered me into an office to see eight bins of toys.

The clients they served had problems. Drugs. Poverty. Violence. They wanted to alleviate those problems by providing clothes and books. Some things people donated didn't quite fit. When I opened the first bin, I was eight years old, my eyes wide. I couldn't believe what was inside and I couldn't believe the price.

I couldn't say no.

The bins were so large I had to get the truck to haul them back to the warehouse. When I had a big enough area swept and the bins all popped open, I completely forgot about Rusty and what he was up to that day.

When you're a boy, you get army men, cars, tanks. If you were really lucky you got a helicopter or two and maybe a boat. No matter how many you got, you arranged them, set them up for war, and you always had room for a few more. Back up another foot and there was a table or a chair where you could place a sniper or line up a new squad. Running out of army men was a sad reality of kid life.

Until you turned forty-something and opened up a bin packed with stuff that totally blew you away.

A helicopter caught my eye. Shiny. Gleaming. Green. Working rotors and a big white star. It was better than any helicopter I'd ever had as a kid. The metal felt heavy in my hand. I chose a spot way back near the windows for my airbase. And then I lined up my helicopters. Not one or two. Or even a dozen. I started with eighty. Unbelievable. Eighty matching helicopters. There were more in the other bins for sure, but after getting those all lined up I moved on to tanks, personnel carriers, planes, earth movers. Any military toy you could imagine, I had fifty of them. If you've never had that much shiny metal in one place, you have no idea how much it rocks.

I had more soldiers than lots of countries. No kidding. Clear bags stuffed full of plastic men in all sorts of poses. Shooting. Marching. Talking on portable radios. If I was ten, I might never have gone home.

It took an hour of sifting to get an inkling of what I had.

The junk game isn't often about what you have fifty of. It's what you find one of. Maybe two if you're lucky. Something unusual that people want because they are scarce. The place I put a value on this stuff was eBay. What better place to see what something was worth than an auction that ran twenty-four seven. If I thought I'd found a valuable piece, that was the first place I went to check.

In among all my goodies were seven military police vans. The wheels were in mint condition. No kid had played with these, and they had to date back to the sixties. I plugged them in to the search box, and bingo, I paid for the whole lot of stuff just like that. The cars were selling for twenty bucks apiece. I found one hundred forty bucks just like that.

I started a box of items to take home, photograph, and list online. The longer I played and dug in the bins, the better my deal got. I kept finding gems. Cars worth twenty, fifty, a few worth three hundred bucks. Not to mention the thousands of pieces I could bundle and sell for a buck a bag.

Pretty soon the old carton that had once held reams of paper was half filled with two-inch cars at twenty bucks a pop. I was so excited I left the opposing armies aligned on the floor. One defending the airbase underneath the windows, the other surrounding it on three sides. I didn't even consider what Newb and Chris would say when they saw my battle arrangement.

My excitement disappeared halfway down Coggeshall Street. I noticed something odd about the two cars following me and detoured away from my house. I circled one block then turned right and continued in the direction I'd been going. Both cars followed.

Less than twenty-four hours after my meeting with Rusty, I had two cars full of thugs on my tail. It was fast for a leak. Not so fast for a tip off. Either way, I had a big problem.

Chapter Forty-eight

"Kid, I've got a problem. You dressed?"

The clicking on the other end stopped and I could hear him stand up. "Yeah. What's going on?"

I kept my eyes on the mirror and flowed along with traffic, weaving out to Route 6, where four wide lanes gave me room to maneuver in case they tried to overtake me. "I've got two carloads of goons following me."

"Need directions to a police station?"

A good idea. But the second I pulled in they'd disappear. That would solve my immediate problem, but they'd show up somewhere else. If I wasn't ready when they did, I might end up dead. I needed to deal with them while I was ready and I needed help in a rush.

"Remember last year at the pig pen?"

"Yeah."

"We need to get four maybe five this time. Can you handle them behind that wall you made?"

"You driving?"

"Driving and standing."

"Got it." He thought a minute and told me he'd be ready in twenty.

I cruised Route 6 at the speed limit all the way to Marion, and they followed several car lengths behind. They weren't in a rush to stop me. I hoped they were foolish enough to think I was just going about my business and waiting for me to go home. My route would have made more sense if I stopped to pick something up, but I couldn't risk getting shot in a Cumbie's parking lot. The wide loop I made going east all the way to Interstate 495 and then back north made no sense unless I knew they were behind me, but I had to hope that they were either oblivious or determined enough to chase me no matter where I went.

I took the ramp to Route 105 in a rush and plowed out into traffic. The little downtown streets were too tight to let them get up on me so I barreled along. They seemed to buy that I was running.

I swung into the drive through at the hospital and slammed the wagon into park, leaving my box of rare army vehicles clacking on the seat as I hoofed it in the dark.

Tires screeched behind me, and I hustled down the concrete steps and through the plywood door as fast as I could. I ducked, expecting a gunshot that didn't come.

I whistled the second I stepped inside. Not any whistle, a locating call the men in our family used in the woods. I didn't wait for a response. I had two flights to climb, and after ten steps, all I could hear were my own footsteps and my breath whooshing in and out. I knew they were right behind. They had to be closing, but I had no idea how fast they were.

I was huffing so badly when I stopped on the second floor landing I could barely whistle. Chris gave me a shrill call from so close I should have been able to see him, even in the dark, but couldn't. Footsteps pounded the concrete stairs behind me.

"You're screwed now, Fat Boy," called a voice from below. "No way out for you."

The men climbed more slowly, careful now that they'd announced their presence, but I pressed across the open space quickly in the dark, right between the pile of sheetrock and the flimsy steel. I kicked a metal stud on my way and it clanged. The perfect invitation for them to follow.

"Big mistake you made yesterday. That CD made the boss pretty damned mad."

I found cover at the concrete wall, and leaning against it, was a Browning twelve gauge. Action closed. When I felt a shell at the mouth of the tube, I knew I had four in the mag and one in the chamber. Triple-0 buckshot if I knew my little brother.

Footsteps scurried into the open behind me. They spread out, but Chris and I were perfectly aligned to be firing in the same direction—and away from each other.

Voices whispered coordinating calls, and I counted four shadows in the open area between me and the security desk.

It was Chris' move. I knew what he was waiting for, I just wasn't sure we'd be lucky enough to draw the scenario we wanted.

Feet shuffled by the security desk and my heart sank.

It sounded like Chris came out around to get an angle. Stepped out into the open. He was smarter than that. Getting out front of that concrete wall would get him killed. Four or five guns to two. We'd be screwed.

Nothing happened.

I kept waiting for something. A shot. A punch. Something.

More footsteps by the desk. The others had settled in around the pile of studs. They hung low. Waiting for their eyes to adjust. Searching the corners for me. My five shooter and I were well covered. I'd only be exposed six inches. Me with the twelve gauge. I could mow down two of them before they got a shot off. Without cover they'd go down in a rush. And the kid had an even better angle.

But what was he doing walking around?

More footsteps.

I wanted to curse him, but then I remembered what he always did.

He'd stand still and let a deer walk up within ten feet before he dropped it. Sick patience. Uncle always said never shoot a deer coming toward you and it seemed the kid applied that to thugs to.

Problem was, thugs shot back.

The light and the voice caught me by surprise. Blinding. Ferocious.

The whole scene snapped into focus for me in an instant.

The temporary lights I'd set up with Newb came on all at once. The whole place lit up. A big empty pen with only one way out. When the light came on, the suckers in the middle of the floor realized the pile of studs was way too short to hide behind.

"Move and die." The words were cold. The guy they were directed at was about six feet in front of the security desk, facing the wrong way. Chris was right behind him with his Browning trained center mass. It'd blow a hole right through from that range.

"Drop it. Easy," Chris ordered.

The guy stood frozen. He was screwed, but didn't comply. He waited for help from his friends, but their position wasn't much better.

"Better listen, Assholes. If you all ran at once, my kid brother over there would drop you all before you made the stairs. Even if he happened to miss one of you, I'll give you a buckshot headache from back here."

The five of them shot nervous glances at each other. They were stranded in the open, facing two semi-automatic shotguns from covered positions. They could have scored a lucky shot and maybe hit one of us. They were probably thinking of trying their luck. Winging a bunch of shots and hoping to hit something. But not one of them had a gun on target. We both had a man lined up. At go, two of them were going to drop. They'd be dead before they hit the floor.

They probably had no idea what they were up against. Country boys learn to shoot stuff that moves in a rush. None of those thugs could spin and vanish like a whitetail, and even a whitetail wouldn't have a chance standing in a spot that wide open.

"You take the closest two. I've got the rest."

The order gave me chills. I believed he was going to shoot. My bead was on an ugly guy's nose. When I heard his Browning bark, my guy would hit the deck and it'd be three on two.

I checked my safety and caressed the gold trigger.

What would I say to the cops after we killed five guys?

Dad would be pissed then proud. If he were standing with us, he'd say to make sure we killed them all so we didn't have to face them in court.

I caught one of the guys looking at the lights. If he had ideas about shooting the bulbs he was out of luck. Chris had them in two alcoves, the glare reflecting off the concrete. Still bright enough for us to see like daytime and impossible for them to shoot the glass.

"He's not playing," I said. I heard the fear in my own voice as I held the bead steady on the ugly guy. I didn't want to drill him in the head. I wasn't sure I could live with myself. "Drop the guns or you're going to start hitting the floor."

The thug in front of the security desk broke first. He bent forward and gently set a black pistol on the concrete then stood straight up, his hands slightly raised, in plain sight.

"Lay down. Hands behind your head. Interlace your fingers."

He moved slowly, but as he did, Chris had a clear vantage to the other four. They had nowhere to go. Facing the muzzle of my gun convinced the ugly guy. He knew he was going to die first. No matter what happened afterward, he was toast. The only way to save himself was to move away from the heap of steel and lay down. Once he did, the final three followed suit. It would have been foolish for them to die with no hope of winning. When they surrendered, our problems with the local cops began.

Chris dialed his phone with one hand, his Browning rested over the concrete wall like a fifty caliber on a jeep.

One of the guys looked over while he waited for the call and I barked, "Keep your head down or I'll blow it off." I didn't think he believed me, but he put his head back down and kept his hands on the back of his head as if his fingers could deflect buckshot.

"I've got five armed intruders at the old St. John's Hospital in Middleboro."

There was a long pause.

"I need a black and white and lots of cuffs. Now would be good."

Another pause. Shorter this time.

"They're face down on the floor."

His voice was tinged with disbelief. They should have congratulated him, but I sensed it was something a whole lot less supportive.

"I'm standing over them with a Browning semi-automatic. They're not going anywhere."

They went back and forth a few more times, and I could hear the annoyance growing in his voice. I knew the cops would separate us first thing. He clicked off the line and cursed the dispatcher in a string Grampy would have appreciated not for its length, but its creativity.

"They hate it when you do their job for them," he said.

"Who knew your first night standing watch you'd catch five armed intruders? Must be your lucky day."

Chapter Forty-nine

The wait for the cops felt like an eternity. Every little move tensed a nerve somewhere in the room. The longer we waited the more time the punks had to think of stupid things to try.

"Don't get me with a ricochet."

Chris sidestepped toward me and angled his Browning steeply down at the guy who'd skirted the security desk. The punk stayed facedown, but he fidgeted enough to make us both nervous. If he moved too fast, I knew Chris would splatter him all over the floor. Pure instinct. He was used to swinging on things that moved. I'd seen him whip the gun around on a squirrel running out of the long grass and drop him in mid-jump, the pellets nailing him so squarely they shoved the little critter to the ground. The whole thing happened in the count of two, but in those two seconds, he clicked his safety off, checked his field, shouldered the gun, swung around, anticipated a bound where the squirrel couldn't change direction, and fired.

A whole lot could happen in two seconds. Everything could change.

"Don't worry. The brain splatter won't carry that far."

His message was for the hood lying in front of him. Now that he was out front of the security desk, his cartridge belt was in plain view under the lights. Twenty-five shot shells should have been intimidating enough. Who owned that much buckshot?

The stupid punk kept fidgeting, and it put Chris on edge. At that range the pattern would have been the size of a quarter. An inch and a half wide hole right through the guy. I needed to calm them both down. Dead hoodlums were a lot harder to explain than dead squirrels.

"You remember Jason's Lane?"

"There aren't any trees here." He sidestepped again and I knew he'd gotten my message. One day he'd scared the shit out of me with a ricochet. A few of his pellets deflected off a tree and came screaming through the forest in my direction. I had no idea what happened to pellets when they hit concrete, and I didn't want to find out in such a tight space.

I hated leaving the cover of the concrete wall, but I had no choice but to step out into the clear. Standing closer, I took away their chance to reach for the guns they'd tossed onto the floor. But what I was more worried about was a quick reach for a piece hidden in a belt or a shoe. That would have triggered a bloodbath.

The police station was three blocks away, and it took ten minutes from the time we called the state police until the locals drove in, sirens wailing.

"Fun's over guys. Hang tight a few more seconds, and you'll get some new jewelry," I said.

Doors slammed. Footsteps rushed in the door then came cautiously.

"Put the gun down!" The cop bellowed loud, commanding, foolish.

We were covering five men and the first guy up the stairs wanted to take over before he even saw what was going on. If he had his way, he'd have been outgunned five to one in about four seconds. Luckily Chris wasn't big on listening.

"I'm not a threat," Chris said, never taking his eyes off the man in front of him.

"You better step in officer," I said. "See what you're up against before you ask him to put that shotgun away."

A rigid arm aimed a Sig at Chris. Head high. Another uniform stepped in and turned toward me and the cluster of men on the floor behind the studs and sheetrock.

"Who are you?"

"I own this place."

Dinner at Deadman's

He hugged the corner at the top of the stairs, ready to dodge back to cover. Both cops were in my line of fire and vice versa. Chris had a clear shot at all five intruders, but I couldn't imagine him taking one then.

"If you guys want to start collecting those guns and snapping on jewelry, we'll be glad to cover you," I offered. Still cocky and cool. I was high on what we'd done. Five guys were out to kill me, and we put them on the ground and gift wrapped them for the cops. As proud a day as I could remember.

The cops didn't appreciate my invitation. The first asked Chris again to drop his gun to the floor. He told him it was an eight hundred dollar Gold Hunter and he wasn't about to scratch the finish. He worked the action and ejected five shells on the ground.

When the cartridges hit the floor and rolled, the thug he'd been holding on stiffened. He must have thought the shells would go off on impact. Obviously he hadn't been around guns much.

Chris leaned his baby in the corner, muzzle toward the ceiling, just like he did in the living room at home. The cop motioned for the cartridge belt then almost moved on, but Chris stopped him to show the Walther PK380 holstered inside his belt. He dropped the magazine and set gun and magazine a few inches apart on the floor near the Browning.

"I hope you have a license for that."

"Glad to show it to you once you cuff these nice men who came in here to shoot me."

I lowered my gun and finally the cops started frisking and cuffing the guys on the floor. They weren't done with us by a long shot, but they kept finding guns, drugs, and a few knives on the guys who had followed me. I knew the first thing they'd do was to separate Chris and me, so I slid over and coordinated the one piece of the story we hadn't settled on.

I patted him on the shoulder, blew out a deep breath. "So glad you weren't sleeping on duty. If you'd missed that call, those guys would have killed us both when they followed me in here."

A senior cop gave me the eye. I learned later he was a sergeant. He left the three other officers and escorted me across the open room to my corner of the ambush. He asked for my license to carry and his demeanor changed a little when I produced it and told him again that I owned the place.

He didn't ask more questions while Chris was in the room. He'd produced his LTC, too. None of the guys on the floor had one, so the cops had five illegal weapons charges to start. It gave them their second clue to what side everyone was on, so they let Chris stand within a few feet of his gun while they taxied the now-cuffed men to the station down Main Street.

When they bagged Chris' Browning, I thought he was going to blow his cool. They took both his guns and led him downstairs, protesting all the way.

"You want to tell me what this is all about?" the sergeant asked.

"The place has been vandalized hard. We're building it out, and I hired my kid brother to watch the place at night, to make sure stuff doesn't disappear. I've got forty thousand in materials downstairs."

He grunted and rolled his eyes.

"I was downtown and two cars were following me. I called my brother to make sure he was here. He said he was and I came over."

The cop crossed his arms. I could tell he wasn't buying it, but I couldn't find an obvious hole in my story.

"You mean to tell me your brother stands guard in an abandoned hospital with two twelve gauge shotguns and a handgun?"

"Good thing he does."

The sergeant made a few notes in a pad. Stuff he was going to grill me on later I was sure. The obvious problem was, it was completely impractical to shoot two sporting shotguns at once. Not impossible, but long guns were made for two hands.

"You didn't walk in here carrying?"

"No, Sir. I didn't."

"When exactly did you get the gun?"

"He gave it to me when I came in." Not technically true, but pretty close.

"Was he holding both guns before you got here? Or did he have one locked up?"

"You'd have to ask him. I was running. I have no idea what he did with them before I got here."

The sergeant made another note, grimaced, and chewed his lip.

He asked me where Chris was when I came in. When I told him, he walked across the room and stalked all around the security desk. He found two trigger locks behind the wall and came back with them in a bag.

"This isn't adding up for me. It looks a whole lot like an ambush."

He let me stew a bit.

"You want to tell me the real story?"

"You mean why these guys were chasing me?"

"You can start there."

"There's a pimp and drug dealer in New Bedford who's trying to kill me."

"This keeps getting better and better," he said.

"Yesterday I gave a recording of ten or fifteen drug deals to a vice cop in New Bedford."

"Does this cop have a name?"

"Rusty."

He sobered a little, but when he asked me for a last name or a phone number, I couldn't supply one.

"Are you aware it's a crime to lie to police? We call it obstruction of justice."

"I met him in a donut shop last night." I gave him the address and told him about our meeting. "The exchange is probably on their security tape. I handed him a CD over the table. About ten thirty P.M."

The sergeant took down the address and ten minutes later he drove me to the station to get Chris. They let us walk out with our guns, but we had a much bigger problem. Why were these guys chasing me twenty-four hours after my meeting with Rusty?

Chapter Fifty

A far away tinkling danced at the edge of my consciousness. Beta snored, his big jowls flapping on the power of his exhaled breath. My hand hovered over the butt of the .38 special tucked into the cushion. I'd have held it flat on the armrest, but Beta loved to jump up and lick my face. If the stupid dog shot himself, Roxie wouldn't sleep with me for two months.

The loaded gun. The dog at my feet. My spot on the recliner watching both doors. They all needled at me through the fog of a dream. Slowly I surfaced. If the dog had stirred, I'd have snapped awake. But nothing was wrong, not while the dog slept.

My brain finally registered the ringing phone. I found it and I flipped it open.

"Still up?" Chris asked, bright as if it were noon.

I squinted, the backlighting of my phone poking my eyes as I tried to read the time. "Do you know it's three?"

"Not quite."

The kid was nuts. He worked until I was ready to get up for work then slept all morning. He said it was quiet in the middle of the night. "Why are you waking me up at this ungodly hour?"

"You've got a problem. The video feeds are all down."

I wasn't a technical genius. I read my email and posted items on eBay. Beyond that I was pretty much lost. That didn't stop me from taking a stab at the problem. "Could the Internet be down?"

"The cameras are on different connections. I doubt all three networks are down. If they were, your tenants would be screaming."

"What are you saying?"

"Someone found your cameras."

I closed my eyes. Could the residents have stolen them? They weren't worth much on the street. Ten bucks each maybe.

Chris got tired of me avoiding the obvious answer. "Nobody found those cameras by chance. They were too high to see from the street. And no one saw us mount them inside the attics. Whoever messed with those cameras saw the video footage and followed it back to the hardware."

My eyes beamed wide.

"If Findley saw the video already, your cop friend isn't your friend."

"Findley knows what I did," I said, talking more to myself than my brother.

My heart thumped enough blood to force me awake. Jake and Roxie were sound asleep in their rooms, safe as long as Beta and I were standing guard, but I couldn't stay home day and night. I needed to get them out of the neighborhood. Findley had been there once. There was nothing stopping him from coming back. Or from intercepting Jake on his way to school. The scum tortured girls and forced them into prostitution. He wouldn't treat Jake any better.

I thought about what he'd do with Roxie and absently pulled the .38 from the cushion.

"You okay?" Chris asked.

"Yeah. Thinking I need to move Roxie and Jake."

"Good plan."

Details ticked off in my mind. The hardest was convincing Roxie to go.

"You've got another problem."

"God. What?"

"The cops grilled me pretty hard about the Tin Man."

"Oh crap." I remembered what Chris said about the original Tin Man dying from the silver paint. "They're okay, aren't they?"

"If they died we'd have heard about it before now."

"So what did they say?"

"They knew a big fat guy beat the crap out of those kids and left them on a sidewalk in New Bedford. And you are one big, angry, fat guy."

"Sounds like they've got nothing."

"They weren't too sympathetic about the vandalism. I reminded them about the kids doing drugs and stealing copper. That didn't slow them down at all."

"If they gave a shit, they would have caught the punks already. How hard could they be to find?"

"You better watch yourself over there. The cops aren't fond of you, and at least three neighborhood punks would like to smack you around. Maybe tie you up and paint you purple."

Beta sensed the change in my tone and went on alert. He rolled up on his beefy front paws and swiveled his head from the back door to the front. The squawking phone deafened me to anything happening outside, but Findley wasn't coming that night. Five of his guys had been locked up for attempted murder, and if he really wanted Roxie and Jake, he'd come for them when I wasn't around.

I hung up with Chris and watched the front porch half an hour before I picked up the phone again. No doubt Angel was sleeping. But I needed answers.

"Dude, do you know what time it is?" The big guy was more annoyed than I'd ever heard him, but he had to be used to getting calls like this in the middle of the night.

"I do. Sorry, man, but I've got a problem."

I heard Angel wiping his face with his hand to wake himself up. "This better be good."

"How well do you know Rusty?"

"What do you mean? We're not friends or anything."

"How do I get in touch with him?"

Angel hesitated.

"He is a cop, isn't he?"

"Yeah. He busted three kids I know. What's the problem?"

"I think he's helping Findley."

"Oh, shit."

That was all I got from Angel.

He didn't know where to find him. Who he worked for. Nothing. He recognized the guy from court and flagged him down on the street.

I wished I'd known that before I handed Rusty that disc.

Chapter Fifty-one

The next thing I saw was gently-jiggling, manmade cleavage.

Most days waking to those fleshy orbs gave me a perma-grin, but my head buzzed. Sort of like a ringing in my ears, but more centered, like a vibration deep in my head. Pain throbbed behind my eyes. I felt dehydrated. Numb. And I hadn't even considered telling her about moving yet.

"Bad enough you sleep out here. You going to sleep through breakfast, too?"

"I'm up. I'm up." I leaned forward and opened my eyes wide.

She kissed my head and said, "Waffles are almost ready."

I fell back as soon as she swished away. My head hit the leather cushion and my eyes closed. I remembered another time I slept in. I ran the water to fill the bathtub before school. Instead of waiting in the bathroom, I went back to bed. The next thing I knew my mother was screaming. I jumped out of bed when I remembered the water, but it was cascading downstairs like a fish ladder.

The memory of scrambling down the hall that morning back in high school sent adrenaline rushing through me. I had a lot more to lose than waterlogged floors and ceilings. The stress sent a tingle down my arms. I eased the .38 from the cushion and crossed the dining room with it tucked in my pants.

She stood before the stove with a sexy little tilt in her hips she had when she knew I was watching. I wasn't the quietest guy rumbling around, but you'd think I'd slip by once in a while. That hip thing stops me every time.

She gave me a snicker over her shoulder. "You know how I feel about you playing with your gun alone."

I thought I'd been careful. I hadn't wanted her to worry, but now that she'd seen the .38, our breakfast conversation would be a lot easier.

I showered my bulk in the old claw tub. A modern shower would have been a lot easier for a guy like me to step in and out of, but the cast iron tub had character. No way I'd trade it for a fiberglass shell.

Clean and dry, I hit the table just behind the waffles and bacon. Jake wandered out of his room in blue sweatpants, rubbing his eyes, blindly taking his seat around the corner from me. Roxie delivered two thick waffles and four slices of bacon. The kid guzzled water and munched rabbit food like a one-hundred-pound chick. But he loved bacon. The smell was enough to get him up in the morning. That and his white-hot aggression on the football field assured me he was mine.

Roxie filled the waffle iron again and sat with a single waffle and two strips of bacon. Beta rolled over and lumbered to a post beside her chair. "Did you miss me last night, Boy?" she asked in a singsong voice.

What she saw in the drooling slob I didn't know, but he sort of reminded me of me.

She gave me a *what's-up* look.

"What's happening at school, Jake?" I asked.

"Same old. Lacrosse practice next week."

The kid never missed a day. He got straight As, but never talked about what happened there unless it was a new girl or a sporting event. Maybe he knew where my interest was. I didn't think he knew how lousy my grades were. If he did maybe he was sparing me the details, but probably not. Kids aren't that kind.

He carried his plate to the sink and trucked off to the shower.

Curtain hooks clinked over the rod. Water sprayed. And the interrogation began.

"You plan to tell me what's going on?"

"I need you and Jake to stay at your mom's for a few days."

"That's a request, not an explanation."

The water rained down on the other side of the door. I could count on Jake to be in there at least five more minutes. I wanted this conversation to be over when he walked out with a towel around his waist.

"I've got a problem with Findley."

"Yeah. The brick through the windshield was a clue."

"A bigger problem."

She froze. Her eyes stopped short of accusing me of doing something stupid. It was on her mind, but she gestured for details instead.

"Chris and I recorded some video."

She covered her mouth.

"We thought it would get him sent up."

Her words refused to come.

"Some guys tried to follow me home last night."

"Oh my God!"

"It's okay. I led them to the hospital. Chris and the cops met me there. They're in jail now."

Her eyes shot to the bathroom door. Her baby. Muscled as he was. Rugged enough to slam through an offensive line. Jake was her baby, and she'd protect him with her last breath.

"I need you to go until I get this sorted out."

"If he touches Jake, I'll kill him myself," she said.

I believed her.

The water shut off and so did our conversation. She cleaned up the kitchen and made lunch while I threw on some jeans for work.

"I'll drive you to school, Kiddo," I said as I passed Jake.

He didn't answer. When I returned to the kitchen, he sat studying his mother's worried look. She gave him a hug that was a bit tighter and longer than a typical morning.

He didn't ask what was going on when he climbed in the car, but I knew he was waiting for news as we drove the first few blocks.

"Your mom is taking you to grandma's tonight."

"No can do. I'm meeting some kids at the mall and we're going to spit some game."

"What?"

"If you've got game, you spit it."

I still didn't understand.

"Talk to girls, Dad."

I couldn't have sounded that ridiculous when I was a kid.

"Listen," I said. "Remember that brick?"

He waved it off like it was no big deal.

"I've got a big problem with that guy. You and mom need to get out of the way for a few days until things get settled."

"It's not a big deal," he said.

"You're not hearing me."

"That brick was nothing."

"What about the guys who followed me home last night?"

"I think you're imagining things."

"Tell that to the Middleboro cops."

He looked at me like I was out of my mind. Like I'd just told him I was Superman or something. I didn't want to tell him about the guns or the arrest because eventually we were going to have to come back to the house.

I wished I'd said more on that quiet drive.

When I stopped in front of school, he told me again the brick was no big deal. He was fine. And he needed to go to the mall.

Teenage boys never think anything is as important as teenage girls.

I called Roxie to make sure she picked him up immediately after school then I sped over the bridge into the city.

Chapter Fifty-two

My phone rang as I rolled down to Cove Road.

"What's up, Newb?"

"You picking me up?"

"Not today. I've got something to take care of."

The kid never revealed much, but I heard the whine in his voice when he asked about tomorrow. He'd cashed his grandmother's social security check, so he couldn't need money. And he had an offer on a house he paid nothing for. I didn't know how long it would take for the will to be processed, but pretty soon the kid would have more free cash than me.

Newb couldn't see three weeks into the future. That was his problem. Maybe I shouldn't have been so hard on him. Maybe he needed the money for lawyer's fees or something, but I couldn't help feeling that all the kid ever did was screw up and the world turned around and gave him what he needed to make it all better.

It riled me to work so hard and see him have things so easy.

I turned onto another street packed with people I worked hard to support in one way or another. The halfway house. The sober house. The detox. I suppose you could argue that they paid my living. Maybe I even profited off their misery courtesy of the state. But the houses I rehabbed were part of the solution. Helping them, or at least giving them a chance to get clean and go straight whether they decided to take it or not.

Some days I felt really proud of the work I did. Other days I fumed at the arrogance and ingratitude of people who received so much simply because they'd managed to totally screw up their lives.

Today was one of those days.

I pulled up to the curb just past the sober house and looked back at the gable. Chris and I had done some clever handiwork, hiding the camera inside the attic vent where it filmed through a gap between the slats.

We'd been careful not to let anyone see what we were doing. We did the entire job from inside the attic, even hiding our equipment from the staff on the way in and out. I hadn't told anyone at the program about the camera. And no one accidentally discovered it, because I was the only person who went up there. The only way Findley knew about the camera was if he'd seen the video.

No question, he had.

And no question why the camera wasn't sending images anymore.

Rocks or bricks had smashed every slat on the square vent. Strays cracked four baseball-sized holes in the vinyl siding. I imagined Findley and his cronies standing on the lawn pelting the place for ten minutes. No one called the cops and no one called me to report the damage.

Five hundred bucks and half a day's work to fix. If I didn't do it before the next rain, I'd have a wet attic and second floor inmates —the state liked to call them clients—complaining about a leaky roof.

I was about to move up to the detox to check the damage on the second camera when I got lucky.

Findley's Audi with those Olympic rings on the front rolled right past me. I saw the goatee and thick sideburns and spun the station wagon around in the next driveway.

I chased him to Cove Road. His tail flashed into a turn I guessed had him headed for Rodney French. He drove too fast to be looking for someone. He was on a mission. And if I was right, Morgan had told me exactly where he was headed.

I blew through a red on Rodney French to a horn from an angry black dude in a little gray car. I weaved in and out, hauling faster than the wagon had ever been on a road so narrow.

Findley hit eighty on Route 18.

I followed, my knuckles hard on the wheel until he hit the Interstate 195 West ramp. I knew where he was going then even if I didn't believe I could be that lucky.

We raced through Dartmouth. He topped at ninety-five and held it there mile after mile. For a while my little, blue, junk mobile threatened to shimmy apart, but somehow I kept him in sight all the way through Fall River.

I wasn't made for going fast or climbing high. It was completely unnatural for a guy my size. My dad said he was part Indian. He'd climb twenty feet up in a tree stand and sit there all day long. Not me. I liked being near the ground. So when Findley weaved in and out, climbing the Braga Bridge one hundred thirty-five feet over the Taunton River, he opened a huge gap between us. I stayed in the left lane near the center of the bridge, behind a green Ford pickup, while Findley rushed down the other side.

Safely back on the ground in Somerset, I stomped the gas and caught sight of his Audi just east of Providence. He hugged the curves like a NASCAR driver, and I kept up until he hung left and took Interstate 95 South. He could have been going to either casino, but Morgan had told me he'd had a problem with nosy cashiers at Mohegan. I could have been wrong, but I let off the gas and let my blood pressure return to normal while Findley sped on.

Forty-five minutes later, I cruised down winding Route 2, through a deep pine forest to where green-trimmed concrete buildings sprouted up and dwarfed the trees. The Mashantucket Pequot ancestors would have fought the monstrous casino that brought billions in revenue to the tribe.

I parked on the fourth level, took the elevator down, and walked along the wide concourse. The sparse crowd offered no cover for a big guy like me, but downstairs, the poker room buzzed even on a Wednesday morning.

The floor man gave me a one-two no-limit seat. I avoided the cashier line and laid a hundred on the table in front of me. The stack of twenty red chips seemed like nothing compared to the mountain of red and green amassed by the dazed guy across the table. He could barely focus well enough to see me. I bet he'd been playing all night and was playing purely on instinct. I might have been able to take advantage of him. He might misread the board or even his own cards, but my tiny stack couldn't put a dent in the three grand he had in front of him.

I paid the blind so I'd be dealt in, but I mucked every hand and watched until Findley joined the short line to the teller windows. I couldn't hear the woman in the green vest, but I saw the bloated stack of bills he took from the belt under his shirt and I watched how long it took her to count it all out. He changed a heap of twenties for yellows and wandered off past the bigger tables to my right and then behind me and up the stairs.

I'd chosen my seat near the higher limit tables where cash played. Any amount of cash you wanted to put down as long as it was in hundred dollar bills. I knew what he was up to, but I hadn't imagined the scale. Findley had other cashiers to visit. Spreading his chip purchases out so he didn't attract attention.

I played a few hands while he was gone, watching anyone who walked around the high stakes tables until Findley slinked through the crowd and sat into a five-ten no-limit game.

The next two cards that came to me were the two and three of hearts. It didn't make sense to most people, but I loved that hand. I took the timing as a sign and called a ten-dollar raise. Findley didn't seem interested in his game. He folded and watched. I was floored to flop trip deuces.

The original raiser pushed in after an ace hit on the end.

I called and turned over trips.

"You called twelve bucks with two-three?" He whipped his cards into the middle and sent them skidding through the pot past the dealer. He fumed, glaring at a pot that should have gone to his aces up. He never showed his big ace, but he didn't have to. I'd beaten tons of predictable players like him.

"They were suited," the dazed guy said.

He was mocking me. People laughed at the cards I played, but it was impossible to put me on two-three after I'd played tight so long. You wouldn't find my strategy in any book, but I was sixty bucks ahead.

After that I laid low and watched Findley play. Or rather not play. He called pre-flop a few times, but mostly just sat around. In about thirty minutes I saw what I'd come to see. Someone at the table needed change and Findley offered up a stack of greens and a handful of yellows. I thought about wandering to the men's room and checking his stack on my way, but I was just too easy to spot, so I settled for watching through the crowd.

A band held the stack of bills tight. Neither Findley nor the dealer bothered to count it. I bet it was ten grand directly from the cashier's window. The players wouldn't trust a bundle of cash from anywhere else.

An hour later Findley traded chips for another bundle. He barely had enough chips in front of him to get involved in a hand, but he hadn't come to play cards. He was doing exactly what Morgan had described.

I took the long way to the cashier, and cashed in my chips while Findley was still at the table so I could get back to the city first and wait for him.

Chapter Fifty-three

"I've got a place about two miles from here."

I took my eyes off the traffic for the first time in an hour. Mouth wide open. A dozen cars whizzed by, but I was too stunned to look for the Audi.

The skinny guy standing outside my window was completely serious. He wanted to take me home. We'd never met. Never talked. The first words out of his mouth propositioned me for sex. I was three hundred pounds in a station wagon loaded down with junk. Not exactly a sex symbol.

"Are you shitting me?"

What a lousy choice of words. I had no idea what he intended to put where. Thinking about it I felt violated and dirty and sick. My butt cheeks clenched.

The guy threw up his hands and backed away.

In moments like this, macho guys picture themselves slugging the queer, but the whole thing took me by surprise. Who knew rest areas were a hotbed of homosexual activity? I'd never given it a thought. I've picked up girls in clubs and at the beach, but a rest area off the highway? Talk about sleazy.

As I sat there waiting, I realized men were sluts. Straight. Gay. Wow were we sluts. Put two gay guys together and there was going to be a lot of sex. For the next hour, I couldn't get that disgusting thought out of my mind.

Two more cars pulled into the rest area while I waited. I watched them as closely as I watched the traffic and fortunately neither of the drivers came over to talk.

When the Audi raced by, I stomped the gas, glad to get out of there.

This time down Interstate 195 the speed didn't scare me, probably because every mile put that rest area farther in my rearview.

Findley swung onto Route 18 much closer to the speed limit and turned off downtown instead of going all the way to the south end. We curved around to Union Street in heavy traffic. I stayed back half a block. When he clicked his blinker to parallel park, I dodged down a side street.

The first open parking space was all the way around the block. I hustled back to Union and lurked among the cars. Two blocks down the hill I saw Findley push through the revolving door into the bank.

I was no crook, but I couldn't stop the ideas from coming.

He kept over twenty grand cash in his apartment. If I knew his schedule and when it would be there, I could take him down. I had my own key. All I had to do was time his Foxwoods trips. I could take him at home or sabotage his Audi and take him along the highway.

I stood on the curb thinking of ways to hit him, dreaming of the places his money could take me, when an odd thought struck. How could Findley be dumb enough to put his money in the bank? If the state found out about his income, they'd never give him a subsidized apartment, and transactions that big got reported.

Ten minutes passed and I wondered if I'd been duped. I crossed the street and walked casually by the bank, trying not to look too interested in what was happening on the other side of those big glass windows.

Findley wasn't in the teller line.

I kept walking and settled into a doorway across the street.

For another ten minutes, I fumed thinking Findley had spotted me and slipped out the back door. I waited and watched. I couldn't risk another pass by the bank. The place had cameras everywhere, and I didn't want to be photographed anywhere near Findley, not with what I planned to do.

I was about to give up when he strutted out of the bank, more casual since he wasn't so heavily laden with cash. It took a few seconds, but I understood what he'd done inside, why it took so long, and how he avoided reporting his cash to Uncle Sam.

Chapter Fifty-four

By the time I got back to my car, Findley was gone. His car wasn't parked at his apartment or on the surrounding blocks. I cruised back downtown to Union, Pleasant, Williams, and County, circling random blocks hoping to catch a glimpse of Findley or Rusty on the street.

Rusty didn't walk a beat, so it would have been a miracle to spot him driving around, but I needed to pass the time until I took care of Findley. Sooner or later Findley would go back home. When he got there, I was going to beat him senseless and make sure he never bothered Jake and Roxie again. This time I'd be ready for his goons.

I never got the chance to stake out his place. My phone rang while I was still downtown, and I couldn't believe who was on the other end. He directed me down Route 6. The address turned out to be an abandoned used car lot. My station wagon seemed lonely in the wide parking area that once held fifty cars. Three closed garage doors, dark windows, and the for sale sign nailed to the front door told me I wasn't meeting the owner.

I parked in the center of the lot, expecting Rusty to pull up alongside and explain what he'd done with the video. Instead, the center door rolled up and a hand waved me inside. If I went in without backup, I just might disappear. I called Angel and left a voicemail telling him where I was and who I was meeting.

I rolled in and parked. I could control Rusty, but what I didn't expect was the crew waiting for me inside.

A dented old sedan lurched behind me and stopped, blocking my way out. Findley leaned against the cement block wall at the back of the building. To his right, Rusty sat on the hood of his unmarked, eyeing me with a disdainful look that said he'd kill me if he could, but right now it would be inconvenient. Findley didn't appear to have any such reservations and the two guys blocking the back door took their orders from him.

"Is this the guy giving you all the trouble?" Rusty asked.

My seat behind the wheel was a death trap, so I stepped out and measured the four guys ahead of me. A fifth stepped out of the old sedan directly behind me. Heavily muscled, almost my height, with a whole lot less spare baggage in the middle. I couldn't watch him and Findley at the same time, and as soon as I turned away, I felt him creeping up behind me.

The large pipe wrench in the backseat would have made an excellent club, but I didn't go for it.

"He's the guy," Findley said. "Escaped a good beatin' last night."

"No reason we can't take care of that now," the big guy behind me said.

Findley nodded and I heard footsteps closing.

Rusty's car and my own wagon hemmed me in. With four guys together at the front ends of the cars, the easiest way out was obvious. Through the biggest, toughest guy on Findley's payroll.

He closed right in on me. Fists clenched. Jaw tight.

I took a tentative step back. Let him get almost on top of me before I leaned out of his reach like I was afraid. He took the bait, stepping in for a cheap shot as I turned away.

I spun and threw the hardest spinning back kick of my life. The big guy kept coming even after my heel crashed into his ribs. I heard them crack. Three maybe. The guy folded around my leg. His head whipsawing toward me then away. He wobbled. Sick looking. Deflated. He dropped to his knees.

The other four couldn't comprehend what had happened.

I skipped up a step, grabbed his nearest shoulder, and wailed an uppercut through his cheekbone. With his shoulder anchored, his head had nowhere to go, so it absorbed the full force of my strongest left.

The guy flopped to the floor and slid a few inches away before going completely still.

Nothing stopped me from running out the front door.

"Don't even dream of it," Rusty hollered.

I spun around and froze.

He wasn't talking to me.

Findley stood, arms extended, one eye facing me over the muzzle of a black handgun.

Rusty stood off to one side, his arms raised. He didn't want any part of Findley shooting me, but he didn't dare step into the line of fire.

"Shoot him we're both going down," Rusty said.

Findley held on me center mass. He was used to muscle doing his fighting for him. I outweighed him by more than a hundred pounds. If it came down to the two of us, he didn't have a chance and he knew it.

"You're on the wrong side of this one, Rusty," I said. "This punk has been trying to kill me for weeks. The Middleboro cops have four of his guys locked up for attempted murder, and when they see the surveillance video from that donut shop, they're going to be looking at you, too."

Rusty sighed then took a step closer to the line of fire.

"Put it down."

Findley didn't lower the gun until Rusty reached for his.

"I didn't try to kill him. Stupid redneck thinks he's a cop. You saw his video. Vigilante shit. He deserves what he's got coming."

Rusty swung toward me and back to Findley.

"He dimed me and sent me up. He's going down. If not today, soon."

Rusty motioned Findley to relax. He glanced at my car, the sedan blocking me in, and the muscle collapsed on the floor, still not moving.

"You let me take care of the vice in the city, Junk Man."

"You think I care about drugs and girls? Why the hell would I dime some punk I never heard of? This moron tried to poison me. He threatened me and my family. What am I supposed to do?"

"If I poisoned you, you'd be laid out in an alley somewhere. You think you'd be alive if I shot you full of smack? What am I? An amateur?"

The punk had a point.

The guys by the back door spread out and flanked Rusty. The vice cop was smart enough to get what was going on, but Findley was a wildcard. In seconds I could have been unarmed in the middle of a firefight with only my legs to save me from getting perforated.

Twenty steps to the front door. Down an alley between two cars. The guys with guns had all the cover, and I was stuck in the open. Even worse, I'd supremely screwed up and gotten myself in the middle of this for nothing. Findley didn't poison me with a diuretic. He would have shot me full of heroin and made it look like an overdose.

So who wanted me dead?

The whole scene slowed down while my brain tried to make sense of the situation. Voices argued. Thugs moved into position. If I got out of the garage alive, I still needed to figure out who was trying to kill me.

Findley seethed from the back wall. He wasn't smart enough to see the misunderstanding for what it was. He'd done almost two years. Time he blamed on me. That was enough to make us enemies for life. The video took away any chance I had of us ever coming to a truce.

Without Rusty I'd have been dead. The guy had a career to protect. The Middleboro cops wouldn't let go if I turned up dead and he knew it. He waved one of Findley's guys to move the sedan.

The thug waited for a nod from his boss then backed the car out of my way and opened the overhead door. As I rolled out of the lot, I saw the big guy propped up over the shoulder of a smaller comrade. He was pissed enough to eat me raw.

I cursed myself all the way back to the city for making a bunch of enemies over nothing, but I had learned something that changed everything. Findley hadn't tried to kill me. That condescending, pissed off look on his face couldn't be faked. If Findley didn't poison me, every step I'd taken since falling off that toilet had been in the wrong direction.

Chapter Fifty-five

I didn't go to the warehouse to hide from my problems. Findley wasn't looking for me anymore. Roxie was bringing Jake back to the house that night, and I was really looking forward to my conversation with the boy. Something bigger had me stumped. I circled to the back corner of the warehouse to dig through Mrs. Newbury's stuff one more time.

The bed. The silver tea service. The electronics. They needled me. They told me something was wrong, but I couldn't put it together.

I looped around and stood under Findley's spray-painted warning.

The little deer caught my attention from its place atop the clutter. The cheap wooden frame wasn't worth a buck. No one bought used paint by number pictures to hang in their home. I should have tossed it, but I couldn't. Grandpa West spent hours painting by numbers and he was really proud of his creations. When I held the crude painting, I could smell his pipe tobacco and I was a little boy in knee-length shorts running around his chain-link-fenced yard.

Mrs. Newbury had taken extra time to highlight the odd little painting on the day she showed me around her home. I didn't know if she'd made her decision before showing me the deer or after hearing about Grandpa West and his love of paint by numbers, but Mrs. Newbury knew this worthless painting meant nothing to Newb and made certain it ended up in my hands. Exactly how she did that I can't be sure.

I felt nostalgic holding that picture and I stood looking at it a long time before I turned it over. There on the back was my name. *Lorado.* Her careful cursive script low in the corner, pointing the way to a gouge in the backing.

Paint by numbers were done on cardboard and didn't usually get much of a frame job. Most people wouldn't consider framing one, but Mr. Newbury's deer had a decent frame and a backing that had been removed recently.

I whipped out my multi-tool and pried the back off.

Inside I found something that changed my thinking about estate sales forever. Every estate began in death. Someone died and left valuables to their kids, grandkids, or more distant heirs. I'd worked dozens of them. Always someone older. When an older person like Mrs. Newbury died, we all assumed it was natural causes. She'd broken her hip. Many elders didn't survive a year after an injury that serious. The rehab was brutal, and once they stopped moving around, the downward slide began. It was easy to believe pneumonia killed her. For me and everyone else.

I'd been completely convinced until I read her letter.

Sweet Mrs. Newbury was afraid. She didn't say who she was afraid of or what they might do to her, but she said she'd become closer to Trig and Delilah in the last year and that had caused problems. She warned something bad was going to happen and begged me to get to the bottom of it. She knew I'd only find her letter if I was hired to clean out her house after she died.

Her letter was dated November 2011. She died three months later.

An image from an old movie flashed to mind. I saw a kid push his mother down the stairs and wondered how Mrs. Newbury had broken her hip. She was a tiny woman with wrists that fit easily in the palm of my hand. It wouldn't have taken much to knock her down. After the fall, she was at the mercy of her caregivers.

I walked in circles. Away from her stuff then back around. I couldn't stay close without fuming and I couldn't turn my back and walk away.

Newb cheated the government out of her social security check. He tried to steal her microwave before he realized it was his. But would he really kill her for the inheritance? Did his blank face hide a ruthless sociopath? Did Newb think of his own grandmother as just another victim?

The pieces started falling together. Newb had called out of work the entire week his grandmother died. I found him whacked out days later. Maybe he killed her and got a conscience after seeing her dead. He ran to heroin like he did whenever he had a problem. Self-medicated. Running from his emotions was so much easier than dealing with his mistakes.

But how did Newb kill his grandmother without getting caught?

He was about as bright as your average sixteen year old.

I rummaged around the boxes for her medical records. I found neat folders of electric bills, car payments, cable bills, but when I dug through her medical file there was nothing within the last six months.

No wonder Mrs. Newbury didn't say more in her letter. How do you accuse your own grandson of murder? I wondered what he could have done to make her so nervous. How she knew she was in danger. Then I saw the scratches in the bed frame, zigzagged through the boxes, and brushed my fingers over the worn finish.

I imagined the scene and wanted to puke as badly as that first night in her house. The official cause of death was pneumonia, but how closely did they examine her?

The wear marks told the story.

Newb had strapped her down in her own bed and kept her there for days on end. If he'd wrapped her in enough blankets, he could have tied her down without bruising her frail skin. Even if the coroner found bruises, she was recovering from a bad fall. More bruises wouldn't be surprising. And after hip surgery, she'd have a hard time moving. It wouldn't have taken much to immobilize her. And keep her there alone, terrified, slowly dying.

I remembered the little boy saying "Grandma, drink." And the disconnected phone wire in the basement.

I wondered if Newb forced drinks down her throat to drown her, or if he'd starved her until her body gave in. She hadn't looked emaciated in the casket, so I figured he'd drowned her and blamed her death on pneumonia.

I couldn't look at her stuff anymore. I folded the letter and left.

Chapter Fifty-six

Roxie didn't bring the boy home that night. She thought she was punishing me. Making me sleep alone. Just me and a slobbering one-hundred-pound dog. As punishments go, being deprived of her hot body under the sheets was pretty serious, but I wouldn't change anything I'd done. Jake and Roxie were in danger and getting them out of town was the right call. She could pout all she wanted. She'd be back.

The boy would give me attitude about missing his friends at the mall. I'd put up with about ten seconds of that crap before I straightened him out.

That night was a bit of heaven in the midst of two pretty strange weeks.

Every guy needed a little frozen pizza, Coke, and television time. Solitude and complete dominion over one's surroundings did something for a man's soul. I could watch as many episodes of American Pickers as I wanted without a single complaint. I got three in before the dog jumped for the meaty face in the front window.

I carried my pizza to the door and let Angel inside.

"What brings you all the way over here?"

"Making sure you're still alive."

"No thanks to you."

Angel frowned and reached down to stop Beta from nudging him with his big slobbering head. "The guy's a cop," he said, petting the dog as gently as a Pomeranian. "I couldn't know they'd send five guys after you."

The mistake could have cost my life. I didn't make a big deal out of it, but I let him marinate in his guilt while I took my seat in front of the widescreen and gulped a few mouthfuls of soda.

"You should have seen their faces when the lights came up. Facing a twelve gauge will shrink your butt up real tight."

"What if they started shooting? They had guns, too. Didn't they?"

"We would have killed them all."

"Five against two? You're insane." Angel's head reeled.

"We were both covered behind concrete walls. They'd have been lucky to score a hit. With buckshot, at a stationary target, the kid and I aren't going to miss."

"But there were five of them." Angel just didn't get it.

"Trust me, Angel. We'd have pumped out ten shots in about three seconds. And the kid was behind them. The first two guys would have gotten it in the head before they could blink. That's how he rolls. The kid loves headshots."

Angel turned toward the television and watched two kids making buttery popcorn so he could avoid thinking about my war with Findley. "What about Rusty? You can't shoot him if he backs you into a corner."

I patted my big round belly. "Findley wanted to take me out in that garage today, but Rusty wouldn't let him. I think I'm safe for now."

"You trust a crooked cop?"

"Not really, but the Middleboro cops know he passed the video to Findley. If anything happens to me, he's going down."

Angel looked back at the television. His way of telling me I was sticking my head in the sand. He was right, but what choice did I have? No one in the NBPD was going to take my word that Rusty was dirty. More likely if I went over his head, he'd hear about it and I'd end up with a .38 poked in my spine. Right then the best thing for me to do was to stay away from those two and try to figure out what happened to Mrs. Newbury.

Angel sighed four times during the next five minutes of the show. He thought I was making a mistake. Thought I should do something about Rusty, but he didn't have any more confidence in his advice than I did.

My biggest problem wasn't what he wanted to say, but the uncomfortable news I had to deliver. Angel was going to take it hard. The next ten minutes were the worst time I have ever had watching Pickers.

When the episode ended, I clicked off the TV. "I need to talk to you about Newb."

"You're not firing him? He can't take that right now."

"It's worse than that. A lot worse."

Angel's cockeyed expression told me he had no idea what was coming. I put him straight out of his misery. "I think he killed his grandmother."

"Are the cops investigating?"

"They will be."

"Don't tell me you're bringing them in on this?" He was angry. Why was he angry at me? It was Newb he should have been upset with.

"That sweet little lady is dead."

"We can't do anything about that. Can we?"

"Are you insane?"

"What good does locking him up do?"

"I know you love these kids, Angel. They remind you of Mark. I get that. But Newb isn't your kid. He can't control himself when he wants a fix. We can't let him kill people for drug money. Don't you get that?"

"Newb is no killer."

"You want me to show you the scuffs on the bed frame from where he tied her down? You know anyone else who could drown his own grandmother? Or starve her to death?"

I let the image sink in. I figured it would break him, but I was wrong.

"How do you know it was him?"

"I can't prove it yet. But she left me a note saying something bad was going to happen. She was scared."

"Did she say she was scared of Newb?"

"The kid didn't show up at work for a week right before she died. Add that to the scuffs on her bed frame, and you've got a drug-abusing grandson killing his grandmother to feed his habit."

"I don't buy it."

"How much proof do you need?"

"Newb's not a killer."

"I caught him stealing her microwave."

"Big difference between stealing a microwave and killing someone."

"There is." I let the words settle. "But there's a lot more money in a house than a microwave. Far as I know, Newb's getting everything."

He looked at the blank widescreen because he couldn't avoid the clarity of my logic. The little old lady didn't have enemies. Someone killed her and made it look like natural causes. If not for the letter and the scuffs on her bed, they would have gotten away with it.

I thought Angel would come around and help me, or at least accept what needed to happen, but I had no idea how hard Angel would fight to protect Newb.

Chapter Fifty-seven

"I have to work three days to pay the guy an hour."

What could I say to the kid? I paid him ten dollars an hour because that was the bottom of the pay scale. Sometimes he slowed me down more than he was worth. I kept him around because I felt bad for him and wanted to help him out. It wasn't total charity on my part. He worked cheap and he'd do stuff that would have made my elbow scream, but it was ludicrous for a high school dropout to compare himself to a practicing lawyer.

Driving down Route 18, I wanted to haul off and slap him for whining about lawyer fees after his grandmother had just dropped so much money in his lap. Not that she had a choice in the matter. If I read her sentiments correctly in that letter, she'd been thinking about including Trig and Delilah in her will. She just hadn't had the chance to make the changes. If she had, Newb would have been whining a whole lot more.

"Do you know anything about probate? He keeps saying we might have to probate the will. What'll that cost?"

I looped onto Interstate 195 west.

"That depends. Is there someone else with a claim? Trig or Delilah?"

I wished I could have seen the kid's face.

"They aren't in the will."

The deadpan, zombie voice didn't sound like a guy who'd killed the old lady off to get the estate for himself. I couldn't see his face, but he didn't sound nervous.

"They were your brother and sister."

"Half."

"What does the lawyer say about that?"

"A whole bunch of crap."

"Like?"

"She doesn't have to mention them because they're grandkids."

"And?"

"Because they're not mentioned, they could say she didn't know about them. They could ask for a third."

"Bummer."

"Lawyer says probate could avoid problems later."

Sixty or seventy grand in the balance and I still couldn't tell what Newb was thinking. No one would be happy losing two thirds of an inheritance, but the kid showed no sign he cared either way.

"He says we could force DNA testing."

"Do you believe they're related?"

"Pretty sure."

I wondered for the rest of that drive if Trig had weaseled his way into the old woman's good graces. If he'd slipped past Cynthia and Newb to befriend the old lady. He and Delilah were nothing like Newb. What if they were posers? What a great scam. Swooping in. Befriending the old lady. Killing her and walking off with two-thirds.

A great con, but Trig and Delilah had both been out of town when Mrs. Newbury died. They could have lied. It wasn't my place to get in the middle, but I was pretty sure if I confronted Trig about where he'd been, he'd produce a plane ticket. I couldn't remember where Delilah had said she'd been, but I didn't have a reason to doubt her.

We parked at the hospital and lugged five-gallon buckets of paint out front. Newb hauled the ladder over from the back shed while I hooked up the sprayer and tested the hoses.

He looked innocent climbing up, sprayer in hand, but I couldn't help thinking about kicking that ladder and watching him fall twenty feet to the concrete. I pictured him in the weeds at the base of the wall, sprawled and twisted on the ground. I'd wait to call 911. Let him bleed awhile.

The sprayer's buzzing reverberated down the plastic line.

I kept my foot on the bottom rung and watched red paint rise up the tube. Up above, graffiti disappeared in broad swipes. Newb worked his way down a few steps, sweeping the sprayer back and forth, then traded tools and worked the paint in with a long-handled roller.

"That's low enough, Newb. Keep it to a big square."

The gang tags had labeled this place a haven for drugs. When I realized the graffiti outside my building advertised heroin, I decided it was time to cover all the tags.

The paint really helped. With freshly mowed grass and the brush cut down and chipped, the place looked respectable. It was time to replace the broken windows and make the place look inhabited.

That'd give me and Newb work for another few weeks while the plans were finalized. The new look might finally stop those emails I kept getting from town leaders about the state of the old place. And maybe they'd start taking my complaints about vandalism seriously.

I was feeling good about the project, especially that I was on the ground while Newb was twenty feet up the ladder, until a guy stepped over the chain that blocked the back driveway. He strutted across the grass like he had an axe to grind.

Chapter Fifty-eight

"You're the guy, aren't you?" He shouted from fifty feet away.

Newb turned and saw the guy then looked down at me.

"Why don't you come down a minute while I give this nice man an attitude adjustment."

I kept my foot on the bottom rung until Newb was five steps from the ground. When I turned, the dude was on the cracked drive that ringed the building. Still strutting right for me. He got bigger as he crossed the yard, but so did I.

"You're the asshole who was messing with my kid."

He took a few more steps and I could see his bravado shrink just a bit when he got a good look at my forearms. Pulling on heavy stuff every day had its advantages.

My bouncer training was invaluable at times like this. Daytime, when I didn't want to explain to a cop why I'd busted some guy's head in. I put my hands in my pockets and kept my voice low and steady.

"Do you realize you're on private property, sir?"

"Do you realize assault and battery is a crime?"

"I don't know what you're talking about, but you're on my property approaching me in a threatening manner. That's assault."

"You think you're getting away with what you did to my son you're out of your mind."

He stopped five feet short of me.

"I don't know what happened to your son, but if you don't relax I'm going to ask you to leave and ban you from the premises." I spoke as calmly as I ordered my coffee in the morning and that irritated the crap out of him.

"Screw you."

"You want to tell me what happened to your boy?"

"He was jumped by a fat guy here at night. Looks like you qualify."

"What was he doing here after dark? This is private property."

The guy got angrier, but didn't have a response. His son was a pothead, or worse. The guy knew it, but felt an obligation to stick up for his kid no matter how much of a loser he was.

"Your kid do drugs?" I asked.

"That's none of your freaking business."

"Actually it is. The punks around here are advertising drugs on my walls. All this labor today, I'd like to charge them for it."

The guy backed up half a step.

"The graffiti's nothing compared to the damage inside."

"That doesn't give you a right to strip my kid naked and spray paint him."

"Never said I did."

He knew it was me. Only a few guys worked around this hospital and most of them looked anemic. The guy would have pressed charges if he had proof. We also knew if it came to blows, the angry father was going to wind up on the ground with his head bloody. This was all bluster. That was all it was ever going to be.

"You think it's funny picking on kids?"

"Nothing about this is funny." I took my hands out of my pockets. The energy drained out of the guy then. "You said your kid was here? What's his name?"

"Who the hell do you think you are?"

"I own this place and the punks around here have stolen fifty thousand bucks worth of copper. I'd like it back. I'd also like them to pay to have the wiring and piping reinstalled."

The guy put his hands on his hips, puffing himself up.

"It's going to cost about two hundred grand to get it all put back."

He wanted to tell me I was full of shit, but couldn't find his voice.

I waved him inside. Opened the padlock and led him down to the electrical room. My materials were all piled neatly in the center of the room. The racks of circuit breakers were all still empty except for tiny pieces of wire where the punks had snipped off the ends.

I showed him dozens of crudely broken pipes and the drug paraphernalia littering my floors.

The guy stood silently at the top of the stairs when I led him back outside and padlocked the door.

"Your kid comes back and touches those pipes or that wire down there, two things are going to happen. One, I'm going to break both his fucking legs. Two, I'm going to sue you for the cost of replacing it all. By the time you're done, it'll be a quarter mil minimum."

His bravado had evaporated somewhere on the tour.

He nodded and left a lot more quietly than he'd come.

I wasn't sure if I made another enemy that day or not, but at least I didn't lay the guy out.

Chapter Fifty-nine

It irked me that the kid still expected me to pay for lunch.

The skin on my face burned.

He barely noticed the waitress slip the bill onto the table. Didn't pretend to reach for it. Just sat there gnawing his last piece of crust.

My fingers clumsily pulled my wallet. The twenties stuck together. The killer across the table was worth plenty. He didn't deserve a free lunch. But what could I do? I'd been buying every day for years. I didn't want to do it anymore now that I was on to him. And since he had all that cash coming. My sense of justice fought me while I paid the bill and left a decent tip.

I resented driving him back. My gas. My lunch. My job. The kid had everything handed to him, and it still wasn't enough. I couldn't look at him without turning red. Good thing he went back up the ladder.

We finished the high stuff after lunch. All those billboards the gangs tagged on my building, gone. The place started looking presentable on the outside. The inside still needed its guts replaced, but progress felt good.

Working alongside Newb didn't feel good at all. Especially when he got down and worked the sprayer with me on the roller right beside him. Every time I looked over, I pictured him torturing his sweet old grandmother. He was less than human, and I avoided looking at him whenever I could.

The only other thing to hold my attention was the graffiti we were covering. Those big curvy letters were like another language. I couldn't read them, but I recognized a few of them on sight after Angel showed me which ones advertised heroin.

"What do you think I should do?" Newb was still obsessed with his inheritance and the idea that his half brother and sister might get a piece.

"Why not call them and see what they want?"

"And invite them to take a share? That's nuts."

I wondered if I'd be so greedy in his place. If I'd try to get the will approved any way I could. It's got to be hard for anyone to see that much money slip through their fingers. I shouldn't have been so hard on the kid, but no matter how much I thought about the problems Newb faced, I couldn't shake the feeling he was beneath me. An animal. And raised by his father, why wouldn't he be?

Drips of red paint cascaded down behind the sprayer and I imagined Bernie Newbury Senior's seed, spraying out in bars along the waterfront. It was a bummer for Newb's half brother and sister to show up now. I hid half a grin wondering if there were more. How Newb would have felt if there were ten kids bucking for a piece of the old lady's money.

That thought would have stressed him out. I didn't tell him how lucky he was. Or how greedy. I didn't say another thing until we finished a ten-foot high section along the entire front of the building.

Angel pulled up and snarled on his way over.

"Clean the sprayer and put this stuff up," I said to Newb then signaled Angel I'd meet him over at the cars.

He gave me a look when I walked off. It bothered him to see Newb picking up the tools by himself. Angel thought I should have helped the kid put away the tools so he didn't have to work so hard. Wasn't that why I paid the kid?

All Angel did was try to make things right for these kids. Pick up their messes again and again. He'd come to drive Newb to his meeting so he could make his ninety meetings in ninety days. Growing up in my house if you wanted something, you did it yourself. I didn't think Angel was helping the kid. Not at all.

By the time we got to the cars, I was ready to give the fat guy a good slap and wake him up.

"You haven't done anything. Have you?" His voice practically begged.

I couldn't believe he wanted me to look the other way.

"We're talking murder."

"They'll give him twenty years."

"If he killed her that's what he deserves. Don't you think?"

He cocked his head and stared, disbelieving.

"Are you totally out of your mind? You want me to look the other way? Let him get away with torturing a little old lady?"

Angel didn't say so, but that was exactly what he wanted.

"How many people has he robbed? And what good is he anyway? He's a charity case. Useless without help every fifteen minutes."

"Don't be such a hard ass. The kid's had a tough way to go."

I threw up my hands and turned for my wagon.

He grabbed my shirt and spun me around. "Don't you get it? With his record, you accuse him, he's sunk. They'll lock him up and he'll never see the light of day."

"What if he killed her?" I yelled then snapped my head around to see if Newb or anyone on the street had heard.

"He couldn't. You don't know him like I do. He's a sweet kid."

"I work with him every day, Angel. I know him pretty well. Good enough to know he'll steal from anyone who turns their back."

Angel didn't dare tell me robbery didn't hurt anyone, but I knew that was what he was thinking.

"The rules don't mean anything to him. He's out of control Angel and if he gets locked up, we'll all be a little bit safer."

"Give the kid a break. It's not his fault he got hurt playing football."

I'd had enough of Angel's bleeding heart. I got in the wagon and drove away without waiting to make sure Newb locked everything up. The kid might not have been to blame for that first prescription, but he graduated to stealing pills. When he couldn't find painkillers to steal he moved up to breaking houses and buying heroin. Angel might not have considered him responsible, but there was no one else to blame.

I certainly wouldn't let him off the hook for murder.

Chapter Sixty

I fumed all the way to the north end and parked in front of Mrs. Newbury's, now Newb's, house and walked over to the Carters'.

The door swung open and Mr. Carter greeted me with a smile and a wagging finger, reminding himself of something just beyond the reach of his memory.

"Lorado," he said. "I've got something I want to show you. Got a minute?"

I looked down at my one-dollar GiftsToGive jeans, splattered in red paint, and my work boots coated in paint and mud then met his eyes again.

He waved me in.

"Sure." I followed him into the kitchen. "Is Mrs. Carter home?"

"She's upstairs." But rather than lead me to her, he opened the basement door and urged me downstairs. "I've got a few things I want your advice on. Do you mind?"

That's like asking my brother if he minds trying your double fudge brownies. What's better than checking out some old stuff? I lowered myself down the wooden treads, squeaks begrudging every step of progress.

The last time down these stairs, the old guy ambled along to the collection of old bottles with barely a look in my direction. This time he apologized for the mess and led me along with the respect due a foreign dignitary. The old guy had the junk hunter's gleam in his eye. Once someone handed you a thousand bucks for something you were going to throw away, it was hard not to get excited about old stuff.

The boxes he led me to were mostly disappointing. A bunch of old clothes that wouldn't sell curbside for a buck a piece. A few stained dresses. A bunch of cotton shirts. Then I stumbled upon something I'd seen online, but never in person.

The pale green one-piece suit was extremely well made. The tags dated to the sixties and yet it showed no wear aside from its color fading over the years. The pockets and zippers looked exactly like the one I'd seen online. I set it aside and dug deeper. Settled in the bottom of the box was a shark-fighting knife. Standard issue for pilots in the Vietnam War.

Mr. Carter's eyes twinkled expectantly.

"Do you know what this is?" I asked.

He ran his fingers over the fabric. "Too thin to be a ski suit."

"There was not a lot of skiing going on in Vietnam."

He still didn't get it.

I could have offered him fifty bucks for both pieces and he would have handed them to me in a second. But the old guy was growing on me and I wanted information from him and his wife.

"It's a pilot's flight suit, probably from the Vietnam War. And this is a shark-fighting knife. See this hole here? It's for a strap so you don't lose it while you're sleeping."

The old guy gestured for me to put a value on his treasure.

"Two maybe three hundred online."

His hand covered his mouth.

"Each."

"Are you kidding me?" He stepped forward to hug me then reconsidered. His face soured a bit then said. "I don't know anything about computers. Could you help us sell these?"

I hesitated. Taking photographs, researching keywords, writing listings, packing, shipping. It was a headache. Too big headache for a simple favor.

"Same deal as before? Thirty percent," he offered.

I shook his hand and we went back upstairs to find his wife.

When she came down into the kitchen, he held up the flight suit like a trophy. Mrs. Carter winked at me and I smiled as he told her how much the suit and the knife could be worth and how they wound up in the basement after a rummage sale.

The couple didn't want for much. They didn't need the three hundred. It was the thrill of the kill that had Mr. Carter aglow.

When he settled down, I pointed to the kitchen chairs and asked Mrs. Carter if we could talk. The gravity in her nod told me she understood I wanted something important. I tried to keep it light, not wanting to cast suspicion on Newb until it was time to get the cops involved.

"I'm curious about something," I said. "Do you mind indulging me for a minute?"

"What's on your mind?"

"Did you visit Mary near the end?"

"When she broke her hip, I started going over regularly. I'd bring flowers. Or just go talk. Once a week maybe."

"Was anything troubling her?"

"She was in a lot of pain of course. And being stuck in bed was hard for her. She loved tending her garden and getting outside. The last few weeks I didn't see her at all."

"What about her grandkids?"

"We saw a lot of Trig. Seems like a nice boy."

"Doesn't he live in Boston?"

"Somewhere up there. He's a big executive or something. Just found Mary six months ago. I guess he never had a father, and by the time he found Bernie, he'd been dead a few years. Mary was all he had left of that side. And Bernie Junior of course."

If Trig had helped kill the old woman, he would have required a huge payoff. By the looks of his car and his suits, he had more money than the Newburys combined.

"Sad timing. Or maybe fortunate he got to know her at all. Depends how you look at it."

"What did Mary think of him?" I asked.

"She adored him. Delilah, too. She was so proud."

Not surprising given her only legitimate grandson was a drug addict.

"Did you see Newb around much?"

"Not really, no."

I stood up and was about to walk out when I remembered an old line from a TV detective show. "Do you remember the last time you saw her?"

Mrs. Carter shook her finger at me like her husband did. A family memory trick. Or a gesture they copied from each other. "I do," she said. "It was Friday before Valentine's Day. I brought her some flowers before we went away for the weekend."

I did some math in my head. It was four or five days before she died.

"How did she look?" I asked.

"I don't know. Cynthia wouldn't let us in."

That was a surprise. I was expecting her to say Newb was there. I tried to hold onto my poker face, but couldn't tell how well I did.

"Did she say why?"

She looked at the ceiling while she tried to remember. "She was sleeping I think she said. But that would make sense. She must have been really sick by then. She died less than a week later."

"Makes sense."

She frowned and bobbed her head gently.

"Did you see anyone else around the house that weekend?"

"We weren't here. Like I said, we went away for the holiday. A little B & B on the Cape."

I thanked her and took the flight suit and knife from Mr. Carter.

Mrs. Carter eyed me at the door. "Do you think something's fishy?"

"I'm always curious about the families I work with."

She didn't believe me, but she didn't press.

Chapter Sixty-one

The flight suit and knife warranted the seat of honor in the wagon. Up front away from the rest of the clutter, the suit would stay clean long enough for me to photograph it and list it online. I smiled all the way around the car, thinking how great it was when money fell into my lap. My two hundred dollar share would buy a nice dinner, and my end of the work wouldn't take two hours.

Mrs. Carter had even given me a glimmer of hope for Newb. If she was right and he hadn't been with his grandmother that weekend, my call to the cops would be a lot easier.

Cynthia, Trig, Delilah, all three of them gave me a vibe and it wouldn't hurt my feelings to see them locked up. Cynthia proved herself a criminal when she stole the sugar bowl. Trig had that upper-crusty attitude that anyone would like to see ruffed up a bit. And Delilah was just plain freaky.

When Cynthia trudged across her lawn in front of me, I had the perfect chance to check Mrs. Carter's story. I wandered to the corner of Newb's house and eyed the line of the corner boards from the sill to the soffit. I pretended to inspect the exterior while she made her next trip to the car. When she closed the trunk I turned and met her on the lawn.

"Just getting back? How was your trip?"

"Nice. We haven't been away without Nicholas for months." She barely slowed, her expression less inviting than her words. She passed me and headed for the door with only a modest attempt to make eye contact.

"Need a hand?" I asked when she faced the door with both hands full of disposable bags.

She gave a weak smile and extended a fistful of plastic handles. I took them and followed her inside to the kitchen.

A grumbling voice boomed down the hall. The words unintelligible. I listened for a scampering Nicholas, running for his life from the big monster, but the rest of the house was quiet. She noticed my head turned toward the bedroom. "That's just Chuck. He's not a fan of long car trips."

She went to work at the kitchen counter with her back to me, pulling out enough fruits and vegetables to make it clear Chuck was staying. I knew my time was running short. We barely knew each other, and for a second, I wondered why she'd let me in at all.

"You'd think he'd sound happier to be home."

She smiled and packed kiwis and avocados into the crisper.

"I was talking to Mrs. Carter," I said. "She said she came over with flowers two weeks ago and you wouldn't let her in."

She straightened up with a hand on her hip.

I tried to soften my tone. "Was Mrs. Newbury that sick already?"

"She was confined to bed."

After seeing the scrapes on the bed frame, I didn't like the word choice.

"We were packing to leave," she said. "I didn't want her hanging around an hour while we were waiting to go."

Something bugged me about that trip, but before I could recall our earlier conversation, she filled it in for me like she was reading my mind.

"We were taking Nicholas. Chuck doesn't like going away. Less so if he's got to share me with Nicholas the whole time."

"It was Valentine's weekend. Wasn't it?"

"Yeah. Newb volunteered to watch Mary, but we couldn't find anyone to take care of Nicholas. It's a romantic weekend for everyone."

The Carters also went away that weekend, and I remembered Trig saying he was out of town as well. Newb had been alone with his grandmother in the little house next door. My stomach turned sour. I felt

Cynthia looking at me, but was lost in thoughts of the old woman being starved by her grandson.

"Where did you go?" I asked more to fill the space than anything.

I looked up for her answer, but she looked past me. The hulk filled the doorway behind me, his bulging arms hanging in matching semi-circles, almost as wide as he was tall.

He eyed me up and down and scowled at Cynthia. His eyes bounced from his chest to mine. The comparison wasn't as ridiculous as he wanted to believe, unless you compared abs. I got the feeling if I were in better shape he'd have been insanely jealous, but he looked at Cynthia with contempt for her poor judgment rather than jealousy for an imagined betrayal.

The big guy stepped into the kitchen, crowding me toward the table.

You might think I left because I was afraid, but the guy was so pumped up he could barely raise his arms. Big as I am, I could have kicked him in the face before he could block my foot. Yeah, I can get my leg that high. At least I could the last time I tried. I didn't intimidate easy, but the way he looked at Cynthia I worried there would be trouble after I'd gone.

I wanted to know why she'd chosen Newb to watch Mary instead of a nurse. When he'd come to take over and how sick the old woman was that Friday when they left, but there wasn't time for my questions.

She explained to Chuck that I'd been working next door and helped bring in the groceries. The guy had the manners of a toddler. He responded with a grunted hello and a quick glance at the food piled on the table.

I took my cue and headed for the front door. In the mirror ahead of me, I saw her stroke him with a soothing pat on her way by.

The big guy didn't come out to the front steps, but to my surprise, Cynthia followed me all the way out onto the concrete walk.

"He's not always so intense."

"Don't worry about it," I said. "I don't scare easy."

"It was the Cape Codder," she said.

I must have looked really confused.

"Where we went for Valentine's weekend. They had a special deal."

The Cape seemed an odd destination in February. Maybe because we lived so close it didn't hold the mystique it did for tourists.

"Why'd you leave her with Newb?"

"We wanted to keep the money in the family. She didn't need much, just meals and help to the bathroom and back. Newb jumped at the job when I told him we were going away."

Newb could barely take care of himself. I had to drive him everywhere and keep reminding him to be ready for work. How could she leave a bedridden woman in his care?

"He wasn't here when we got back."

"Were you the first ones to find her?" I knew the answer from talking to the funeral director. And I knew she'd done the right thing and called the cops. I still wanted to hear it for myself.

"She was dead when I went to check on her."

"What did Newb say?"

She bit her lip and measured her words. "I couldn't find him."

My heart sank as the pieces of her story came together. Somewhere far below the surface, Newb had some decency left. He couldn't handle killing his own grandmother. The guilt sent him on a binge and he didn't come down until I found him boosting the microwave.

"I don't want him to get in trouble," she said.

I was already scripting my call to the cops.

Chapter Sixty-two

"Welcome home, Rambo."

I whipped out my pretend bowie knife and said, "Nothing's over until I say it's over."

"You're lucky I like you or it would be over."

I couldn't tell if she got my movie reference or not. She stood in the doorway to the kitchen, hand on hip, pout on her lips. After a day on my own, I was glad to have her hotness back in the house. I scanned for the boy, but didn't see him.

The bathroom door was open. Jake's door was cracked and Beta stood with his head pressed where the basement door met the casing.

"How was your mother's?"

"You know how it was. You going to tell me what happened?"

Roxie and her mother couldn't stand being in the same house very long. That much personality refused to be contained in a small space. No wonder Jake was hiding in the cellar.

"Turns out I stepped into a hornets' nest. Otherwise it would have been nothing."

"Just like you to turn a ticket for vagrancy into an all out war."

Her plot knowledge was impressive. I'd seen the movie half a dozen times and it took me a second to realize she was keeping the analogy alive.

"They drew first blood. I was just confused about who *they* were."

"Okay," she said. "Now I'm lost."

"First I got sick at Mary Newbury's house. I thought I was poisoned during the day. I was sure someone put something in my big blue sippy. Turns out I was wrong."

"So you went after Findley and pissed him off?"

"Not until the brick. Then I went after Findley."

"So it wasn't Findley who threw the brick?"

"I don't think so."

"So who was it then?"

"I'm going to find out in two minutes."

She cocked her head and threw out her hip even farther. Totally confused.

"I thought you said Findley's guys tried to kill you?"

"They did. After I barged into his place."

"So it's all your fault," she said. That's not hard to believe. But if they tried to kill you, why are we back? Are they all locked up?"

"Not exactly."

The arrogant look faded. She liked to play tough, but at one hundred twenty pounds, she couldn't stand up to an angry man, never mind four or five. I think that was the reason she stayed with me. When we went out, people didn't give her any crap because I was too big to mess with.

I told her about the meeting in the garage and how Rusty protected me from Findley. She relaxed a little. I think she believed we were safe from Findley for a while, but she was glad she had me around at night.

When I told her what I thought about the brick, she led me to the cellar stairs so I could test my hunch. She didn't follow me down. This was guy talk.

If you think the places I take on for estate sales are packed with junk, you've never been in my cellar. I've got your everyday garden variety junk, but I've also got rows of shelves packed with the best unsold stuff from years of sales. I hold yard sales once in a while and when I do, the best junk dealers from all over the city come and browse.

No one is happier than Roxie when I have a good day, because that means so much less stuff gets crammed back into the cellar.

The boy stood near the washer with the nearest bulb turned off. Three empty red and blue boxes sat on top of the dryer, the reddish shavings clumped on the white lid. He'd been down here a while, practicing a game I'd invented after I bought the toy cars and army men.

He let go of a tiny paper and it popped when it hit the floor. The mini explosion sparked in the dark, and if you had some imagination, it was a mortar round blowing a hole in the battlefield.

A jagged crack ran through the cement at Jake's feet. Tiny soldiers faced each other from opposing sides of the crack. The battlefield littered with exploded white papers and fallen men.

Jake dropped another white bomb. This one exploded less than an inch from a green soldier, and a tiny rock knocked him over. If we were playing competitively that would have been cause for celebration.

"Practicing?"

"Yeah." He took another snapper from the pile of shavings and twisted it tight, a trick I'd taught him to help more of his bombs explode when they hit the cement. In our game, a dud meant a missed turn.

"You're still never going to beat me."

"We'll see," he said.

He didn't know I kept winning because the green men were a bit bigger than the tan men. That slight advantage made his guys easier to hit.

He dropped two more bombs. Both misses.

I tried one and scored a hit.

His grimace was more about missing his friends at the mall the night before than my skill with the bombs.

"Have fun with your mom last night?"

"No."

"Not happy about staying at grandma's?"

"No." His tone was on the edge of getting a slap to the head and he knew it, so he stepped away to get another bomb.

He missed by three inches.

"It's your fault, you know."

"My fault?" He started hostile, but stopped himself from going on. He sensed my trap. He was as street smart as his mother.

"You want to tell me about the guy who threw the brick?"

"What does that have to do with grandma's?"

"I thought someone was after me and I started a whole lot of trouble. Now I know I was wrong. The question is why would a guy throw a brick at my car if he wasn't after me?"

His fingers searched the shavings for tiny bombs.

I remembered his apologetic tone when I dropped him off at school two days earlier. And the time he was trying to tell me something on my way out to chase Findley. I should have listened.

"What are you into, Jake?"

He shrugged.

"Guys don't throw a brick through a windshield for nothing. And the black eye. What was that about?"

"Marissa Elliot."

"She must be hot if her boyfriend is that mad."

That was the first smile I got from the kid that day.

"Smokin'."

"What about this other guy?"

"He's a senior at Stang."

"Need help with him? Seems pretty serious."

"Nah. The team's got my back."

I took a bomb and killed another of the green guys. Nearly a direct hit.

"Next time you're in trouble, tell me what's going on before I start world war three with a bunch of drug dealers. Okay?"

He hesitated.

"I won't go busting heads without you. Promise."

"Deal."

We counted out twenty soldiers apiece. As I dealt him another sound defeat, he told me why Marissa was worth risking black eyes and bricks.

Chapter Sixty-three

The boy was exhausted from a sleepless night at his grandmother's. There wasn't much going on at her house to keep him awake, but he was so angry at missing his new girl, he tossed and turned the entire night. By ten o'clock that first night back at home, he disappeared into his room and started snoring soon after.

Roxie took a long hot shower and came out in a robe that barely covered her curvy little backside. Those smooth silky legs broke my focus on the television. I listened to her open drawers and pad around the bedroom on the other side of the wall, wondering what she'd be wearing when she came back out.

She didn't keep me guessing long. In five minutes she leaned into view with a hand on the door casing, her robe fluttering open, hair hanging down. She lured me out of my chair with a naughty grin and a wiggling finger.

She locked the dog outside the bedroom and tossed the robe toward the bureau. She pulled my shirt over my head and caressed my arms and chest. In those first few moments, the thrill for her was as much about feeling my protection as it was about my love.

She helped me forget my problems with Findley for the next thirty minutes and left me breathless, sweaty, and content, lying back with her tiny figure pressed against mine. Mostly against the big round belly that kept her at arm's length.

She snored lightly with her head propped on my shoulder. Pretty soon she drifted deeper. Her breaths only a whisper on my cheek.

My conversation with Cynthia rolled over and over in my mind. The two vacations nagged me. Something about that whole thing wasn't right. Maybe it was all that talk about steroids short circuiting one's manly equipment. Or maybe it was his attitude. The romantic weekends with Chuck bugged me. Not that she could do better. She wasn't the friendliest or the hottest. Maybe he was the best she could do. Whatever the state of his equipment, he was definitely a step up from Newb.

And why would she leave the old lady with Newb. Why not a nurse? Was Mrs. Newbury broke? I wondered if Cynthia was collecting her pay while she was on vacation. I doubted that would be in the records I got from Newb, but it was worth a look.

Even if saving money was the goal, leaving a feeble old woman with a known drug abuser didn't make sense. Sure he was her only grandson, but anybody would have been more qualified to care for her.

All the loose threads surrounding Mrs. Newbury's death plagued me, and even post-coital sleep escaped me for hours that night.

Cynthia's pointy beak haunted me. Newb, the bodybuilder, the two half-siblings they all kept me tossing and wondering what had happened to poor Mrs. Newbury.

No wonder when I finally started dreaming, I found myself snuggled under the rose comforter with the little lady herself. A short, bony, old version of Roxie. Her stringy blue hair peeked out from under the comforter. She groaned in agony, holding herself and rocking back and forth.

Long bony fingers shook at me. Blaming me for letting her die.

Guilt stole my breath.

"I didn't know," I mumbled in my sleep.

"You wouldn't listen," she wailed.

I couldn't push away across the bed. My limbs were anchored to my sides, the comforter restraining me like a straight jacket.

"You let me die." She waved an accusing finger.

"No," I moaned.

"Punish..." The blankets swallowed her voice, but not the anger in her sunken eyes. Dehydration, starvation, pain, something evil had befallen her.

She blamed me for letting it happen. For letting her killer get away. Her bony fingers stretched for me. To maul me and make me feel her pain.

"Punish..." It was barely a whisper, but the single word sent quivers through my body.

I shivered despite the heavy covers.

I couldn't escape the angry eyes. I felt myself rocking faster and faster until finally I heard Roxie's voice. "Quiet."

Her hand gripped my shoulder. Long fingernails digging in.

She was annoyed at being woken so early, but her hostility paled next to the anger I felt from the old woman herself.

"I'm up. I'm up."

She rocked me a few more times.

"Who were you talking to?"

My cheeks were red hot. Would the little woman want me to punish her killer even if it was her grandson? Her letter hinted that it was someone close. Maybe she knew Newb was going to do her in. Maybe she was so angry because she knew I was contemplating Angel's advice. Considering letting him go. Giving him another chance in a very long string of chances to get his life together.

"You're not fantasizing about someone else?"

"No."

"What then?"

"I've got to call the cops."

"You're not going to have Findley crashing in here again?"

"Not this time."

Chapter Sixty-four

The phone rang four times and went to voicemail as it had on my last ten attempts. I turned down North Front, found the little bakery that marked Speedy's street, turned the corner, and pulled up in front of his place. Cars lined both curbs at 6:00 A.M. not leaving a single space, so I nosed the wagon into a driveway. I blocked the sidewalk, and my bumper hung out beyond the line of cars, but it didn't matter. Not a soul moved up or down the street as I made the ten steps to Speedy's front porch.

Paint flecks dropped off the flimsy door as I rapped.

The window flexed and rattled as I banged, but no one came down the steep stairway. I told myself he could be asleep. I searched the casing for a doorbell. Not finding one, I banged louder.

Speedy lived with two guys, but they weren't any more reliable than he was. All three of them could have been nodded out somewhere. Standing on his porch, I knew he was in trouble. I didn't chase help. If I wanted another body, all it took was a phone call. Speedy had grown on me in the six months he'd been around. The guy made it his mission to make everyone on the job look slow. He did it easily, and in the process made the other guys work a whole lot faster.

But where was he that morning? No doubt he'd been using. Guys didn't disappear for days without a reason. The best I could hope for was him being nabbed in a sting, sitting in jail. But I knew he could have overdosed or been stabbed while he was nodded out. I hoped he was whacked out at a friend's house somewhere. High and safe.

I walked off the porch, wondering if I'd ever see him again. Wondering if he'd freeze to death in a park. And wondering if my visit was about more than salve on my guilt for what I was about to do to Newb.

I considered bagging work that day. Calling Newb and the hired gun I scheduled and calling it off. I wasn't planning on staying with them very long and that meant low productivity without Speedy around. These guys knew how to milk an hourly job, especially Newb.

My hands fought each other on the wheel as I rolled into the south end. These jobs were about more than finishing a project. The budget would have been better served hiring specialists like Greg to hammer out jobs and walk away. A businessman would have waited until all the approvals were in and then whipped through the building with wave after wave of contractors.

What I did with Newb was a good thing, keeping him busy with a trickle of work, teaching him all sorts of trades a little at a time. He may have only made ten dollars an hour, but it was steady work and what he learned would serve him well someday. Not many employers would have put up with him disappearing the way he sometimes did. They wouldn't pay him to hang drywall either.

I let my friends snicker at my methods and my thin margins. If they pressed, I told them hiring guys like Newb earned me a lot of business with the state. It was true and usually I was proud of what I did, but that morning driving to Newb's apartment seemed like an affront to Mary Newbury's memory.

He didn't plod down the stairs that morning. It was more of a trot. He even smiled at me when he slid into the passenger's seat.

"Hey," I said and backed the car out.

Looking at the kid was painful. Anyone would be happy to inherit a hundred grand, but the way it happened disgusted me. Sitting in the car with him, I could feel Mrs. Newbury suffering. Gasping for breath. Writhing in pain. Sitting in the car with her killer, breathing the same air made me ill.

We drove all the way to Interstate 195 in silence. Not unusual for the kid. He never said much. Usually I filled the time with chatter about the job or the economy or whatever was on my mind. Sometimes I felt like a lecturer filling the kid's mind with useful stuff to replace his cravings for drugs. That day my mind kept coming back to the cops and what I had to do.

"Were you close with your grandma?"

"Not really."

The kid didn't have an ounce of regret.

I thought of Chris. How often he said he was the least favorite grandchild and how much that bugged him. It was true. You'd have to be blind not to see it. There was no telling why she didn't like him. He was shy as hell. Never caused any trouble. She favored all the other kids over him, but he would never have killed her. Not for a hundred grand. Not for a million.

"You were the only grandchild, right?"

"Until two months ago." He didn't betray a hint of jealousy, but Mrs. Newbury's note told me the problems had a lot to do with Trig and Delilah coming out of the woodwork.

"How'd you feel about that?"

"They were accidents. Chicks my father banged while he was drunk down by the docks." If the kid was trying to hide his motive for murder, he wasn't doing a very good job. I wondered about recent changes to the will. Newb had let me pack all her records into boxes and take them to the warehouse. Maybe he'd already searched her place for copies of the will. Or maybe he'd known exactly where to find them.

He'd had four or five days alone with her in the house. Plenty of time to find what he needed. Something about that didn't fit though. He seemed too at ease. Clueless as Newb was, I doubted he could fake innocence that well.

"Did your father tell you they were accidents?"

"Didn't need to."

It made no sense. "How did you find out about them?"

"They just showed up a few months ago."

"Your father's been gone a long time. How can you be sure they're even related?"

Newb said his grandmother was convinced they were legitimate and that was good enough for him. Newb's father had been a heavy drinker and his mother had often complained about his flings when he came ashore. It only made sense that a few of those flings resulted in children.

The whole thing was casual to Newb. He didn't show any anger toward his half siblings, but from what I'd seen, he hadn't worked hard to embrace them either. He showed them the same indifference he showed everyone else. I wanted to blame the newcomers for what had happened. Maybe that was just me trying to make it easy on myself. Trying to avoid turning Newb in. But no matter how I tried, the pieces refused to fit.

Trig and Delilah were both out of town when Mrs. Newbury died. I told myself they could have lied. It seemed no one was around the old woman's house that weekend, and anyone could have slipped in and out. The biggest problem I had was that Newb wasn't bright enough to mastermind a murder and get away with it. These two were in a different league, though. Polished. Educated. Either of them could have put this together.

The puzzle gnawed at me with each passing mile. My resolve stiffened as we parked and reviewed the blueprints with Greg. He was a hired gun. He could handle framing and hanging sheetrock without me. I didn't need to worry about the kind of expensive mistakes Newb would make on his own. My biggest fear was that little to nothing would get done while I visited Quincy. If I was going to understand the role Trig and Delilah played in Mrs. Newbury's death, that was where I had to go.

Chapter Sixty-five

If the density of German cars in the parking garage wasn't proof enough the place was raunchy with money, when the elevator launched up so fast it sent my stomach turning inside my gut, I was convinced. It took real money to put a sleek new elevator in a two hundred year old brick factory. If Trig could afford the rent here, he didn't need the old lady's money. Or maybe that was precisely why he needed it. Maybe his plan was to come after it when the old lady had been dead and buried awhile.

I stepped into the office of Discoverable Enterprises and saw the upgraded headlights on the blonde behind the desk. Roxie had nothing on her. At second look I wasn't sure if she'd had work done or if she'd been endowed as one of God's most magnificent creatures, but I could tell by her horrified look at my one dollar, grease-stained jeans we'd never get friendly enough for me to find out.

She scanned a page on her computer screen and said, "I don't have any work scheduled today."

Too bad. I would have liked to work on her. "I'm here to see Trig."

She didn't say I couldn't afford his services, but it was in her snicker.

"It's personal." I'd learned those magic words in my investment sales days. No gatekeeper wanted to be chastised for keeping a guy's fishing buddy waiting. I didn't look anything like one of Trig's buddies, but those words proved timeless.

Trig came out in jeans, but instead of grease stains and work boots he showed off shiny loafers and a sport jacket. "Hey, Lorado."

He waved me back into a wide office with a view of the marina. I couldn't help walking to the window and looking down at the miniature version of New Bedford harbor, minus the riffraff.

"Looks like the Internet business is booming."

He beamed a smile that couldn't be faked.

"What do you do again?"

"SEO, social media, Internet marketing strategy."

"It's all about keywords. Isn't it?"

"Discoverability is key."

I wasn't sure if he agreed with me or not. "The right keyword in one of my eBay listings can make me a hundred bucks."

Trig shrugged and gave me a patronizing look. A hundred bucks was lunch money in his business, but it was the same game. A curb alert could bring a slew of shoppers to a yard sale. The only difference between my sales and the boutiques Trig worked with was the price tags on the merchandise. And his office. And his hot blonde receptionist.

"So what brings you all the way up here?"

I was running out of time. If my business was selling rooms in the hospital I was renovating, Trig would have relaxed on the couch or leaned against his desk, but he wasn't going to make any money on my estate sales, and his small step toward the door was more than symbolic.

"I was talking to Mrs. Carter. She says you were really close to Mary Newbury."

"She was my grandmother."

"But you didn't know that until recently."

"Lucky? Isn't it?"

"How do you figure?"

"I almost didn't get to know her at all. I took my mother out shopping for her birthday and we bumped into Ruth and Delilah. Seems I was the only one who didn't know about our father."

"Did she hide him from you all these years?"

"She told me he was a no good bum. She was right."

"So why get in touch with the family?"

"Delilah was a little much. She was always calling, wanting me to go to Provincetown."

"For a trip?"

"She lives there. Makes pottery in a little shop."

He looked down on her pottery shop as much as he looked down on my estate sales. The guy needed to be on top, and I wondered how much of that had to do with having a no-show, alcoholic father.

I could understand how a flower child like Delilah would be a little weird for him to embrace. What I couldn't understand was Bernie banging a hottie like Trig's mom and then a butch mess like Ruth. I asked him if they'd done a paternity test.

"All we wanted was to get to know our family."

"Are you sure Mary was your family?"

"Sure as I need to be."

He told me about Bernie in the dockside bars. How his mother happened down there drunk and had an accident. Ruth had gone down looking to get pregnant then her lover left her when she discovered they were going to have a baby. The whole thing was convincing especially because Trig and Delilah hadn't asked for anything. I still couldn't help thinking that Mary Newbury and her grandson were easy prey. I should have believed Trig didn't need the money and that Delilah didn't care about money, but I didn't want to leave his office without proof.

"Did you see Mary the weekend before she died?"

"No. It had been two weeks I think."

"You were out of town, right?"

His eyes locked on me for the first time in our whole conversation. He wasn't afraid, but the insinuation was serious enough to get his attention.

"Hang on a sec."

He skirted his desk, tapped a few times on his computer, and the printer buzzed to life. He handed me the single sheet, his travel itinerary to Las Vegas for an Internet show.

"I was featured on the program," he said.

As fast as my thoughts turned to Delilah, he turned back to his computer, clicked a few times, and turned it to face me.

Delilah held a colorful vase under a banner that read, Colorado Craft Festival, February 13-16.

She could have flown in after killing the old woman, but that didn't fit the starvation-torture scenario I'd cooked up. Whoever slowly killed Mrs. Newbury needed a week to get away with it and the time Trig was in Las Vegas and Delilah was in Colorado was ideal. I wondered how Newb had known they'd be gone or if he'd just gotten lucky.

Delilah might have had answers for me in Provincetown, but I didn't have four hours to drive down and back. Trig walked to the door while I was thinking it through then stood there holding the knob.

I'd been handled. He'd figured out what I wanted, proved it, and now he wanted me out. He had more important things to do and he didn't seem to share my suspicions about what happened to Mrs. Newbury.

The blonde barely looked up when I passed.

Chapter Sixty-six

Vince Gorman had to be the most junior guy in NBPD Homicide. He looked at me across the desk as another screwball tip his superiors pawned off on him so he could do the paperwork while they were out investigating gang shootings and other cases with blood on the ground. In their minds, Mrs. Newbury was an old lady who died of natural causes. I couldn't have convinced them otherwise even if I could have gotten them to listen.

Lucky for me Gorman didn't have their swagger. He listened and even took a few notes, but once I slid Mrs. Newbury's letter across the desk, I had him hooked.

It could have been coincidence, but how many people hid a note about being killed then died a few months later? The more he read, the straighter he sat in his chair. He practically jumped up when he finished reading.

"Where's this warehouse of yours?"

"North Front Street."

"I'll drive," he said, balking back toward his desk for a camera and a bound notebook.

Ten minutes later, Gorman watched me unlock the overhead door and followed me inside to the back corner of my warehouse. The shelves stacked with old treasures overwhelmed him so much he slowed in the aisle, turning in circles, probably trying to imagine how he was going to catalog thousands of items.

"Mrs. Newbury's stuff is back here," I said to hurry him up.

"Nice friends you got." He gestured to the spray paint.

"Yah."

I led him to the bed frame.

"This all her stuff?" He asked.

I backed up to the second shelf and made a corner with my arms, fencing in what remained of her belongings. Then I waved him forward. "Come take a look at this."

He came over when I kneeled down. Not a pretty picture when my belly escapes the bottom of my shirt, but it's the only way I can get low enough to see the underside of the bed frame.

"It looks like someone strapped her in bed and kept her there."

He leaned in close to examine the scuffmarks I believed to be from some sort of straps holding Mrs. Newbury down. He didn't betray his thoughts, but the intensity of his examination and the set of his eyes told me he believed something awful had happened.

Gorman kept his hands clear, lowering his head to get a good view. He mimicked the action to drill a screw into the bottom of the frame so he could figure out what he wanted printed.

"You handled this right?"

I told him I had.

"Anyone else?"

"I think the killer helped me move it here."

Breath whooshed out of him, and he glared at me like I'd been leading him on then dropped him cold.

"Prints aren't going to do you any good. He helped me move all her stuff."

His glare got harsher.

"He works for me. I hadn't found the note yet. I had no idea." I heard myself whining. But how could I have known she was murdered? If Gorman knew how guilty I felt about the other estates I cleaned out, he might have gone easier on me.

He paced a circle under Findley's spray-painted warning. The first loop he kept his hands on his hips and muttered something about luck. On the second lap, he flailed wildly, forgetting, or not caring, I was there. I figured this was his first real case. Losing would have been a bad thing for his career. I didn't know how important a win-loss record was to homicide cops, but I didn't want him to give up.

Gorman was Mrs. Newbury's last chance. Already in the ground, haunting me for justice, I couldn't let her down even if I let Newb contaminate all the evidence with his prints.

Not after she pleaded for my help in her note.

"Come over here for a second," I said.

I showed him the picture and the backing still lying against the shelf.

"The note was inside?"

"Yeah. See my name there in the corner?"

He took a photograph, scribbled something in his notebook, and looked toward the other items stacked beside the shelf.

I pointed to the answering machine, careful not to touch it and mess up any prints, not that it mattered. Any prints still on it were probably mine "There are several messages about missed appointments on here."

He photographed and bagged the machine, but did so mechanically. His enthusiasm drained away.

"That's important."

He didn't appreciate my telling him how to investigate.

"She was isolated with him for a week."

"How do you know that?"

"The note was bugging me. I started poking around."

"And?"

"The neighbors were away. Two of her grandchildren were out of town. And her usual caregiver left her with the guy I think killed her."

"Who is he?"

"Bernie Newbury Junior. A recovering heroin addict. He works for me. That's why he helped me move her stuff here. Mrs. Newbury was his grandmother, and she left him everything."

When I told him Newb missed work for an entire week before his grandmother died, the sparkle flashed in Gorman's eyes. He bagged a few more items and headed back to the station to check it all in.

Chapter Sixty-seven

Being around drug addicts was an infuriating experience you could only understand if you'd been there. Conflicting emotions rattled around and some days you just didn't know what to feel. I parked outside the hospital that day with guilt and pride having a tug-of-war inside me.

Gorman's enthusiasm gave me hope Mrs. Newbury would finally get justice. It made me sick to think about that frail woman suffering, but the picture of Newb in handcuffs felt wrong. The kid had been with me almost a year, and he was too hapless to lock up. He was trying to get his life together. Futile as his attempts were. He was sure the world owed him a living and that he could take whatever he wanted, but the kid had never been taught better.

I couldn't imagine how hard it was to be related to someone like him.

When Newb fell down, he looked completely helpless. You wanted to help the kid as much as a puppy who'd strayed out of his yard. The night he tried to steal the microwave whacked out on dope, Cynthia walked him home, ignoring his pawing hands as they went. She could have called him a lecherous bastard, smacked him, and let him fend for himself, but she didn't. Newb was lucky to have Cynthia and Angel, and even me, I guess, but he never realized how lucky he was.

He needed us all because he couldn't help being stupid. Cashing his dead grandmother's social security check, stealing from family, killing a helpless old woman. Sometimes you couldn't help but want to pound him.

My heart pumped as I climbed the concrete stairs. Whether from thinking about the beating Newb deserved, or the exertion of carrying my bulk up two flights, I couldn't be sure. Breathing heavy on the landing, I couldn't believe what I saw.

Gorman had asked me to watch Newb for mood changes and stress. Any sign he realized the investigation was getting close. It was too early for a sign, but there it was. The kid hustled drywall like it was his first day on the job. I'd only met Gorman hours before. No way Newb knew what was up, but he worked like he knew. Proving he was valuable to me by busting ass the whole time I was gone.

Greg had framed the open space on the second floor landing into smaller rooms. The two of them had hung more drywall that day than I thought possible. I'd expected a solid hour's work in the five hours I had been gone and they'd completed twelve.

The whining screw gun reminded me of a pit crew changing tires during a race. Greg poked in screws as easily as pressing buttons. Newb hurried down the hall so quickly to get the next sheet I felt a twinge of guilt for turning him in. He was trying to keep pace with Greg. Speedy had never had that effect on the kid. No one worked faster than Speedy, but even when he was around, the kid plodded along. I wondered what Greg had said to make Newb want to impress him so much.

Maybe he'd offered him a job.

I followed the maze around the corner. They'd framed the innermost parts first and worked their way to the hall so Newb didn't have to maneuver drywall through the new corridors. Five or six more pieces and they'd be done. Greg zipped the screws in fast and flush. Not reckless, but quick enough to finish far more work than I expected. Quick enough to fasten the sheets as fast as Newb brought them.

"Hey, boys. What's shaking?" Angel's voice boomed from the bottom of the stairwell.

I peeked back out of the maze to see Newb rushing across the face of the open stairs. He looked down toward Angel and said, "Five more pieces to go," never stopping, blinded by the eight-by-four sheet the size of a small sail.

The subtle turn toward his mentor caused him to stray off track. He wobbled with the gypsum, and instead of crossing in front of the steps, his right foot missed the landing and dropped eight inches to the first stair. That first step is no problem if you're expecting it, but it threw Newb forward. He landed hard on his right foot, the shock travelling up his back. His old injury buckled, the eight-foot sheet shifted up over his head, and threw him down the stairwell.

In that instant I saw a kid trying to please everyone to get what he needed, but he couldn't impress Greg and be on time for Angel to take him to dinner and his meeting. The rush sent him flopping down the concrete stairs still holding the drywall as if it could keep him afloat.

Angel and the kid screamed together.

The sheet covered the opening and slammed down. Newb's hand holds broke free. A hard crease sliced down the middle of the board.

Thuds and wails followed.

Angel cursed.

By the time I pulled the sheet up and threw it aside, Newb lay still halfway down the stairs with Angel's hands on his shoulders keeping him steady. Newb's hands clutched his arched back and that's the way they stayed until the ambulance arrived.

The first paramedic hustled up the stairs and stopped before touching him. The kid was in serious pain.

"He's had two discs fused," Angel said.

The two paramedics fastened the collar and strapped Newb to a backboard with the care due a senator. He didn't budge when they hoisted the gurney and carried him down.

"See you at the hospital in an hour?" Angel asked.

My plan that night was dinner and a good movie with Roxie. The kid looked fine, and I told Angel so on my way back up the stairs.

Chapter Sixty-eight

Walking down that tiled hallway, I was twelve again, being forced to sit through my great aunt's birthday party. Nothing but old ladies yammering on about nothing, blowing cigarette smoke while the cousins were held captive in a cramped living room.

The emergency room waiting area on Friday night was much the same, except every fourth person was bleeding and no one knew each other. The locked double doors stopped me from going back to find Angel and Newb. The ambulance ride jumped Newb up in the queue and got him seen minutes after he'd come in.

A skinny kid wheezed in the front row. He looked scared, and I wondered how long he'd been waiting and why he wasn't being looked after. I was sure they would have come running if the kid turned blue, but that was little comfort to his mother who looked just as nervous as the kid.

A guy in the second row cradled his right hand. The sleeve of his blue work shirt was rolled up to his elbow. Bloody gauze hid a wound that needed stitches at least. He watched the TV news on the set mounted high in the corner, his biggest concern after getting the hand fixed up was learning how soon he could get back to work. He was the calmest guy in the place, but I felt for him. That hand had to hurt.

I dialed Angel on my cell, and a minute later, the double doors opened and he waved me past admitting, into the hall. Newb lay on a gurney against a wall between two small treatment rooms. Angel took up a position behind his head so he didn't block the hall. I stood beside the movable bed and looked down at the kid still in the collar.

"You doing okay, Kid?"

"Yeah," he said, tracking me with his eyes.

His arms relaxed by his sides. The panic I'd seen on the stairs had been replaced by a resignation to stay in bed until he was told what to do next. I couldn't help feeling the kid struggling to breathe and the guy with the cut hand should have been treated before Newb.

Angel caught my attitude and gestured with his hands open. He wanted to ask what my problem was, but wouldn't in front of Newb.

I thought of my grandfather with ten kids way back. His wife needed an operation he couldn't pay for and the state stepped in to cover the bill. He worked hard to pay the state back. He didn't need to, but he felt it was the right thing to do. What a difference from a kid like Newb.

Newb took free health care and a twenty-five-dollar-a-week apartment in stride. How could a kid who screwed up so badly be so damn entitled?

Angel scowled and I wondered if the kid knew what I was thinking.

Was Newb worth any less than that kid in the waiting room? Maybe not, but I couldn't get over the feeling that all he ever did was take.

I checked out a couple of nurses to help me relax. Those blue hospital scrubs didn't show off much, but when a contour sticks out, it really sticks out. I had my eye on a curvy little brunette who passed in and out of the treatment rooms with a smile for us every time.

A young guy with a clipboard, shirt, and tie came down and stopped at the foot of the bed. He introduced himself as Dr. Campbell.

"You're a lucky guy, Mr. Newbury. Your X-rays came back negative and aside from a little bruising, you're going to be fine."

I should have asked if they'd given him anything for the pain, but Angel had been with him the whole time. He wouldn't let them make that mistake.

"Take it easy this weekend," the doctor said. "You can go back to work on Monday." The nurse would be by with release instructions in a few minutes. In the meantime, the doctor removed Newb's collar and had him turn his neck side to side.

When the doc walked away, Newb sat on the bed as if he were waiting for the bus.

Angel saw how pissed I was and tapped my arm. "Newb, we're going to go outside for a minute. Come on out when you've got your papers together."

The kid nodded and sat obediently.

Down the corridor and through the double doors, the characters I remembered waited in the same seats, looking as hopeless as before. Angel trudged along, through the automatic doors and sat on a bench against the brick wall just past the soda machine.

"What's your problem?" he asked when his generous backside stressed the wooden slats almost to their breaking point.

"You're not seeing what I'm seeing."

"The kid is trying, Lorado. Cut him some slack."

"He works three days a week. You want to give him a medal for that?"

"He's clean and he's working."

"Didn't you see what happened today?"

"The kid nearly killed himself."

"Killed himself?" I threw up my hands. "Come on, Angel. He fell, yeah. And if he really hurt himself, he would have sued me for everything I own."

"He wouldn't sue you."

"That's what he does. Take. Take. Take. You think he needed to tie up two paramedics, an ambulance, and the emergency room staff for a bruise?"

"He didn't know—"

I cut him off. "If he worked for what he had, he wouldn't pull shit like this. People like you cater to his every whim. No wonder he's useless."

"You've got something against him because you think he's got it easy. You can't imagine how hard his life is. Just getting up and going to work is an achievement."

"Stop making excuses. The kid's got a drug problem. That doesn't give him the right to do whatever he wants. He won't live long enough to pay back what he's already taken."

"What should we do? Give up on him? Send him to an island somewhere?"

"He's going somewhere all right."

Angel jumped up from the bench so fast his man boobs shook in front of me. "What did you do?" he yelled.

"It's out of my hands."

His hands flew to his hair and he spun away. "Are you out of your mind?"

The guy couldn't see the basic facts. Couldn't accept them because he was using Newb as a crutch to get over losing his own son.

"Tell me you didn't go to the cops."

I couldn't.

Angel buried his face in his hands, and when he raised his head again, his skin was pulsing red. "Do you know what they'll do to him? They find out he's a recovering addict and they'll lock him up for good."

"That old lady didn't deserve to die. Not like that."

"Newb couldn't kill anyone." He turned and slapped the soda machine with both hands. "What makes you think he could do something like that? He's not a bad kid."

"Have you seen his arrest record?"

"He's never hurt anyone."

"He was alone with her for a week. When he left, she was dead. What more do you need to know?"

Angel stormed around in a wobbly circle then stopped and pointed a finger at me from ten feet away. "He wasn't with her when she died."

"How do you know that?"

"You had me looking for him, remember? He was with some chick in the south end. Only he turned up at his grandmother's before I could grab him and bring him to you."

Angel wasn't bullshitting. It was there in his eyes. If he was right about Newb not being at the house, I was wrong about the murder, but he'd do anything to help the kid and that included lying about where he was.

"Tell the kid I'm glad he's okay."

Chapter Sixty-nine

I hated paperwork. Not because it was boring. Or because I preferred working with my hands. Both of those things were true, but my real problem was that my mind played tricks on me when I looked at strings of letters. Sometimes they appeared backwards or upside down. It wasn't dyslexia exactly. The doctors didn't know what my problem was. All I knew was that I sucked at spelling and that it was a lot easier for me to work a pipe wrench or a nail gun than a pen and paper. That's why I hired my kid brother to write grants. And that's why I was so miserable in the warehouse late that Friday night.

What I lacked in writing skill, I made up for with people. Angel couldn't fake desperation that intense. He was so wound up about Newb he convinced me to take another look, and that's how I found myself sitting in the warehouse with boxes of Mrs. Newbury's records spread around me. I started with what I knew and set out to prove Newb wasn't alone with his grandmother that weekend. If I could do that, I'd go to Gorman and admit my mistake.

Mrs. Newbury died on February fourteenth. A Tuesday.

I'd seen the death certificate. It wasn't in the boxes of records on the floor because Newb needed it to take over her financial accounts.

Cynthia Newbury found her ex-grandmother when she came to work that Tuesday morning after a long weekend with her boyfriend. I had no confirmation of her trip, but didn't think it was important enough to snoop around to find it. Cynthia was with Mrs. Newbury every day. If she wanted to do something, she could have done it anytime. And killing the old woman meant losing her job.

I moved back in time to the previous Friday.

Mrs. Carter said she came to the house and was turned away by Cynthia.

Cynthia left that Friday, and for the next four days, Mrs. Newbury was alone with her grandson.

Trig went to Las Vegas.

Delilah went to Colorado.

My own payroll records showed that Newb hadn't been in work from that Wednesday until he got clean two weeks later.

I remembered the calls on the answering machine from the nurse asking about cancelled appointments. Mrs. Newbury was already sick. It didn't make sense for Cynthia to leave her in Newb's care, but she married the guy. She had to believe he was capable of feeding a little old woman.

Gorman had the machine so I couldn't verify the dates. I thought I remembered a call the Wednesday before she died, but the timing didn't seem to matter. She was alive on Friday when Cynthia left and dead on Tuesday when she returned.

She wasn't alone all that time. Or was she?

My heart sank as I dug through the box of papers. Could the whole thing have been a horrible accident? Could Newb have gone out for the night and forgotten to come back? What if she'd died in her sleep while he was gone? If he came back, found her dead, and freaked out?

I was getting as bad as Angel, making excuses for the kid. But I believed in Angel enough to dig through five boxes of miscellaneous paper Newb and I had shoved together when we packed up her things.

All I needed was a delivery receipt or a signature for a nurse's visit to tell me who was in that house. I found utility bills and bank statements going back years. She kept the instruction booklet for every appliance in the house. I found letters from her dead husband. Pictures of her dead son and his wife, cars, pets. Not one scrap of paper created in February of 2012.

Who could vouch for Newb if I couldn't find proof in the boxes?

He hadn't been to work.

Angel hadn't seen him.

Cynthia said he'd been at the house.

Was there anyone else? He had roommates and neighbors at the program, but they'd cop to any story for ten bucks. Even if they could remember what they'd seen on that weekend, I couldn't trust them to tell me the truth.

My face pressed onto the desk.

Something about the phone nagged me. The call records might tell who was in the house by which numbers they dialed, but even Newb had a cell phone. I wondered if Gorman could pinpoint Newb by the GPS in his phone. I thought of the loose wire I'd tightened and the messages on the answering machine. The thoughts drifted together. None of it making sense. None of it pointing to anyone in particular.

I shook myself awake and realized why my dreams were filled with phones and answering machines. I'd been dozing, thinking about the case in my sleep, while my own phone rang on my belt.

"Do you know it's eleven thirty?"

I told her I'd dozed off.

"You better not be playing with your gun again."

I told Roxie I'd be right there then looked down at my desk.

We had packed five boxes of paperwork from Mrs. Newbury's house. I'd been through all but a thick handful at the bottom of the last box without finding a single receipt that would help Newb. I tossed the last bit back into the box and locked up. If Newb was going to be redeemed, the evidence wasn't going to come from my warehouse. The kid was in deep. I'd done what I could and now it was time to let Gorman sort it all out.

Roxie had plans and we were long overdue.

Chapter Seventy

The next morning I woke up with a perfectly-engineered breast in my right hand, happy as a baby with his pacifier. The tight contours of Roxie's backside pressed against my thighs. Beta, notorious for burrowing between us during the night, had been content to stake out the edge of the bed with only Roxie's legs for human comfort.

Roxie left and I dozed until I smelled fish omelets in the kitchen.

She hated the smell of fish so much she refused to cook it fresh even though catching fish and shellfish was in my blood. I'd had a commercial shellfish license in my teens and my dad had caught lobsters and scallops commercially when he was out of work. We still fished often. Mostly for stripers and blues, but we hadn't been out lately. I wondered where she'd gotten the fish. More than that, I wondered why.

My one-dollar jeans from GiftsToGive were just right for a day of chores at home. I pulled on a fifty-cent work shirt and left my boots in the corner for later.

The boy was asleep when I passed his room. Fish omelets didn't hold much attraction for him and even the scent of bacon couldn't wake a sixteen year old at nine on Saturday morning.

My plate and I arrived at the table simultaneously. Roxie's robe dipped curiously low off her shoulder, like she'd pulled it open a bit extra when she heard me coming. Undercooked bacon. A three-egg Fish Omelet. Coffee steaming. She wanted something, and there was only one button she hadn't pressed to get it.

Three forkfuls of eggs and a bite of bacon later, her hand traced my shoulder and down my spine. "It's nice to have you around. We haven't seen much of you lately."

After mainlining guilt about turning Newb in, I didn't have anything left to fight off Roxie's assault. Sending her to her mother's was bad enough. After working Mrs. Newbury's estate for weeks, then the trouble with Findley, I'd been away too much. Add to that my quest to prove Newb was guilty then my late night search the night before to prove he wasn't, well she had some big favors coming. Whatever project she wanted me to do would keep me from obsessing over Newb. She'd won before she started.

"I've had that surround sound package for a month now."

I nodded and chewed another bite of bacon. I didn't want to give in too quickly or she'd have me fixing things all weekend.

"Movies will sound so much better."

She had both hands on my shoulders now. I smiled, but she couldn't see my face. "Good idea," I said. "I know just which movie we should watch first."

She bounced off to the kitchen victoriously, and I let her enjoy her win. Working a few hours then watching a good movie or two was a great way to unwind. As long as she kept thinking it was her idea, I'd keep getting fish omelets when she wanted something. Not a bad trade.

She washed the fry pan before she made her tiny omelet with cheese and eggs. By the time she started eating, I had the speaker boxes opened and started laying them out at the four corners of the room.

When he finally got out of bed, the boy helped pull the entertainment center out far enough for me to crawl behind. The place was old, but I wouldn't run wires over the floor, not with a hundred pound dog dashing around the place.

I spent two hours in the cellar looking at junk from old sales, stuff I was thinking about putting online. She probably didn't believe running wire was such a big job, but when she finally came down to check, I was hard at work with the drill chewing through the bottom plate of the living room wall.

She came over and looked at the small hole up through the ceiling. She didn't ask how the wire was going to get to the speakers, and I kept the mystery of fishing wires to myself for a while.

When I went back into the living room, she hovered in the wide doorway while I cut a square hole in the drywall behind the couch. Roxie nodded with recognition when I left the boy there to catch the wire I fed him from the cellar. By the time we had the final wire pulled, Roxie had vacuumed the concrete dust from the floor.

Fish tacos and cleanup help. She really was a find.

I'd been installing electrical boxes since high school, so it only took a few minutes to mount all four boxes and wire them up.

The speaker company included a test to prove the surround sound was working, but I had a test of my own in mind. I slipped in the Matrix DVD and forwarded to the scene where Neo and Trinity walk into the security complex to battle the guards.

The wide screen wasn't squared up yet in case I needed to move some wires around, so the scene was hard to see from my seat on the couch, but the sound was awesome. Shell casings tinkled to the floor behind me on both sides like I was walking down the wide hall with Neo on my left and Trinity on my right.

The boy and I squared up the TV, and Roxie walked in with a large linguica pizza before we even sat down. Not frozen, fresh from the little place down the street. She poured sodas all around, brought a pile of napkins, and plunked down on the couch for a Matrix series marathon.

God must have loved me to put so much hotness in a package that also enjoyed sex and action movies.

The day couldn't have been more perfect until Chris walked in near the end of the second movie with a grant I needed to review before deadline.

Chapter Seventy-one

"Are we being piggish?" Dangerous phrasing given how much I resemble a well-fed boar.

"By the time this thing is decided, your work on the hospital will be cruising along. You should be managing these projects anyway. You're too old to be lugging tools."

"Imagine what he'd look like if he didn't work out?" Jake chimed in.

"Watch it, Smart Guy, I know where you sleep." I'd trained Beta to growl at anyone who came in to my room at night and that included Jake. He didn't have a dog of his own, and I wasn't above dipping his fingers in warm water while he slept. Or worse.

Chris and I moved to the dining room table and spread out the printed pages. We'd been over the specs on the building, so all I really needed to look at was how he'd written up the treatment programs. He was the expert at winning grants. I just read them because I was the guy who had to deliver. These dining room table sessions were where I really made my money, but reading was a chore, and if I could have left it all up to him, I would have.

I guess I stared at one of the pages a bit too long.

"You okay?" he asked.

I waved him off and started reading again.

"Findley's guys after you again?"

"No, but thanks for reminding me."

"I know you hate paperwork, but this grant is big. Whatever's going on has to be pretty important."

I shuffled the pages back together.

"I think someone killed Mrs. Newbury."

He perked up. Intrigued, but clearly thinking I was imagining things. "I thought she died of pneumonia? Pretty common after a broken hip."

I told him about the scuffs on the bed frame, the other clues I'd found, and how seriously Gorman was taking it all.

"No shit. You think it was, Newb?"

"I think he starved her to death."

"I think it takes a month to starve a healthy person."

I hadn't checked how long it took someone to starve to death, but Mrs. Newbury was frail. "She was a little old lady. She didn't have an ounce of fat to begin with."

"I'm not buying it," Chris said. "Someone would have come around and seen her. Why not poison her? Something to speed up the process."

His writer's mind was spinning with ideas. The killer, if there was one, had convinced everyone she'd died of natural causes. If she hadn't left me that note, no one would be looking for a killer. The idea was irresistible to Chris, but for him to be happy, it had to be more clever than simply starving the old woman. That was too low tech and offered too much chance of being caught.

Maybe he was right.

"She was alone with him for about five days."

"That's not long enough," he said. He'd be Googling starvation as soon as he got back to his computer.

"Got a better theory?"

"I'm sticking with some sort of poison. If you're feeding her and she's dependent on you, she's eating whatever you give her. Couldn't be easier to poison her if you could find something tasteless."

"I think she was strapped to the bed and kept there."

He gripped his chin the way he does when he's working. "Why would you do that?" he said, not really looking for an answer. "You're keeping her from something. Food. Water. Medicine. Would she have died without her meds?"

We'd tossed all her medication. She didn't have anything valuable. If she'd been on Oxycodone, Newb would have taken it long before I arrived. "I don't think so. I can't ask her doc. HIPPA and all. Newb probably wouldn't know. Or he might lie," I said. Cynthia would have known what Mrs. Newbury was taking, but I wasn't sure she'd tell me.

"Where did her stuff go?"

"I sold it on the lawn."

"I mean her real assets. Who got those?"

"Newb."

"Hard to believe," Chris said.

"What?"

"He seems like a harmless kid. Zoned out, like the life was sucked out of him, but I never believed he'd kill his own grandmother no matter how much money she had."

"It's unbelievable what drugs can do."

"Whoever ends up with her stuff, the house, the bank accounts, her real assets, there's your killer." He spoke like Sherlock Holmes. Like he'd written the book on murder investigation.

I wanted to make fun of him for being so smug, but in things like this, the kid was usually right on. The old woman's will left Newb everything of value and that helped clear my conscience about putting the cops on him.

Chris walked me through the changes he'd made to the grant, so I didn't have to wade through the whole document on my own. I gave him the go ahead to submit just as my cell rang.

Detective Gorman told me what the lab had found in that silver sugar bowl I pulled out of Cynthia's trash.

"Anyone's prints on it?"

"Yours, matched from the FBI database."

I remembered wiping the outside clean. How I admired the silvery shine that gloomy day in the warehouse. It didn't matter which of them had stolen the sugar bowl from the old lady's house. What mattered was what the lab found inside. I still felt like a dope for wiping it down. I'd yelled at Newb for doing the same with the paint can. Had I known more about drugs and fingerprints, we might have solved the whole thing right then.

I hung up with Gorman and the reality of me being right about what had happened to Mrs. Newbury started to sink in. A killer was going to be punished because I saw those scuffmarks.

"What's up?" Chris asked.

"Gorman asked me to call Newb and convince him to sign an exhumation order."

"You going to do it?"

"What choice do I have?"

"If they find what they're looking for, Newb's going away for a long time."

Gorman wanted me to lie to the kid. Tell him the testing was routine.

Newb was street smart. If he killed her, he wouldn't make it easy for the cops to dig her up. It seemed common sense to me. He had to know the exhumation order meant trouble, but he hadn't graduated high school. Gorman was sure the two of us could outsmart him.

I wasn't sure I could lead him to slaughter.

Chapter Seventy-two

It took me forty-two minutes to call Newb. I counted every tick of the clock. I wrung my hands. Paced the floor. Kept bouncing between the image of Newb in cuffs and his poor grandmother strapped down into her bed, starving, pleading for help.

Grandma Newbury won out.

Newb didn't answer my first three attempts.

As I was dialing again, my brother's face came up on my screen.

"Win that grant already?"

"Not yet, but I've got something a lot more interesting."

"Gonna tell me how long it takes someone to starve to death?"

"Nope. But I can tell you Mary Newbury wasn't the first in her family to die unexpectedly."

"Okay, Little Brother. You got my attention."

"Newb's parents died in a car crash five years ago. You'll never guess who got the house."

"Newb."

"Careful what you say to him," Chris said. "He might be more dangerous than you think."

The next call to Newb was a lot easier. He finally answered. Said he was out with some girl, but he'd meet with me and Gorman in the morning.

I hung up and sat back on the couch, piecing together what I knew. Newb inherited his parents' money and blew through it. No wonder he gave

Cynthia such generous terms in the divorce. He hadn't worked for that money. And when things got tough, he found another way to cash in.

Chris' final words kept ringing in my ears. "Whoever ends up with those two houses is your killer. Guaranteed."

I couldn't have been more disgusted, or less happy to see the round face at my door.

Angel tapped the glass like he always did, his meaty face lit by the living room lights. My phone was still in my hand. The instrument of Newb's death. More correctly his incarceration. The government didn't kill people in Massachusetts no matter how much they deserved it.

Roxie saw Angel and retreated to the computer in our bedroom. She'd heard enough of my conversation with Chris to know what was going on. She saw a storm coming and was smart enough to hurry out of its path.

Angel took half the couch, and I felt my half rise.

"I want to talk about what's going on with Newb," Angel said.

"No surprise there."

"You've got him all wrong. He's not a bad kid."

"He's not on my list of favorite people right now."

"What did he do? What have you seen him do?"

The big guy couldn't help seeing Newb as his own kid. No matter what Newb did, Angel would back him up to the end. No use arguing with him.

"You want a drink?" I stood up to get myself a soda.

Angel grabbed my arm and turned me toward him. If a punk on the street did that, he'd get a hard left to the chest, but Angel was a solid guy, trying to help a kid who sorely needed it. Unfortunately, Angel was a couple years too late.

"Don't blow me off, Man. I know what you're doing and you've got it all wrong. Those cops see the kid's record and they'll be done investigating. A jury, too. Newb'll get fired in jail faster than you can blink."

I walked to the kitchen and poured myself a Coke to give Angel some time to cool down.

I sat back down on my half of the couch and got comfortable because I didn't want Angel to think his guilt trip was working. What was about to happen to Newb was shitty, but it was his fault not mine.

I sipped my soda and let Angel chill.

"I know what you're doing."

"Do you know Newb inherited his parents' house when they died?"

"And that bitch of an ex-wife took it from him."

I couldn't believe how blind he was.

"You think he killed them, too?" Angel demanded.

"Don't you think so? The kid's whole family died."

"He's a good kid."

"You just said yourself he's got a record that's so long a jury will throw him in jail. He didn't get that record being a Boy Scout."

"He didn't kill his parents and he certainly didn't kill his grandmother."

"Get real, Angel. You weren't there. You can't know what happened."

"He wasn't there either."

I threw up my hands and fell back in my chair. The big guy had completely lost his grasp on reality. It was sad what happened to Angel and his family, but I wasn't about to cancel my plans with Gorman so Angel could live his fantasy of saving his dead son.

I couldn't look over to my right. I stared ahead and thought about the meeting in the morning. How Newb would sit across the table like a sheep and sign whatever I told him to.

If Angel was at that meeting, he'd go berserk.

Telling him would have been throwing my investigative work away.

"You couldn't be more wrong about this," Angel said.

"You don't know what you're talking about. You weren't there."

"Were you?" he asked.

The guilt slammed me into my seat. I was about to send the kid up for a long time. I wasn't testifying against him. I was doing the right thing. Giving the evidence to the cops and letting them do their job. Still, with Angel staring at me across the couch, I couldn't help feeling I was making a mistake.

"The kid wasn't there," Angel said again.

"What are you talking about?" I asked, even though I didn't want to hear it. Not after what I'd set up for the next morning. I wanted Angel to give it up and go home. I couldn't handle the back and forth, but that's what those kids did to you. After a while you started to see they were human. They were weak and needed help. But in a short time, you'd also see the power the drug had over them. They'd sell your car for drug money. Or stab you in the back. Or strap you to a bed and let you starve.

"He wasn't with his grandmother."

"The kid will say anything to keep himself out of trouble. Don't you know that?"

"I can prove it."

"How?"

"He was high with a girl."

"That doesn't prove anything. He was supposed to be taking care of his grandmother for five days. He strapped her down and starved her instead."

"He wasn't even there. He was with this girl for a week."

Chapter Seventy-three

Saturday night at ten o'clock, I sat in the passenger's seat of Angel's red Toyota and cruised to the south end feeling like I'd made a huge mistake. You couldn't help being swayed by Angel's passion for the kid, so I didn't fault myself getting in the car, but when we walked into the first dive bar, I knew we were on a fool's errand.

The fiasco with Rusty should have taught me not to listen to Angel.

He led me to the dirty cop simply because the guy worked on the force. If he'd had a clue what he was doing, he wouldn't have almost gotten me killed. Was this chick he was leading me to any better? So what if Newb got some chick to say she was with him when his grandmother died. What did that mean? Worse, what kind of trouble would we find down here?

Angel wasn't the best judge of character. And by the looks of this bar, he hung around in some scummy places. Whether it was to help guys like Newb, or to meet prostitutes, I wasn't sure. Probably a little of both.

No matter what happened, I'd be meeting with Gorman and Newb in the morning then it would be out of my hands. Still, I walked along the dingy tile floor behind Angel and scanned the crowd for a girl that would stand out even in a room full of derelicts with full color tattoos. Colorful arms and chests were bared even in February.

I scanned a sea of bandanas for a head of long black hair streaked with florescent pink and green. The nose ring wouldn't have stood out, but the hair would have been easy to spot if she'd been there. Angel told me she also wore neon beads around her neck to match her hair.

"Newb said she'd be here."

"And you believed him?"

"Give the kid a break, will you?"

"That's all he gets. He screws up and someone fixes it. Over and over and over."

Angel turned away frustrated and shoved off into the crowd, determined to prove me wrong. At his size moving in a crowded bar was like swimming neck deep in partially dried cement. He stalled in front of a scruffy-haired guy with a goatee who eyed him and refused to move. I'd started to my right, to circle the far side of the bar, but stopped and watched in case he needed help. Angel could barely move himself around, never mind fight. He'd be little more than a punching bag for the guy, though, I remembered from football that fat didn't bruise. At his size, Angel could take a few punches.

I almost stepped back to help, but a guy in a Red Sox jersey thrust his hand toward Angel and pushed his friend out of the way. They shook hands and the guy threw an arm over Angel's shoulder. They talked. I assumed Angel asked about the girl and where to find her. Seeing he was okay, I pushed on to my right.

The fifty people crammed into the small bar clogged progress in every direction. I could see over most of them. This girl would have stood out even with the neon lights. Most of the guys hadn't shaved in a week and more than a few of them smelled. The music blared from my right, but they weren't dancing enough to sweat. They were standing around drinking, looking to score sex or drugs.

Around the corner, a little alcove held a scratch ticket machine and a pool table. Two guys played eight ball. One carefully lined up a shot on the fifteen in the side. He had an easy lag to the eleven in the corner and the eight was almost hanging in a corner at the opposite end of the table. I didn't see cash on the table, but there had to be money involved for him to hesitate over such an easy situation.

Half a dozen people watched. Mostly men. A few ten-fifty blondes hung on the edges of the room, good bodies, boobs hanging out, long straight hair, but their faces would stop you cold unless you'd had ten beers or were traveling fifty miles an hour. That day I wasn't looking for blondes.

The guy made the shot and rolled the cue smoothly down to kiss the rail and come back half an inch. His next shot was a bunny and with a little topspin, the cue would roll down for a gimme on the eight. The guy sitting with the stick between his legs didn't pull any bills out of his wallet. He stared at the cue and the three solid balls clustered against the rail by the side pocket. He kept hold of the stick, but we both knew he wasn't going to need it in that game.

I moved around the corner in case the girl was tucked in by the jukebox. Making out in the corner or on her knees making a few bucks.

The back door was cracked a foot to let in the cool night air or maybe to let dealers slip in and out. I looked around at the dreck that filled the place. The city should have shut this place down long ago. I was wondering why they hadn't. Whether they'd been paid off, or were just too lazy to deal with places like this when I heard, "That's not cool, man."

Three heads focused on the space beyond the door. I only saw bricks out there, but my heart started pounding. The vile tone was unmistakable. To disgust this crowd took some doing. The only thing I could picture sent me scrambling for the alley. I imagined a young girl out there. Whether she was being raped or serving a few clients for drug money didn't matter.

I pushed my way through to see a guy rifling the pockets of a familiar coat. Farther down, three guys shared hits on a joint. They eyed me considering they might need to run, but not considering the idea very seriously. No girl. Nothing but dented barrels and a pair of stocking feet behind the guy with the coat.

I looked up and down for the girl, maybe I was just focused on a girl because I was looking for one, but it finally occurred to me that the guys smoking the joint and the people in the door were looking at me and the guy rifling every pocket in the coat.

The guy in the stocking feet, lying against the wall was being robbed.

I pushed past the thief to see if the guy on the ground needed help.

His chin pressed down into his chest. I recognized the thin brown hair, the sinewy muscles that defied his age. Even the blue tank top. Speedy was nodded out against the brick wall and the punk had taken his shoes and coat. Not a big deal in summertime, but February in New England is rough without a coat, especially if you can't afford a new one.

"A lousy ten bucks!"

Disappointed, the guy kicked Speedy hard in the thigh. His leg bucked with the impact, but he was so wasted his expression didn't change.

Why would Speedy nod here? Was he trying to kill himself?

One of the punk's friends thought it was funny and kicked Speedy from the other side.

Angel was lost in the crowd by the bar. Even if I could have called him, he wouldn't have been much help.

Laughter spilled out from the door behind me. The thief had at least three friends in the narrow alley behind the bar, and it sounded like more just inside. If I stepped in, it was going to get ugly, but I couldn't let them keep pounding him. "I'll take the coat, the ten bucks, and his shoes," I said, stepping right up in the guy's face.

"Hell you will."

From the corner of my eye, I saw a guy stomp his heel down on Speedy's fingers hard enough to break them. Another guy came up for his turn. "Piece of shit. Blocking the alley." The guy unzipped his pants and pissed a wide stream over Speedy's legs.

The guy in front of me kept feeling around inside Speedy's coat like I hadn't said anything.

"That's my friend on the ground," I said so all of them could hear. "You're not taking his coat."

The two guys standing beside Speedy stopped and measured me up. The pissing bandit was stuck in place by his stream, but his face turned, unsure whether he should continue or run, not that he could move.

The thief glared. "Fuck off while you can."

Before I could decide which guy to hit first, a blade glimmered in front of me. The thief snapped it open and poked it toward me left-handed. He assumed I'd turn and run. Big mistake.

I yanked and turned his wrist. His elbow locked, and as I twisted, his shoulder dropped. His right hand turned away so whatever else he had under his own coat was useless. I owned him then. I could have taken the coat back and figured out what to do about Speedy, but I had a hunch this guy wasn't the type to give up easy.

I took a deep breath and hammered my palm down just below his elbow. Tendons snapped as I exhaled.

He squirmed and flopped and screeched.

The aspiring kicker came running with a roundhouse at my head. I caught him by the wrist and elbow, flipped him over my hip, and slammed his head into the brick wall. His momentum sent all his weight on a collision course with the bricks. His head the brake.

Vertebrae crunched.

Gravity claimed him with a thump on the cement floor.

The pissing bandit wanted to run, but couldn't head for the street with his unit flapping in the wind. He backed up slowly, the spray of urine shield enough to keep me from chasing.

The rest of the friends stayed inside the threshold.

No one dared step outside until a round face asked me if I thought I was Batman.

Chapter Seventy-four

Angel cleared the cluster of people from the doorway, and I hauled Speedy inside by the armpits, his feet dragging behind him. He was so out of it he didn't know where he was, who I was, or why I was moving him. Left against those bricks without his coat and shoes, he would have died of hypothermia.

At fifty-two he worked harder and faster than any guy I put on the crew. He was smart enough to know he'd die out there. I couldn't tell if he'd been high before he shot up or if he'd shot up in that alley to end it all. But I wondered how stupid he'd have to be to shoot up and leave himself vulnerable, outside, surrounded by a horde of scumbags.

The bartender sneered at me over four empty tables.

Angel's 911 call sent a few people up the alley. By the time we got Speedy's coat and shoes on, the place was half empty. Not everyone left. Probably just the ones who had outstanding warrants or who'd stolen something recently. No matter who they were or what they'd done, the guy had just lost half his tips and maybe some kickbacks on drug deals he let go while he worked.

I caught a goateed snicker at the door as Findley shuffled out. He'd been waiting there, wanting me to see him leave. Twenty minutes later I knew why.

The jacket thief cradled his left arm and sat low against the wall as the paramedic examined him. He winced at every touch. I'd snapped at least one tendon, but didn't offer my assessment because I didn't want to incriminate myself.

The paramedic carefully strapped the elbow down so it couldn't move.

"Ah. That kills. I'm going to sue your ass," the kid whined.

The punk probably couldn't afford treatment and was looking for someone to pay his medical bills. The paramedic didn't flinch. He'd barely touched the kid. I could tell it wasn't the first time he'd played this game.

The second guy sat with his knees drawn up, head buried in his hands. When he went down, I would have bet I heard something in his neck pop, but he was content to sit there and wait for his headache to subside.

The paramedic shined a light in his eyes, moved his fingers back and forth in front of his face and told the kid he was going for a ride.

The uniformed cop who'd bagged the knife passed the gurney in the alley as he made his way back. He locked on me, and I made a point of staying put, waiting for him to come. He'd figured the score pretty quickly and hadn't pressed me too hard over busting up the two punks. I was happy about that because I'd had enough legal trouble for the next few years.

Before he reached me, a raspy voice called from behind.

"Nice work. Assault with a deadly weapon. Aggravated battery. Should get you five to ten."

Rusty smirked down at me from the doorframe.

"You cause trouble everywhere you go, don't you?" he asked.

"Your colleagues didn't see it that way." I nodded to the uniformed cop approaching.

"You're talking to a lot of cops these days. I think you'd be better off if you kept your mouth shut."

Angel watched from the doorway as Rusty and I traded veiled threats. My size and fighting experience led me headlong into trouble. I could have been smarter about a lot of things, but I was damned glad I wasn't Angel. Guilt lit up his round face and helplessness filled his eyes. I hoped I'd never fall to the point where no one feared me.

"What's up with Gorman?" Rusty asked.

"Homicide's a little off your beat, isn't it?"

The uniform stopped between us and eyed me suspiciously. He knew Rusty on sight, and it seemed he knew Gorman, too. My connection to both cops left him wondering who I was. He probably suspected I worked undercover or something. I let him go on thinking that.

"I could use some help," I said to Rusty.

"I'm not your friend," he said. "You can't go busting people up and expect to get away with it."

"Officer," I gestured for the uniform to supply his name. It was Ryan. "Officer Ryan has bagged a knife that puke," I pointed to the kid with his arm splinted, "tried to stab me with. You're going to find one set of prints and they're not mine."

"Seems you don't need my help," Rusty said.

"Not for that." I led Rusty inside to Speedy.

"This guy works for me. He hasn't been around for over a week. We want to do a Section Thirty-five."

"You family?" Rusty asked Angel.

"He doesn't have any," I said.

Rusty glared at me. He didn't want to process Speedy any more than he wanted to close down the bar. He'd gotten way too cozy with drug traffickers. What they needed down here was a few more kids like Gorman who were excited about the job, eager to do the right thing and get the drugs off the streets.

It didn't take a rocket scientist to find drug abusers in New Bedford. The problem was helping them. The bar was going to fester like an open sore until the city figured out how to help people like Speedy.

Rusty was all we had. He wasn't enthusiastic, but between him and Angel, we got Speedy headed to a detox bed.

Chapter Seventy-five

The fifth time Angel called I shut my phone off and stuck it in the glove compartment. I'd spent the night before looking for the girl with the neon-striped hair to give Newb's alibi a shot. As far as I knew, she didn't exist. Newb wasn't above lying, and Angel wanted to believe the kid so badly he'd swallow anything.

The night wasn't a total bust. We'd found Speedy alive. He might have died out in the cold if we hadn't brought him in. He'd be pissed at me if I saw him that day, but in two or three weeks when he came back to work, he'd be thankful.

I double-parked the wagon, and Newb came hustling outside without me even having to get out and knock. The kid was downright jovial. Most of the time his expression was so lifeless you had to wonder if he was awake. The kid had half a smile as he walked around the hood. He climbed in with purpose on that cold Sunday morning, eager to get the meeting done.

I started toward Belleville Avenue and Newb asked, "Why's this cop working Sunday?"

"You think they let criminals run free on weekends?" I wanted to pull my words back as soon as they escaped. Newb had been a criminal most of his adult life. It took me a long time working with him to realize that my heavy-handed, anti-crime rhetoric irritated the crap out of him. Normally I didn't care too much about bothering the kid. He worked for me, and there was a certain amount of brainwashing that went along with his pay. I considered it a public service. But that day, I needed his cooperation.

He kept smiling so I guess my comment didn't bother him too much. I remembered he was out with a girl the night before. It didn't happen often, and I assumed that either he'd gotten some, or he saw the prospect coming soon. He didn't share his nighttime exploits on the way to the coffee shop and I didn't ask.

Newb went straight to the counter, ordered coffee and a donut. When the cashier asked him if that was all, he pointed to me. I stepped up, ordered a coffee and a donut, and by the time the woman asked for six bucks, Newb was two steps back. The kid had money falling from the sky, and he still expected me to buy his food everywhere we went.

I felt a little less guilty helping Gorman deceive the kid, but not enough to stop the twirling inside my gut.

Gorman came in, breezed through the line, and sat down across from Newb. I introduced them and they shook hands.

Gorman thanked Newb for taking time out on a Sunday and told him what would happen during the exhumation process. The kid listened as the detective talked in intricate detail about everything that would happen to his grandmother's body from the time she was removed from her grave until she was returned, but the detective was fuzzy on why she needed digging up in the first place.

Newb was puzzled and said so.

He didn't seem nervous about the whole thing. Certainly not in the way you'd expect a murderer to act. I'd expected him to be shaking with worry when Gorman told him they wanted an autopsy, but like most things in life, Newb didn't seem to care what happened one way or another.

Gorman stammered his way into explaining the need to exhume Mrs. Newbury. "The mortician called us..."

Newb was baffled.

"The guy at the funeral home," I said.

"He left a message," Gorman said, "and I didn't get it until after the funeral was over. He was curious about a mark on the body and we didn't get a chance to examine it before she was buried."

"You think something bad happened to her?"

I couldn't read what Newb was feeling, but it wasn't the outrage I would have felt if someone just told me my grandmother might have been murdered.

"The mark could be nothing. We won't know until we run some tests."

Newb accepted the bold-faced lie and looked down at the paperwork Gorman had given him. The detective indicated where Newb had to sign and the kid scribbled his name above the solid line.

Gorman took the papers and sat back wearing a smug grin. If he found drugs in the old lady's tissue, he'd have broken his first homicide. A case the medical examiner missed. He wasn't a rookie, but this would be a huge push for his career.

Before he got up, he asked me if I had the letter he needed. It was a printout of hours my crew worked the weeks around Valentine's Day. It showed Newb missing work while Mrs. Newbury was suffering in bed. Another nail in the kid's coffin.

The detective took the envelope, and Newb and I watched him go.

Newb turned to me, "Don't you think that's weird?"

"What's that?"

"Digging her up? She was an old lady. She got sick and died. Why waste the time?"

"I don't know," I lied.

The kid trusted me, and I'd thrown him under the bus.

"She was lucky," he said.

"Lucky?"

"She was seventy-something."

"Eighty-two," I said.

"Whatever. No way I'll live that long."

The kid was right. His body had been through hell, and it would be a miracle if a relapse didn't take him to an early grave.

His phone rang. He answered, then handed it to me.

"You didn't do it, did you?" Angel asked.

"I did."

"Well now you're going to have to undo it."

Chapter Seventy-six

Not only did she exist, she had the smoothest porcelain skin I'd ever seen. The most penetrating blue eyes. And a hot little figure that withered up to five feet six. Too bad she'd messed up the package with a silver nose ring and a heavy stud below the corner of her supple young lips. Why? And the hair. Gorgeous long, straight black hair. Shimmering. Radiant. And streaked with pink and florescent green. At least that was fixable. Even if she shaved her head, it would eventually grow back.

I didn't have to see beneath the long sleeve shirt to know there were tattoos lurking. I wasn't a fan.

Angel was much less discriminating. Can't blame the guy for drooling. He didn't get any attention from women he didn't pay. This girl didn't have many miles on her, but there was the desperation men like Angel preyed on. I hate to lump him in, but I could see how turned on he got when he saw her. She'd come to a point where she needed more drugs than she could pay for with a nine to five, and then she'd welcome Angel and dozens of guys like him.

I shuddered and tried to imagine what this girl was doing with Newb.

She was way out of his league, but if he was paying and she was desperate, I could see it. At least they were about the same age.

"Don't tell me you were out to breakfast and stumbled across her."

"A friend hooked us up."

"Interesting choice of words."

He looked down at his feet, shaking his head.

Buying sex was desperate. I wanted to stop poking him about it, but it made me so sick I couldn't help myself. The friend he mentioned was a hooker no doubt. That's how she knew the little emo chick we were meeting. I bet her rate was pretty high, and I bet Angel would make an offer the minute I left.

She looked bored and nervous. Angel had been standing in front of the lone cashier. Between breakfast and lunch, the place was dead and the neon-haired girl didn't take well to being left alone in a fiberglass booth.

Angel led me over and introduced me to Alley.

"You a cop?"

I told her I wasn't.

"What do you care what I'm doing then?"

"That's a question for Angel. I'm not sure I care about you at all."

"Tell him what you told me."

"About Newb?" she asked.

"How do we even know she's talking about the same guy?"

Angel pulled out his smart phone, tapped a few times then laid it on the table in front of her.

"That's Newb," she said.

I sat down across from her. "How do you know Newb?"

"I spent a week with him," she said. "A little more. Maybe ten days."

She saw the astonishment on my face. It wasn't a fling. It wasn't charity. Newb couldn't have afforded her for ten days.

"Tell him why," Angel prompted.

"Twenty-seven hundred bucks."

Morbid hooker math took over my brain for a moment. What did three hundred bucks a day buy? Was Newb doing her day and night for that? I thought about my raunchiest escapades. How many times I'd done it with a woman in twenty-four hours. When passion and testosterone were running high and physical needs were priority one.

"It wasn't like trickin'," she said.

I gestured with open hands.

"It was like dating," she said.

"He didn't pay you to go on dates?" I was confused.

"He didn't pay me. It was his friends. They said the cops were after him. Wanted me to keep him out of trouble for a while. Help him lay low."

"So he wasn't too demanding," I mused.

She shook her head. They'd stayed at her place. She came onto him in a bar and he thought she wanted him for dope. She kept him high and he slept most of the time. They'd had sex, but I got the feeling Newb had no idea she was paid for and he could have had as much as he wanted. He thought he was scoring big time, but the kid really missed out.

I felt for him and I felt something else. Adrenaline surging. My brain coming on full alert. Telling me something was wrong. That I'd made a huge mistake.

"When did you two split up?"

"Right before Valentine's Day. The Friday before I think."

"How was Newb?"

"Messed up. Hooked bad. I expected the cops to pick him up quick. He was out of cash. Doing smash and grabs to score his fixes. I even checked the papers once, but didn't see his name."

"They were keeping him out of the way," Angel said.

I didn't have to ask who, but I did.

Alley described the two people perfectly.

I used Angel's phone to call Gorman as we hoofed out of the place.

Chapter Seventy-seven

Angel was full of questions when we got back into the car. Bringing him along was a risk, but he loved Newb so much I couldn't tell him no. When he finally understood what was happening, we rolled the last few miles in silence, both wondering if we'd find the guy we were looking for in his usual haunt.

The boxy industrial building was ringed with aluminum siding one step up from corrugated tin. Thirty cars waited in the parking lot around back, a bunch more than we'd find later in the year when all those New Year's resolutions had petered out. We found the guy's car, and I blocked him in against the low concrete wall that separated the parking lot from the swamp the place backed up to.

My dad says he can predict the future. Standing there looking at the car and the swamp I wasn't sure what was going to happen. The scrubby trees in the wetland provided enough cover to run to and hide for a while, but the strip only went so far. The guy was too top heavy to run very far and his bulk would make it hard to slip between trees. I wondered if he'd pick up the wagon and move it. He was strong enough.

I didn't share my worry with Angel on the way across the lot.

Walking through those glass doors, we couldn't have been more out of place. The spunky girl behind the desk in the bright blue T-shirt must have been laughing inside.

"Welcome. I'm Sandy. Are you gentlemen new?"

Between us we carried over seven hundred pounds. I was pretty sure she didn't know all the club members, but we'd be memorable. They'd probably have to put a rider on their treadmill insurance policy if we started using it.

I told her we wanted to look around. That we were thinking about getting in shape and wanted to see their equipment. She wouldn't let us go unsupervised even when I told her how embarrassed we were to be visiting for the first time.

We each got a glossy brochure and a great view of her tight little shorts as she led us into the cardio room. The first woman we saw walked on a treadmill and watched a movie on an iPad. She wasn't going any faster than I'd walk, probably to keep from sweating and smudging her makeup. I couldn't tell yoga pants from spandex or whatever the girls wore, but she might as well have held up a sign that said, "I'm looking for a hot guy." She glanced over her shoulder when we came in, but never looked back. I didn't think we qualified.

I wondered if Sandy parked us there to sell us on the hot babes in their membership. She explained the gym had seventy cardio machines. Mostly treadmills, but also stair climbers, bikes, and ellipticals.

We passed the rooms they used for yoga, aerobics, and spinning classes and listened to her spiel at each stop. When she led us into the weight machines, I gave Angel a nod to keep her busy. Sandy showed him how to adjust the weight for a lat pulldown, and I slipped around the corner and disappeared.

I felt like an escaped prisoner who'd accidentally run into the hall of mirrors at a carnival. A heavy grunt stopped me cold.

The muscled face straining over bicep curls belonged to a woman. Not a woman I'd ever date. Bulging neck, red face, sweat pouring down. She was a hot blonde before she bulked up so much her jaw muscles swelled.

I skirted black pleather benches. Racks of dumbbells, numbered plates, and bars lined up along the wall. There in the back, Chuck checked himself in the mirror while he held two weights way out to his sides, shoulder height, the muscles on top of his shoulders rock hard.

"What are you doing here?" He grunted and eased the weights down to his sides then the floor.

"Checking the place out. Saw you and thought I'd offer you some advice."

With every passing second, his muscles recovered from the lift. I had him in the corner with no way out, but I couldn't keep him there. Not without help. Those dumbbells weighed sixty-five pounds each.

"I've seen enough of you. Get lost."

"They have plenty of weights in prison, but I don't think they have your brand of protein shakes."

He stood tall and took half a step toward me. Big as I was it was all I could do not to back up. I'd squared off against a lot of guys as a bouncer, but most of them were drunk and none of them approached Chuck's size.

"I know what you did and why."

"You accusing me of something?"

The blonde behind me stopped doing curls. Even though we were back to back, our eyes met in the mirrors. She was curious, trying to figure out if I needed help. Sadly, she was probably tougher in a fight. Definitely stronger, hard as that was to imagine.

"I'm trying to help you stay out of prison."

"Why don't you get the hell out of here and never come back."

"Shame she's turning you in to save herself."

He grabbed for my shirt and missed. Big as he was, his muscles made it hard to move fast. I dodged aside and grabbed for a weight to whack him with. The one I picked was half the size he'd been lifting, but I could barely move the thing. It was useless as a weapon.

He shoved me from behind and I toppled onto the dumbbell rack, iron poking me everywhere on my way to the floor.

He picked up a forty-five pound round plate and hoisted it over his head like a pizza box. His red tank top advertised Ida's Gym. In the face of sure death, I chuckled that a woman made the hulk that was about to crush me.

"I know there's no money in bodybuilding competitions. I know it sucks. But those drugs from the old lady lead straight back to you. If you don't cooperate, you're going down."

Sandy and Angel appeared in the doorway. She screamed, "Chuck! Put that down!"

The titan stood there trying to decide what to do.

"Don't add a second murder," I warned.

He could have cut me in half with that plate, but Sandy knew him on sight. Anyone in the gym could identify him in a lineup. Killing me in front of three witnesses was a lot different than killing a little old lady he thought no one would miss. I was pretty sure he hadn't even done that.

Angel saw me down and rumbled right in. He didn't realize that weighing four hundred pounds wasn't much of a deterrent to a guy who could bench press nearly double that.

Chuck tossed the plate aside. It bounced off the concrete floor, crumpled the carpet into a deep crack, and smashed the mirror next to me. Fissures zigzagged through the glass. The plate clattered to the floor before I could move.

Chuck launched himself toward Angel, and in two running steps, my friend collided with a shoulder larger than his own. The impact of raw muscle on bulk sounded with a heavy thud and the whoosh of Angel's breath escaping. Chuck pancaked the big guy and ran right through him out into the maze of weight machines.

Chapter Seventy-eight

An octagonal dumbbell jammed into my ribcage when I tried to get up out of the tangle of weights. My back arched wide and threw my big belly way out front. Angel looked even more ridiculous trying to roll over. He rubbed his head, but he wasn't hurt. His big problem was getting his sheer bulk hoisted back over his feet.

The manly woman by the entry surveyed the damaged mirror and smirked.

"It's not over yet," I said, getting to my feet and rushing out.

She didn't comment on my chances for stopping the raging bodybuilder alone, but I didn't need her to tell me to call for help.

Around the corner into the weight room, Sandy had rounded up three staff members, guys who'd been using the gym a lot more than I had. They snapped to attention when I hustled in among the machines.

"Where'd he go?" I yelled, not stopping.

An older guy stopped his lift and pointed urgently to the front door.

I paused long enough to recognize the exit and hustled down the carpeted aisle with the staff chasing me.

"Are you a cop?"

The crisp dry air braced me as I ran over the narrow strip of pavement onto the grassy bank. Chuck didn't waste time trying to move the wagon. His red tank top plunged down into the trees.

I stopped. Not because I could see the cattails and knew the whole place was soaked and that I'd be wet to my knees. And not because I knew

Gorman would surround the big guy and haul him out. It was the combination of not wanting to be wet and pummeled and left to drag myself out of a swamp on my own in the dead of winter.

I whipped open my phone. Gorman answered on the first ring.

"He's running," I said. "Into the swamp behind the building. He's between Nash Road and Route One Forty."

"We're not far. Give me a description."

"Seen the Incredible Hulk?"

"Yah."

"He's that guy, just not green."

Gorman laughed.

"He's wearing a red Ida's Gym tank top, but I'm pretty sure he's going to be the only guy that big wandering out of the swamp."

"We're on it," Gorman said. He told me to stay put, but I didn't listen.

The guys from the gym stood around listening, and from my conversation with Gorman, they decided I was a good guy. I wasn't sure what they'd have done if I turned out to be a gang hit man. I guess when you're that bulked up you think you're invincible and do some pretty stupid things.

I knew I wasn't invincible. I let the big guy trudge his way through the brush until his red shirt was hard to see.

Angel lumbered over and stopped, looking for a place to sit down. He decided that getting up off the grass would be too hard, so he stood and followed our eyes into the swamp.

"How'd you know he was connected to the drugs?" Angel panted from the walk outside.

"He's a competitive bodybuilder."

"Obviously."

"They use diuretics to make their muscles look dry."

"What does it matter if they look wet?"

"On the inside. Dry muscles look leaner. More sculpted. Bigger."

The staff on the bank listened intently, but they'd have a hard time leaping from a diuretic drug to murder. Angel slowly made the leap himself.

"She used him," I said.

Angel smiled at me for the first time in days. "Thanks for believing in my boy."

The truth was I hadn't, and I felt sick about it.

Sirens sounded in the distance. We couldn't see the lights over the trees. Neither could Chuck.

"Let's help the boys out," I said and started down the bank for the trees.

Angel glanced at the swamp and parked himself heavily on the bank. "You go ahead," he said.

I went in hard, cracking branches for ten or fifteen yards, and then I started my best beagle imitation. I howled and pushed through the trees, the muck slurping over the tops of my boots.

When I stopped to listen, the crashing ahead of me was easy to follow. He turned west toward the highway. I kept on his heels for a few more yards then climbed up on a hummock to rest.

When I had my breath, I called Gorman and told him where his man was going to come out.

Chapter Seventy-nine

One-way mirrors in the police station were cool if you were looking through the glass and not wondering who was on the other side. Gorman was giddy standing with me and Angel while we waited for Cynthia to be seated at the small table in the interrogation room.

His boss was skeptical that Gorman had discovered and solved a homicide on his own, so he'd interviewed Angel and me personally to make sure we weren't a couple of crackpots. The warrant followed quickly, and when Cynthia was escorted in, Gorman couldn't wait to take his seat.

Gorman shook our hands vigorously when he was ready to go. "Push this right here." He indicated a button on a stick microphone on the counter. "And I can hear you. I'm going to get as much of her story out as I can. Then we'll have something to compare later when she realizes she's in trouble and starts covering her tracks."

Gorman left, and a minute later, he appeared on the other side of the glass.

"How'd you know it was poison?" Angel asked.

"My first night at Mrs. Newbury's I got really sick."

"I remember."

"I thought Findley was trying to poison me."

"So the whole thing with Findley and Rusty was nothing?"

"Not nothing, but he didn't try to poison me."

Angel hadn't gotten there yet. He gestured for me to catch him up.

"I had cereal and sugar. Lots of sugar."

"Gross. You ate the dead lady's food?"

"There was nothing wrong with it."

"Everything in my grandmother's house was stale. She never ate cereal, but she never threw it away either."

"You obviously don't take after her."

"Funny. Still disgusting."

"I would have never figured it out if the sugar bowl wasn't silver."

"Huh?"

"I set it aside, then Cynthia swiped it from the house while I was there. They had been poisoning the old lady with Chuck's drugs and a heavy dose of laxatives. It was all mixed in with the sugar so when I dumped it on my cereal, wow. That stuff hit me hard."

"That must have sucked." Angel laughed.

"You have no idea." I didn't want to relive that morning passed out on the linoleum. "When I found the sugar bowl in her trash I knew something was up. But I thought Newb threw it out because he was there."

Angel and I quieted while Gorman and Cynthia squared off in the next room. He told her we'd found the Furosimide in the sugar. That it had been tested and that Chuck had admitted to giving it to her. Once they found it in the old lady's system, it would be over.

Cynthia had to be reeling inside, but she feigned composure.

"That's still gross," Angel said. "Eating a dead woman's food."

"The food's not any different," I said. "The cereal didn't know she was dead."

Gorman put a paper on the table. He didn't say what it was but Cynthia's mouth dropped open in horror.

"We'll have her exhumed by tomorrow. Testing will take a day, maybe two. You want to make this easier?"

She glared at him. I'd never imagined she could be so nasty. All that time, I assumed Chuck was intimidating her and that Newb was taking advantage of her. Seemed I had both situations backwards.

Sometime soon she'd realize it was me who'd put the whole thing together. But I wasn't afraid of her. And it wouldn't matter for much longer anyway.

"Why'd she do it?" Angel asked.

"I think she married Newb for the money."

"What money?"

"That house she's living in. It's paid off."

"Newb's never had a job."

"His parents died about the time they got married. I think she seduced him, got pregnant, and ended up with his inheritance."

"The bitch."

"She made one mistake. She thought Newb could keep paying."

"Why would she think that?"

"I don't know. But their settlement, the child support is huge. Way more than Newb could ever pay."

"So she went through the money."

"Had to. She went to work taking care of the old lady and somewhere along the line, she remembered how great that first inheritance was and wanted another. Newb owes her so much money she assumed she'd get everything from the inheritance."

Angel didn't tell me how wrong I'd been about Newb. I guess he appreciated that I'd helped clear him. And maybe he understood I'd been trying to do the right thing all along.

I didn't feel guilty at all about burning Cynthia.

She didn't submit. Maybe because Gorman wasn't a pro interrogator and couldn't trip her up. Or maybe she was that hard to crack.

"I want a lawyer," she said.

That ended our fun behind the glass.

Chapter Eighty

My next experience with a cop was in a paneled room in the back of the courthouse. There was no one-way mirror this time. Even with my top button open, with only my tie holding the collar of my best white dress shirt closed, I could barely breathe.

My red face had nothing to do with the judge's questions.

"How much did you see changed?"

"Twenty thousand."

"Cash?" The judge straightened, incredulous.

Morgan smiled her thanks to me. She could tell the judge was outraged by the amount.

The cop nodded solemnly for his part, assuring the judge that this was what he expected.

"How did you arrive at that amount?"

"They band bills in stacks of ten thousand. He had two at least."

"How does a man with no bank accounts, no job, no means of support, come up with that kind of cash?"

"He runs drugs and girls," I said without pause.

The judge snapped a stern look at the officer.

"It's consistent with his record," the officer said.

The judge pulled the warrant over his desk and studied the language.

Morgan wasn't getting it all. Findley had fathered children with other women and they were entitled to their share, too. I might not have sent him to prison, but when this warrant was executed on his safe deposit box, the cash he'd been hiding would be drained to support his children.

I didn't know if they'd confiscate what was left since he'd been living off the state since he'd gotten out of prison, but whatever the outcome, Findley wasn't going to be happy.

I considered asking the judge's advice about Rusty the crooked vice cop. If Findley got put away, my problems with Rusty might disappear, but there was a chance my problems with Findley were about to get a whole lot worse and I'd have to deal with Findley and Rusty myself.

I watched the judge read and didn't interrupt. Before he signed, he asked me if I was sure it was the correct bank. I told him I was, and he still asked me to check the form again.

When I assured him a second time, he signed the paper and the cop ushered us out.

Morgan jumped all over me in the hall. She must have needed the money badly and couldn't imagine someone handing it to her.

Getting even with Findley felt mighty good.

Chapter Eighty-one

A couple days later, I had my suit on again.

Family court this time.

For any other father this would have been a slam dunk, but Newb had a long record of arrests and trips to detox and rehab. The judge was a military guy. Sat erect and wanted everything just so. He had issues with the change in custody, but with Cynthia behind bars, his choices for Nicholas were limited. Newb was the kid's only living family unless you counted Trig and Delilah. They weren't exactly lining up to take the kid.

"Mr. Newbury, you are regularly employed?"

He pointed to me in the seat beside him. "Yes, Sir. In construction and maintenance."

"And you make ten dollars an hour. That's hardly enough to pay for housing and childcare. Is it?"

"I'll be helping out, Your Honor," Angel offered from Newb's other side.

The judge asked if they were family or if they worked together. When Angel said no the second time, the judge was confused. He wondered if it was a gay love thing, but was trying hard not to ask.

"If I may help, Your Honor," I said.

"Please."

"Angel lost a son to drug abuse. He was about Bernie's age. He's worked hard to help area kids put their lives back together. This is a chance for Angel to experience what he missed with his own son, and to give

Bernie the support and guidance he never received." It sounded eloquent to me. Must have been the suit.

I think the judge liked my speech, but he wasn't buying the idea of a middle aged, overfed guy and a recovering addict working together to raise a kid. It was going to be a bumpy road, but like I said, the judge was short on options.

He granted a temporary order for Newb and Angel to share legal custody of Nicholas until Cynthia was released from jail, or prison if it went that way. With luck, Nicholas would graduate high school before Cynthia was released. She deserved to be in that long.

Newb and Angel were all smiles, but as they strapped Nicholas into his car seat, I could tell they were in for hard times.

Newb was on his way to selling the house. It was even possible he'd get the old house back to help pay for support, but the kid didn't even have the most basic tools to raise a child.

I pictured Newb struggling through a bedtime story and thought how good it would be for both of them.

I felt Mrs. Newbury smiling down on me as I walked off the courthouse steps. Cynthia was behind bars and her great grandson was back in the hands of her family where he belonged.

Chapter Eighty-two

The next morning I got a fish omelet on a Wednesday. I knew something was up by the way she kissed me at the door. For a minute, I thought she'd been gambling again and was planning to tell me she'd blown a bundle, but she let me go out the door and head off to pick up Newb without giving me a hint what the special treatment was all about.

The ignition cranked and I mentally adjusted my route. To Angel's house today as it would be for a long time.

I looked in the mirror and there it was. My fat ass on the linoleum floor. Dark windows. Puke all over the vanity. My face out of the frame.

Below the picture she'd written one word.

Sexy.

That wasn't the last time I'd see that photo.

Not by a long shot.

Other Books by CJ West

The End of Marking Time (standalone)

<u>Randy Black Series</u>
Sin & Vengeance
A Demon Awaits
Gretchen Greene

Addicted to Love (standalone)
Taking Stock (standalone)

WE HOPE YOU ENJOY THE FOLLOWING PREVIEW

The End of Marking Time

A Psychological Thriller
by CJ West
available now

Chapter One

I wasn't surprised when the Plexiglas partitions shot up out of the floor and locked me in front of this window. I had seen the breaks in the tile floor and I knew what was underneath because Wendell has done this to me before. I know this time is different. I'm not going to pretend I'm not scared to face your decision. If you were on this side of the glass, you would be scared, too. You can tell yourself you're too good to end up where I am. That you're not like me. But how different are we really? I wish I could see you, to see the difference for myself, but I understand why Wendell is hiding you. You probably have a steady job, a house, and credits in the bank. You could never imagine doing the things I've done. All you want is to get this over and go back to your life. You might even be ready to push the red button and get on with it, but put yourself in my place. For the next few hours I'm going to tell you my story. I hope you'll give me a chance.

It was my destiny to be trapped in this tiled hallway with you watching me through the one-way window. Maybe not from birth, but certainly from the time I opened the can of peaches I stole on Longmeadow Drive. I had been on my own five years by then and I was at the top of my game. I was cocky, but I had good reason. I chose my targets well and I moved like a ghost when I worked. I hadn't been arrested in three years, not even a close call. Maybe that's why I watched Leno from behind the couch while the middle-aged fat guy drifted in and out of consciousness right in front of me. He snored one minute and laughed at some politician's latest gaffe the next. I watched the show, ate my peaches, and wondered how this buffoon afforded such a huge place all by himself. It wasn't just him. The whole street was full of little kings and I couldn't imagine there were so many kingdoms in America. Don't get me wrong. I was glad to have them around because I worked my way through the royal suburbs week after week. I should have been paying attention instead of wondering why someone with so much money lived by himself. Unlikely he had a mother like mine. Or maybe he was just like my father.

Usually I cleaned up after myself so well that my marks weren't even sure they'd been hit. Plenty of them blamed the shifty-eyed kid next door or raged against a child they suspected of buying drugs. Normally I would have cleaned the fork and put it back, then rinsed the can and left it with the recycling, but that night I left the can on the end table, the fork leaning down into two inches of syrup. I knew I could never come back. I had been through half the houses on this street, pinched a wad of cash here, a diamond necklace there. After I slipped out with the Mercedes that night, the neighbors would take a closer look around their houses and the emails would start flying. There would be meetings with the police, talk of a neighborhood watch, a few of them would even buy guns. Sometimes when I was done with a place like this, I'd tip off a real bungler, a smash-and-grab type hyped up on drugs, and send him stumbling into a hornet's nest of nervous housewives and angry husbands. Sometimes the druggie barged in and out so fast he got away the first time, but eventually he would end up cuffed in the back of a cruiser. That satisfied the neighbors and covered my trail nicely. Everyone was happy except the guy forced to detox in a six-by-nine.

I should have sent one of them in my place, but I wanted the Mercedes. It took me five minutes to creep out of the living room and up the stairs to the master bedroom. The keys to the Mercedes were right on the bureau in plain sight, as was his wallet with five credit cards and six hundred forty in cash. Who carries that much cash anymore? I left him twenty for breakfast and took all the plastic. If he had more cash lying around, I couldn't find it. I checked the sock drawer, then felt under the bureau and along the back edge with no luck. He might have had a safe behind one of the oil paintings, but I couldn't risk taking them down with him in the house. I was sitting at the desk in the corner with his checkbook in my hand when he decided he'd had enough of Leno and lumbered upstairs. The room was massive, but there was only one way in and one way out. I gambled. I could have headed for the door and whacked him when he came in with his eyes half open, but that wasn't my style. I slipped to the floor, crawled into the opening under the desktop, and pulled the chair in behind me. He topped the stairs, trudged past me, and flopped face first on the bed without even looking in my direction.

It took him ten minutes to start snoring regularly. I got back up onto the chair, reassured by the irregular nasal bursts. My gamble paid off. There in the top drawer I found a two-sided sheet of paper that listed every credit card, bank account, and Internet site logon the guy had, complete with passwords. I had his debit card and his PIN, but I wasn't stupid enough to walk into an ATM and use it. I could find some kid I'd never seen before and split the max withdrawal with him, but that was risky. The magic was the plastic. Since I had his list of customer service numbers, it'd take him a day to contact the banks. All I needed was a few hours and he'd be asleep longer than that.

I stopped at the bedroom door to look back and wonder if I'd ever own a place like this. With an eighth-grade education, probably not, especially where I went to school. But for the next thirty minutes, I'd be driving a top-of-the-line Mercedes with a pocket full of cash and plastic.

The garage door opened smoothly. I drove out and hit the remote like I lived there. I was pretty full of myself when I made the corner out of the neighborhood without a soul to see me. I couldn't stop thinking about what the fat guy would do when he woke up. He might not notice his wallet was lighter, but he'd definitely be pissed when he couldn't find his keys. He'd have a fit when he went down to the garage looking for them and realized the Mercedes was gone.

The whole thing would sink in then. He'd call the cops and he'd stomp around the house looking to see what else I'd taken until they got there. It would really hit him when he found the empty peach can on the end table.

Eventually he'd remember hearing the fork tap the bottom of the can. He'd turned around once but hadn't really been looking. He felt safe in his home until that night. All people did. They had to. Otherwise they'd go nuts jumping at every noise and shadow. They knew there were criminals out there, but not in their houses, not while they were home. The poor guy wouldn't sleep for weeks.

He'd turn the night over and over in his mind until he realized he'd picked up the clicker just a few feet from where I was hiding in the shadows against the wall. He'd be terrified then. He expected criminals to be violent and unpredictable. He never expected someone like me. I never panic. I know the cops take twenty minutes to get most places and that's more than enough time to disappear if you're not in a rush. I always plan two exits, a hot one and a cool one. I always keep my head and most of the time, like that night, I glide along the cool road home, careful not to get stopped.

Unfortunately, I had no idea who I'd just hit or the shit storm I was about to set off when I sold those credit cards.

CPSIA information can be obtained at www.ICGtesting.com
Printed in the USA
BVOW012151251012

303987BV00005B/1/P